SIX

G.S. LOCKE

ORION

First published in Great Britain in 2021 by Orion Fiction,
an imprint of The Orion Publishing Group Ltd.,
Carmelite House, 50 Victoria Embankment
London EC4Y 0DZ

An Hachette UK Company

1 3 5 7 9 10 8 6 4 2

A CIP catalogue record for this book is
available from the British Library.

ISBN (Trade Paperback) 978 1 4091 9049 3
ISBN (eBook) 978 1 4091 9051 6

Typeset at The Spartan Press Ltd,
Lymington, Hants

Printed and bound in Great Britain by Clays Ltd,
Elcograf S.p.A.

www.orionbooks.co.uk

For Boy, Karl, Katy, Rosey and Zak

Chapter One

The door to Jon Shaw's office clicked shut with the same finality of a gun jamming. He should have felt triumph for securing the release of an innocent man, the toughest legal gig there was. Innocents displayed outrage, defensiveness and, as often as not, unpredictability. Against all advice, they got shirty under cross-examination, viewed any slur on their character or integrity as a gross imposition and bellowed their blamelessness at judge and jury, thereby scuppering their own chances. As for those well-meaning folk who claimed that if you are innocent you have nothing to fear, they knew very little about the workings of the law. As Shaw was keen to point out to interns, spin it right and the Pope could be found guilty of unspecified crimes. So, yes, Shaw had argued his client's case and won, yet his victory was bitter-sweet. Something deep inside always prevented him from fully embracing the moment.

He swivelled his chair, swung his legs up and parked his feet on the desk. Lamplight cast a dull glow across his highly polished shoes. Tipping his head back, he loosened his tie and briefly closed his eyes. It was churlish but he had no burning desire to join his colleagues and surround himself with fellow poets (piss off early, tomorrow it's Saturday) or get stuck with the shiny-eyed intern on an adrenaline high at landing a month's work placement at Toombs and West, Cheltenham's most prestigious criminal defence firm. The poor kid didn't yet understand that a few weeks mixing with the dangerous, mentally unstable and repeat offenders would soon dispel any glamorous illusions. Had he been so naïve back then? Hard to remember.

Perhaps if he huddled here in the silence, he'd find the certainty and peace he craved. Think of all the good things in life, a cranked-up life coach would say. Shaw harboured a deep suspicion of personal trainers, gurus and individuals who ripped you off to tell you what, in your darkest hours, you already knew. But, right now, he was prepared to give that sort of advice a go. Perhaps he was plain exhausted. His mountainous workload would make a Sherpa stagger. Hours spent reading files, visiting police stations and prisons, taking statements, liaising and negotiating and, yes, arm-twisting, was all part of the job. The law wasn't so much about justice as doing deals. *We agree to this if you give us that*, and usually equated to a reduced sentence. This he could handle. Dealing with clients at the worst time in their lives, and whose liberty was often at stake, gave him a sense of worth and purpose. But he bloody hated repeat offenders.

As he saw it, a squandered chance to get a life back on track was *his* personal failure to turn a felon's life around. Only yesterday, he'd heard that a former client, who'd walked on a technicality twelve months before, had been charged with the same offence: GBH. Bail would definitely be off the menu this time and, although Shaw hated to say it, richly deserved.

White noise, he thought grimly, his mind running full circle. The real mood-killer was Jo leaving. Although he couldn't fault her observation that he had commitment issues, he wished she'd given him another chance. He missed the dimples on her cheeks when she smiled, the mole above her full top lip, her tempestuousness, her body dammit – *really* missed her, to the extent that it physically hurt. Forty-eight hours ago, they'd shared a lovely Regency-style home near the Suffolks, for which he was mortgaged up to the eyeballs, and willingly so. Without her, it felt pointless. Without Jo, his house was barren, cold and empty. He let out a sigh. Sort yourself out, Shaw thought, swinging his legs off the desk. Grabbing his jacket and umbrella, he headed out towards the corridor, snapping off lights as he walked.

Outside, he was greeted by a bloated grey sky pissing rain. Visibility reduced to a few feet, cars aquaplaned down busy St. George's Road and shot great torrents of water over anyone unfortunate enough to be walking past.

Rolling up the collar of his jacket, he set off. It wouldn't hurt to show his face and drop in for a swift drink. Some company might even do him good. It would be a hell of an improvement on letting himself into a house that looked as abandoned as he felt. Then, maybe later, emboldened by gin, he'd give Jo a call. See if she was OK. Find out if she needed anything. Would he have the guts to tell her that he loved her, that he needed her? *Come home. Please. I can change.*

June rain sheeted from dark clouds, bouncing off the uneven pavement, and sprayed the back of his trousers.

People scurried chaotically, heads down, hoods up. Kids ran and squealed and splashed, with water-soaked hair and dripping faces. Another time it would be comic.

About to cut through into Montpellier Walk from Bayshill Road, something indefinable caught Shaw's peripheral vision. His eyes flicked to the right and peered through the gloom. A figure barrelled down the street with a 'who are you looking at?' gait. Something about him felt horribly familiar. Disturbingly so. As Shaw's brain made furious connections, he silently mouthed *Danny Hallam*.

Alarm chased through him.

It couldn't be.

Wasn't possible.

Not even remotely so. Not now, after Shaw had done so much to change. Not after twenty-five years.

Without a word, the figure swept past inches away from him, like an unquiet spirit vanishing as quickly as it came.

Thank Christ.

Chapter Two

It was a good question, if an obvious one, and yet Shaw, shaken by his recent encounter, was reluctant to answer. Because that wasn't Danny Hallam, *was it*?

He took a slug of gin. Mind messing with his head, he'd made a mistake, cooked up an image that didn't exist.

Giving Annie Mayfield his most winsome smile, he determined to give the young intern an honest answer.

'I went into the law because I like underdogs. And winning. Not necessarily in that order,' he said with a short laugh.

'Jon is an underdog's wet dream,' Charlie Toombs, senior partner, showman and bonne viveur, boomed from the other end of the table. The rest of the team, including clerks and legal secretaries, one of whom Shaw suspected Charlie was bedding, erupted with laughter. 'Jon was hugging hoodies way before it became a political slogan. He does more pro bono cases than you've had takeaways,' Charlie continued, very slightly slurring his words. 'Nothing Teflon Jon likes better than sticking it to the cops.'

Teflon Jon. Sticking it to the cops. Charlie made him sound like a sleazy lawyer working for some Mafia don.

Shaw smiled indulgently, a mask for the irritation crackling beneath. Responding to Annie's perplexed expression, Shaw explained that he'd earned the soubriquet by holding the practice record for the greatest number of clients to whom charges had failed to stick. Annie the intern looked unimpressed, as if he were somehow protecting the guilty and shafting the victim. He took another swallow of gin, wondering how in God's name he could disentangle himself.

Annie inclined towards him. He caught a distinct and familiar waft of Miss Dior Original. Jo was fond of it. *Oh shit.* 'About you and the police,' Annie sliced through his thoughts, 'Mr Toombs was joking, right?'

Another burst of laughter exploded from their table. Shaw raised his voice so he could be heard. 'Charlie has a wicked sense of humour, Annie. Of course, I don't set out to thwart the activities of the police. We need them but sometimes mistakes are made and, unfortunately, the police are inextricably linked to the system.'

Annie nodded blankly, the vacancy in her eyes suggesting that a) she didn't have a clue and b) very much feared the intensity of any strongly held opinion.

'Look,' he said, 'Children aren't born bad. They're made. Poverty, neglect and abuse creates angry, pissed-off people who often become criminals when there is nobody significant enough in their lives to deter them. Fundamentally, it's a failure of the system to protect the most vulnerable in society. What's so damned rich is that the same system has the temerity to punish them.'

'Yes, I see,' Annie said, although, from the height of her sculpted eyebrows, he could tell that she saw no further than her own cute little nose.

'It's our job to give those people a voice and a defence, whatever they've done,' he continued.

'I understand, but—'

'And then we negotiate the best outcome for our clients. If you can't get your head around that, you might be better suited to one of the other legal disciplines.'

'Fuck's sake, Jon,' Charlie roared over the clamour, 'get another round in before the poor girl changes her mind and becomes a plumber.'

Relieved to escape, Shaw excused himself, slipped off his stool and, to a chorus of *same again*, headed to a bar thick with customers brandishing wallets like City traders waving bits of papers at the Stock Exchange.

About to sneak into a small gap that had opened up, breath left his body as surely as if he'd been stabbed in the back. Surrounding noise vanished, sucked into a tunnel of nothingness. His mouth dried, filled with tar and sand, it seemed. Condemned, he tried to move. No, to flee, but was tethered by paralysis; nailed to the spot. Every muscle in his body had clenched, except his jaw, which was slack.

There was no mistake, no delusion. What he'd thought a figment of his imagination was all too horribly real. A part of him had always known that Danny Hallam, his one-time closest friend, would materialise and return to haunt him.

Frozen, Shaw could not take a step forward or take one back. Danny didn't look stoked or drunk, but it was still very identifiably him. Despite the passage of time, Shaw would recognise that spitting bundle of human energy anywhere.

And Danny was looking straight at him.

Shaw briefly wondered whether he could slip out of the bar and run. A coward's way out for sure. There was little point. It would be like trying to outsmart a saltwater crocodile intent on grabbing his next meal. Danny would hunt him down and, if Shaw were honest, he couldn't blame him.

A good five inches shorter than Shaw, at around five feet, nine inches tall, Danny had a blocky, powerful boxer's build. The intervening years had not seen him run to fat. Older, with deep lines chiselled into his forehead and carving a trench from his nose to the corner of his mouth, his pale stubbly face was thinner, and his narrow pale blue eyes harder. A serious number-one haircut failed to disguise the flecks of grey in his mouse-brown hair. He looked every bit down on his luck, a loser, some might say, except that Shaw knew better. *Way better.*

He unfolded his fingers and touched the cuff of his tailored shirt, an unconscious response, maybe, to Danny's tatty vest top, grey jogging bottoms that were too short and covered with smuts of dirty rainwater, and plimsolls. Tempting to categorise a man by what he wore, yet Danny was beyond definition. With his edgy undertow, he would always be a paradoxical force of nature. Handed a different set of cards, he could have been a leader, someone memorable, who made a mark on the world. But Danny, like so many, had only Jokers in his pack. A ball of fury at nineteen years of age, he was the epitome of the men and women whose anger mutated their DNA. Shaw was in no doubt that nothing had dulled his old friend's rage. Worse, hardened by prison life, Danny had come to collect.

Without dropping his gaze, Danny lifted his glass. It was almost empty. To emphasise the point, he tipped his chin, a provocative gesture Shaw recognised. Danny had used it extensively as a 'come on' to any idiot kid stupid enough to underestimate him. A 'bit of bother' would start with verbal taunts, *Your mam shags anything with a pulse*, threats and two fingers up (not one back then), followed by extravagant hand gestures, suggesting dickhead. Next – and by now Danny mad for it – fists and boots and, unlucky for some, a blade or razor. One of Shaw's abiding memories was Danny flicking his chin at him in anger. Only that time Danny had done the underestimating. Believed he'd won; just like always, business as usual.

And he'd been so wrong.

But that was then and this was now.

Glancing wistfully back to his current life, which no longer seemed half as bad as it did five minutes ago, to Charlie and the others, with their booze and their bravado, Shaw resigned himself to his fate. Pushing one foot in front of the other, he cut through the scrum of drinkers and walked slowly towards the man he had once loved and, with a greater passion, hated.

Chapter Three

'You thought I'd disappear, didn't you?' Danny pitched an amused smile that did not connect to his eyes.

'I did.' More accurately, he thought that Danny would not find him. Shaw had changed himself, his life, his everything. He'd dumped his old persona, fashioned a new image and become the man he aspired to be. That Danny was sitting here now proved that his efforts had been pointless. You couldn't do a runner from the past.

Shaw reached grimly for his glass and recalled how, twenty-five years before, he'd frantically scoured the news. There'd been a false start when a man's body was pulled from the river. He'd been convinced it was Danny, so certain. And with that certainty had come relief. It didn't last. Days later Danny was picked up, arrested and charged. Throughout that anxious period of time, a teenaged Shaw had expected a dawn assault with a battering ram at his door, police swooping on him in the street, a foot on his back, face in the dirt, wrestled to the pavement, onlookers jeering and spitting at him when bundled into a police van. The pressure was so great that, once, he'd seriously considered giving himself up. As best he could, he'd prepared what he would say if interviewed, or to his young mind, *interrogated*. But then there would be more questions, with answers he couldn't give because it would put others at risk. At least, that's what he'd told himself back then. Riddled with guilt, those were dark and dismal months and yet his worst fears had not come to pass. Amid lurid headlines, Danny was tried and convicted. After that Shaw had compartmentalised the incident in his brain and labelled it with a skull and crossbones: *open at risk of death*.

'You've changed.'

'We've all changed, Danny.'

'Nah, man. Me – I'm the same under the skin, but you?' Danny rolled his eyes. 'Still got your louche blond looks and your swept-back hair, you lucky fucker, but you've lost your Manc accent. All that bleeding hearts shit made me want to throw up. Gone soft in the head, Jon. Mind, I can see you're doing all right for yourself,' he said, casting a sly look to where Charlie and the others were sitting. Shaw followed Danny's gaze and noticed that one of the clerks was missing. Charlie had probably given up on him returning any time soon and had dispatched an underling to get in a round.

'And how's things with you?' Shaw silently cursed how banal he sounded.

'Oh, I'm fine and dandy and ta for asking,' Danny replied with a lop-sided smile. 'You going to get me a lager or what? I'm gagging.'

Shaw ordered a drink for Danny and another gin and tonic for himself. 'Make it a double.' His mouth felt stiff and mechanical as if he were recovering from serious oral surgery.

'See, even your booze is a toff's.'

The drinks arrived. Shaw took a big swallow, rolling the astringent taste around his tonsils, and looked his old friend in the eye.

'What do you want, Danny?'

'Is that any way to treat a mate?'

'Bought you a drink, haven't I?'

Danny grinned. 'That's more like it. Still got your old spark. I'm glad. Really. Besides Carl, I always thought you were the bright one out of the lot of us. Yeah, you were definitely the thinker, the brains in the operation but, fuck me, you a lawyer in your sharp suit, doing all nicely in Ponceville with your bestest mates.'

Shaw could see where this was going. Danny was about to blow his cover, announce in long and loud tones the list of crimes he'd committed, including attempted murder. Thank Christ Jo wasn't around to see the spectacle. He opened his mouth to speak but Danny wasn't done.

'Man, you look like you've shat yourself.' Danny threw back his head and laughed, the noise loud enough to break windows. Shaw was given a ringside view of several missing molars and a couple of decayed teeth.

'Just spit it out and say what you came for,' Shaw growled.

'I don't know what you mean.'

'The fight. The—'

'Nothing more than a lover's tiff.'

Shaw kept his voice artificially low. 'I tried to kill you, for God's sake. And *you* know and *I* know that I meant to.' And if he hadn't dumped Danny in the drink, would Danny have escaped the attention of the police? Neither of them would ever know.

A dark light entered Danny's pale eyes. It was like the mood music suddenly changed from pop to Wagner. 'I almost drowned, you cunt.'

An image of them knocking the shit out of each other careered through Shaw's mind. Brawling on the side of a riverbank in the driving rain, throwing punch after punch, receiving blow after blow, Shaw finally doubling over, wringing wet and in severe pain. Triumphant, jacked up on cocaine and Christ knows what, Danny had whooped and crowed and thumped his chest, king of the fucking jungle. Shaw remembered it like it was yesterday.

Danny issued a cold stare, raised the glass to his mouth, took a deep drink and wiped underneath his nose with the side of his hand. Shaw noticed the short fingernails, hard-bitten at the edges, like the owner. He briefly wondered whether his old friend was armed.

'You're here to collect, Danny. And if I don't do whatever it is you want, you're going to destroy my reputation and my comfortable life. I get it.' He was surprised how calm he sounded. A few moments ago he was thick with fear and didn't mind admitting it.

Static filled the air. To Shaw's ears, the bar fell silent and it was just him and Danny and a threat that hadn't yet made good on a promise. Still, Danny didn't speak. Shaw tried to read him and found he couldn't.

'I've come,' Danny said, at last, 'because I need your help.'

Chapter Four

'You're in trouble?' He wished to God that Charlie hadn't called him *Teflon Jon*.

'Not just me.'

It wasn't what Shaw expected, although he never knew what to expect from Danny Hallam. His unpredictability was what had made him the most thrilling friend he'd ever had.

'Who else?' Shaw believed it unlikely that Danny had ever moved out of criminal circles.

'Remember Mickie?'

'Fuck's sake, Danny . . .'

'It's OK, I'm not a grass, Jon. You're in the clear.' Shaw would never be in the clear. His conscience wouldn't allow it.

'We did something indefensible.'

'For which *I* paid,' Danny said darkly.

Shaw felt like a man who had pushed his way through a blazing basement fire to the one emergency exit only to find it bricked up. Turning back and faced with the unthinkable, he had no alternative but to confront what had happened all those years ago on that awful night.

'Let's go somewhere quieter.' He pointed to a free table at

the back of an adjoining room and away from the main bar area.

Danny followed. Shaw scraped back a chair, sat down with a thud. 'When did you get out of prison?'

Danny snatched a smile as if applauding Shaw's powers of deduction.

'Three weeks ago.'

Shaw guessed there was a supreme irony in that, despite his legal career, he had failed to check Danny's precise release date. To do so would be like admitting an association. It would create bad karma. He felt a vein in his jaw pulse. Danny had wasted little time in tracking him down.

Danny took a long draft of lager, pinched the bridge of his nose between his fingers. 'Never expected you to do what you did. Never thought you had it in you.'

Shaw briefly closed his eyes. While Danny had celebrated knocking the crap out of him, Shaw had feigned defeat and, gathering the last dregs of his strength, straightened up and, balling his fists, smashed Danny with everything he had straight into the seething waters of a river in full spate. With cold detachment, he'd watched his friend carried away by strong currents, his head bobbing, mouth open in shock, before quickly disappearing beneath the surface. The reason for the argument was the only thing Shaw could not bear to recall. It's why he'd spent so many years trying not only to forget, but attempting to make amends.

Danny spoke in a dull monotone. 'After I hauled myself out of the drink, I went to ground. Stayed local, slept rough, lived on my wits.' To which Danny was well suited, Shaw recalled.

'Police found the blade?' It was more of a rhetorical question.

'With my prints all over it. Why the fuck didn't you get rid?'

'Someone was coming.' And he'd panicked, Shaw remembered. Back then, he was just another kid running wild on a council estate in Manchester, his mates were his family because he, like the others, didn't really have one. Mam dead. Father drunk. An all too familiar picture.

Shaw took another slug of booze and tiptoed up to the memory. Poor as hell, Danny and his crew intermittently ran drugs for Aaron Waterhouse, a man who, at thirty years of age, seemed old and wise and provided a route out of destitution. At least they had enough money to eat and, yes, to drink, which was all that mattered. But Waterhouse was a hard guy and Michelle Ashton, or Mickie, as everyone knew her, owed Danny drug money, which, in turn, meant Danny owed Waterhouse. It was Danny's idea to put the frighteners on her to force her to pay up. 'Nice one,' Danny had said. 'Waterhouse will be chuffed when he recognises we can sort things out for ourselves, and we'll be minted.'

Shaw had seen the logic. Only ever going along to get along, he had not foreseen the danger. His eighteen-year-old self had thought in terms of verbal warning, not physical attack. It was a woman they were scaring shitless, after all, not some hairy-arsed bloke.

They'd outflanked Mickie walking along a riverbank at around ten o'clock one summer's evening. After a long spell of hot weather, it was pissing down, just like tonight, and the sky had roared with thunder and flashed with lightning.

Mickie was as spirited as she was desperate. Threatened with violence, Mickie spat back that she didn't have the money and they could go fuck themselves. When Mark, egged on by Danny, gave her a little slap, Mickie screamed. Next, Kenny and Carl piled in and went to work. The pack in action is a fearsome sight. Like fire, it has an unpredictable energy and power that consumes everything in its wake.

Shaw remembered grabbing Carl, receiving a rib-breaking elbow in his chest for his trouble. Wolf restrained Kenny. Still Mickie screamed. If Shaw closed his eyes, he could hear her; sometimes at three in the morning, pouring with sweat, and him shouting and waking anyone who happened to be sharing a bed with him at the time; most recently, Jo.

'Fuckin' shut her up,' Danny had yelled, his rage morphing into something tangible, vicious and satanic. In that finely tuned moment, Shaw had sensed a step change. He'd shouted for them to stop, to sort themselves out. Nobody could hear and, even if they could, nobody was listening. Next thing, Danny barrelled into Mickie from behind and, as if *he* were hurt, let out a foul-mouthed curse, but it was Mickie who was doing the screeching. Then Danny lunged and the noise cut out immediately.

With big eyes, Mickie half twisted and pressed a hand to her back. Shaw saw blood blossoming through her jacket, seeping through her fingers. He'd never seen so much, despite a life in which he'd witnessed more of the stuff than he should have done.

And that was never part of the plan.

Staggering, Mickie went down on one knee and, clutching her stomach, pitched over. Sweat beaded her forehead.

She was white-paper pale and her breathing was rapid and ragged.

Shaw recalled each of his mates' reactions as clearly as the jury's the day before to a description of a sexual assault on a young man. Stunned, slow and lumbering, Kenny clawed at his hair with his great big hands. Mark stumbled about too stoned to utter a coherent word. Wolf shrank back, his voice pegged to a whisper, 'Man. Fuck. Man.' Only Carl looked as though it was the best entertainment he'd seen all year. He had smiled in sick fascination until a shout from a walker a long way down the riverbank had made him scarper.

When the others fled, Danny had stood over Mickie and, jutting out his chin, demanded that Shaw roll her into the river. A roar, like the tide before it breaks and smashes against the rocks, erupted from the back of Shaw's throat. The rest was a flurry of gouges, blows and kicks until, finally, one deliberate and perfectly pitched punch catapulted a grown young man into a seething and angry river. After that, Shaw ran. Mickie Ashton died a day later and he'd been running ever since.

Shaw glanced at Danny. From the strange, distant look in his eyes, Shaw guessed that he too was travelling back through the murderous terrain of that dreadful night. Mickie's death had not only spelt the end of her life, it had irrevocably damaged the lives of everyone involved, not least because she'd been pregnant. They hadn't known it at the time. No excuse. Christ, how bad could things get, Shaw had thought, when he'd made the discovery, courtesy of a sensationalist tabloid headline?

Shaw took another long drink to steady his nerves. How

could they have been so stupid, so reckless? They were just kids and yet he understood only too well the malign energy a bunch of teenagers can generate. He saw it up close and personal, day in and day out. And despite not laying a finger on Mickie Ashton, under the current law of joint enterprise, he could still be regarded as culpable. This mattered less than, in his own mind, he was guilty.

He turned back to Danny. 'If you want money, I can get you enough to start over.' And go far away, get out of my life, and leave me the fuck alone.

Danny shook his head. 'I'm not on the cadge.'

'So?'

'I visited Kenny and Mark.'

It was typical of Danny to be obtuse. 'How are they?'

'Dead.'

Chapter Five

Kenny and Mark dead?

'Murdered,' Danny said.

Shaw shot him a penetrating look. Consumed by the revelation, Shaw almost missed what Danny said next.

'Kenny was killed two days ago, Mark some time last night.'

Shaw's mind was a carousel of questions. 'I need another drink.' He downed what was left in his glass, which wasn't very much. 'You?'

'Jack Daniels,' Danny replied. 'Make it a double,' he added, in a pompous piss-take of Shaw's accent.

Shaw went to the bar, ordered refills, paid and returned.

'Tell me what happened,' Shaw began, once seated.

'Kenny had his head smashed in.'

'What? Where?'

'On the farm. Came off his quad bike.'

Relief stampeded out of him. 'That's an accident, Danny.'

Danny shook his head. 'It's not what you think. You don't get it.'

Shaw was accustomed to clients taking labyrinthine routes.

An internal logic existed in there somewhere. Part of his job was to work out the sequence of events. 'Then help me out.'

'Kenny stayed *loyal*,' Danny began in a tone designed to needle. 'He picked me up from prison, took me briefly to me mam's and then back to his uncle's farm in North Devon.'

Shaw vaguely remembered a relative who farmed land near Ilfracombe. Kenny was always telling them stories about him. To those who lived on a run-down estate in the north, where the residents numbed their pain with drugs and cheap cider, a place like that was nirvana.

'His dad had him shipped out there after what happened,' Danny explained.

What happened felt a poor way to describe the cold-blooded murder of a pregnant woman but Shaw went with it. There was no question in his mind that, had Kenny's dad known his son was in trouble, however serious, he'd have kept his mouth shut. That's the way the community, as fractured as it was, worked.

'Happy as a pig in shite, he was.' Danny's eyes ghosted to the rain-soaked window. 'Getting up at the crack. Spending half the night in a lambing shed. Building fences, feeding animals – I couldn't see the appeal myself.

'Anyways, I stayed there a couple of nights. It was good. We talked about the old days.'

Shaw briefly tuned out. He had a gag reel in his head of their escapades. Play-fighting that, like as not, erupted into real fighting; Danny nicking pies from corner shops while the others distracted the shopkeeper and Shaw kept lookout; lads against the world.

'Kenny mentioned he'd been in touch with Mark and that he wasn't doing so well,' Danny said.

Shaw recalled a baby-faced kid with a gap-toothed smile. The class comedian, Mark had fooled around when he wasn't stoned. Weed helped take the edge off regular beatings by his dad. Looking back, Shaw saw that Mark and Kenny were the vulnerable members of their group. Kenny because he was slow and Mark because he was bullied by a cruel and odious father. It wasn't a stretch to picture them staying in contact.

'Mark disappeared to the Midlands,' Danny continued, 'worked in a warehouse and then as a school caretaker until the booze got the better of him. After that, he wound up in a series of dead-end jobs. Drinking spiralled. Hard drugs followed – not that I'm one to judge,' Danny remarked in a rare moment of insight. 'When Kenny said I could borrow his motor so I could see him, I took off.'

Typical of Danny, Shaw thought. For all his faults Danny was a cause merchant. If he believed in you, you couldn't ask for a more loyal friend. His drink felt suddenly sour on his tongue.

'Kenny was right,' Danny said plainly. 'Mark was living in a shithole you wouldn't keep a dog in, in a back street of Wolverhampton. I swear to God I almost didn't recognise the guy. Thin as a whippet. Lost all his hair. Bald as a baby's arse.'

The sour taste in Shaw's mouth turned noticeably bitter. While he'd been living a comfortable life, a friend, who had once made him laugh at the bleakest of times, had fallen through the cracks in society's thinly laid pavement.

'He were that pleased to see me,' Danny said. 'It was fucking heartbreaking, man.'

'When was this?'

'A week ago.'

'Then what?'

'I slipped him a few quid and promised I'd be back. I drove to Kenny's. His uncle wasn't best pleased, thought I'd taken advantage of his nephew, or some such bollocks. Fuck him,' Danny snarled. 'Kenny was my mate. Remember how upset Kenny could get?' Shaw did. For a big man, Kenny Sharples could become agitated by the smallest change in his existence.

'So Kenny tells me I can take his motor and sleep in it while he talks his uncle round. Me? I wasn't bothered. No way was I shovelling shit on some fucking farm in the land that time forgot. I took off for a few days, did some sightseeing.'

Danny's version of sightseeing meant eyeing up a property with a view to robbing the owner blind. As if reading his mind, Danny wagged a grubby finger, 'No way was I going back to Her Majesty's vermin-infested hellhole. I mean proper tourist stuff, eating ice-cream and fish and chips, and walking along the beach and that.'

'How the hell did you get around the probation system?' All released prisoners serving lengthy sentences had to stick to certain conditions, including residing at an address approved by a supervising officer. Staying away meant prior permission had to be obtained.

'Give over,' Danny said, with a wolfish grin. 'My probation officer doesn't know his arse from his elbow. If I see him this side of Christmas, I'll be lucky.'

Shaw stifled a sigh. Unfortunately, he could believe it. The probation service had reached crisis point some time ago. It had been made worse because some authorities placed services in the hands of private companies.

'How did you manage for money?'

'Kenny saw me right,' Danny replied, snarky with it. Shaw had long ago learned that it was better to suck it up than react. 'His dad died back end of last year and he was hoping to collect,' Danny added.

Shaw thought about that. Money was the root of so many crimes but, contrary to what Danny claimed, Kenny hadn't been murdered. He was simply a sad accident statistic. Shaw nodded for Danny to continue.

'This morning, I drove to see Mark. Door was open. Inside smelt to high heaven but that wasn't unusual. I called out. Nobody answered. So I took a look. I thought he was out on the streets begging, and then I saw him curled up, mouth open.'

'Drunk? OD'd?'

Danny shook his head. 'He wasn't foaming at the mouth or nothing, then I noticed.' When Danny took another pull of his drink, his hand shook.

Silence trailed around their feet like smoke from a recently tamped down campfire.

'Noticed what, Danny?'

'His scalp. Someone had decorated it with nails.'

Chapter Six

Detective Inspector Samantha Deeley checked herself in on the crime-scene log and entered the inner cordon. Flea-infested, littered with empty bottles of spirit and stinking of piss and shit, the place was not the kind of home you'd find on Rightmove, she thought grimly. Not only was it a junkie's dream location, but also a fire hazard. One dropped match and the whole lot would go up. Once they caught up with the owner, Mr Khan, who was currently residing in Islamabad, she intended to introduce him to the good people of Health and Safety and Environmental Health.

Fighting the strong temptation to scratch, she moved tentatively from one stepping plate to another, along a route least likely to have been taken by either victim or suspect. Bright yellow crime-scene markers, adhesive labels highlighting the presence of evidence, flanked her path like flowers along a woodland walk.

The scene was not a hive of activity and personnel, as often depicted on film and in novels. In a limited space like this, it was essential that crime-scene examiners were restricted to the chosen few. Only the particular rhythm associated with working a crime scene, whether it was vast or small, remained the same.

Accompanied by the flash and click of a camera, slow and methodical evidence gathering went on quietly all around her. Unlike many of her colleagues, Deeley respected that she was one cog in a bigger machine. She appreciated that, without Scenes of Crimes officers identifying, securing, protecting and preserving evidence, her job would be impossible, which was why she knew her presence, despite being dressed in a scene suit, mask, gloves and overshoes, was not exactly welcomed at this precise moment.

Focus, as it should be, centred on the deceased, a homeless man whose head had been used like a dartboard by a maniac. The forensic pathologist had estimated that thirty nails had been driven into the victim's skull with a nail gun. Aside from the brutality of the killing, any blood associated with the injury was limited, the extensive damage contained inside the unfortunate man's head.

'Where are we at?' Deeley asked Lisa Harvey, the crime-scene manager, a stout woman with laughing eyes.

'Slow but sure. We don't yet know the identity of the victim.'

Deeley gave an inner groan. She hated the nameless ones. Too often the unidentified were the unloved. If nobody cared enough when they were alive, why make a fuss when they're dead? It made her job harder. On the plus side, the dispossessed tended to stick together. There was a chance that someone among the town's vagrant population knew him. She made a mental note to instruct uniforms to make approaches at known homeless hideouts.

'Nothing in his belongings?'

'Afraid not.'

So it would be down to DNA, Deeley thought. 'Any distinguishing features?' She was thinking of tattoos with a lover's name scrawled in ink.

Harvey looked to one of the SOCOs who, assisted by another, was stripping the body. 'Nicole?'

The young woman looked up. She had striking blue eyes and plain girl-next-door looks, unadorned by make-up. Nothing, however, could play down the frown that left two indentations between her eyebrows. Deeley had long thought that disturbing a SOCO at work was like breaking the concentration of a tennis player serving for the match.

'The victim has a congenital nevus. Here,' she said, indicating an area of a skin the colour of old bone.

Deeley craned her head and saw a large dark hairy mole on the dead man's torso. The SOCO was right about the state of emaciation. The man's chest was a set of ribs encased in a thin veil of flesh. As for his scalp – *Jesus Christ*. She'd once seen a picture of a young Dinka boy who'd received a traditional head scarification. She'd stared then as she did now.

The arrangement of nails was precisely positioned in lines from the base of the skull to the hairline. And why thirty when one in the right place would do the job? Was the number significant? Thirty pieces of silver, or whatever? Why not stop at ten or fifteen? The viciousness of a premeditated act of extreme violence spoke of a highly dangerous individual, with a sense of theatre and taste for the macabre.

Tearing herself away from the sight, she asked about

defence wounds. The SOCO shook her head. Deeley bent over the body to see for herself. Satisfied, she said, 'Drug use?'

The SOCO raised the man's left arm, the skin on the underside visibly scarred near a main vein.

'Makes sense,' Deeley said. 'To inflict this much damage without a fight, the victim must have been high. Don't suppose you've found the murder weapon?' She asked more in hope than expectation.

Harvey shot a grin. 'We'll get back to you in a week, which is about the time it's going to take to bag and tag every exhibit.'

Deeley had never witnessed murder by nail gun before. With thousands of the tools used in DIY and the building trade, it would be like searching for a specific blade of grass in a meadow.

'What about nails?'

'Nothing so far.'

Deeley contained a sigh. 'Dr Speight wasn't keen to tie herself down to time of death until she's had a chance to conduct a post-mortem.' Deeley didn't mention that Speight, a cerebral and detached individual who looked as if she had more lively conversations with the dead than the living, had stated that establishing time of death was a mug's game. 'Any thoughts?'

Once more, Harvey looked to the SOCO.

'Absence of rigor suggests he's been dead for around twelve hours, but it's important to bear in mind that the deceased is fairly emaciated. Without muscle bulk he might not appear to display any signs at all. Also a curled position retains more heat, which only demonstrates that estimating time of death is not an exact science.'

'Nicole graduated in Biology before joining us,' Harvey explained to Deeley.

The SOCO straightened up and flashed a winner's smile. 'I didn't really know what to do with my degree afterwards. I more or less fell into forensics.'

'Lucky us,' Deeley said. 'So what's the story here, Nicole?'

The SOCO thought for a moment. 'No sign of forced entry but, in this scenario, it's hardly headline news. This is the type of place random people come and go.'

'You think the victim knew the killer?'

The SOCO nodded. 'Odds-on he didn't feel threatened until it was too late.'

'A drug buddy?'

'Maybe. It could also be someone he owed.'

'That fits with the profile of the killer, except it contradicts any lack of fear displayed by the victim and, consequently, the absence of defence injuries,' Deeley said.

'Whoever it was, a weapon was deliberately brought to the party with the intention of using it,' the SOCO pointed out.

'Perhaps the killer knew there was a fair chance that the victim would be wasted, making him more vulnerable,' Deeley commented, thinking aloud.

'Tox results should be able to clarify to what degree,' Harvey chipped in.

'Have you been able to isolate footwear marks?' Deeley asked.

'Near the body,' Harvey replied.

Hallelujah, Deeley thought. The upper part of a shoe,

and particularly with trainers, could be distinctive. From Harvey's expression, however, she deduced a 'but' was coming. Harvey left it to the SOCO to deliver the bad tidings.

'The footwear pattern suggests a trainer with a very worn, thin sole.'

'Are you kidding?' A pattern scuffed away over time would be a devil to identify. Deeley felt the stirrings of a headache behind her eyes. 'What about size?'

'Around a nine, certainly no smaller.'

'OK, well, I guess that rules out a female killer.' Which, Deeley was aware, was a pretty stupid thing to say at such an early stage in the investigation. In truth, the choice of weapon was a bigger factor. It simply didn't seem the type of crime committed by a woman.

'Further tests could throw up more information,' Harvey said. 'If you think of anything else, Nicole,' she said, addressing the SOCO, 'write it up in the crime-scene notes.'

Her cue to leave them to it, Deeley traced her steps back towards the cordon. A determined and organised killer, armed with a nail gun, and a thing for patterns and numbers. The more she thought about it, the more bizarre it seemed.

Chapter Seven

'Extremely bad news for a convicted murderer to be within spitting distance of a dead body,' Shaw said in consternation.

He knew of all kinds of methods employed to wipe another human being off the planet, but even he had to admit to shock. He'd also learnt, over the years, a certain measure of detachment. However fucked up things were, stay calm and, above all, focused. Whatever his emotional state now, he needed to concentrate.

'Did anyone see you go in?' he asked.

'Nah, I was careful.'

Careful in what way? Careful not to get caught? 'Did you touch anything?'

Danny issued an enormous pissed-off sigh. 'I looked and then I legged it.'

'Any CCTV cameras?'

'Not ones I noticed. Anyway, I wore a hoodie.'

Shaw sparked with suspicion. 'Why?'

'Because it was fucking cold this morning, knobhead, and it was raining.'

'OK, then what did you do?'

'I went back to the car and phoned Kenny. His uncle picked up his mobile. That's when he told me Kenny was dead.'

'In very different circumstances to Mark,' Shaw reminded him.

Danny pulled a face. 'You don't really believe that.'

'In the absence of evidence to the contrary, it's the *only* thing left to believe. Have you any idea how many people are killed on quad bikes every year, quite apart from those who sustain serious injuries? It's right up there with flying helicopters.'

'Kenny knew the risks.'

'He might well have done but you can't mitigate against bad luck.'

'Answer me this: why would someone that careful drive at speed down a hill with a 70-degree gradient?'

'For fun. For kicks. I don't know.' Shaw failed to mask the scepticism in his voice. 'Maybe he was driving away from a lunatic?'

'That's my point.'

The trouble with Danny: once he got an idea in his head, he was obsessed and nothing could distract him. Judging by his mutinous expression, Shaw knew he had to come up with a more persuasive argument.

'As far as Mark is concerned,' Shaw said, intent on staying on point, 'unfortunately, people who live rough often operate on the margins of criminality.' Something he felt well equipped to discuss. 'It's practically an occupational hazard, especially if they're using, which, according to you, Mark was.'

32

'Someone fucking did him. Kenny too.'

A tall, good-looking brunette sashayed past. Danny glanced up and followed her with his eyes in the way a starving dog drools after a piece of fresh meat. He turned back to Shaw and mouthed 'Stacked.'

'Don't even think about it.'

Danny glowered. 'Why? Think she's out of my league?'

Shaw didn't bother to answer. 'Were either Kenny or Mark afraid or worried about something?'

'Not that they said.'

'How was Kenny's health?'

'What's that got to do with anything?' Danny's expression was one big sneer.

'Did he mention blackouts, dizzy spells?'

'Fuck's sake, Mark had a filthy cough but it didn't mean he hammered his own head.'

Typical of Danny to answer the question he hadn't asked instead of the one he had. 'Did either of them mention falling out with anyone?'

Danny shook his head vigorously. 'Look,' he said, his voice chill with frustration. 'They died two days apart. That isn't a coincidence.'

'One man murdered and another who lost his life in a tragic accident does not represent a pattern.'

Danny shot forward and slammed the table with the side of his fist. Several drinkers looked round, including the brunette. 'I'm telling you someone is rolling the old gang up. This is only the start.'

Danny was the only person who could induce a 'hands around the throat' reaction from him. Shaw checked any

33

physical response, took a breath and prepared to peg his voice to the low tone adopted for the more unruly client. But Danny, whose eyes had narrowed to slits, wasn't done.

'Of all people I thought you'd be there for me, for us. You fucking owe me.'

'I owe you nothing.' A flash of pure anger blurred his vision. 'And if you don't go now and leave me the fuck alone, with every power I have I swear I will end you.' The threat had erupted from nowhere and yet Shaw felt the truth of it with every fibre of his being.

Danny's icy stare was enough to drop the temperature in the bar and surrounding streets by several degrees.

'What happened to you?' Danny was breathing hard. 'Don't you care? Don't you remember what we had, how we stuck together through Christ knows what? Took care of each other? Remember me looking after you after your mam died?'

The mention of his mother's death produced the same effect as if Danny had taken pliers to his fingernails and ripped them out one by one. A low emotional blow, designed to penetrate, it hurt. A lot.

Danny kicked back his chair and stood up. 'I thought I could rely on you. Seems I was wrong.' He pushed his hands into his pockets and made to leave.

'Sit down,' Shaw said. Pulsing with restless energy, Danny danced from one foot to the other.

It was true that Danny had protected him when he'd needed someone most. Kids could be brutal, but impoverished kids could be vicious and cruel. Small for his age, Shaw had been bullied directly after his mother's funeral, following her miserable and extended fight with cancer. His first aggressor had received a broken nose, the second a broken arm. After that, nobody ever bothered Shaw again and he had worshipped Danny Hallam. But a lot had changed since then.

Shaw looked up. 'Danny, for God's sake, sit down.'

Danny glared and sat with the force of a building under demolition.

'I'll help,' Shaw said grimly. 'But let's get two things straight. If you've committed a crime, I will not defend you. Secondly, I talk, you listen.'

Chapter Eight

'I'm not in the speculation business,' Shaw continued remorselessly. 'I'm only interested in facts and, until I have a clearer picture of what actually occurred, as opposed to what you *think* occurred, we're not jumping to unsubstantiated conclusions.'

When Danny opened his mouth to protest, Shaw dropped him with a look designed to have the same cutting precision as razor wire.

'I'll use the weekend to make enquiries. I need you to give me addresses and phone numbers. I also need to know exactly where you've been, where you've stayed and who with. In the meantime, you stick around and lay low. You will not, *repeat not*, ask questions or attempt to dig up information about Mark's death. You leave that to me. You will not contact Kenny's relatives. You will not speak a word of this to anyone.'

Danny's knee jived. 'Fuckin' hell. Yes, sir, no, sir.'

'Where's Kenny's car?'

'I ditched it when it ran out of petrol.'

'Yes, but specifically where is it? You must have some idea.'

'Between here and Wolverhampton.'

'Danny—'

'I set light to it, all right? It's burnt out on waste ground, somewhere near Tividale, a place that's a lot less pretty than it sounds.'

Shaw gaped at him. 'You torched a vehicle in broad daylight?'

'Don't get on your high fucking horse with me, or have you forgotten?'

An image of a burning Ford Escort flashed through Shaw's mind. It had been Danny's idea but Shaw had been happy to go along with it. They'd set light to a lot of stuff back then for the thrill.

'That was different and you know it.'

Danny shrugged. 'Getting rid of Kenny's motor seemed like the best plan at the time.'

'Did anyone see you?'

'Nobody who would talk.'

'Don't you understand the risk you took?'

'What does an arse-covering lawyer know about risk? It had my DNA all over it. You know what the pigs are like. I didn't want to get framed.'

'You really believe it, don't you? You really think there's some deep conspiracy at work?'

'It's what I've been trying to tell you, only you're not fucking listening. According to you I'm supposed to keep my gob shut and my ears pinned back.'

Shaw could see that he was getting nowhere. He tried to humour him. 'OK, hypothetically, let's say you're right.'

Danny glanced furtively towards the bar. 'I need more drink. Got any cash?'

Shaw sighed and fished out his wallet. 'Here,' he said, slapping a twenty into Danny's hand.

'Nice one,' Danny said. 'Do you want a refill?'

'Kind of you to buy me a drink,' Shaw said facetiously.

Danny flashed a grin and winked.

While he was gone Shaw considered the timing of the deaths. If there was a shred of truth in Danny's conviction, why now and after a quarter of a century? Was it really possible that someone was hell-bent on seeking revenge for a twenty-five-year-old murder in which the accused had paid his debt to society and done his time? Shaw frowned. Maybe Danny was right. Maybe he *was* thinking too much like a risk-averse lawyer.

Danny planted two drinks on the table. Shaw stuck his palm out. 'Change?'

'I bought crisps.' Danny tore open a packet, removing a fistful. 'Food,' he said, munching happily. 'First thing I've had to eat since yesterday.'

'You should have said.'

Danny hiked an eyebrow. 'Going to take me out to dinner, were you, love?'

Shaw was thinking more in terms of takeway food from the Co-op on the corner. Time to cut to the chase.

'Did Mickie Ashton have any surviving relatives, brothers, sisters?'

Danny shook his head. 'Her mam died years ago. Didn't have a dad. Well, obviously she did,' Danny said, 'but not one that stuck around.'

'What about the father of the child?'

Danny frowned, gave it some thought. 'Nah,' he said, plunging his hand back into the pack. 'The little shite would have come forward.'

'What about Mickie Ashton's kid?' Shaw couldn't bring himself to articulate the fact that the child had been delivered early in an emergency procedure.

'Word was it didn't survive.' Shaw balked at yet another stain on his conscience. 'Aside from her mam,' Danny continued, 'nobody mourned the death of Mickie Ashton.'

How pitiable was that? And yet, *if* Danny was right, someone not only cared but knew that five other people were complicit.

And then it hit him.

With Danny's release from prison, someone could be tracking his movements in the hope that he'd expose other members of the gang. Jesus, Danny could have inadvertently led a killer to his door. Hold up, Shaw thought. This was just a hypothesis. *Wasn't it?*

'Have you heard from Carl or Wolf?'

'Nobody's seen or heard from Carl in decades. Last I knew of Wolf he was shacked up with an American blonde.'

True what they say about leopards not changing their spots, or in this case, wolf, Shaw thought. Terence Whittaker aka Wolf had always been a magnet for female attention, something to do with his moody, mercurial manner. Once he'd cast his spell, his girls became powerless to break it. He was the first of the group, allegedly, to lose his cherry. Conversely, Danny held the record for first smokes, booze and drugs.

'Do you know where?'

'A guesthouse in Clevedon. The Yank runs it.'

'Clevedon, near Bristol?' He knew the area well, courtesy of a former girlfriend who'd put up with his lack of commitment for a lot less time than Jo.

'In Somerset, yeah.'

'You don't have a specific address?'

'What do you think I am, Google?'

'Fair enough,' Shaw said mildly. 'How about the woman's name?'

'Lori. Don't know her surname.'

'It's a start and it's not a very big place. I'll make sure Wolf's OK and then I'll find Carl.'

'If they're still alive.'

Shaw pretended not to hear.

'So what happens next?' Danny tipped the last remnants from the packet into his mouth, scrunched up the cellophane and licked his fingers.

'You go your way. I go mine. We'll meet again once I have news.'

'I don't have a phone, muppet. What are you planning – pigeon-post?'

Shaw pulled out his wallet, counted out three twenties. 'Get yourself a Pay As You Go.'

Danny swiped the money out of his hand with the speed of a viper-strike.

'And where am I supposed to sleep now I've ditched the car?'

'Wherever the terms of your license stipulate.'

'I'm not going back to me mam's tonight.'

'Danny, you can't afford to take the risk. If you're not where you're supposed to be, they'll throw the book at you and send you straight back to prison.'

Danny crossed his arms. 'I'd like to see them try.'

'I'll pay your train fare.'

'Nah,' Danny said, tipping back on his chair. 'I've got a way better idea.'

Oh crap, Shaw thought, knowing exactly where Danny was going with it.

'I'll book you a room.' Although God only knew where. Danny wasn't your usual hotel clientele.

'Why can't I doss at yours?'

'Because you're asking me to risk my career.' No way could he assist an ex-offender, and what if Jo came back? But then, oh Christ, what if it wasn't safe for her to return?

'Only if they find out, which they won't,' Danny said, bullish. 'Nobody will know I'm there. I don't mind kipping on the sofa. I assume you have a sofa,' he said with a crafty smile.

'It's absolutely out of the question.'

Adopting the faux accent of the aristocracy, Danny mimicked Shaw.

'Look,' Shaw said. 'What if you're right? What if the killer is here? Now. In this bar. Watching. The best thing we can do is split up.'

Danny was having none of it. 'You've got right up yourself, you know that?' He tapped the side of his nose. 'Safety in numbers, that's what I say. Be like old times.'

Yes, Shaw thought. That's very much what he was afraid of.

Chapter Nine

Taking no chances, Shaw deliberately took a circuitous route home. He couldn't help but glance over his shoulder. If they were followed, would he be able to spot it?

The rain had abated and the air, once again, felt muggy and warm. Shaw could feel the weight of it pressing down on his shoulders. They were cutting down Montpellier Terrace, in Cheltenham, between a park with a bandstand and café on the left and a row of terraced houses on the right. Raindrops slid off spiked railings. Water dripped from plane trees.

'How did you find me?' Shaw asked.

'Where do you think? The internet.'

Shaw glanced across in surprise.

'No need to get your knickers in a twist; I didn't leave a digital trail in prison, if that's what you're thinking. Went to a café after I got out, didn't I?'

'You know how to use a computer?'

'Learnt inside. It goes down well with the screws if inmates better themselves. With twenty-five years to look forward to, I thought I might as well. Not that it helped reduce my sentence.' To emphasise his frustration, Danny stamped through a particularly deep puddle. 'I've done courses in bricklaying, numeracy and IT. Supposed to make us ready for the big bad world once we get kicked out. Fat chance.'

Shaw knew what prison did to people. It institutionalised them. It often brutalised them. It screwed with minds already screwed. It rotted souls. Stepping out after all that time would be a frightening prospect. More terrifying: the fact that the world had moved on at speed, without them.

'I guess you must have seen a lot of change.' Shaw winced at how crass it sounded. Danny was not an ex-pat returning to Blighty.

'Well, let me see.' Danny's tone suggested that Shaw was in for a long list. 'Obviously, prices have increased. A packet of fags when I went inside was under three quid. Now they're nearer a tenner. There's more noise. More people. More immigrants. Nobody talks to each other. Frightened of their own shadows, most of them. I mean what's that Woke bollocks all about? Half asleep, more like.'

Shaw tried to interject but was cut off at the pass by Danny in full flight.

'Then you've got fuckers just plain out for themselves, dog eat dog, especially on the roads – drivers pulling all kinds of lunatic shit – and you can't even walk on a pavement without being knocked over by some tosser on a bike. And,' he said pausing for dramatic effect, 'since when did women dye their hair blue? I mean, what the fuck?'

Shaw tried to speak for a second time but Danny was unstoppable. Was he on drugs? Shaw asked himself.

'Don't matter where you go,' Danny opined, 'high streets are full of empty shops, and fields are full of housing nobody can afford – and they call that progress,' he said with a sneer. 'There's cameras everywhere snooping, but cops nowhere to be seen – not that I'm bothered – and when they do get off their bony arses and show up, they've all got long chin beards, like fucking garden gnomes.'

Shaw dived in, briefly interrupting Danny's flow. 'They're visible enough when it comes to enforcing the law, I can assure you.'

'Oh yeah?' Danny said, sucking in his cheeks. 'You've got little kids acting as lookouts and mules. Some, as young as eight, carry knives. Girls too. It's a disgrace. And that's because there's nobody around to give them a good slap.'

Shaw understood only too well the consequences of giving a pumped-up teenager a 'good slap'. The evidence could fill an entire filing cabinet in his office.

'You've only got to look sideways at the wrong person,' Danny grumbled, 'and you get a blade in your gut.'

Danny had always been good at seeing things in isolation when exercised, Shaw remembered. It seemed to escape him that he, too, had also shoved a blade into a woman and killed her and, indirectly, her child. Shaw blanched at the memory. Born at seven months, the baby hadn't stood a chance. Maybe it was for the best. There was nothing bleaker than a motherless child.

'Fuckin' hell, I thought you said this was a short walk.'

'It usually is.'

'Well, I'm hotter than a tart's fanny.' Danny bent forward and slipped off his top.

'For God's sake, put your vest back on. You can't walk up Bath Road half naked.' Danny was acting as if he'd been raised by wolves, which, Shaw guessed, was not far from the truth.

'Ooh, do I embarrass you?' Danny laughed and flicked Shaw in the face, catching the corner of his eye.

Shaw stopped dead. Danny's incessant homespun bar-room philosophy had driven him to the brink. 'You're a child, Danny, and if you think catching up with me is one big laugh, then take your cobbled together story of murder and mayhem and piss off.'

Cars travelled up and down the road. Light from an overhead street lamp bathed Danny in ghostly hues, turning his torso green and mauve, like a collection of bruises. No more laughs. No more jokes. No more smiles. Both palms up in surrender, he looked stricken.

'I'm sorry, man. I didn't mean to make you angry. I thought, you know, with everything.' His voice petered out. Obediently, he slipped his vest back on. 'It's not a story, Jon,' he said quietly. 'I swear.'

Shaw felt a shiver run along his spine. 'I know,' he said.

Chapter Ten

Danny's astonished expression was a first. Shaw got it. This was planets away from their childhood homes in cramped flats that reeked of mould on the eighteenth floor of a tower block. The first time Shaw had stepped into the tall and imposing proportions of what was to be his new home, it had elicited a similar response.

A grand and elegant house, with many period original features, including sash windows, deep skirting boards, cornices, it had that whole moneyed, Regency vibe going on. He only wished that Jo were there to complement it. But then, did he really want her to meet Danny? How could he explain about his old life when all she knew was his new? Shame smothered him for his deceit to her and his lack of loyalty to a friend. A friend who drove him crazy. A friend who had turned murderer and he'd wanted to kill, admittedly. And that led to another big question: how would Jo feel about his association with a convicted killer? How did *he* genuinely feel? The answer came back in a shot. He wanted Danny out of his hair and his life.

But if Danny was right, he had little choice other than to stick with him. It was a matter of pure survival.

Shaw shook raindrops off his coat, hung it up and parked the umbrella. Out of habit, he wanted to call out to Jo that he was home before remembering with a wrench that she was gone.

'The living room is here.' Shaw crossed the hall and indicated a room opposite an imposing staircase.

Danny tilted his head towards a door to his immediate left. 'What's in there?'

'My study. Out of bounds,' he added, making a mental note to find the key. 'Go into the living room. Fix yourself a drink. Are you hungry?'

'Nah.' Danny patted his washboard lean stomach. 'Maybe a fry-up in the morning, if you're not vegan,' he said, teasing.

Shaw wasn't, although it had been a long time since he'd eaten bacon and eggs for breakfast. 'I'll get you a towel for your hair and throw some bedding together for the guest room.' He braced himself, waiting for Danny to mock him, but he was too awestruck by his surroundings, or, as Danny would say, *gobsmacked*.

Upstairs, Shaw went straight into the bathroom, ran the cold tap and splashed his face vigorously with water. Staring into the mirror revealed that, physically, he was the same man who'd stepped out of his home that morning and yet he felt as though he were viewing an imposter.

Who am I?

To the outside world he was a forty-three-year-old male with blond hair, swept back from his brow, and neatly trimmed sideburns tinged with grey. He had fair skin and brown eyes, downturned at the edges, which suggested vulnerability. His nose was straight, neat, some might say, and, more often than not, his thin top lip tilted up, suggesting that he was a glass half-full merchant. In short, he had one of those faces that did not look easily disposed to anger.

This man before him had plenty of colleagues who were friends. He had no enemies and was spoken of in warm tones. He commanded respect in legal circles. He had a nice, comfortable existence, a universe away from his upbringing. His choice of holiday was far-flung, expensive and, shamefully, did nothing for the welfare of the planet. Money posed no problem. But these were merely the trappings, the shell of his existence. Deep down, he was not what he seemed, however much he willed it otherwise.

Shaw rubbed his hair dry and found clean linen and towels. Roughly making up the bed, he returned downstairs to find Danny, a glass of whisky in his hand, sprawled out on the sofa. His plimsolls had scuffed the carpet with wet marks.

'Here,' Shaw said, handing him a towel. He fixed himself a drink while Danny gave the top of his head a rub and mopped rain and perspiration from his face.

An awkward silence prevailed. Shaw snatched at his drink. His entire life had been upended. And there was something else: he didn't entirely trust Danny.

'So,' Danny said, clearly settling in for a long evening, 'what became of you?'

Shaw glanced at the neutral-coloured walls, the massive fireplace and the French windows that opened out to a walled garden. 'I'd have thought that was obvious.'

'After you pushed me into the river.' Danny's voice was low and tight, his lips thin.

Shaw didn't want to do this, didn't want to think about it. By a miracle, he'd escaped the badlands of Manchester. For years he'd remembered every case he'd won, every decent deed, every courtesy extended to a friend in the hope that it would expunge the smell of the river, the sight of blood, the taste of bile in his mouth; in effect, blot out the past. And here was Danny dragging him back.

When he finally spoke, he talked so quietly that Danny was forced to crane forwards.

'I went to Old Man S.' Old Man S, or Richard Squire, his history teacher, hadn't known it but he'd saved Shaw from a desperate situation and from himself. Shaw wasn't lying when he'd told Annie Mayfield about the importance of significant intervention. He'd been speaking from the heart.

'Thought so,' Danny said knowingly. 'Always was teacher's pet.'

That's wasn't fair. 'I simply wasn't one of those kids interested in bunking off.' Like the rest of you, he thought, although ridiculously clever Carl had also put in enough hours to ensure high grades. For Shaw, school had provided a routine that was sadly missing from his life. Education had been his salvation. He hadn't inhabited the library only to keep warm. With books, you knew where you were. With Danny and the gang, you never had a clue, which was also the attraction. Mayhem was a knowable entity, familiar and almost comfortable. The irony was that the things he loved the gang for, he also hated.

'I suppose you don't get owt for nowt,' Danny said,

surprisingly philosophical. 'Did Old Man S know about Mickie?'

'Absolutely not.'

'But he knew you were in trouble?'

Shaw gave a shrug. 'If he did, he didn't ask questions. I stayed at his for the night and the next day I picked up my exam results.'

'Don't tell me,' Danny said, 'Top marks.'

'Good enough to secure a place at university. I moved to London straightaway.' Where he could lose himself. He'd worked his arse off to obtain a law degree while bartending and delivering pizzas to supplement his grant.

'Fuck of a long way from Manchester.'

That was the point, Shaw thought. How he'd loved being a speck on the massive urban landscape, where nobody could find him. Whenever he had a spare hour or two, he wandered streets, losing himself in the hustle and anonymity. After a lot of graft, and a little 'right time, right place' luck, he'd reinvented his persona in the same way an orthopaedic surgeon builds a broken body. He'd landed a job, moved up the legal food chain and, bit by slow bit, risen to the top of his profession.

'Long story short, I did my internship there and finally fetched up here.'

'Sweet,' Danny said, taking a deep swallow of whisky. 'Sounds dead easy.'

Nothing had come easy. Like a spy, Shaw had invented an entire cover story, a legend, to help him more easily fit into his new environment. He'd studied how people spoke, how they engaged, even the way they walked. He watched what they ate, how they ate, observed every nuance of what he regarded as Southern behaviour. He studied their passions and obsessions, their dislikes and their hatreds. He tried to think like them, especially those who'd come from what he regarded as privileged upbringings, a universe away from his own experience. There were plenty of other students from the North but he didn't want to be one of them because then questions might be asked. And questions would lead to difficult conversations. To survive, he had destroyed his roots and, like a con man, become an impressive liar. He rarely dropped his guard and, when he did, he put as much distance as he could between him and the situation or person.

Switching back to the present, Shaw said, 'You were going to provide me with Mark and Kenny's details.'

Danny let out a gale of a sigh, rummaged in the pocket of his jogging trousers and pulled out a slip of paper. He stretched across and placed it in Shaw's hands. The writing looked as if it had been written by a five-year-old. Shaw pictured Danny, with the tip of his tongue poking out, pen inelegantly grasped in a fist, like a dagger, laboriously forming letters.

'I'll get started on it in the morning. You must be pretty bushed.' Shaw hoped that Danny would take the hint and go to bed.

Danny had other ideas. He stretched out his limbs, happy, a ridiculously sentimental gleam in his eye. 'Hey, remember us scrapping with the Hanlons?'

'Scrapping' was a daily occurrence. Danny would deliberately pick fights to reset the boundaries, like an aggressor ramping up hostilities and gaining ground immediately before a ceasefire and further negotiation.

'And we rescued that knock-kneed kid?' Shaw couldn't help but smile at the memory. Danny had been furious. 'You put the fear of God into them.'

'Right little bastards. I threatened to string Sean Hanlon up by his toenails, big fat fuck. I would have done and all. I hate bullies.'

'What was the kid's name?'

'Not sure he had one,' Danny said with a laugh. 'Mind, Auntie Maggs was that pleased when I handed him over.'

'God, Auntie Maggs.' Auntie Maggs ran things in their part of the estate. Seer, elder, provider of fags and cheap booze, and the woman girls went to when they were in trouble, Auntie Maggs was an all-round fixer. Shaw hadn't thought about her in years.

'Think she's still with us?' Danny said.

'Unlikely. She looked about hundred and that was then.' Sadly, Shaw doubted Old Man S was still around either. He recalled their last goodbye. There was an unspoken acknowledgement that they would never see each other again. 'Your mam,' Shaw said. 'How is she?'

An image of a blowsy blonde with dark roots floated in front of Shaw's eyes. Danny's mother, Christie, had a generous nature, particularly when it came to men. She liked a drink or ten, too. Memorably, and on more than one occasion, Shaw had scraped her off the floor and put her to bed. Once, when the social came round, he said she'd got the 'flu.

'Same old. Living with some old git from Wythenshawe. At least she's off the game.'

'That's a bit strong.' Shaw liked Christie. She'd been good to him and his dad after he lost the plot when his mam died. She'd brought them a hotpot every week, regardless of the season or the weather.

'The woman says it herself,' Danny said, wide-eyed. 'Oldest profession in the world. It's like a fucking badge of honour.'

A great gut-gurgling sound that Shaw hadn't heard in years burst from the back of his throat. He wasn't laughing at Christie's expense or at Danny's. He was laughing because this was his past and he was connected to something that wasn't all bad. There had been mad and happy times. He hadn't simply fetched up somewhere in the south, like he pretended. Only Danny really understood the real Jon Shaw. He knew the joy and the pain and the tragedy in his life like no other. Not even Jo.

The sound of the doorbell cut through the air like a blade.

Shaw glanced at his watch. Who would be calling at eleven o'clock at night?

'You expecting anyone?' Danny said, immediately alert.

Jo, Shaw thought. 'You stay here,' he said. 'Pour yourself another drink.'

'It's a woman, isn't it? I can tell by that look on your face. Didn't think you'd be living here all on your ownsome.'

'Drop it, Danny.' Shaw headed out to the hall.

'Are you going to introduce us?' He heard Danny call after him.

Hardly daring to hope, wondering what the hell he was going to say if Jo had come back, Shaw glanced through the peephole in the front door. Nobody was there. He drew back. Was it a prank? Or, more worrying, was someone waiting to stick a sharp implement through the lens? No, this was not a scene from a thriller, for God's sake.

Sliding across the security chain, Shaw opened the door and peered across the street and then to his right and to his left. Cars parked half up on the road and on the pavement. Lamplight cast a greasy glow. A cyclist wearing a hi-viz jacket splashed up the middle of the road through the rain, avoiding the gutters. About to close the door, Shaw glanced down. On the step were six black feathers. Two of them were broken.

Chapter Eleven

'It's a warning,' Shaw said. 'Two down, four to go.' After locking the door, he'd picked up the feathers, cupped them in the palm of his hand and showed Danny.

'Believe me now?' Danny said, slow-eyed.

Reluctantly, Shaw supposed he did.

'Did you see anyone?' Danny said.

Shaw shook his head.

'No car driving off at speed?'

'The street's as quiet as a grave.' Then it dawned on him. 'Maybe it's a diversion.'

Danny sprang up.

'You check downstairs,' Shaw called over his shoulder, already hurrying out of the room and towards the staircase. 'I'll check the upper storeys.'

This is crazy, Shaw thought, flicking on every light in the house, moving from room to room. Against all rational thought, he found himself breathing hard. Perspiration coated his top lip. What did he expect? An axe murderer already in the house and ready to strike? But Mark's appalling death was genuine, and the feathers were real and signified more than two lives snuffed out with four to go. They symbolised cowardice. His.

As Shaw returned to the hall, he noticed Danny bowling out of his study. *Damn.* 'Anything?' he said.

'Nah. Everything's locked. No sign of break-in. We need more drink,' Danny said firmly.

They didn't, Shaw thought. Danny's eyes were already filmy with booze, but Danny wasn't a guy you said no to, particularly when tanked up. Shaw filled their glasses. Small for him, large for Danny. Maybe he'd pass out.

Danny took a deep drink and narrowed his gaze as if he were downing cyanide. 'So why muck about?'

'Not sure I follow.'

'Doorbells and feathers. Waste of time.'

'You mean why not break in and...' Not keen to say the unthinkable, Shaw left the words unsaid.

'Do us?' Danny said.

'Well, yes.'

'Because he's mental, off his head.'

Shaw wasn't so sure. He glanced towards the window. 'Because it's part of his game.'

'Drilling holes in a bloke's head is funny?' There was a raw, challenging edge to Danny's voice.

'That's not what I said or meant.' Shaw stood up, went to the kitchen, poured the contents of his glass down the sink and filled a tumbler with water. He needed to clear his head, to focus on facts, without Danny screwing up his thought processes. When he returned to the living room, Danny was up on his feet, swaying unsteadily and studying a photograph of Shaw at a wedding with Jo.

'This your woman?'

'We broke up.'

'Shame. She's hot. What's her name?'

'Never you mind.'

Danny shrugged, turned away, and slumped back down. His left leg jerked uncontrollably. Shaw wondered whether Danny's twitchiness was down to nerves or was symptomatic of his need for a fix. In the past Danny would get hyper-edgy following exposure to one of his mam's boyfriends beating the crap out of her. Later on, it was the prelude to jacking up before an illegal rave. A vivid memory of Danny, arms in the air, jumping to a pumping techno beat, off his head and shouting at a thousand decibels, coursed through Shaw's mind. Back then, Danny didn't speak; he rattled.

Shaw perched his rear on a sideboard, a deliberate tactic to assume authority. 'Aaron Waterhouse,' he said.

A flash of colour raced across the top of Danny's flat cheek-bones. 'What about him?'

'Maybe he's behind it all.'

'Why? I kept my mouth shut and did him a favour.'

'Maybe he bears a grudge.'

'For what?'

'Drawing heat and turning the spotlight of the law onto his patch.'

'Twenty-five years on?' Danny scoffed.

Put like that it did sound ludicrous, but Waterhouse was a man who could crawl lower than a snake's belly; he was capable of anything. 'Maybe Waterhouse is doing quite nicely and doesn't want any former association coming along to ruin things.'

Danny pulled a face. 'Is that what you think *this* is?' His eyes danced around the room, voice surly again. 'Me showing up at your fancy front door?'

'I didn't say that.' Shaw did all in his power to suppress a streak of irritation because, sure as hell, he could see truth in it. 'I simply don't think we can rule a man like him out.'

'Nah, from what I hear, Waterhouse went straight years ago. Owns half of Cheshire.'

This time it was Shaw's turn to mock. 'Have you any idea how many criminals front their criminality with a property portfolio? And how do you know so much about him? Oh, don't tell me, the magic internet.'

Danny glared and fell ominously silent. A quiet Danny was more alarming than a full-on, garrulous Danny. Shaw apologised.

'Fuck you.'

'We're all fucked if we don't get a handle on this.'

'That's true.' Danny clicked his tongue and took another pull of booze. Shaw waited for Danny to settle again.

'So what else do you know about Waterhouse?'

'He divorced Esther and hooked up with some woman half his age. Doesn't seem very likely he'd come after the likes of us when he's happy as a Premier League footballer.'

Shaw disagreed. Men like that never changed and they were easily able to compartmentalise their lives. 'Waterhouse might be regularly getting his end away but business is business. If anyone is capable of carrying out a scorched earth policy, it's him.'

Danny frowned. 'Scorched earth?'

'Destroy anything that might be useful to the enemy. In Waterhouse's case, the cops.'

'Looks like we're on the same page then,' Danny quipped, with an earthy laugh.

Shaw gave Danny a good hard look. Why did he get the strong impression that a big part of Danny Hallam was actually enjoying this?

'You were saying,' Shaw pressed.

Danny issued a monster sigh. 'He lives near Altrincham, not far from Hale Village, in one of them mansions. As well as making money from property, he specialises in cars, rare first editions.'

'Always was a petrolhead.' While most kids on the estate couldn't afford wheels, Waterhouse had swanned around in a silver BMW 328i with a dent running down the side of it.

Shaw pictured him. Tall and lean, older than the rest of them by a decade, Waterhouse had jet-black hair and small features, although his neck was thick and there was a suggestion of a double chin. By contrast, his mouth was small and his lips indistinguishable. It only served to make his eyes, which were the colour of marrowfat peas, stand out. One look from Waterhouse and you'd feel as if he'd drilled a hole in your head. Shaw briefly balked at the comparison.

The man in charge and with a plan, Waterhouse had seemed older and wiser. And he was vicious. There were reports that he'd had a man's hand plunged into a fat fryer for not paying his dues. Was it really possible that a bloke like that could change his ways? Surely, ruthlessness was impregnated in his DNA? It wasn't such a stretch that Waterhouse wanted every connection broken, every loose end tied, despite what Danny said.

Downing his drink, Danny abruptly stood up and stretched his arms above his head. 'Where am I kipping?'

Shaw eyed him. Was Danny really bushed or, more worrying, uncomfortable discussing Aaron Waterhouse for reasons Shaw didn't yet understand?

'This way,' he said, leading Danny to his room.

'Like staying at the Ritz.' Danny smiled admiringly and with a glint in his eye that told Shaw he was going to fill his boots with whatever was on offer.

'None of my clothes will fit, but I'll nip down town in the morning and grab a couple of pairs of jeans and shirts. What are you, forty-inch chest, thirty-two-inch waist?'

'Forty-two, thirty-one, twenty-nine length. Shoe size is eight, if you're interested. Don't forget socks and undies.'

'Right.' Shaw was sharply reminded of how he'd fetched and carried for Danny in the past.

'And mind how you go. Don't want someone knifing you in the back in the middle of the high street.' Danny's grin was wide, seemingly amused by the thought.

'Why are you treating this as one big laugh?'

'Why are *you* such a dick?' The happy expression vanished as quickly as a power outage.

Shaw met Danny's ugly expression. Shaw itched to rearrange it. Was Danny's company rubbing off on him? Was he somehow morphing back into his old defensive self? It wasn't a pleasant thought.

'Get some sleep,' Shaw said coldly. 'We're taking a road trip tomorrow.'

Chapter Twelve

Shaw slept badly. Nothing new. Since Jo's departure, the bed hadn't felt right. Now he was consumed by memories he'd rather forget. How could 9,125 good days, give or take a couple of leap years, be obliterated in the space of a few hours? When he'd finally drifted off, his dreams were filled with Mark and Kenny and a kaleidoscope of people who were more caricature that character; men like Billy Butterworth, a wheelchair-bound pimp, Wes Burgess, a kid at school whose budding football career had been ruined by high expectation followed by crushing disappointment, and Auntie Maggs with her hooded fathomless eyes and her knife-edged cheekbones. Strangely, Danny didn't feature at all.

As soon as it was light, he dragged on a robe and set out to make coffee. He needed it strong. Two sugars. While the kettle boiled, he briefly examined the six feathers, running his index finger along the barbs. He naturally assumed that the individual responsible had worn gloves. Even if prints could be lifted off them, a long shot, Shaw could hardly report what he considered a very real threat to the police. Questions would rightly be asked and then more until

61

connections were made and the truth dragged out kicking and screaming into the blinding light. Goodbye everything he'd worked hard for. Did a myriad of good deeds obliterate one massive error of judgement? If only he could throw away the past as easily as depositing last night's warning into the kitchen bin.

Shaw pulled out two mugs and glanced up to the ceiling through which Danny's heavy snores could be heard. He decided to leave him to it.

Back in bed, Shaw grabbed his laptop and trawled through the latest stories. He didn't find anything on Kenny but, sure enough, a news item reported the murder investigation of an unidentified homeless man in Wolverhampton. The headline ran with 'Killed By Nail Gun'. A crude mock-up of a skull, in which nails were embedded, accompanied the piece. Following a brief description of the victim and the bedsit in which the body was found, a spokesperson for the police, Detective Inspector Samantha Deeley, took a standard police line, and one with which Shaw was more than familiar. He ran down a mental checklist: *barbaric act*: tick; *defenceless man*: tick; *highly dangerous individual:* big tick. *Anyone with information*: usual tick. The piece concluded with a routine appeal to anyone who thought they could identify the victim, or help with the enquiry.

What to do? Shaw ran a hand along his jaw. With one anonymous phone call, he could make a difference. Talking to Deeley in person would possibly aid her enquiry and help his. Such an action would provide an elegant solution.

But what about the risk?

Putting himself in the police officer's shoes, Deeley was

bound to question why a smooth-talking lawyer from Cheltenham would have an association with a down-and-out in Wolverhampton. And it wasn't only his own skin to consider; he had to take into account Carl and Wolf too.

Hoping that caffeine would sharpen his thinking, Shaw drank some coffee. Much depended on how good Deeley was at her job, her approachability, what she was like as a person. Did she only speak police, or was she open-minded and flexible in her thinking?

Most police had a presence on social media. Often they'd make amendments to their name and keep their personal contacts' list private. Shaw knew that they were also warned never to search for offenders using Facebook accounts as the algorithms could then suggest them as 'friends' to the criminal in question. So, he wondered, clicking through a variety of permutations, where was Detective Inspector Samantha Deeley? Five minutes later, he had his answer. The woman appeared to have no social media or digital footprint. Private then, or, like him, did she have something to hide?

Undecided about how to approach her, he threw back the duvet, showered and dressed. He didn't bother shaving.

After a night of rain, sunshine played hide and seek among the clouds. Automatically, he was wary of others as he walked down the street and cut into town, via a long way round, down Sandford Road and then College Road. Cheltenham had its corporate, cosmopolitan look going on: sharp corners, exotic cars and oversized salaries.

A speedy detour into a park allowed him to check whether he had company. He didn't. Yet. He reckoned a certain measure of fear was good, his closest ally. Only a stupid, reckless man was unafraid. He couldn't quite explain it but he felt more courageous now than at any time in the sad, safe life he'd created for himself. Maybe his survival instinct had kicked in.

Shaw bought two pairs of straight leg jeans the second he hit the high street. A couple of pairs of trainers, both black, were purchased from a shop that was closing down. Next stop: a chemist for razors, shaving foam and other toiletries. He bought two white T-shirts and a windcheater in Superdry, despite resenting the fact that he was contributing to its fabulously wealthy founder, who had already bought up a substantial amount of property in town.

Shaw crossed to a shop that sold mobile phones, picking up a cheap pay as you go mobile, then on to the Promenade and to Jack Wills, where he collected underwear, socks, a couple of sweatshirts and a hoodie reduced from sixty-five to forty-five pounds. The kind of sweatpants favoured by Danny Shaw strenuously avoided. Finally, he popped into the Co-op on the corner of Montpellier Street and bought milk, bacon and eggs. Food shopping had been Jo's domain. Booze was more his speciality. With a pang, he examined his phone to see if she'd left any messages. None. Maybe it was for the best, the thought of putting her in danger unbearable.

Cutting through Montpellier Gardens, Shaw thought about Deeley again, coppers and lawyers and how they connected and that's when he hit on an idea that was so blindingly obvious he was embarrassed not to have tumbled to it before.

The house was silent, suspiciously so. He called Danny's name. No answer. Three bags of shopping hit the floor and Shaw edged towards the kitchen, picking up the largest blade he could find from the knife block. He moved with stealth on the balls of his feet and glided upstairs. Pushing open the door to Danny's room, the bed was empty; the duvet piled on the floor alongside Danny's clothes. A heavy smell of body odour and alcohol clung to the walls. No sign of a fight. No sign of blood. Shaw tightened his grip on the blade. About to turn, a fierce blow from behind connected with his kidneys, shooting a tidal wave of pain along his spine and down his legs.

'What's wrong with you?' Danny shouted.

Shaw spun round and found himself eyeball to eyeball with Danny, who stood in front of him, pumped up and naked.

'Wrong with me?' he gasped, doubling over.

'You're the one with a knife in your hand,' Danny yelled. 'What were you going to do with it?'

Shaw tried to answer but found he couldn't speak. His back was one raging ball of fire.

'Can I trust you, Jon?'

Bile flooded Shaw's mouth. Had the pain lost some of its intensity? He didn't think so. 'I came back and you didn't answer,' Shaw spluttered. 'Where the hell were you?'

'Where do you think I was? Having a crap. Next time, I'll send a memo.'

Shaw dropped the knife and attempted to straighten up. 'Did you have to hit me so bloody hard?'

Danny's stance relaxed and the rawness in his voice disappeared. He reached out and playfully pinched Jon's cheek. 'You've gone soft, Jon Shaw.'

'And you stink. Go and take a shower, for God's . . .' Shaw stopped, transfixed by the inks on Danny's bare chest.

'What?' Danny said. 'Like what you see?' he added with a fake salacious grin.

'Fuck's sake, Danny. I'm not staring at your junk.'

Danny glanced down at his chest. 'Oh, you mean that,' he said, suddenly sheepish.

'What on earth possessed you to have the names of everyone in our gang tattooed onto your torso? You're a walking encyclopaedia, a mobile bloody clue.'

Danny hiked a shoulder. 'Seemed a good idea at the time. I don't normally walk around without my vest on.'

'Apart from last night.'

'Oh yeah. But I was battered. Got any aspirin?'

'You'll find some in the medicine chest in the bathroom. Help yourself. Now go and shower and cover yourself up. We need to talk.'

Danny made to move and then stopped. 'That breakfast you mentioned last night?'

'On the table in fifteen. Be there.'

Chapter Thirteen

Danny, clean-shaven and wearing his new clothes, looked almost respectable. Shaw watched as Danny mopped up bacon and eggs with a slice of bread, as if it were his last meal before facing lethal injection.

'When you spoke to Mark, did he mention any problems he'd experienced with the law?'

'What sort of problems?' Danny mumbled, his mouth full.

'Issues with a former landlord, maybe.'

'Not that he mentioned. Got any toast? I'm that starving.'

Shaw scraped back his chair, extracted two slices from the bread bin and banged them in the toaster.

'What about theft?' Shaw had occasionally defended those who stole because they were too poor to pay for goods.

Danny's eyes brightened. 'He mentioned something about a shopkeeper he'd fallen out with when he half-inched some cans.'

'You mean alcohol?'

'Don't think he was ever prosecuted, just barred,' Danny said.

Which was a pity, Shaw thought. Had there been a case

to answer, he could justifiably say that Mark had paid him a professional visit. Then again, if a record existed, the police would be able to match it to the identity of the victim but, so far, they hadn't. Maybe the shopkeeper would come forward in due course. More likely, he would not. People were protectionist when it came to involving themselves with the dead, particularly when a crime has been committed. By reporting a disagreement, the shopkeeper could fairly assume he would join the suspect list. The good news: Shaw could weave a story based on fact that would give him the plausibility he required. Only Shaw would know that Mark had never consulted him. He stood up.

'I'm going to Wolverhampton.'

'What about our road trip?'

'Later.' Shaw glanced at his watch, worked out the time-scale, including the possibility of an hour spent with the police. 'I'll be back to pick you up at three o'clock.'

'What am I supposed to do in the meantime?' Danny's voice was a flat whine.

'Watch a film. Play some music. Read a book. There's enough of them to choose from.' Danny gawped at him as if he'd suggested he learn Mandarin. 'Whatever you do, don't go out and don't answer the door.'

Before Danny could complain, Shaw scooped up his car keys and headed out of the house.

He could have driven straight to the cop shop. He could have made a phone call, but Shaw needed to see where his old friend had died.

*

Even if Shaw hadn't had an address, the level of police activity, crime-scene tape and rubberneckers was a giveaway. Shaw parked a way down the street and, for once, wished he drove something less eye-catching. The whole area was down on its luck and here he was about to plant a forty-six grand motor in the middle of it.

Shaw locked the Macan and walked towards the building where Mark had met his gruesome end. He guessed it was what you'd describe as a maisonette. The shop below sold saris, the one next-door sex aids. It had a grille over the window. A neon light above the door flashed 'Adult Shop' in red and sickly green. You'd think there would be a plethora of CCTV cameras to clock a killer on the prowl but there were fewer than expected. Shaw suspected that a fair proportion of them, in common with quite obviously disconnected burglar alarms, were only there for show.

He sidestepped observers and sauntered past the property to get a feel for the terrain and to find the nearest convenience store. He found one seven minutes later. Retracing his steps, past an overflowing rubbish bin, he skirted a voluminous amount of vomit on the pavement. Poverty stalked the streets. Despite the sunshine, so many closed doors; so many closed lives. People who lived here had the odds stacked against them from the moment of birth, Shaw reflected. It was the kind of place where a drug dealer was guaranteed to be available within a hundred feet of any house or school. Education, which could provide a way out for those who didn't play truant, was only available to those lucky enough to have well-qualified teachers who didn't mind living in rough areas themselves. Those residents fortunate enough to be given a local authority flat were not exactly made either. Even a shot at a decent job from a place like this was hampered by the little obstructions that many prospective interviewees took for granted: the borrowed unaired clothes that stink because there is nowhere to dry them properly; the fact you can't drive and might need to take three bus rides to an interview, which means you arrive late and sweaty, or you never arrive at all because you couldn't afford the fare in the first place. Add this to the wrong postcode address that marks the jobseeker out as one of life's losers, and, like it or not, snap judgements are made, the post given to someone else, *better suited*, and the poor get poorer.

A lone uniformed officer stood outside the outer cordon. Slipping his official card from his wallet, Shaw introduced himself and revealed that he had information that might prove useful to the investigation.

The officer, who seemed a foot shorter than Shaw, puffed out his chest in a similar fashion to a male pheasant displaying itself to attract the attention of a mate. Of stocky build, he had thick hairy arms. 'What sort of information would that be, sir?'

Shaw automatically clocked the four-digit number on the officer's collar and adopted his most professional smile. 'Regarding the identity of the deceased. He consulted me as a potential client.'

The chest swelled a little more. In common with the expression on the man's face, the sinews in the arms hardened. Maybe he didn't like lawyers, Shaw thought. 'You need to speak to Detective Inspector Samantha Deeley and, as it happens, you're in luck.' The officer spoke into his radio and, less than a minute later, conversation drifted down the stairs and a woman in a navy trouser suit appeared, followed by an equally tall androgynous-looking figure in full crime garb. All Shaw could make out was a blizzard of blue through the gap between the facemask and hood. The SOCO was speaking to the woman, Shaw assumed to be Deeley, about working the scene. He quickly deduced that she was female.

'I'm OK, as long as I can be left to get on with it. Lab technicians should be here soon to carry out luminol treatment. Long shot but it might throw something up. I'm going to take a breather, update my notes.'

'Thanks, Nicole.'

Shaw turned and watched the Scenes of Crime officer walk away to a SOCO van.

'Mr Shaw,' the woman said, addressing him with the kind of authority he would reserve for the higher echelons of the judiciary. 'I'm Sam Deeley.' She stuck out her hand.

'Jon, please,' he said, feeling the firmness of her grip in his.

She was big-boned and well built. He couldn't tell whether she went to the gym in her spare time, but it was possible. Had to be around five feet ten and she wasn't wearing heels. Chestnut-coloured hair grazed her shoulders. Her features were petite and cat-like, which made her body seem out of proportion to the rest of her. She had creamy pale skin sprinkled with freckles, like a dusting of chocolate on a cappuccino. Her piercing hazel-coloured eyes were directed straight at him. Shaw quickly picked up an aura of 'not a woman to suffer timewasters'. Fortunately, she was smiling. He liked her on sight.

'So, Jon, I gather you can help us. Shall we talk?'

'My car's up the road.'

Deeley followed his gaze. 'Perfect.'

She had a good stride, Shaw thought, easily matching her steps with his. Neither of them spoke. A police helicopter flew slowly in loops above their heads. The sound reminded him of the air ambulance that had cut through the sky to transport Mickie Ashton to hospital, in a doomed bid to save her life.

Once they were inside the leather-bound interior, Deeley said, 'So what have you got?'

'I believe your murder victim is Mark Platt.'

He explained how Mr Platt had sought his help with a legal matter.

'What sort of legal matter?'

'Mr Platt had stolen goods from a shop and he worried what would happen to him in the event of a prosecution.'

'So he wasn't actually charged?'

'That was my understanding.'

'A bit of an overreaction, isn't it? I'm surprised he didn't visit Citizen's Advice first.'

Shaw agreed.

'And why would Mr Platt seek the services of a solicitor from Cheltenham?' The smile remained but the note in her voice had changed. She's switched on her bullshit detector, Shaw thought, which was exactly as expected.

'I carry out pro bono work.'

'Are there no pro bono lawyers in the West Midlands?'

Shaw spread his hands. 'He chose me. That's all I can tell you.'

'You didn't ask?'

'Initially, I assumed he lived in town.'

She nodded, processing the information. He wasn't sure she bought it but that was all right.

'When was this?' she asked.

Shaw made a play of thinking. 'Around two months ago. I'd have to check my diary.'

'And how did Mr Platt seem at the time?'

'Troubled, obviously.'

'Needlessly so?'

'I generally only get involved if a client has been arrested, not when they think they might be.'

'Odd, isn't it?'

'Odd comes with the job description,' Shaw said lightly. 'Out of the ordinary for sure.'

'Was he upset about anything else, do you think?'

He could see where she was going with it. 'I really couldn't say, but he did seem a little paranoid.'

'Fearful?'

'Yes.'

'Did he mention falling out with anyone?'

'Not in so many words.'

'But you thought there was more to his visit?'

Shaw kept his expression neutral. Underneath he ripped inside. If only Mark had really come to him, he'd have done everything he could to help and protect him. He might have been able to save him.

'How was he dressed?'

'Pardon?'

'Was he clean and tidy?'

Shaw frowned, deliberately creating an impression that Deeley wasn't really asking the right question. 'I believe so.'

'But?'

'He wore jeans and a leather waistcoat. It was quite odd. No shirt at all.'

Deeley looked at him in disbelief.

'I know,' Shaw said.

'In April?'

When it was unseasonably cold, Jon remembered, realising that there was an immediate inconsistency in his account that required clarification.

'The temperature in our offices is on the warm side. Of course, he had a coat. Not very clean, as I recall.' While she was on the back foot, this would now be the time for her to switch direction, and get her balance back.

'This shop that Mr Platt mentioned,' Deeley said. 'Where was it?'

'Lowe Street, the convenience store.' Recalling the street he'd visited no less than a few minutes ago, Shaw repeated it parrot fashion. Deeley nodded, filing the information away.

'How did you leave things with Mr Platt?'

'I invited him to contact me if there were any developments.'

'And you never heard from him again?'

'I assumed there was no evidence.'

'And this was two months ago?'

She was checking to see if he was about to change his story, Shaw registered. 'Correct.'

Deeley briefly looked straight ahead. Shaw followed her gaze to an Asian family dressed in brilliantly coloured silks. It felt symbolic, a moment of light in the darkness.

'I'm impressed with your powers of deduction.' Deeley's eyes locked onto his. 'How did you join the dots between a random client, who showed up at your practice months ago, with the man murdered down the street?'

Shaw waited several beats, as if giving the matter his full consideration. 'I suppose because he stood out from the usual crowd and, of course, Mr Platt gave me this address,' he said with a firm checkmate smile.

'Which was false,' Deeley countered. 'There is no evidence that Mr Platt had ever owned or rented the premises in which he was found.'

'It happens,' Shaw said as if this were no big deal. 'Together with the appalling nature of his death, something chimed.'

Deeley smiled back. Shaw couldn't tell whether it was genuine or fake.

'If I can schedule a viewing, would you be prepared to come to the mortuary to identify him?'

For all his forward thinking, he'd failed to factor it in. Shaw's salivary glands packed up and his mouth dried.

Deeley picked up on his fractional hesitation. 'Now would be good.'

Clearly, she wasn't going to let an important step in her investigation slip through her fingers.

'I understand,' Shaw said. 'Of course.'

Deeley slipped out her phone and punched in a number. Judging by the line of conversation, it became quickly clear that it wasn't straightforward. Apparently, the mortuary was closed on Saturday apart from exceptional circumstances, which, Deeley vociferously argued to someone on the other end, was one of those occasions. Eventually, a call came back stating that they were good to go. With a heavy heart, Shaw arranged to follow Deeley in his car.

Chapter Fourteen

Shaw did his best not to heave. The dead don't resemble the living, Mark no exception. It didn't lessen Shaw's revulsion.

Viewing photographic evidence of the dead for legal purposes was something he carried out with cool professional detachment. It was his job to interpret a scene in relation to his client's defence. The corpse inches away from him created an entirely different reaction, neither cool nor detached. It stirred the deep and murky well of latent fear within him, a taster of what was to come, the dread of whether he would be next.

Was this really his old childhood friend? What if Danny were wrong? What if someone else had walked into the bedsit that night and Mark was someplace else, shooting up or drinking himself into oblivion and beyond?

Then how did those feathers fit?

The sheet that covered the deceased was drawn tight and up to the neck. In the filtered light the punctures in the man's head resembled a game of peg solitaire. They were perfectly arranged, Shaw observed with dismay. He'd used a nail gun once to make a small shed. Not a natural with DIY, he'd been bewildered by the variety on the market. Some required compressors, other batteries; each had specific uses. From a killer's point of view, the firing mechanism would be important. Dual contact allows for the user to hold the trigger and press the nosing against a surface and fire before moving onto the next. It's speedier than sequential firing, but far less safe, which wouldn't matter a damn in this case. The average length of a nail varied up to three and half inches. Such deep penetration to the skull, and presumably to the brain, would inflict massive internal injuries. Christ, how could someone mete out such punishment on a helpless and vulnerable man? And then Shaw remembered why.

'Are you all right?' Deeley's voice carried an anxious ring. Shaw wasn't sure whether she'd picked up on his trepidation or whether she viewed him as her current and, possibly, only hope of identifying the man lying on the gurney. 'Take your time, Jon.'

Shaw glanced at her. She looked at him with intensity. He swore she was holding her breath.

'I told you that Mr Platt wore an open leather waistcoat.'

She nodded and her eyes shone.

'He had a large birthmark, a mole, quite dark and hairy about here,' he said, touching the left-hand side of his body and the space between his ribcage and pelvis.

Deeley let out a breath and, with a flourish, rolled back the sheet. 'Like this?'

Shaw gazed in stupefecation. 'Like that,' he said.

'You're certain?'

'I am.' He spoke with more clarity than his mind allowed.

A distant part of him had hoped that this was all one great mistake, but the evidence was incontrovertible.

'Are you OK to drive?' Deeley said once they were back outside and in the open. She seemed concerned. Maybe his skin had paled. He certainly felt as if blood had drained from his face. There was a sharp buzzing sensation in his temple. He snapped a smile and assured her that it would not be a problem.

'I may need to stay in touch in case we have more questions,' she said. 'Is that all right?'

'Fine.'

She turned to go. The body language and bounce in her step told him that he had delivered and she was now a person with purpose and focus.

'Could I ask you a question?' Shaw said.

She turned back. 'Yes?'

'Was Mr Platt tortured?'

'According to the pathologist, the first nail into the base of his skull killed him.'

'So the murderer knew exactly what he was doing?'

'Oh yes,' she said evenly. 'You can be sure of that.'

Shaw didn't go directly home. He called Charlie Toombs from his car and arranged to visit him at his lavish neo-Regency villa in Pittville Crescent.

Set well back from the road and behind electric gates with a gravelled drive, Charlie's place made Shaw's look like a Portacabin.

Shaw pressed the entry phone and listened for the click

and whir of machinery as his friend and colleague granted him safe passage.

By the time he parked, Charlie was already at the front door. Dressed in an old pink and blue rugger shirt, three-quarter-length trousers and flip-flops, the only style accessory was the crystal glass in his hand, presumably filled with gin and tonic, judging by the slice of lemon.

'Drink?' Charlie said. 'You damn well look as if you need one.'

'Straight tonic would be good.'

Charlie pulled a disappointed face and indicated for Shaw to go into the study, which overlooked the landscaped and mature garden.

Dog-tired, Shaw sat down and watched a wagtail speed across the grass.

Charlie returned and handed Shaw a tall glass. 'Marsha isn't about. Spa day in the Cotswolds,' he added, in the resigned way successful men often speak of high-maintenance wives on the loose with their friends. 'I shall be bankrupt by this evening,' he said with a not so wry laugh.

Charlie plumped down into a leather scroll-winged chair that had clearly seen action. It creaked and yawed like an ancient tree in high wind. He fixed Shaw with a shrewd expression.

'You disappeared very quickly last night. Is everything all right, Jon?'

Shaw knew his failure to answer would tell its own story.

'I don't wish to be rude,' Charlie leant forward in such a way that even his eyebrows looked conspiratorial, 'but that fellow you were with ...'

'Oh, him?' Shaw said with forced jollity. 'No, he's a former client. From way back.'

'I see.'

And that was the problem. Toombs no more believed him than Shaw believed that Mark Platt was *not* lying on a mortuary slab in Wolverhampton. Shaw knew it and Charlie knew it.

'He wasn't bothering you?' Charlie pressed.

'Not at all.'

Charlie leant back. The leather groaned and crackled. 'Are you in trouble, Jon?'

To be an effective criminal lawyer you needed to be quick-thinking and street-smart. Time to bring his smarts to the table. Sometimes that actually meant telling the truth.

'I might be.'

'Can I help?'

'It's why I'm here. I need time off work.'

Charlie nodded slowly. 'How much?'

'A week.' If he hadn't cracked it by then, he'd be dead.

Charlie stood up and took a legal pad from his desk. 'You'd better bring me up to speed with any cases pending.'

Shaw let out a sigh of relief. 'Thanks, Charlie.'

Gone the bon viveur, and maybe even his friend, Charlie Toombs said, 'Shall we begin?'

By the time Shaw reached home, it was late afternoon. Letting himself into the house, he walked through to the kitchen where Danny was speaking to someone on his newly acquired mobile. He looked up with a start at Shaw's return.

'Yeah. Sound. I'll check in next week.' Danny cut the call and slipped the phone back in his pocket.

'Who was that?' There was no mistaking the accusatory note in Shaw's voice.

'What's it got to do with you?'

'Given the current situation, it has everything to do with me.'

Fly and sly, Danny scratched his chin. 'I was talking to a mate.'

'What sort of mate?'

'Someone I shared a cell with.'

'Why?'

'Because I was bored. You've been gone frigging hours.'

'It took longer than expected.' Shaw leant his back against the work surface. He had the beginning of a crucifying head-ache and felt nauseous. 'I think it best if we get an early night and start out first thing tomorrow morning.'

'Suits me. So what's the craic?'

Shaw told him he'd identified Mark.

'Fuck,' Danny said.

Next, Shaw told him about his conversation with Sam Deeley.

'A woman on the job?'

'What's wrong with that?' Shaw decided not to waste his breath on a lecture about sexism. He guessed in the twenty-five years Danny had been inside, this was another one of those big changes. More women were taking senior roles in every aspect of society. And thank God for that. 'She's no fool and not a woman to be underestimated.' And he had the impression that she was someone who didn't conform to rules. She'd been happy enough to sit and have a conversation in his car instead of parking him in the back of a police vehicle, for a start.

Danny, it seemed, would take rather more convincing judging by the sullen look in his eyes.

'Did you tell her about Kenny?'

Shaw shot Danny a penetrating look. Was he dumb as well as obsessed? 'I didn't. Even if Kenny was murdered, Deeley, like most police officers, is unlikely to connect cases.'

'Thought you said she was clever.'

'She is, which is why she would have asked me a ton of difficult questions.'

Danny appeared to consider this. 'So you think she's in with a shout of finding Mark's killer?'

'Why not? It would be the best outcome.'

'Sure, and then we can all move on and go back to our nice cosy little lives.'

Danny's cynicism was as great as his own. Shaw very much doubted anything would be nice and cosy ever again.

Chapter Fifteen

'Rise and shine.' Shaw tapped the sole of Danny's naked foot and planted a mug of fresh coffee on the bedside table. He hoped it might provide an inducement. This was the third time of asking and each time Danny had barely stirred and gone back to sleep. 'It's past nine o'clock.'

Danny groaned and turned over, a barely audible profanity masked by an expanse of Egyptian cotton.

'Shift. We've a long day ahead.'

Danny stuck out an arm and shuffled out from beneath the duvet. Twisting his head, he opened one eye, the other a slit. Overnight stubble clung to a pallid complexion. His skin glistened with sweat, emitting a nasty sour odour.

'I'm not feeling well.'

'You'll be fine after a shower. Come on. You need to get cracking.'

'I told you I'm ill.'

'It's called a hangover.'

'Nah.'

'What's wrong then?'

'The 'flu.'

Shaw crossed his arms. 'You'll have to do better than that, Danny.'

'I'll get in the way and piss you off.'

Fair point, but the idea of leaving Danny on the loose in his home lacked appeal.

'You said yourself it's better we split up.' Danny was adept at sneaking into the space left by Shaw's momentary hesitation.

'I didn't mean . . .'

'It's a no-brainer. I'll man the fort.'

Shaw thought about it. His plan was to first drive to the farm where Kenny had died. Danny was persona non grata with Kenny's uncle so he'd need to wait in the car. So leaving Danny behind made sense – apart from the small fact that it was Danny's idea. Perversely, a rational, sensible Danny alarmed Shaw more than a knowable reckless Danny. It meant only one thing. He was up to something.

'I'm not comfortable leaving you here alone.'

'Didn't seem to bother you too much yesterday.'

Again, true. 'OK,' Shaw said reluctantly. 'Leave your phone switched on. I'll check in at regular intervals.'

Danny rolled over and closed his eyes. 'Suits me,' he mumbled. 'See ya.'

With one last look back, Shaw went downstairs, collected a pair of Wellington boots from the stand in the hall for the journey, then, gathering keys and wallet, let himself out of the house and drove straight down the M5 to North Devon.

Two and a half hours later he was cresting a hill that led to a farm a few miles outside Ilfracombe. Fields of cows flanked a long, rutted drive that badly needed resurfacing.

The farmhouse itself was single-storey, gable-ended and built from stone. It stood lengthways down a steep-sided hill on which sheep grazed. Traditionally, the family would have lived in the upper end, with animals tethered in the lower area. Without a tent or yurt in sight, the landscape indicated a working farm, not the kind of place that embraced glamping.

Shaw slowed right down and glanced up to see a range of barns at the very top of a hill, indicating that there could be an access road higher up.

Pulling across a yard muddy from recent rain, he parked a short distance away, climbed out and was hit by the pungent smell of fresh cow muck, straw and roasted meat and vegetables. He'd forgotten it was Sunday. Good news: the family were at home; bad news: they may not welcome the interruption.

The path to the house was a series of uneven and broken paving slabs, the garden a mixture of rosemary and thyme, which grew freely, scenting the air and cutting through the overriding stench of farm animals. Two pairs of muddy Wellington boots stood either side of the front door like sentries. Up close, Shaw noticed the downstairs window frames were in disrepair. Had there been an upper storey, he realised, views would be good. Somebody might then have witnessed exactly what happened to Kenny.

He'd barely stepped up to the front door before ferocious growling and barking erupted from inside. Next, a chair scraping across flagstones and stern admonitions to 'bloody well shut up'.

Seconds later, a bone-thin man emerged. He had a quizzical

and guarded expression. No taller than Shaw, his extremely slender physique created an illusion of great height. A shock of thin white hair framed a deeply lined face. Button-brown eyes sat astride a hawkish nose and competed with thread veins that patterned the man's cheeks. He'd recently cut himself shaving and had missed several white hairs on his chin, which matched the several white hairs on his chest. His trousers were old and worn. His open collarless shirt, faded to light blue, had cuffs rolled up to the elbows, exposing wiry arms covered in liver spots. The man stood in his socks. A hole in the big toe on his right foot revealed a yellow, thickened and flaking toenail.

Shaw immediately apologised for the intrusion, introduced himself and, hating the deceit, asked to speak to Kenny. Suspicion pinched the old man's cadaverous features. 'You must be Mr Sharples, Kenny's uncle,' Shaw pressed on. He aimed for a warm, respectful tone. Judging by the man's stony expression, he'd missed it by a mile.

'Says who?'

'I'm sorry, I understood...'

The old man made to close the door.

Shaw inserted his head into the gap. 'Please, I'm an old friend of Kenny's.'

The door inched open.

'Shaw, you say?' the old man cut in.

'That's right.'

He pushed the door wide, crossed his arms. 'You look nothing like him.' His accent was pure Devon, no trace of northern roots.

'Excuse me? There must be some mistake.'

'Don't think so.' The old man took a step forward. 'Jon Shaw visited Kenny no more than a few weeks ago. Borrowed his car and all. I spoke to him myself days ago.'

Shaw gave a jolt. Danny had given a false name: *his*. Worse, Kenny had gone along with it because Kenny went along with anything Danny said.

Shaw slipped a card from his wallet. 'If you don't believe me, you can phone my business partner. I assure you, I *am* Jon Shaw.' He watched as the old man took it and silently mouthed and processed the information.

'A lawyer, you say?' The brown eyes fastened onto Shaw's. 'Now what would Kenny be wanting with the likes of you?'

Shaw cleared his throat. 'I believe he expected to inherit from his father's estate.'

'Poppycock. There was barely enough money to go round to bury the old bugger. Not that it matters a damn now. Come to pay your respects, have you?' His gaze narrowed. Shaw had an image of the man shooting a pheasant out of the sky with a twelve-bore.

'I'm not quite sure . . .'

'Kenny died in an accident on the farm a few days ago.'

'My God, I'd no idea.' Shaw loathed lying through his teeth, but could see no other way. 'I'm so sorry. Is there anything I can do?'

The old man's upper lip curled. 'Reckon so.' He hooked his thumbs into the waistband of his trousers, jutted out his scrawny chest and tipped back on his heels. 'Would you be willing to cover the funeral costs? Seeing as you're an old pal.'

Shaw met the old man's sly expression. Whoever he was, he was definitely no fool.

'The name's Finner,' the man continued. 'My late wife was a Sharples.'

Shaw forced a smile. 'Why don't I come inside?' he said smoothly. 'I'll take your details and make a payment direct into your account.'

When Finner asked Shaw to call him Jeffrey, he knew he was home and dry.

Chapter Sixteen

I stand here naked before twenty people. Moderate pain runs along my neck, down my left shoulder, to my waist. My left eye is fixed on one spot, a stain on the floorboards, and I must not move.

I have stood here for nearly six hours, with all sorts of random thoughts wandering through my mind. *Six*. The significance is not lost on me. And five sixes equal thirty, the same number of nails I hammered into a vagrant's skull. I wonder how many of those who capture my body in pencil or pen and ink have sat in a room gazing at a killer. Can they smell the sweet undertone of death leaking through the pores in my skin? Do they notice the tight musculature in my biceps, the sinews in my arms and hands? You need strength to kill, not courage.

Naturally, I scrub my body whiter than white before disrobing. You don't need a fine figure to be a life model; only the ability to stay still and with a willingness to bare your all to a bunch of strangers. I'm not embarrassed. It's really no big deal. I don't do it for art's sake. Nor do I pose for the thrill. I'm no narcissist or exhibitionist. There's nothing sexual in what I do. I perform (for this is how I regard it) by fixing my limbs and torso in one position, in complete silence, because it gives me the perfect opportunity to tune out. Only in that pure state of calm and composure can I contain my rage and reflect on my real life's work and specialist subject: getting away with murder.

They say your first killing is the biggest psychological divide to cross; the taking of another's life, allegedly, as tough for the perpetrator as the victim. It's due to basic biology. Survival dictates that we are not primed to kill unless attacked. Every would-be murderer should bear this in mind because the instant a murderous intention becomes clear there is the heavy risk of a counter-assault, which could prove fatal. Happily, my first victim was of limited intelligence, my second hopped-up on heroin. Put more bluntly, one was stupid, the other weak. And did I feel destroyed by what I'd done? What do *you* think?

A novice to the game, I made sure I knew my limitations. I saw no shame in bailing if the conditions weren't right. I took care to avoid elementary mistakes. Leaving a crucial piece of evidence can sink you and I'm not talking about obvious things like fingerprints – all those oils and acids we carry on our fingertips – and shoeprints, fibres and DNA, but trace evidence. Naturally, an element of risk is inevitable, especially if plotting more than one murder. It's all about minimising, without overthinking it.

An itchy piece of skin flares a millimetre below my chin. The bane of the life model, it takes everything I have to resist the urge to move and scratch. I can literally feel blood bashing through the veins, heating up the capillaries and prickling the hairs on the surface. To the outside world, I bet there is nothing to see. Like me, really. Nobody would dream of my extra-work curricula. Concentrate, I tell myself. Damn it. What I'd give to tear at the skin with a finger. I take a breath. *Calm*, I think. Mind over matter. Where was I? Oh yes. Homework. Important, naturally, but gut reaction is essential, especially if things don't go as expected. I didn't think idiot-brain would flee on his quad bike, for example, but I'm so glad he did. Originally, I'd considered luring him to the slurry pit but the personal risks were too great. Dismissing that idea, I came up with a way better plan. I wonder how long it will take before a pathologist notices that the decisive fatal blow to the head was inflicted *after* injuries were sustained in the crash.

Not that anyone will make the connection to my handi-work in Wolverhampton. It occurred to me some time ago that if you really don't want to get caught, do *not* adopt a signature. This is no time for ego. You know what I'm talking about: those killers, often serial offenders, who always use strangulation, or a blade to the throat, or the sick perverted creeps that fuck their victims after they're dead. If you're that self-indulgent, you deserve to have a forensic profiler dissecting your psyche, looking for patterns, and working out which way your dirty little textbook mind ticks before they catch you. Similar applies to those dumb enough to favour railway stations, parks, nightclubs or whatever to select their prey. Don't they get it that they leave themselves open to experts triangulating their kill grounds, resulting in sting operations and capture? The dim-witted murderer who has an identifiable MO *and* is also attracted to a specific type of victim might as well shove a neon light over his head that says *Murderer*. I mean WTF. Mix it up, guys. Diversify. Vary your methods. It's way more creative and fun and, importantly, guaranteed to confuse the cops.

And how do I know this stuff? I've studied, lived and breathed it. Killing is as valid an art form as the artists sketching my naked body on a Sunday morning.

Chapter Seventeen

Jeffrey Finner led Shaw down a narrow corridor with a low ceiling, into a kitchen in which two yellow-eyed border collies glared from a metal cage. Mean swelled their arteries. One word from Jeffrey and each slunk into their respective corners.

Smelling of damp and dog, the kitchen was similar to the outside of the farmhouse: tidy and ordered but seriously down on its luck.

Jeffrey cleared his plate from the table, dumping it in the sink and indicated a straight-backed kitchen chair with a vinyl seat. Shaw thought it circa 1950.

'There's tea in the pot, if you want it.'

Shaw thanked him and sat down. A thick-rimmed mug was placed alongside a bag of sugar, a bottle of full-cream milk, and a large metal teapot already on the table. Jeffrey poured out a brew for Shaw and topped up his own. It wasn't particularly cold outside but Shaw was glad to be seated with his back to a working Rayburn. The interior of the old building was cold to its core. God alone knew what it was like in the depths of winter.

'You said it was an accident,' Shaw said.

'Quad bike. Dangerous machines.'

'Could there have been a mechanical failure?'

'Kenny was careful with maintenance. There's only one explanation. He must have been going at a lick. No idea what possessed him to tear down Lark Hill, daft sod.'

Shaw let his gaze fall towards the window. 'Is that near here?'

'The other side of the barns.'

'At the top?'

'That's right.'

'Your land?'

'All fifty acres.'

Shaw nodded, sipped his tea. Waited. All people talk. Eventually.

Jeffrey tilted his chin, his eyes full of guile. 'Funny business that man pretending to be you.'

'Very strange,' Shaw agreed, madly underplaying it.

'But why would my nephew agree to such a deception?'

Shaw spread his hands. 'I can't answer.' *What the hell was Danny's game?*

'Up to no good, that's what it was.' Jeffrey put his mug down on the table as if laying a bet. 'Thick as thieves, they were. I didn't like it. I didn't like *him*.'

Shaw held his voice steady. 'You think there's a connection?'

Deep lines creased Jeffrey's brow. His mouth fell very slightly open. He was giving it serious consideration, Shaw thought, and not liking where it was heading. Shit, *Shaw* didn't like where it was heading.

'Might Kenny have fallen out with the man?' Shaw pushed. 'It could explain why Kenny was driving too quickly.'

Jeffrey shook his head.

'Someone else?'

Jeffrey stared morosely into the depths of his mug of tea, in the same way a plumber stands over a blocked drain.

'Mr Finner?' Shaw prompted.

The old man glanced up, eyes full of pain. In that moment he seemed like a sinner who was carrying every wrong he'd ever done in his expression. '*Me*,' he said. 'He was upset with me.'

Shaw did his best to smother any obvious reaction. Inside, his brain was crackling with ideas, none of them nice.

'May I ask why?'

Jeffrey gave a deep sigh. 'We argued.'

'That morning?'

'No, not then, a few days before.'

'What about?'

'Stupidity.'

Kenny was not the brightest but it seemed an odd reason for dissent. There had to be more to it. He waited for Jeffrey to continue.

'Kenny went to a café in town in his spare time – not that he had much of that,' Jeffrey said firmly. 'The place was run by a right rum crowd.'

'How do you mean?'

'Illegal gambling dens. Unlicenced so they don't pay tax like the rest of us. Kenny, well, he's easily led and I thought they were bad for him.'

'Bad in what way exactly?'

'They got him hooked and, Kenny, God bless him, wasn't that bright.'

This possibility opened up a whole new line of investigation, Shaw thought. 'What's the name of the café?'

'The Seashell. Not very original.'

'Was he in trouble with them?'

Jeffrey's brow furrowed. 'How do you mean?'

'Did he owe them?'

'He wouldn't have told me if he had, but he'd have sold the family silver, if we'd got any, to keep them happy. They were his *friends*.'

Derision and jealousy punctured the old man's voice. It must have come hard for him to see Kenny right for so long and then watch as he fell in with what he considered a bad lot.

'So he was generally upset, not quite thinking straight. Would that be a fair assumption?'

'He wasn't upset. He was bloody hysterical.'

Shaw blinked. 'I'm not sure I follow.'

'You see,' Jeffrey continued, as if settling in for a gossip, 'Kenny went everywhere with Fred.'

Who the hell was Fred?

'A cross-breed ratting terrier,' Jeffrey explained, responding to Shaw's perplexed expression. 'Anyway, Fred went missing the morning of the accident. Kenny got in a right lather.

'It was market day so I left him to it. Told him to calm down, find Fred and look after the farm.' The old man let out a gloomy sigh. 'Never gave him another thought until I came back. The house was that quiet,' he said with a shiver. 'No Fred and no Kenny.' He took a drink of tea. 'Searched high and low, I did.' A shadow passed behind his eyes. 'I found Kenny on the other side of the hill at the bottom of a ditch, the bike on top of him. Stoved his head in, it did. Nasty business.'

An image of blood drenching Mickie Ashton's clothes flashed before Shaw's eyes. He clenched his hands. 'I'm sorry.' He meant every word.

'Nothing I could do. I saw that straightaway. Life, isn't it? It comes and it goes.' Jeffrey stared past Shaw, as if trying to locate a thought that, so far, had eluded him. Shaw could see the man was crushed by a weight of guilt. He recognised that look. 'Right,' Jeffrey said finally, slapping his bony thighs. 'I'll get my details.'

Shaw sat back, reflecting on what he'd heard. Superficially, it seemed like a straightforward accident and yet there were anomalies, not least the café crowd.

While the old man thumped around upstairs, opening drawers and shuffling papers, Shaw pictured uncle and nephew living side by side. He thought of the two men sitting companionably at this same table, sharing a Sunday roast. Conversation, he reckoned, would have been minimal, but that wouldn't matter. He wondered at the old man's loss. Superficially, he seemed matter of fact, heartless almost. Farmers saw life and death on such a regular basis perhaps it inured them to it. But Shaw recognised that, from some deaths, there is no recovery. The loss of his mother had devastated him, his grief for her as enduring as the depth of his love. The death of Mickie Ashton and her child was on a different level. It had messed him up for good.

Jeffrey returned, brandishing a chequebook. A pair of

small round reading glasses perched on the end of his hawk-ish nose.

'Here we are. Account number and sort code, it's all there.' He laid the details before Shaw. The tip of Jeffrey's tongue poked out of the side of his mouth and he ran the heels of his hands down his trousers. 'I was thinking of along the lines of five grand.'

'Fine,' Shaw said crisply. He pulled out his phone, scrolled down and did the deed. He showed Jeffrey the screen. The look on the old man's face was one of wonder.

'I'll give Kenny a right proper send-off. You'll come, of course,' he said.

Shaw's smile was tight. 'Let me know the arrangements.' He drained the contents of his mug – tannin and metal and old teabags – and stood up. He had one final question.

'Did you find the dog?'

Jeffrey slowly shook his head. 'Another damned funny thing about the whole sorry business.'

Chapter Eighteen

Shaw climbed into the Porsche Macan and traced his way back along the road, up the steep hill and down the other side. He pushed away all thoughts of Danny impersonating him. For now, he had headspace for only one thing: to find a killer before a killer found him. For any chance of success, he'd need to acquire the mind-set of half the people he defended. Wasn't such a stretch; he had a working knowledge of the criminal mind. If he required assistance, he'd look no further than Danny.

Forensics was a different ball game. Shaw's knowledge was probably greater than most due to the nature of his work (nightly viewings of contemporary crime dramas, with flaws and inconsistencies, didn't count) but was far less than the experts he often bumped up against. It seemed to him that the adage, 'a little knowledge is a dangerous thing', richly applied. Still, he had to start somewhere. Maybe he could find a way back onto the land.

Driving slowly, Shaw scoured the countryside for a separate access point to Jeffrey Finner's farm. Incessant rain had resulted in a growth spurt of greenery. Foliage was dense and he almost missed a gap in the hedgerow. Barely visible, a grassy track, too narrow for a car, too muddy for a motorbike but fine for a horse, mountain or trail bike.

He pulled off onto the side of the road, parked and got out. Narrowing his eyes against a squally wind, he stood still for a moment and surveyed the lonely path before him. Flanked on either side by high unruly hedges, anyone walking up here would be concealed from view, he reasoned. The only obstacle might be another walker, although judging from the state of the earth it would be a determined person to skirt the volume of mud and puddles. Had a killer stood in this same spot and made the same calculation?

Shaw returned to the car, popped the boot and took out a pair of Wellingtons and changed out of his sneakers. He returned to the mouth of the trail.

First, he circumnavigated a pool of water that had drained from the top. Clinging to the odd branch of a low-lying tree, he found progress slow, slippery and precarious. The ground beneath was severely rutted and, like a human game of snakes and ladders, he expected to slide, fall and roll down to the bottom. Plastered in mud, he'd be forced to start all over again.

The higher the climb, the less soft the ground beneath and easier to traverse, or so he believed. Yet he was wrong. And was he also wrong about a killer passing this way? Had Danny's obsession infected him? Was guilt screwing with his brain?

By the time he'd clambered halfway up, his calves were burning and his pulse rate soaring. He continued trudging uphill as fast as he could. Signs declaring public rights of way led seemingly nowhere. Some paths were so overgrown free passage would be impossible. Stiles had been removed and replaced with gates topped with barbed wire. The track narrowed and brambles clawed at Shaw's clothing as he squelched his way through. It was like travelling up a flume the wrong way, against a tide of swimmers, and as equally claustrophobic. He couldn't breathe, not from exertion but of what might lie ahead.

At last, cresting the peak, he found more solid ground. The barns lay straight ahead in an open field populated by sheep that scattered in panic at his approach.

Like a mountain climber planting his flag at the summit, Shaw stopped to look around him. The views from the top were magnificent. He could see for miles around and the little farmhouse, nestling in the valley below, looked a great deal more attractive and homely than in reality.

But he hadn't come to sightsee.

On one side, the land plunged away down the kind of hill that would be good for cheese rolling. So why, Shaw wondered, had Kenny chosen this route and not the gentler slope back to his home? What had possessed him to drive at top speed? Kenny, a simple-minded, easily led individual, was also a big man. He could inflict serious damage if he had to. Wondering if there had been an altercation or a fight, Shaw dropped his gaze to the ground and walked back and forth. The earth didn't look particularly displaced or disturbed but, after incessant rain, it was hard to tell.

He ambled over to the nearest barn. Used for storage by the looks of it; one end piled high with furniture and junk, including an old upright piano and a job lot of metal filing cabinets. A couple of dinghies lay upended. An array of farm tools, some rusty, hung from brackets on a nearby wall in the same way a spider stockpiles flies. Shaw checked to see if any had been used recently. He didn't think so, but then again, farming equipment wasn't his forte.

Outside, the wind had picked up and, with it, a strong smell of dung that pricked his nostrils. Glancing to his right, he noticed an area cordoned off by broken railings. Drawing near, he stopped, frozen. A fathomless stretch of slurry, around ten feet in width, sat like a poisonous bog. Imagined or real, a pall of toxic gas appeared to hover over the surface ready to snuff out the life of anyone who drew near. Shaw quickly backtracked.

The next barn was more traditional in content: a tractor, various pieces of farm machinery, bags of sheep nuts and cattle feed, and a concrete floor strewn with remnants of straw and hay bales. There was no sign of the mangled quad bike and Shaw wondered what Jeffrey had done with it.

Deciding he could do no more, doubt once more crept in, the lawyer in him playing devil's advocate. It was entirely possible that he was riffing with a scenario that never existed. Maybe Kenny simply made a stupid mistake. People did and he should know. But if Kenny didn't . . .

Something or someone had deliberately frightened the shit out of the man enough to push him to take an absurd risk with obvious consequences. Reminded of his conversation with Jeffrey, Shaw understood what that might be.

Shaw returned to the first barn, unhooked a shovel hanging on the wall and, eyes down, walked slowly along the ridge like a soldier detecting unexploded ordinance. Sheep shit was expected. A bare patch of turf and a bump in the land was not.

Shaw swung the shovel down and dug around the perimeter of the mound. The earth was claggy. Although recently disturbed, it came away relatively freely. Edging his way in, Shaw detected a strong smell of rotting meat. Automatically, he glanced over his shoulder and experienced an icy chill ripple down his spine. Half of him wanted to pack it in and go home, the other felt crazily driven to discover what lay beneath.

Throwing the shovel down, he pushed the earth away with his bare hands. At last, matted hair grazed his fingertips. Next, a number of tiny teeth. Shaw clawed away more stones and soil and found what looked like an undocked tail, and not from a lamb or sheep. With a roiling gut, he examined it. Despite the mud and gore, it was clear that it had been roughly cut from the animal's body. Was this what had freaked Kenny out?

Shaw returned to the shallow grave and his grisly task. Eventually, he found what he'd been looking for: the putrid remains of a small dog.

The missing Fred.

Chapter Nineteen

'How's progress on the nail-gun case?'

DCI Nick Dillane hovered over Sam Deeley with a predatory expression. He couldn't help it. Craggy-featured, cadaverous in build, with dark receding hair in the shape of an arrowhead on his scalp, he looked as if he were descended from a long line of Transylvanian counts.

Rather than looking DCI Nick Dillane in his beady eye, Deeley glanced at the printer next to her computer. Maybe if she stared hard enough it would spew out answers. God knew she needed them if she were to prove herself, not just to Dillane but to her colleagues. She glanced up, caught the eye of her biggest detractor, DI Angel Finch. Single-handedly, Finch had run a whispering campaign against her. Deeley had believed a transfer from West Mercia signalled a brand-new start. Instead it had heralded more of the same.

'Not great,' she replied honestly.

In a long list of other cases, it was the one that most obsessed her for its random brutality, and yet was the one most elusive. Mark Platt had no gang affiliations. He had no family. A drunk, by all accounts, and a drug-user, for certain. His profile, such as they'd managed to cobble together, indicated a harmless character who drifted around, living on what was left of his wits, and had friends with similar lifestyles and no enemies. Following a lead provided by the nice-looking lawyer, she'd wasted no time in visiting the shopkeeper where the alleged theft had taken place, and asked whether he'd intended to bring charges. Mr Singh had stared at her as if she were cracked.

'You seriously think I would report the theft of six cans of lager to the police? We were broken into last year and it took you lot a week to visit. For my trouble, all I got was a log number so that we could claim on the insurance.' Revved up, Mr Singh waggled a finger at her. 'Any idea how much my premiums are now? And, no, you didn't find the culprit.'

Several hours later, Mr Singh's stinging words still turned her ears red. The incompetence and failure to which he referred was a reminder of a terrible chapter of her life she'd sooner forget and the reason she'd transferred from West Mercia to West Mids. The memory acute, Deeley felt as if someone had poured wet concrete over her soul.

Dillane shifted his skeletal frame from one foot to the other, his way of telling her to get on with it.

'We've carried out door-to-door enquiries,' she told Dillane, thinking she ought to, at least, look as if she was in control. 'The Tactical Aid Team pulled apart the crime scene.'

Which meant ripping off kickboards, lifting skirting and checking through nearby wheelie bins.

'According to tox results, there was no alcohol in the victim's bloodstream but there was a significant amount of heroin, which had been cut with fentanyl. Basically, he was a heavy user.'

'Christ, I'm surprised he wasn't dead already.'

Deeley agreed. Eighty times more powerful than morphine, the additional opiate was lethal.

'I've got Griggs and Salter checking DIY stores and hardware shops within a fifty-mile radius.'

'Any attempt made to conceal the body?'

'None.'

'How are the SOCOs doing?'

'We've got a team on the case.' And, so far, nothing to show. She wished she was at home, in her two-up, two-down end of terrace, admittedly in a lousy part of the city, curled up with a good book; something funny, or romantic and undemanding. It was Sunday, after all, not that murder made allowances for normal shift patterns.

Dillane sniffed the air, as if scenting blood. Deeley idly wondered if Dillane and Dr Speight, the pathologist, hung out together. Speight and Dillane had a certain ring about it. Like a couple of Victorian grave robbers.

'Any ideas on motivation?' Dillane shifted his stance, his bony torso displacing the cheap fabric of his suit.

Deeley registered the SOCO's remark. 'It would seem Mark Platt was deliberately targeted. I'm more inclined to think that any homeless man or druggie would have fitted the bill for the killer.'

'You're not suggesting a serial offender?' Dillane's expression darkened, which was a pretty unpleasant sight from Deeley's perspective. She dropped her gaze. Put like that, she had to agree it sounded worrying. She'd always believed that the likelihood of crossing paths with some deranged serial killer in a police career was as likely as her being chosen to take the lead in a Broadway musical.

'I guess we'll only know,' she said, 'if there's another murder with a similar MO.'

'Might be an idea to warn the homeless community,' Dillane said.

That won't be easy, she thought. 'Fine. I'll see it's done.'

'You'll keep me up to speed?'

She nodded with a smile. When Dillane was out of sight, no doubt teleporting from one part of the building to the other, she ignored the muttering of those around her and picked up right where she left off, back to her computer search of Jon Shaw, lawyer and all-round do-gooder.

It had been a long time since she'd felt an immediate attraction to a man. Risky for her and dangerous for him.

Chapter Twenty

Shaw had got the worst of the muck off his hands on a patch of lush grass growing in a clump at the side of the road. He'd cleaned the rest off with wipes that Jo had left in the glove compartment. Fearing discovery, he took the precaution of taking the shovel with him and slinging it into the boot. If the police ever got involved, he didn't want them arresting him for a crime he hadn't committed.

A fruitless detour into Ilfracombe revealed that The Seashell was closed – bar stools parked upside down on tables – and that the town, once a favoured seaside destination, had lost much of its glamour and charm. Silo-style architecture on the seafront did little to improve it.

Caning it up the M5, he reached the Victorian coastal resort of Clevedon in under an hour and three quarters, at around 4.45 p.m. Gut feeling told him that his search would best be served by parking in Hill Road, an attractive part of town with local shops, cafés, pubs and restaurants.

Before he moved a muscle, he called Danny. He'd no intention of telling him about his visit, or the discovery of Kenny's pet dog. That could keep until later. He simply wanted to know if he was all right.

The number rang out several times before going to voicemail. Shaw tapped the steering wheel in frustration. Probably asleep, he said to himself, in direct opposition to the other voice in his head that told him there was a problem. Unfortunately, the negative won out and, rattled, Shaw headed for the nearest pub, a double-fronted building in trendy grey that chimed with the appearance of the mostly retired clientele. In stark contrast to the punters, the bar staff looked several generations younger and even made Shaw feel ancient.

Inside was a noise machine; how anyone hard of hearing, or suffering from tinnitus, could make out a single word was beyond him. Memories of him and Danny crashing into every noisy gathering, to snatch at what was only ever transitory happiness, Shaw squashed by ordering half a pint of guest beer. He asked the lad serving if he knew of any guesthouses in the area run by an American woman.

'What, mate?'

'Guesthouses,' Shaw bellowed. 'Run by an American lady?'

'Nah. Sorry, mate. That will be four pounds sixty.'

Shaw paid, took his drink and, with nowhere to sit, cast his gaze around the bar for the most likely prospects. Truth was, there weren't any. No matter the age, Brits at play were singular and territorial. No way was he going to blunder into an animated conversation between friends. Besides, he was pretty sure he stank of farm and sheep and, quite likely, dead dog, so he gave up, drank up and headed out. His only passing regret was that he hadn't used the loo before he left.

Crossing the road to a Sainsbury's Local, he bought a cheese sandwich and a packet of crisps and, avoiding the self-service till, made straight for a manned checkout. The woman serving was chatty with the female customer in front of him, clearly local, judging from her accent, and looked about his age. Promising. Her nametag declared she was 'Debbie'.

Shaw stacked the goods on the conveyor built and waited his turn. The second she glanced up, he killed her with his warmest smile and went through the same spiel.

'Big hair? Big smile?' Debbie beamed back at him.

'Erm, yeah,' Shaw replied. How many American Lori's could there possibly be?

'Comes in here sometimes when she's run out of milk or loo rolls.'

'That sounds about right.'

'Two-minute walk from here. Not far up the road,' she said, indicating. 'Can't miss it, actually. It's the big pale pink house set back into the hill.'

Shaw thanked her, paid, and delivering his goods to the car, thought about calling Danny again before dismissing it.

Setting out up the road, Shaw tried to gauge what sort of reception he'd receive from Wolf. His old friend's legendary success with the opposite sex did not preclude him from being one of the lads. If it were a straight choice between hanging out with the gang and banging a girl, Wolf tended to choose the former for in truth, Shaw suspected, Wolf, deep down, feared women. And that fear meant he didn't respect them. Wasn't rocket science; Wolf's mam was a hard-bitten old witch, with a vicious tongue. Didn't matter what Wolf did to try and get on her right side, she'd verbally lay into him. More than once, Shaw had witnessed her annihilate her son and then confound him, and anyone else in close proximity, by playing nice.

But Shaw was open to the belief that Wolf had changed. People did and, by Danny's account, Wolf was now in an established relationship. He had a home, a life, a companion. Oddly, it was Wolf who stepped in, alongside Shaw, to try and protect Mickie Ashton. That had to count for something.

The shop assistant was right. The handsome double-fronted, gabled Georgian-style building looked down from its commanding position on the high street with an air of benevolence. It had that old money thing going on and Shaw couldn't help but admire the fact that Wolf had done well for himself. Or at least, he'd fallen on his feet, which was probably nearer the truth.

Standing in front of a shiny charcoal grey front door, he wished things were different and that he had better news to impart. But this was not a social visit and they were not close friends. There was never going to be any sitting together over a drink, reminiscing over old times and shooting the breeze. They'd forfeited that a long time ago.

He rang the bell. Seconds later, he heard movement on the other side. The door opened and a small-boned woman smiled at him. She had a mass of dark, curly, shoulder-length hair and eyes the colour of fresh conkers.

'Hi, can I help you?'

'You must be Lori,' Shaw said.

'Lori Bryant, that's me.' Still with the smile.

'Terry's other half?'

Her eyes opened wide in delight. 'You're a friend of Terry's?'

'We go way back. I'm Jon, incidentally, Jon Shaw.'

'Well, Jon Shaw, come in, come in.'

Shaw followed Lori through a large arched entrance hall with some decidedly non-PC antiquities, including a full-size statue of a Blackamoor, and a stuffed wolf's head. The large open-plan kitchen was more traditional and professional. A vast gas-fired catering range took centre stage. Above it, copper pots and pans in every size. At a glance, Shaw could see that each area had a purpose. At the far end, a large refectory table and chairs, where he assumed Lori and Wolf ate.

'Terry's out on a run,' Lori explained.

Shaw muted the frown that threatened to pull his eyebrows together. Wolf must have changed a great deal over the years. The only activity known to Wolf twenty-five years before was the one that took place up against a wall.

'He should be back soon. Can I offer you a cup of tea, or coffee?'

Shaw wondered if anything ever got this woman down. With her pixie smiling features, she seemed permanently thrilled to be alive.

'Tea would be great. Would you mind if I use your loo? It's been a long drive.'

'Sure,' she said, pointing back towards the hall. 'The door under the stairs.'

Shaw did what he had to do while thinking how to play it with Lori. Don't ask too many direct questions, he thought, especially about Wolf.

By the time he returned to the kitchen, Lori had laid out dainty porcelain teacups and saucers, milk and sugar and a plate of biscuits.

'Help yourself to cookies,' she said.

Shaw thanked her, took one. 'I'm guessing you're not from around here,' he said, taking a bite.

She trilled with laughter. 'Seattle, originally. The climate's similar but that's about it.'

'Long way from home then.'

'This is my home now. Has been for many years, so much so I think of myself as an honorary Brit. Do you like your tea strong or weak?'

'Strong.'

'I'll put in an extra scoop.'

'Proper tea. I'm honoured.'

'I like to do it right. All part of the service.' She beamed at him. Caught in her slipstream, a pessimist would become an optimist, Shaw thought. Maybe that's why Wolf had hooked up with her.

Lori glanced at her watch. 'Terry should be back by now.'

'Is he a serious runner?'

'I should say so and in every sense.' She let out a laugh and pressed a hand to her chest. 'We met in a bar and the first time we fell into conversation, I seriously wondered whether he was on a WITSEC program.'

'Nomadic then?' Shaw was certain his face had contorted into a rictus smile.

'I need roots. Terry is always ready to move on. We've been here four years. Frankly, it's a record. Any moment I expect him to up and go. Milk first or after?'

'First, please.'

He watched her pour out. 'You run this place together?'

'We do. I'm front of house and Terry's more of a backroom boy. Not what you call a people person.'

'Who does the cooking?'

'Definitely Terry's department. I need three shots of espresso before I can even greet a guest for breakfast, let alone prepare food.'

Shaw nodded amiably. 'How many rooms do you let?'

'Four. We have another two rooms at the top that I call our Harry Potter floor.' She leant towards him. 'They're kind of secret. If you didn't know how to access them, you wouldn't have a Scooby. Once we get enough loot together, we hope to convert them into a honeymoon suite. So where are you from, Jon?'

He told her.

'How did you meet Terry?'

'We went to school together.'

'You don't sound as if you're from Manchester.'

So Wolf had come clean about that much. Shaw wondered what else he'd told her.

'I moved away in my teens. Never went back.'

She glanced up at the clock on the wall. Shaw thought he caught a glint of anxiety in her eyes. 'I've no idea where he's got to.'

'Please don't apologise.'

'But you've come all this way.'

'It's fine. Honestly.'

She leant towards him. 'He's going to be so thrilled to see you.'

Shaw sipped his tea. He didn't share her optimism. About to say something, Lori stopped and inclined her head towards the hall and the distinctive sound of a key in a lock. She stood up. Almost seemed to dance from one foot to the other. Nervous, Shaw thought.

'Lori, honey . . .' Wolf's eyes swivelled straight to Shaw's. In seconds, Shaw read it all. Recognition, shock and forced warmth.

Chapter Twenty-One

Wolf had changed substantially over the years. So had his voice, which was a blend of smooth Americana and Home Counties. Still had those smouldering, raw-boned looks, care of his mixed-race parentage, but he'd bulked up and toned up. His physique was nothing short of impressive. Christ knew how many hours he spent weight-training to achieve that kind of dedicated perfection, Shaw thought. 'Well hard,' Danny would say. Interestingly, there was no evidence to suggest that Wolf had worked up a sweat. Super-fit, Shaw concluded.

Wolf strode towards him. Shaw stood up and felt himself enveloped in an iron-man hug. Not especially tactile, he did his best not to recoil. 'In all my days I never expected to see you, Jon. How are you, buddy?'

'I'm good,' Shaw said, clapping Wolf on the back.

'How lovely is this?' Lori said, obviously enjoying the show. 'You want tea, Terry?'

'This calls for booze.' Wolf's eyes were feverishly alight with what Shaw read as a mixture of dread and anticipation. He realised that Wolf's reaction mirrored his own response to Danny's sudden relaunch into his life. 'Bourbon, Lori. Get the Maker's Mark from the dining room.'

'Thank you, but I'm driving,' Shaw pointed out politely. This was no celebration. This was anaesthetisation.

'We have a spare guest room,' Lori said brightly.

'No, I couldn't. It's very thoughtful of you, but it's such an imposition. Besides . . .' Shaw trailed off. The look of terror that passed behind Wolf's eyes was instantly recognisable. So you feel it too? Shaw thought.

'Really, it's no trouble,' she said.

'Leave it, Lori.' Wolf's voice was firm enough to swipe the smile from her face. It was like watching a puppy being kicked. Shocked less because he'd seen the cruel attitude on display before, Shaw was disappointed nonetheless. Like a child dressing up in his parents' clothes, Wolf could alter his appearance but the personality beneath remained unchanged.

Shaw coughed, something he did when the dynamics didn't sit right. It had the desired effect. Reading the cue, Wolf assumed a gentler tone, reached out and touched Lori's hand.

Gratitude flooded her features. 'Jon probably has things he needs to get back to.'

'Perhaps one small drink and then I'll be on my way,' Shaw said.

'I'll get it,' Lori said, eager to please, 'then leave you guys to catch up.'

'She's lovely,' Shaw said the second Lori scooted out of the room.

Wolf turned to him, his expression hard, as was his accent,

which was pure Manc. 'What are you really doing here?' No pleasantries, no banalities, straight to the chase.

If that's how you want it to roll, so be it, Shaw thought. 'I came to warn you.'

Wolf's mouth pinched into a frown. 'About what?'

Shaw took a breath. At any moment Lori would come back. With little time to say it, he took a less than scenic route. 'You know Danny's out of prison?'

'Three weeks ago, yes.'

'Ever visit him?' Shaw asked.

'Never.'

'See the others?'

'Saw Kenny a year ago.'

Shaw raised an eyebrow.

'I looked him up. Call it curiosity.'

'Taking a risk, weren't you?'

Wolf opened his mouth, closed it again. Lori had appeared like a wraith. Two tumblers and a bottle of bourbon were set on the table. Wolf thanked her stiffly, following her with his eyes as she left.

He poured out three fingers of booze for him and two for Shaw. 'A *calculated* risk,' he said.

'Because?'

'I wanted to know about Danny. I wanted to know when that bastard was going to be released.' He took a swig of booze. 'I heard you tried to kill him.'

'Yes.'

'Pity you failed.'

Shaw lifted the glass to his lips, felt the heat and the roar of neat spirit in a single sip. Rolling the conversation back to a less controversial footing, he said, 'About Kenny.'

'Met him at a café in Ilfracombe. Vile place. Coffee tasted like liquid bitumen. The blokes running it were a dodgy crew.'

Kenny's private hangout, Shaw remembered. Interestingly, Wolf's view of Kenny's friends corroborated Jeffrey Finner's story.

'In what way?'

'Couldn't give a flying fuck what they said to him. Treated him like shit. Not that Kenny saw it. I got the impression he was in pretty thick.'

'Was he afraid of them?' Shaw asked evenly.

Wolf thought about it. 'Maybe. In awe, for sure.'

'Other than that, how did he seem?'

'Proper sorted. Lively, even. Definitely looking forward to Danny coming out of prison. He kept going on and on about Danny this and Danny that. The muppet had got it into his head that Danny had money set aside. He said one or two other things too.' Wolf looked away.

'Like what?'

'Doesn't matter.'

'Everything matters.'

Wolf looked at him straight. 'That Danny wanted to kill you.'

'What the hell are you talking about?'

Wolf took another pull of Bourbon. He had the contained look of a man who harbours secrets.

'C'mon,' Shaw said with a shaky laugh. 'Why on earth would he want to do such a thing? What's his motivation?

He's just done a twenty-five-year stretch in case you hadn't noticed.'

Wolf shrugged. 'Maybe he holds you responsible for not getting rid of the blade. Maybe he resents the fact that you threw him in the river.'

Shaw thought back to his conversation with Danny. Sure, he'd been angry but there was no sense of threat. Danny had been sitting in his home when someone had delivered those feathers. Wolf must be mistaken.

'Did Kenny say that?'

'No. He told me that Danny was going to get a gun when he got out. If you don't believe me, you can speak to Kenny yourself.'

'Except,' Shaw said, 'I can't.'

Chapter Twenty-Two

Shaw brought Wolf up to speed on recent events. Mute, Wolf stared out of the window to the steep-sided garden, his expression changing like the seasons. Gone the cagey manner, the open aggression. Eventually, he picked up his glass, took a long deep swallow.

'You ever think about that night?' Wolf's bottom lip quivered.

He was terrified, not of what was to come, but of what had been, Shaw realised. 'Often,' he replied.

'I can go for weeks, months sometimes, and then, suddenly, out of nowhere, it comes back and slams me in the face.' He leant towards Shaw. 'I replay every second, every moment, thinking and thinking whether we could have done it all differently, whether we could have stopped what happened.

'It's like,' he said, faltering, 'it's like there's no joy. Know what I mean? Like anything good is tainted, like I'm not allowed to be happy. Something like that changes you in your soul.'

Shaw felt the same darkness and absence of hope on occasion. Was this why Wolf continued to behave so badly towards the women in his life? Did a deep black part of him believe he didn't deserve Lori? Shaw wondered if this was what had gone wrong between him and Jo.

'You and me,' Wolf continued, 'we are not bad men. We did nothing wrong. We tried to stop it.'

'We shouldn't have even been there, Wolf.'

A sad smile spread across Wolf's face. 'I haven't been called that in twenty-five years. Even Kenny called me Terry. Christ,' Wolf said, pitching forward, stricken. 'Poor bastard.'

Shaw wished he didn't have to drive. He could use another drink, maybe two or more.

'What happened after Mickie?' Shaw asked softly. 'Where did you go?'

'I went home. Thought I'd sit it out. Cops came to question me.'

This made Shaw sit up. 'What the hell did you say?'

'I acted dumb. Mam vouched for me and so did my Uncle Gordon, said I'd been working late at his garage.'

'And the police bought it?'

'Seemed so.'

'Did they name names?'

'They did. Yours wasn't among them. You were always on the periphery, Jon, never at the business end.

'Afterwards, I fled to the south-west, got a job in a hotel where they didn't ask questions and I didn't need references. It's how I fell into catering. The rest, as they say, is history.'

Shaw considered what Wolf had said. Kenny wouldn't make up a lie about Danny, but he might well have misunderstood.

'Do you know where Carl is?' he asked.

Wolf's face registered disgust. Like Shaw, he'd never

forgotten Carl's expression when Mickie had bled out. Out of all of them, he seemed to be the least affected. 'Not a clue, thank Christ.'

'Ideas?'

'Mercenary. Trauma surgeon. Running a major criminal organisation. To be more charitable, and if I had to take a punt, look for a snake in a suit.'

'That doesn't really narrow the field.'

Wolf lifted the bottle. 'Another?'

Shaw shook his head. 'Better not.' Wolf poured out a liberal measure into his own glass.

Shaw inclined his head. 'I hope I haven't made things awkward for you with Lori.'

'It's fine,' Wolf said shortly.

Shaw slipped out his phone, suggested they keep in touch. Wolf agreed and gave his number, taking Shaw's.

'What will you do?' Shaw said.

'I've got plans.' Wolf's gaze was steady. His voice contained a definite ring of certainty.

'Sounds mysterious.'

Wolf glanced towards the door. 'They've been in place for a while. You know me – a rolling stone.'

'Don't run. Not yet, at least.'

'I'm not,' Wolf said flatly. End of.

Shaw rested his hands on his thighs. 'I should go.'

Wolf didn't stir. Didn't look. Didn't speak much above a whisper. 'You seriously think someone's out to get us?'

A day ago, Shaw wasn't certain, but not any more. 'I do.'

'Who?'

Shaw ran through the possibilities discussed with Danny,

every one of which led to a dead end. 'You should be on your guard, particularly with the business you're in.'

'You mean the psycho guest?' Like a bloodstain on a wooden floor, a wide grin spread across Wolf's face. 'Better add arsenic to the salt and pepper then.'

'I'm serious.' This was no time for jokes. His tone seemed to have a sobering effect.

'Do I need to look out for Lori?'

Shaw thought about it. The killings were deliberate and targeted. Six feathers. Six men.

'I'm sure she'll be fine with you around,' he said pointedly. 'It's us who are in the firing line.'

Wolf took another pull of his drink. 'What about you?'

'Me?' Shaw said. 'I want to stay alive long enough to figure it out.'

Chapter Twenty-Three

Shaw sat in his car, mechanically eating a late lunch. One thought plagued him: Danny wanted a gun, possibly for protection, probably to use against whoever was carrying out the killing. But what if . . .

Shaw had to put himself out of Danny's reach; he had to make him leave.

With this in mind he arrived back in Cheltenham just before 9.00 p.m., and home shortly afterwards.

Inside it felt too quiet, but after his error of judgement the day before, he wasn't going to assume that something bad had already happened. The sitting room told a different story.

Several cans of lager had ringed and stained the pale ash coffee table. Two empty bottles of wine from his vintage wine collection sat next to several glasses. He picked one up, noticed the lipstick mark. Frosted pink. The ashtray swam with roll-ups and filters. Flecks of tobacco randomly scattered the wool carpet. A pungent scent of weed hung heavy in a room deeply resentful at being dragged into a stranger's idea of a good time.

As Shaw's eyes raked the scene, he noticed, to his fury,

that the remains of a Pepperoni pizza lay, discarded, on the mantelpiece. Tomato sauce smeared the antique mirror, a present from Jo's mother, in a final 'Fuck you'.

Shaw tore out into the hall and bellowed Danny's name. Noise and laughter erupted above his head, followed by hushed whispers, giggling and the sound of two pairs of feet hitting the floor. Shaw stood his ground, stony with cold fury. He crossed his arms and adopted the stance of a parent waiting for his teenage son to extract himself from the bed of an impromptu adult guest.

After a lot of scrabbling and scraping, Danny emerged, pulling a T-shirt over his head, and sauntered down the stairs. Shaw never expected contrition but he didn't expect full-blown cock of the north either.

'Whoever that woman is, get her out of here,' Shaw said icily.

Danny glanced over his shoulder and upstairs. 'You take your time, love.' He looked back at Shaw, his expression taunting and brazen. 'You want to watch that mouth of yours.'

Shaw didn't stop to rationalise, didn't consider that, while he'd been busting his balls, Danny had betrayed his trust and hospitality by inviting a random woman into his home to shag. Thought didn't enter into it.

In one move Shaw lifted Danny off his feet and, hands around his throat, slammed him hard against the wall. Close up, Danny's breath was rank with booze, nicotine and garlic.

'What are you waiting for?' Danny goaded him, eyes sliding left and right, fixing on something over Shaw's shoulder. 'I'm buzzin' for it. Go on, squeeze a bit harder.'

Stilettos clacked feverishly across the porcelain-tiled floor. Shaw did not look round. The door slamming shut finally brought him to his senses.

'Are you planning to kill me, Danny?' There it was. Despite Shaw's belief that Kenny had got it all wrong and Wolf had wilfully misunderstood, Shaw didn't entirely trust Danny either. His unpredictability was never in doubt. Neither was his tendency to extreme violence.

'If I had, pal, I'd have done it.' Danny's voice was a rasp. He tried to struggle but Shaw was stronger.

'So you only want my help, that right?'

'We're helping each other,' Danny spluttered. 'That's the deal.'

'And is carrying a gun part of the deal?'

'Who told you that?'

'Wolf – and Kenny told him.'

'For protection. That's all. I can prove it. Fuck's sake, Jon, let go.'

Shaw stared deep into Danny's muddy-coloured eyes. 'You've just got out of prison. They'll throw the book at you if you're found with a firearm.'

'Better than being dead.'

Shaw took a breath. Dealing with Danny was like juggling with chainsaws.

Shaw's hands released and his arms dropped to his sides. Without a word, he strode through to the sitting room, poured a drink and sat on the nearest chair. Danny followed him and slumped down on the sofa, legs apart.

'Sorry about the mess.'

Shaw couldn't speak. He took a long swallow. How did they move on from here?

Silently, Danny stood up and gathered up the empties, taking them and the ashtray into the kitchen. He returned with the pizza box into which he scooped the remains. The mantelpiece and mirror received a cack-handed wipe with a damp cloth. Shaw could see that Danny's domestic skills were limited but his pathetic and belated attempt to make amends did little to damp down his fury. In truth, he felt shame that he'd lost it. He needed to keep it together. At this rate a killer would only have to drive him to the brink of insanity. Job done.

Shaw glared at Danny. 'That woman you brought here could have been a killer.'

'Give over. A slip of a thing like that? I wanted some fun and she was up for it. Have you any idea how long it's been since I got laid?'

'Don't expect any sympathy from me. What was her name?'

'Fuck knows. Lorraine, Loretta, Laura, maybe.'

Different world to the one he lived in, Shaw thought.

'And the bloody gun – what were you playing at? Where the hell did you get it?'

'Same way most ex-cons get their hands on stuff. I didn't order it from Amazon.'

'Funny,' Shaw said, not laughing.

Danny lifted his T-shirt and scratched his belly. 'So how did you get on?'

'I discovered you wanted to kill me.' Shaw issued a thin smile.

'Not that again.'

'Did you say it or didn't you?'

'I was showing off or something. You know what Kenny was like.' Shaw did and it came as a relief. Wolf had let his own animosity towards Danny twist his thinking. 'He loved all that macho shit,' Danny laughed.

Shaw raised an eyebrow. 'So you don't deny it?'

'Turn of phrase, that's all. You looked frigging serious about ending me a moment ago, but you didn't.'

'*And* you impersonated me.'

Danny pressed a finger to his temple like he was tapped in the head. 'Yeah. Sorry about that. Me coming out of prison, and all, I thought it were for the best.'

'The best for whom? Did you know that impersonating a solicitor is a criminal offence?'

'Can't say I did. Consider me told,' Danny said, with a dry smile. 'Now are you going to tell me what you've done all day or not?'

Shaw did the mental equivalent of counting to ten. Marginally composed, he gave Danny a brief rundown of his conversation with Finner, including his grim discovery near the barns. Immediately, his mind conjured up the smell of rotting flesh and old blood.

'Not Fred?' Danny said, open-mouthed. 'Kenny doted on that dog. It was like his kid.'

'My guess is that the dog was used as bait. Once the killer had Kenny's attention, he docked the dog's tail, blatantly causing the animal severe pain. Had it happened to you or me, we would have gone on the attack.'

'But Kenny was different,' Danny said, sparking with

sudden knowledge. 'Kenny must have flipped, panicked and fled.'

Shaw agreed. 'You have to hand it to the killer. Whoever he is, he knows how we tick.'

Danny sat back, viewing Shaw with wary eyes. Shaw wondered whether they were thinking the same thing: someone close.

'Mind if I have one?' Danny said, eyeing the decanter.

'Help yourself.' Shaw was past pointing out that Danny had had plenty already.

Once Danny was settled, he asked after Wolf. Shaw gave him the straight facts.

'That it?'

'How do you mean?'

'Well, you said he'd altered his appearance.'

'Overstating it. He got fit, that's all.'

'Why?'

'Because he cares about his health, I presume.'

'Not because he needed to get strong, toughen up?'

'What are you saying, Danny? Wolf might be a narcissist but he's not our killer.'

'How do you know?'

'Because I had a conversation with him.'

'You didn't pick up any vibes?'

Shaw thought about it. Theirs had been a necessarily highly charged meeting. Wolf was obviously taken aback, disturbed possibly. He was also guarded.

'Only one thing that struck me and it isn't exactly breaking news.'

Danny leant forward. 'Let's hear it.'

'He plans to leave the woman he lives with.'

Danny's grin was broad. 'Same old Wolf.'

Predictably, yes, Shaw thought. He stretched out, reflected on the day's events. Both Finner and Wolf had mentioned Kenny falling in with a bad lot. 'Did Kenny ever talk about his mates?'

'Kenny didn't have mates. He had users. Never shut up about them. I tried to tell him, but he wouldn't have it.'

'These are the guys at the café?'

'Right skanky place.'

'You visited?'

'Didn't need to. Load of low-lifes, from what Kenny said. Bet most of them have done time.'

'Maybe those low-lifes can shed light on Kenny's death.'

'You think?'

'Kenny might have mentioned someone hanging around, or something off. A long shot is better than no shot. Fancy a trip tomorrow?'

'Thought I was supposed to be laying low.'

Which was true. 'Your unique insight could prove useful.'

'Never heard that one before.'

'What do you say?'

Danny shrugged his sturdy shoulders. 'I'm in.'

Chapter Twenty-Four

Sam Deeley sloped into work, hoping to avoid Dillane. The only good news she had to offer her creepy boss: there were no repeats of the nail-gun case. Ergo no serial killer on the loose and thank God for that.

Since Mark Platt's murder, she'd watched as others covered suspicious deaths and domestics, robberies and hate crime. There had been a number of successes, from which she had been shut out. Nobody asked her to join them at the pub for a drink. Nobody spoke about 'the' case and the reason for her hasty escape from West Mercia. They didn't need to. She could read the condemnation in their expressions. Nothing overt was ever said. But she knew. My god, she knew. Which was why the murder of a vulnerable individual in a filthy bedsit rankled. She couldn't fail this time. She couldn't afford another screw-up.

Reaching for her phone, she called Toombs and West, asked to speak to Jon Shaw and was told he was on annual leave. She'd enquired about a meeting of his with former client (and recently deceased) Mark Platt. The receptionist went all preachy about client confidentiality before Deeley cut across her.

'Does Mr Shaw have a secretary?'

'She's not in this week.'

'Then who *can* I speak to? This is an urgent police investigation.' I need to speak to someone higher up the food chain, Deeley insisted, without spelling it out, the threat in her voice usually enough.

In seconds she was talking to a paralegal called Julie Strong who had, to Deeley's ears, an officious manner. Repeating the question elicited a smooth response that confirmed to Deeley why she had a pathological dislike of secretaries.

'It's possible that, due to the nature of the enquiry, no record of Mr Platt's meeting exists.'

'You're surely not telling me that you have walk-in clients?' It wasn't like going to the hairdressers, Deeley thought, bristling. 'You're saying it wasn't in the diary?' Deeley wanted to be absolutely sure.

'That's right.'

'Seems very unprofessional and unorthodox.' Deeley had suspected that something about Shaw didn't stack, and now she knew.

'May I assure you that Mr Shaw is one of our most highly regarded and assiduous lawyers.'

'In that case you'll be able to supply a record of any telephone transaction.'

'Only if one was made. I'd be happy to confer with Mr Shaw's secretary when she's back next week.'

'Do that.' Deeley left her number and signed off.

On her second cup of coffee, she stared at the sheet of

doodles in front of her. It looked like a mathematical equa-
tion, which was a laugh because numbers had never been
her strong suit. Thirty nails. Three times ten. Five times six
equals thirty. At odds with a Chinese interpretation, suggesting that the number six is lucky, Biblical teaching had it
that the number six means imperfection, sin and weakness.
Deeley's stomach seized. Six times a desperate woman had
warned her. Six times she'd failed to act.

Tearing herself back to the here and now, Deeley asked
whether the number six was significant within the context of
Platt's murder. How desperate was she to even contemplate it?

She put her hands above her head and stretched. Resorting
to numerology was akin to talking to clairvoyants. If her colleagues ever found out, she'd be in for a right royal piss-take.

But you didn't need to be a Biblical scholar to understand
the significance of the number thirty and Judas's pay-off. So
who had Platt betrayed, with what, and when?

She pulled up Platt's file on her computer and ran through
the shout lines. Originating from a poor background in the
north, he'd moved twenty-five years ago and led a life that
was unremarkable, if sadly predictable. He had no criminal
record but, operating within druggie circles, didn't mean that
he hadn't committed a crime. Deeley wondered what had
brought him to this part of the world. A series of dead-end
jobs didn't suggest a career move.

She stood up and headed off to the office where the SOCOs
hung out. Sharing her thoughts on Platt wouldn't elicit a forensic breakthrough but it might help to clarify her thinking.
Part of a wider team, SOCOs didn't work in isolation.

Belting down a set of stairs, she met Angel Finch halfway

up. Finch was a woman who, in the civilian world, turned heads and got people, mostly men, to listen. Here, she commanded tacit respect because she'd been in the force since graduating and her dad was a Chief Super in Devon. Deeley's dad was a postman and she hadn't seen him since she was six years old.

Natural ash-blonde hair swept back to better display her perfect skin, brown eyes, the lids slightly heavy, sexy, men would say, and with a ready smile for anyone other than her, Finch adjusted her position so that Deeley either had to move aside or return to the top of the flight. Deeley maintained course, no deviation. A collision was inevitable, but Finch stopped short, tilted her chin, her gaze planted firmly on Deeley's head.

'Excuse me,' Deeley said.

Finch's lips drew back, revealing small piranha short teeth as if they'd never properly developed. 'Shift. In fact, why don't you do us all a big favour and hand in your notice? Become a traffic warden or something. You'll be less of a danger to the public.'

This isn't happening, Deeley thought. Suck it up. Pretend. Smile. Keep cool. In theory, she should be able to report Finch for bullying in the workplace, resulting in a disciplinary and black mark against the woman. Practically, Deeley didn't dare make a fuss or complain. It would only draw unwelcome attention and prevent her, the new girl, from fitting in. Besides, Finch was smart, choosing her opportunity to strike well out of earshot of others. Unable to prove anything, it would be a case of Deeley's word against hers.

A measure of restraint was often needed when questioning

a rapist, child abuser or murderer. Pretend she's one of them, Deeley thought, standing her ground and resisting the temptation to fold her arms even though she wanted to wrap them around her for protection.

Deeley said, 'I'm sorry you feel that way. Now can we, please, both move on? I'm sure you have important things to do.'

Finch's eyes darkened to the colour of wet slate. The features that had made her seem alluring looked decidedly grubby, Deeley thought.

'Think yourself smart, don't you? Getting away with murder.'

Had Finch raked the back of her nails with a jagged blade, Finch could not have wounded her more gravely. Pumped with a sudden surge of hot adrenalin, her stomach churned and, damn it, her body shook. She'd spent the last couple of years defending her actions to others, from her now ex-husband to her superiors. Things, she told herself, would get better. After the inquest. After the divorce. After the transfer when she could start fresh. She was a good police officer. It was only a time issue, she'd told herself. Standing here, receiving insults from a detective who clearly hated her, she understood that nothing had changed. Wanting to howl her regret, her disappointment, while knowing that she was, indeed, guilty, although not literally of murder, Deeley stepped aside, the heels of her shoes pounding the steps like gunfire as she made her rapid descent.

Harper, the Crime Scene Manager, was monitoring jobs coming in on screen. Dark shadows pouched underneath her eyes. Deeley wondered if she was ill.

'You good?'

Harper looked up. 'Sure. *You* don't look too good though, if you don't mind me saying.'

'It's nothing,' Deeley said breezily. 'What's the latest?'

'This and that bubbling. Nothing we can't handle, which is just as well because we're short-staffed. After pulling an all-nighter, Nicole wasn't happy to be given the dubious task of swabbing the hands of a woman charged with the attempted murder of her partner. I'm surprised you haven't heard her yelling her rights from the other side of the building.'

'Nicole, or the suspect?'

Harper rolled her eyes. 'Ha-ha.'

'I've had fresh thoughts about the nail-gun case,' Deeley said. 'Platt moved to the Midlands in the mid-nineties. As far as we can tell, he never went back.'

Harper shrugged. 'Loads of people move away from their roots.'

'Accepted, but when people fall as low as Platt, they tend to go back to familiar territory. He didn't.'

'On the run, is that what you're saying?'

'Bearing in mind the nature of his death, it's a possibility.'

Harper looked unconvinced. Deeley knew what she thought. When a detective speculated, it was usually a sign of desperation. As if to confirm it, Harper said, 'Is Dillane giving you a hard time?'

'Nick simply wants the job done. Our clear-up rate for random murders isn't as good as it should be.'

Except that this wasn't random, she thought, as she scurried back to her office. Of that, she was certain.

Chapter Twenty-Five

Dark and early, Monday morning hit Shaw like a derailed train. The mother of a hangover pummelled his frontal lobes. Hot as hell, he staggered to the bathroom, downed two pain-killers with water straight from the tap, and returned to bed to catch another hour of fractured sleep before daylight.

Sifting through layers of consciousness some time later, he vaguely registered the town awake and on the move. Traffic throbbing. People jogging. Cafés stirring. His mind thick and parked in dreamland, Shaw became aware of pressure at the foot of the bed, as if a dog had suddenly padded into the house and chosen a cosy place to lie. In confirmation, he heard a breath in and an exhalation out. *Shit.*

Bolt upright, he found himself snared in Danny's twisted gaze. It was like being sucked into a deep black hole.

'What the fuck are you doing?'

'What's it look like? Sitting on your bed.' The odd expression on Danny's face had vanished.

'*My* bed,' Shaw said. 'You've got your own.'

'I was thinking.'

'Well, do your thinking somewhere else.' Social boundaries in prison didn't exist. Perhaps Danny had yet to relearn what was acceptable and what wasn't. Unless there was another reason for Danny parking himself on his duvet, when dawn had only recently thrown its clothes on. The after-effects of too much booze and too little sleep instantly became a distant memory.

'You're just pissy 'cos you're hanging.' Danny raised his arms above his head and stretched, giving Shaw a full view of rope-hard musculature. He wasn't certain that it was an entirely casual gesture.

'What's on your mind exactly?' Shaw asked.

'How you pulled all this off.'

'All what?'

'Anyone can get a nice house with nice furniture and a nice garden, but what you've done here, Jon, is buy yourself a life. You've frigging performed a miracle.'

'Divine intervention never came into it. And now your curiosity is satisfied, you can go.'

To emphasise the point, Shaw staggered out of bed and reached for a robe. Distant and preoccupied, Danny stayed put. *Danny wanted to kill you.* Ridiculous, Shaw told himself, annoyed that a single inflammatory statement without basis should crawl under his skin. There was a perfectly sound explanation for Danny's weird mood: a killer on the loose, two of their friends picked off, and the possibility that they could be next.

Danny suddenly snorted with laughter.

'What's so funny?'

'When you woke up, I swear to God you looked as if you'd found broken glass in your bacon buttie.'

'Funny.' Shaw made for the bathroom, Wolf's warning words trampled beneath his bare feet.

Danny talked about the car he would buy when he got rich, where he would live and the house he wanted to live in, 'Detached, four bedrooms minimum, and a sea view.' *When*, Shaw noted, not *if*. It was like going back to when they'd sit and dream as kids.

'And will there be a wife in the shiny big house?'

'Not likely.'

Shaw glanced across.

'I had enough nagging and ordering about inside. Maybe I'll let me mam come and stay, as long as she doesn't bring the wanker from Wythenshawe with her.'

After that, Danny fell silent. Shaw couldn't tell whether he'd inadvertently hit a nerve or whether Danny's expressed hopes for the future were limited by whether there was a future to be had.

'You good?' Shaw asked.

'Mint,' Danny said, without enthusiasm. He seemed to collapse in on himself; face pressed against the window, hand on the door, as if poised to open it and throw himself out. The omens were not good. When Danny went flat, he would either snap out of it with a smile or lash his way out with a fist.

By the time they reached Ilfracombe, it was spitting rain, the kind of thin drizzle that glazed your face.

Shaw drove into the main car park, with its view of a grey

and sullen Bristol Channel, and parked. Danny seemed to perk up now that they were there. 'I'll get us a ticket,' he said amiably, stepping out of the Macan. 'Be good to stretch my legs.'

Shaw waited inside, glad that Danny's brief 'black dog' moment had passed.

'Good to go,' Danny said jauntily on his return.

Together, they walked up towards the town and a row of shops along the front.

'What a shithole,' Danny said. 'Like one of them reality stars hooked on cheap applause and who thinks they're it.'

The café was a place that tried to be too many things to too many people. Outside gave the impression of sea shanty, inside looked chrome and modern and soulless. They had their pick of tables because, despite being lunchtime, it was empty of customers. Danny chose a table near the window. Shaw sat, picked up a menu, handed it to Danny, and looked across to a man at the bar, expecting some form of greeting or a nod of acknowledgement. The guy continued to focus on a TV screen with the latest horse-racing results. It gave Shaw time to clock the dark hair, high cheekbones, almost black eyes, as if he came from Italian descent. He had a diamond stud in his right ear. He looked spare and tight, like he was ready to defend with attack at the first sniff of trouble.

Shaw looked across at Danny who had his head down, engrossed in the menu. 'Coffee?' Shaw asked.

'Lager.'

'Anything to eat?'

'Hamburger and chips.'

'Cheekbones' was now drying glasses with a tea towel.

An aura of intensity and unapproachability surrounded him – not great if you're in the hospitality business. At Shaw's approach he turned away, called out the back, 'Jack, customer.' Shaw noted a foreign accent. 'Coming, Leo,' a British voice fired an instant reply.

Jack was a broad-shouldered man whose T-shirt was too small. He wore a black pork pie hat on his head, Shaw suspected, to conceal male-pattern baldness. His warm smile was genuine enough, indicating that he was the hired help, not management.

'What can I get you, guys?'

Shaw gave his order and Jack smiled once more, murmured something to Leo, who didn't seem pleased to have his busy day interrupted, then sped back to the kitchen as if his life depended on it. Maybe it did. Meanwhile, Leo operated a complicated machine, working it in slow motion as if he had until next Christmas to deliver a cappuccino.

'Is it always this quiet?' Shaw said.

Leo's shrug was epic. 'It's Monday and it's raining.'

Shaw tamped down the facetious reply that was keen to trip off his tongue. Maybe Leo was stoned. Maybe the 'can't be arsed' slow-eyed expression and banal response was a façade designed to conceal the fact that Leo was weighing him up. Did he notice the expensive clothes, the *posh* accent, the trappings of well to do? Shaw ignored the electric sensation of Danny's eyes lasering a hole in his back. *I've got this*, Shaw wanted to say.

'So what do people do around here when it's not raining?' Shaw asked amiably.

'How do you mean?'

'For fun?'

'The amusement arcade is three doors along.'

'I was thinking more in terms of roulette, rolling the dice, chasing the dime.'

Leo's liquid dark eyes shone. His face lit up like someone had placed a cheque for a million quid into his hands. Then, as if someone had made a salacious remark about his mother, his expression darkened, eyes thinning with suspicion.

Shaw leant in and lowered his voice. 'I'm not police, if that's what you're thinking.'

Leo breathed in as if he were sniffing the air for a lie. 'I think nothing, friend.'

'I'd heard on the grapevine I could get a game.'

Leo was now at the penultimate stage of coffee production – whizzing up the milk.

Adopting his coolest expression, Shaw murmured, 'Poker.' He didn't know the first thing about it, other than what he'd read in books and seen in films. Big stakes. Booze. Smokes. Glamorous women. It was difficult to imagine that Kenny had got himself embroiled in a game that demanded intellect, nimble thinking and front. Kenny didn't have the capacity to play 'Brag', never mind anything more sophisticated. But, eager to please and easy to impress, he would have been a pushover because, more than anything in the world, Kenny needed friends. His biggest desire was to fit in, in a world that had no room for the simple-minded. For a man like Leo, Kenny would have been an easy mark.

Leo leaned across the counter. 'How did you come by this news?'

'We have a mutual friend.'

Mistrust tightened Leo's features.

'Kenny Sharples.'

'I heard he died.' Leo's expression defaulted to pissed off and bored. A mug of coffee hit the counter like a badly landing hang-glider.

'An accident with a quad bike,' Shaw confirmed. 'Seems it was his fault, wasn't thinking straight. I wondered if he were under some kind of pressure.'

'Couldn't say.' Leo reached for a bottle of lager from the chiller, popped the top off and put it on a tray. 'Do you want a glass?'

'No ta, mate,' Danny called out from his place near the window.

Shaw homed in again on Leo. 'Did you ever see Kenny with anyone in particular?'

Leo shook his head.

'Never noticed somebody hanging around?'

'You mean a woman?'

As far as Shaw knew, Kenny had never been interested in women, or men, for that matter.

'Anyone at all.'

'No.'

'Nothing out of the ordinary then?'

A shifty light entered Leo's eyes. 'Your coffee's going cold and I have much to do.'

'Fair enough. If anything springs to mind, I'd be grateful. We won't be leaving for a bit.' Shaw picked up the tray and took it back to the table.

Danny gulped half the contents of the bottle, wiped his mouth and grinned. 'The bloke's a dickhead,' he muttered.

'He is, but it doesn't mean he's a know nothing.'

Danny gave a non-committal shrug, looked around him, still with the grin. 'It's a long way to come for a drink and a bite to eat.'

Shaw took a sip of coffee. Wolf was right. It was the beverage equivalent of freshly laid tarmac. Danny's meal arrived, along with cutlery.

'Can I get you anything with that?' Jack said. 'Tomato ketchup, vinegar, mustard?'

'Got any brown sauce?'

'I'll have to check with the kitchen.'

'And another lager.' Danny jutted his chin in Leo's direction, an indolent nod from the man with the attitude suggesting that the message was received and understood.

Seconds later, Leo strolled over, placed a bottle of Becks on the table.

'Ta,' Danny said. 'You're not from round here, are you?'

Leo shook his head.

'So where are you from, pal?'

'Bucharest.'

'And where's that when it's at home?'

'Romania,' Shaw chipped in.

'Nice place, is it, Leo?'

'It is my home.'

'So why did you leave *home* and come over here then?'

'Danny . . .' Shaw began.

Danny flicked up his palms. 'I'm genuinely interested is all. I mean maybe the economy isn't so good. Maybe Leo here wants to improve his language skills and better himself. Isn't that right, Leo?'

Leo's full lips twisted into a cold smile that put Shaw on edge.

'You have to hand it to him,' Danny continued wide-eyed, 'his English is loads better than my Romanian.'

Shaw held his breath, fearing that either man could lose it. He looked from Danny to Leo and back to Danny who, thank God, had picked up a chip and was chewing away happily.

'Well ta for that and I wish you luck with it. Nice to natter,' Danny said.

Dismissed, Leo languidly turned on his heel. Danny shoved another chip in his mouth then swept the plate of food, knife and fork cartwheeling, onto the floor.

'What the . . .' Words failed Shaw as he saw exactly what Danny was about.

On his feet, Danny grabbed his beer and dashed it against the edge of the table. Advancing on Leo, Danny held the neck of the broken bottle in his hand.

Chapter Twenty-Six

Shaw stared, aghast.

Leo was flat out on the grubby floor, face twisted to one side, broken glass perilously close to his right eye. Astride him, Danny gripped Leo's wrists in one meaty hand and he was not letting go.

'Right, you little fucker, you're the mate that took our friend for a fool and ripped him off so when you're asked a question, you fucking well answer.'

'I wasn't rip . . . Ow, *Futu-il*.' Blood dribbled down Leo's ear where Danny had nicked it.

'Danny, mate, stop.' Shaw made a move towards him.

'Stay the fuck back. I'll stop when I get what I want, otherwise I swear to God pretty boy here is going to need a plastic surgeon.'

'OK, all right,' Leo garbled. 'We let him run up a few debts.'

'You mean you encouraged Kenny, that right?'

'That's right,' Leo stammered.

'And threatened him if he didn't pay up. That right too?'

'Yes, yes. Sorry.'

'Good, it's important to recognise when you've done wrong. Now my friend here,' Danny gave a backwards glance at Shaw, 'asked if you'd noticed anything out of the ordinary.'

'I did not know what he meant. I . . .'

'Now let's try it again,' Danny said nastily, the jagged edge of the bottle moving a centimetre closer.

If Leo didn't give Danny something soon, Shaw feared Danny would lose all sense of reason. He scanned across and noticed Jack, white-faced, a bottle of Sarsons in his hand. Shaw cast him a look that said, *Don't be a hero*. He wondered what the exit strategy was. Knowing Danny, there wasn't one and he'd bet a decent wedge that Leo had mates who could run faster and fight meaner.

'Danny, let him go,' Shaw pleaded. 'The guy hasn't a clue.'

Leo squirmed. 'Your friend is right. I don't know nothing.'

'He's lying,' Danny yelled. Another jab. This time Leo screamed as blood sprayed from a wound to his cheek.

'For God's sake, stop it.' Shaw stepped forward and found the jagged edge of the bottle pointed at him. Danny's eyes flashed. Out of it. Operating on pure instinct. Fight mechanism switched to full-on.

'DANNY.'

'Shut the fuck up.'

A torrent of words poured from Leo's mouth in a language nobody understood; the tone, however, universally recognisable.

Danny drew his hand back. 'Right, you little—'

'Kenny thought he was being watched,' Jack piped up.

Danny stalled, whatever demon had possessed him taking flight.

Keen to lower the emotional temperature, Shaw asked Jack when it had been happening.

'Been going on for months, off and on.'

Danny exchanged a backwards glance with Shaw, who wondered why Kenny had never mentioned it to Danny.

'Where?'

'At the farm. In town. Whenever he was out walking his dog. Kenny thought he was imagining things until, one day, he found a peacock feather on the seat of his pick-up.'

Leo lifted his head. 'It is an omen of death.'

'No shit,' Danny said.

Shaw noted Danny was less confrontational. Keen to keep the conversation rolling at a vastly reduced temperature, he asked Jack if there was anything else.

'That time in the truck, his dog was inside, which really freaked him out. Reckoned the feather was some kind of calling card, or something.'

'He never saw a soul?'

'Nobody.'

'Was the vehicle locked?'

'That's the bit he couldn't understand. Kenny was that scared he reported it to the police.'

Chapter Twenty-Seven

'I can't believe it,' Danny exploded. 'Going to the cops. What was Kenny thinking?'

'What were *you* thinking?'

They were back in Shaw's car and driving out of town. Fortunately, Leo was more concerned about patching up his face than retribution. For now.

'That little scrote had it coming to him. He's got a right dodgy outfit going on. I smelt it the second we walked through the door. If you hadn't been there, I'd have glassed him good and proper.'

Shaw sat in stony silence. The narrow space between them crackled with hostility.

'Where's the problem?'

'The problem is you can't control yourself. One minute, you're all smiling, the next you completely lose your shit.'

'I got a result, didn't I?'

'Exactly the same information could have been gained without leaving blood all over the place.'

'Fuck him. Anyway, pretty boy is hardly going to report us to the police. Bad for business.'

'And what if a community-minded citizen had witnessed the assault and reported it? You'd have been back in prison within the hour.'

'Well, nobody did, did they?'

Danny hunkered down, crossed his arms and made a big pretence of sleeping for the next two and a half hours. Shaw was grateful for the silence. It saddened him to think of Kenny being stalked and terrified. Why Kenny hadn't taken Danny into his confidence seemed strange, unless Kenny feared losing face. Perhaps he'd already visited the police by then and they'd told him that, without solid evidence, there was nothing they could do. Shaw could imagine how dismissive they would be and that would have embarrassed Kenny.

They arrived back in Cheltenham late afternoon. Unusually, Danny stamped off to his room and stayed there. Embracing the silence, something lifted in Shaw. His priority was Carl and how to trace him. A duty to deliver a warning was not the only reason that Shaw needed to find him. *'Snake in a suit,'* Wolf said. *'Nobody's seen or heard from Carl in decades,'* Danny told him. How come? Carl might have dropped off the face of the planet, but in a digital world it was impossible to go to ground completely.

Shaw opened up his laptop and tried a basic Google search. The list was not long: an electrician in North Wales, a landscaper and a US singer-songwriter who'd dispensed with his Christian name, preferring initials. Dicking around, Shaw tried Lord and Sir before the name. Nada. Remembering Wolf's quip about Carl becoming a trauma surgeon, he tried Doctor. Negative. Could Carl be dead?

Shaw pictured a twenty-year-old Carl. Not easy because Carl was one of those individuals who was instantly forgettable. He had no particular distinguishing features. Brown hair. Average height. Average build. *Vanilla* best described him. He'd once boasted that he was impossible to identify let alone photo-fit because his skin was like glass and his face too generic. Passing him in the street, nobody would give him a second glance. Unsettled, Shaw came up with a plan. He only prayed that Hope Castleman had not entirely lost the plot and was back in the game. Most importantly of all, he hoped that her meds were working.

Chapter Twenty-Eight

Outwardly, I have all the patience of an outreach worker with a mouthy adolescent gang member. I tell myself I can stand here all night, for as long as it takes for someone to capture my likeness and the essence of who I really am.

The greatest lie is the one we tell ourselves.

Like a modern piece of conceptual art, I'm a mess. Have been for as long as I can remember. When someone kills, it's not only the victim who dies. The souls of those they leave behind are forever blighted. In twenty-five years, I've had a couple of hours' relief if you measure out the time it took me to dispatch my first victim and decorate the head of a second. Not much, is it? Not enough to compensate for what that pack of animals did to her and then to me, not sufficient to make up for my smashed-up life.

Voices from the past snap and worry and bite at my heels. Always angry. Always shouting. As if it were all my fault.

People say time heals. That's another big fucking lie. Time corrodes and festers and eats you alive.

If you let it.

Despite the buzz of bloodletting, the messy method

employed at the farm was, I admit, not my finest hour. I'd done my homework as usual. Aside from timing my trip so that it coincided with market day, I waited for the weather to turn nasty. Human debris is less likely to stick to a water-proof jacket and walking trousers, and outside crime scenes are always more difficult to navigate for the humble SOCO. All that trudging through thick mud. All that human soup mixing with animal excrement and DNA. I'd ensured my victim was pliant and in a high enough state of agitation. But, despite bashing that moron's brains out being the nearest thing to joy, as uplifting as it was, it lacked elegance. I'll be honest (not a word I use lightly), I was less happy about the dog. That trusting look in its eyes as I grabbed its scrawny neck, and then the noise it made, squealing and yowling and wriggling, as I docked its little tail, set my teeth right on edge. And what did Kenny Sharples do? He stood frozen, like he'd been injected with succinylcholine (now there's an idea). Snot pooling grotesquely on his thick top lip, he bawled his eyes out. *Top one.*

Half blind with irritation, I resist the urge to flex my fingers. Careful, I tell myself. Frustration leads to mistakes. I haven't waited this long to get sloppy and balls it up now.

Chapter Twenty-Nine

'*Gone fishing. Have taken cash from drawer in study.*' Next to the note, the phone Shaw had bought for Danny. The message could not be clearer: Danny was in the wind. He must have left during the night or in the early hours. Shaw had been too bushed to notice. His immediate reaction was one of relief. He was glad Danny was no longer around to bug him. On the downside and perversely, he felt isolated and alone.

The door to Danny's room was closed. He pushed it open and walked inside. Instantly, his eyes zeroed in on the bed: a gun and what looked like a magazine, presumably containing bullets.

Shaw could probably lay his hands on a firearm if he wanted to. For Danny, it would be as easy as ordering a take-away from an Indian restaurant. So how was Shaw supposed to interpret Danny's gesture? A symbol, a gift or a threat?

Charitably, Shaw guessed it could be viewed as a genuine act of goodwill, a peace offering. *Just maybe* Danny genuinely believed that Shaw needed protection and this was the best he could come up with. After Danny's firework display the day before, Shaw wasn't sure he bought it.

He crept close. No expert, he easily identified the gun as a Sig-Sauer because it was imprinted on the stock. It had a stainless-steel frame, with the model number P365 engraved on the slide. The grip looked like it was manufactured from polymer. Shaw didn't think that Danny was stupid enough to leave his fingerprints on it, but he took no chances. No way did he want the thing within a supplicant's breath of him.

Darting into the bathroom, Shaw swiped a fresh hand towel from the shelf and, returning to the bedroom, wrapped it around the weapon, picking it up as if it were dog shit to be put in a disposal bag.

It felt lighter than expected.

Tracking back downstairs, he went into the study, unlocked the bottom drawer in his desk and discovered that Danny had indeed stolen two hundred pounds from his personal stash of cash. Annoyed, he lowered the Sig, still bundled up, and secured it. For good measure he locked the door to the study too.

A shower and shave later, he drank juice from the fridge straight from the carton (something Jo detested) and made the coffee he'd promised himself an hour earlier.

Sharper now, an unwelcome thought returned to scratch at the back of his brain.

The killer was someone who knew their weaknesses, which buttons to press, how they ticked. Someone close.

Hope Castleman lived in a less affluent part of town where builders were swiftly moving in and going full Art Deco. In a newly gentrified area, houses remained competitively priced for Cheltenham and it was fast becoming 'the' place to buy. But Hope's fall from grace, together with her offbeat and unfortunate manner, condemned her to the cheap seats for eternity. Consequently, she lived in one of those homes that had not been done up. Run-down and neglected – a bit like Hope – someone, who had once taken up her fight, as Shaw had done several years before, rented the place to her well below market value.

Shaw pulled up outside. Gaining access was like crossing a demilitarised zone. Attached to the gate and front door were large magnetic boards. Copper coils hung from trees. If you looked closely enough you could see magnets attached to the branches. A necklace of interlinked copper bracelets straddled the guttering. Glinting in the wet light, they resembled an attraction at Blackpool. Scaring birds and deterring cold callers might be assumed. In Hope's brain, the volume of scrap metal was designed to upset electromagnetic fields and stop 'the bastards from listening in'. Conspiracy theorists – and there were a lot of them – believed she was a folk hero. Others thought she was a nutter. Shaw knew otherwise. Frighteningly intelligent, Hope had worked for GCHQ until she was chucked out on what Hope described as 'unspecified grounds'. Indignant and defensive, she'd approached Shaw with the fervent and touching belief that she could take on the government and Ministry of Defence, or rather he could. Had Shaw not delicately explained her position and the futility of such an action, she'd probably still be doing time in a special facility for those who dabble illicitly and above their pay grade in the digital dark arts. As it was, he'd managed to convince enough bodies in powerful places that, although brilliant, she posed no threat to national security. The new 'right on' interest in mental health, and thanks to an autistic British hacker receiving a fair-ish hearing in the States from the safety of the UK, had aided Shaw's case in his fight for Hope. 'Mitigating circumstances', that all-encompassing and obscurely applied phrase, had done the trick. Since then, she'd lived virtually as a recluse.

Shaw rapped at the door. Windows had received the same metallic treatment so it was impossible to see in. Scuffling from somewhere inside convinced him that he'd been heard. 'Hope,' he called out. 'It's Jon.'

Seconds later, he heard several locks, including a dead bolt, release. A security chain briefly rattled and the door opened a crack. Following carefully laid down protocol, Shaw telescoped his body and slipped in sideways.

He stood in a narrow corridor, with a door off to the left, another leading to a kitchen and stairs at the back. Copper entrails, stripped from old television sets and washing machines, hung in elaborate arrangements from the ceiling. If you could get past the fact that the interior decor consisted of boxes piled high with provisions, the house had all the normal attributes associated with a three-up, two-down, apart from the fact that every light was switched on because blackout blinds and metal shutters were permanently closed.

Hope peered at Shaw while munching her way through a large bowl of cereal. Spectacles with big frames and thick lenses obscured her blue eyes and sat astride her face like anchor plates on masonry. Pasty-faced, due to a lack of direct sunlight, her lips were ghostly white and ill-defined so that they blended in with the rest of her skin. Shaw briefly wondered whether she was anaemic. Sure as hell she was deficient in vitamin D.

He knew his reassuring smile would fail to ding on Hope's emotional spectrum because she was incapable of comprehending facial expression. Speaking fluent Geek, Hope was only socially at ease with data, codes, encryptions and algorithms.

'Want some?' she said, mouth full. Self-enforced incarceration, coupled with boredom, meant that Hope had put on a couple of stone in the intervening years. The smartly dressed young woman he'd first encountered now wore baggy clothes to hide her burgeoning physique.

'I'm good, thanks. How are you doing?'

Hope pushed in another mouthful, by way of a response, and reloaded her spoon.

'Got a job for you, Hope.'

A spoonful of Mr Kellogg's finest paused midway to its destination. The surprise and gratitude on her face would make a thug cry.

'I need you to locate someone,' he explained.

Hope looked madly around her and, seeing nowhere suitable, plonked the bowl on the floor, spilling milky cereal on the carpet. She stepped over it. 'In here,' she said. 'Quick.' Shaw did as he was told.

The room was large, a citadel of monitors and screens and plasma perfection. Against every wall and window, and arranged in alphabetical order, were hundreds of books on computing, defence and the military and, surprisingly, on astrology. Running underneath a window, a long executive table bristling with technology and a row of widescreen Mac computers that sat like ruthlessly ambitious young scientists discussing how they, alone, were going to tackle the world's numerous ills and redirect the course of humanity. Astonishingly, the centrepiece of the room was what, on a first glance, appeared to be a massive American-style refrigerator. Shaw craned his head. Through a transparent door, a rack of electronic components, similar to circuit boards, and attached to cables. The mid-section looked more complex, with circular thick wiring. 'Is that a mainframe computer?'

'No.'

'Well, what is it?'

'The altar and where the magic happens.' Grabbing a chair, she sped over to one of the Macs and beckoned Shaw, who was none the wiser. 'So what you got?'

He provided Carl's basic details. He didn't tell Hope why he wanted to locate him, only that he had to. 'I've carried out a search online and got nowhere.'

Hope made a facial expression that Shaw interpreted as *This is no job for an amateur. What did you expect?*

'Snare was born in mid-November in Salford,' he added, hoping this would help.

'Scorpio,' she said. 'Secretive.'

Shaw had no belief in the less than scientific study of the planets, no more than he believed in Father Christmas, but he had to admit that Hope was right about Carl.

'I may need to access the dark web.' Her pale lips thinned in concentration.

'How long will that take?' he said.

'How long will *what* take?'

Yes, I can help, her face seemed to say, *but I need you to get out of here before 'they' get me.*

'To locate Snare?'

'Two minutes, two days, who knows?' Her bare foot tapped the floor with impatience.

Shaw spiked inside. 'I don't have two days.'

'Then push off.' She crouched over a keyboard, hands poised, resembling a concert pianist gearing up to play a concerto.

'I'll drop by later,' he told her.

'Don't. I'll contact you when I'm ready.'

'How are you going to do that?' Phone calls and texts were off limits, according to Hope.

'I'll drop an encrypted email to your work address.'

'I'm not at work.'

'Home phone then.'

'How am I supposed to decipher it?' Shaw said.

'Private key.'

Shaw's technical abilities were passable, but he had absolutely no idea what she was talking about and said so.

Hope twisted round and gave him a pointy look very similar to the one Jo had flashed him before she'd angrily walked out.

'I send an email with a digital signature attached. Open it. When I send the encrypted email, you check it matches.'

'Right.'

'Make sure you close the doors and gate after you.'

'Hope?'

'What?' In a huff, she did not look up.

'Are you still taking your tablets?'

'Go away.'

With nothing more to say or do, Shaw left.

Chapter Thirty

Shaw pulled into his parking spot when his phone rang. Praying Hope had worked her magic, Shaw snatched it up.

'Hello?'

'Jon Shaw, is that you?'

'Jeffrey,' Shaw said in surprise. 'Are you all right?' He didn't sound it.

'I've had the police here this morning. They're saying that Kenny's death wasn't an accident.'

Shaw let out a breath. Thank God for rain and mud and him having the presence of mind to remove the shovel. That was as far as the good news went. If Jeffrey told the police about Kenny's 'lawyer friend', things could get complicated.

'The pathologist claimed his injuries didn't kill him,' Jeffrey said, audibly bubbling with distress. 'They said he'd received several blows to the head. Who would want to kill the lad?' Jeffrey's voice escalated to near hysteria. It was essential Shaw calmed him down.

'Jeffrey, have the police interviewed you formally?'

'They wanted a chat, the copper said. Seemed friendly enough.' There was a hitch in his voice.

'But?'

'Clear as glass he had me down for chief suspect.'

'They're bound to look at those closest to the victim. It's procedure, nothing more. What was the officer's name?'

'Nick Stroud.'

'Rank?'

'I don't remember. Detective, I think. Or maybe sergeant. Does that help?'

Jeffrey clearly didn't realise that the officer could be a detective *and* a sergeant, as in Detective Sergeant.

'Or it might have been an inspector,' Jeffrey said. 'I'm really not sure.'

Shaw pictured the old man's confusion and felt sorry for him. It must have come as an almighty shock. 'Don't worry, Jeffrey. Did Stroud ask where you were on the day of the incident?'

'Between 10.00 a.m. and noon, he said.'

'He was that specific?'

'Yes.'

Must be the approximate time established for Kenny's death, Shaw thought. Stroud was checking whether or not Jeffrey had an alibi.

'And what did you say?'

'The truth,' Jeffrey snapped back, volume control on the increase again. 'A dozen people can vouch I was at the market.'

'Excellent.' Shaw's buoyancy was a lie designed to reduce the emotional temperature. He could see how badly Jeffrey Finner's defensive manner would play with the detectives. He needed him to curb it.

'*Excellent?* They're treating the farm as a crime scene. I've got people in white suits turning up with equipment and all sorts.'

'Again, this is a very normal part of a murder enquiry.'

'But I have to move out.'

'It would only be for a few days.'

'What about my animals?'

Shaw scratched his jaw. 'I'm sure the police will advise.'

'Can you talk to them?'

No way. 'I'm not—'

'You're a lawyer. I might need one.'

'In the circumstances, it's unlikely. The main thing to remember is that you're innocent and you need to stay as calm as possible.'

'But you could represent me, couldn't you?'

'Jeffrey, I live miles away. I'd be more than happy to find someone close to where you live, someone you can trust.'

The line went quiet. Shaw sensed the old man's disappointment.

'All right then,' Jeffrey said slowly, a new edge to his voice. 'I can see you don't want to get involved.'

'It's not that,' Shaw began. 'It's . . .'

'I've been on this earth long enough to recognise a man with something to hide when I meet one.'

The line went dead.

Shaken, Shaw sat back, stared straight ahead into the damp light. He didn't blame Jeffrey Finner. The man had a point and, regrettably, one he'd quickly share with the police.

In his experience, the Devon and Cornwall constabulary were more accustomed to boat theft than murder. Coupled with the savage dispatch of a pet dog, which they were bound to uncover, and the fact that Kenny had already reported the incident with the peacock feather (admittedly this assumed that the report was ever logged and Shaw, somehow, doubted that), it was destined to make headline news. They would get on it, resulting in a connection to Shaw, giving him less time to manoeuvre.

Switching from phone calls to Google, Shaw checked the weather conditions for the day of Kenny's murder. According to the MET Office, between 10.00 a.m. and noon, 90 per cent precipitation was predicted, with windy conditions and a threat of localised flooding. The murk and poor visibility would provide ideal conditions for a determined killer to strike. A fair degree of planning had obviously gone into it. Nearer to home, he wondered how Deeley was faring. Had she yet traced Mark back to his roots? Would she make a more tangible connection? And how long before she rumbled Shaw himself?

In theory, he had a head start on all of them; he knew there was a killer on the loose and why. In practice, he was adrift.

He rubbed his eyes, not sure what to do next, when an email flew into his inbox. Hope had sent a preliminary to enable him to read the encrypted message. He opened it. Another followed. Obeying her instructions, the second message was simple. 'Back here NOW.'

Chapter Thirty-One

Shaw felt as if he'd taken a selfie in a beauty spot and, failing to spot the cliff edge, had plunged fifty feet to his death on the other side.

'Classified?' he said, slack-jawed.

'Yup.'

'Snare is a spy?'

Hope frowned. 'We don't call them that.'

'All right, an intelligence officer.' James fucking Bond, what difference did it make?

'From the scant information you shared,' Hope said in all seriousness, 'Snare seems eminently qualified.'

Shaw sat down with a thump.

'What's your interest?' Hope asked.

'Personal.'

Hope reached for the pack of biscuits handily arranged next to one of the monitors. 'Want one? There's plenty more.'

'No, thanks.' Grimly, he realised that Snare had the means to dispatch them one by one for reasons he could not yet work out. 'I guess this is where it ends,' he said morosely.

'Not like you to give up.' Hope merrily munched through a digestive.

'I don't have a choice. Classified means hands off.'

Hope nodded towards the beast of a machine parked in the centre of the room. 'To me, it's another layer of secrecy to uncover, another piece of encryption to crack.'

'No,' Shaw said shortly. 'You start digging and you'll have a firearms team arriving at your door before you can say GCHQ.'

'Don't be so dramatic.'

'I'm not.' Shaw had forgotten how obstinate Hope could be. He had *not* forgotten the intransigence of shady men and women who served to protect the nation. 'Trust me, it's . . .'

'Too late. I've already located him.'

Oh crap, Shaw thought. This would not end well. He dreaded to think how many protocols she'd broken to access the information. He asked her.

'Best you don't know. Are you all right? You look a little peaky.'

Hope might be brilliant. She was also bat-shit crazy. 'Promise me you'll delete any trail back to you.'

She tapped the desk petulantly. 'You really should have more faith in my abilities.'

'I do but, as your lawyer, I'm also concerned for your well-being.' Despite coming a cropper with the intelligence agencies, she appeared ignorant of the consequences of messing with them. Again.

'There's really no need.' Narked, she lounged back in her seat, folded her arms and stopped eating – a bad sign.

'Sorry.'

She gave her finger a little nibble. 'You should be.'

'I am. Truly,' he said, in an effort to convince her. 'So what did you find out?'

Hope flexed her body, stretched out her legs. Her show. Her expertise.

'Mr Snare has spent the past ten years in and out of Afghanistan. Looks like he's been working in Black Ops, assisting the US on their black sites.'

'Detention centres where people are held without trial.' It wasn't difficult to imagine what line of work Carl was embroiled in. 'And where is he now?'

'Closer than you think.'

'Here?' Shaw streaked with alarm.

'Birmingham. We have a branch of MI5 there.'

'Are you even supposed to tell me that?'

Hope flicked biscuit crumbs from her lap. 'Probably not.'

'Consider it forgotten. Tell me how I get hold of him.'

'Are you sure you want to?'

'I have no choice.'

'The guy knows how to kill.'

Shaw thought about the gun in his desk. 'I still have to talk to him.'

She waved a piece of paper in front of him. 'I've written the address down. It's a loft apartment, very smart and convenient and within walking distance of the Mailbox, the Cube and Grand Central Station,' she said, going all estate agent on him. 'Only the best for our man.'

Shaw took it, stood up and, slipping out his wallet, handed Hope the thick end of five hundred pounds.

'I don't need that much.'

'You do.'

'Give it to me next time.'

There might not be a next time, Shaw thought.

Chapter Thirty-Two

Satisfied he wasn't being followed, Shaw drove to Birmingham from Hope's. He did not call in at home. He did not retrieve the gun. To go armed was an open invitation for trouble. Besides, he'd never fired a weapon – unlike Carl. Better to employ his lawyerly skills and dial down any potential rhetoric than inflame someone who killed for a living. And if Carl was really offing his old mates in his down time, Shaw could do damn all about it.

Parking in a multi-storey near the Mailbox, he walked the short distance to Carl Snare's apartment in a converted warehouse. The first obstacle was the entry system. Shaw hung around doing his best not to look sketchy. Eventually, a young woman appeared.

'You OK?' She was purposefully making for the intercom.

'Erm . . . yeah, I'm visiting a friend.' He patted his pockets as if he'd lost something else other than his bearings.

'No worries. I'll buzz you in with me.'

'Amazing. Thanks. One of those days.' He smiled weakly, sustaining the impression that he was one heck of a disorganised guy.

'Lift's this way,' she said, returning his smile.

'I need the exercise. I'll take the stairs.'

A sympathetic conversion, the building retained many of its industrial features, including bricks walls, painted white signs marking the levels, and metal balustrades. It was the ultimate in warehouse chic. Four flights of stairs later, Shaw reached the door to Carl's apartment. He'd gone beyond wondering what kind of reception he'd receive; too much at stake for that.

He raised his hand to rap at the door when it swept open. Carl Snare's eyes connected with Shaw's like sights on a sniper rifle. Wearing a dark brown leather jacket, he looked as if he'd just got in.

'Jon Shaw.'

'Carl, how are you?'

'Unfortunately,' Carl grimaced, 'I'm on my way out.' No greeting. No pleasantry. No *as I live and breathe, I haven't seen you in a quarter of a century*. Pegged at a low note, Carl spoke slowly, deliberately, with little inflexion. Traces of a northern accent were vaguely identifiable. Shaw wondered whether Carl adapted his accent, depending on the company he was in. Less easy to read: the sub-text behind Carl's response. Shaw couldn't tell whether Carl was pleased, surprised or plain irritated to see him.

'I don't want to hold you up, but I really need to speak to you. Won't take long.' A lie even if Shaw only delivered edited highlights.

Carl glanced at his watch, a big chunky affair that Shaw bet was water-resistant to a hundred metres. 'I can spare a few minutes. You'd best come in.'

Carl opened the door wide into a hallway with coat hooks and a rack below for shoes and boots. Entering Carl's personal charisma-free zone, Shaw glanced down and noticed a black pair of military-style combat boots with laces and thick soles, perfect for traversing deserts and, more tellingly, muddy fields.

The main living space was minimalist meets nothing in it and consisted of a single ultra-modern leather sofa, a solitary armchair, chrome radiators and modern light fittings. This was a place to pitch up in, not to inhabit, a front to conceal the false life loitering beneath.

Big windows revealed extensive views over the city. Shaw was reminded of the wisdom of taking the higher ground in battle.

Invited to sit down, Shaw sat. Carl, he noted, stood. 'How did you find me?'

'Sheer chance,' Shaw lied. 'I happened to be in the city and spotted you.'

'Where?'

'Bull Ring, or thereabouts.'

'Extraordinary coincidence.' Whether Carl bought it or not, his eyes gave nothing away. 'You have work here?'

'Occasionally. I'm a lawyer in Cheltenham.'

'Nice town.'

'And you?'

'I live here.'

'Work?'

'I'm in the export business.'

Yes, that sounds plausible, Shaw thought, if clichéd.

Carl drummed his fingers on his thighs. *Places to be. In a hurry.* 'I take it this isn't simply a social call.'

'I'm afraid not.'

'Is it about Danny?'

'Very perceptive of you.'

Carl's face twitched into what passed most closely for a smile.

'You've seen him?' Shaw said, guarded.

Carl shook his head. 'I was aware that his release date was up.'

Keeping tabs, were you? Shaw thought. Watching him closely, he filled Carl in on Kenny and Mark's murders.

'A nail gun, you say?'

Did Shaw imagine a glint in Carl's eye? It had been a long time since he'd last eaten and he felt vaguely nauseous. Nothing could dispel the thought that Carl's face was reliving the dream.

'What about Wolf?' Carl asked.

Shaw confirmed he'd seen him and gave Carl the shout lines of their conversation. Finally, he told him about Danny's reckless decision to go it alone. Carl listened, his gaze intense, tight-eyed and tight-lipped. Shaw had always thought that Carl was more dangerous than Danny. Some things never changed. After what he'd found out, he half expected Carl to produce a concealed weapon, make a lunge, stab him in the gut, slicing up and wide.

Carl glanced at his watch again. 'I'm sorry,' he said politely, 'but I really need to go.'

Was this it? Was this all Carl had to say? Or behind that cool façade had he already made murderous plans? Shaw got to his feet. The encounter, so different to his conversation with Wolf, left him seriously rattled.

Carl walked with him to the door. 'Jon, are you around later?'

'I can be.'

'Meet me for a drink at The Old Joint Stock, Temple Row, at six.'

Chapter Thirty-Three

Carl went one way and Shaw the other. Starving, he headed back to the Mailbox and nearest chain restaurant where he ordered a Croque Monsieur with fries and an Americano. After using the conveniences, and back at the table, he reflected on his most recent encounter.

Unpredictability ran through the man's DNA, yet Shaw had been surprised by Carl's invitation for drinks. It didn't compute with the less than enthusiastic and muted reaction he'd received on rocking up. Neither did it gel with Carl's seeming disinterest in the information Shaw imparted. The spook showing the inscrutable face could account for it, Shaw guessed, or the news he delivered was actually not news at all; Carl had acted like a man who expected him to show.

Shaw returned to the dining area and checked his phone. There were two missed calls from a number he didn't recognise. *Danny*, he thought, returning it. The line rang out twice and cut out. Cold caller, Shaw presumed.

His meal arrived. He ate slowly, drank his coffee, and paid. With over two hours to kill, he decided to lose himself in the massive shopping centre at Grand Central.

Thick with shoppers and wide boys trying to flog him things he didn't want, the streets were a crush of rush and thrust. Cars hooted. People scooted. Carried along on a sea of humanity, Shaw felt hemmed in on all sides. Out of nowhere, a distinct prickle of unease made the hairs on the back of his neck stand erect.

And it had nothing to do with the volume of people.

Someone was watching him. He was certain. He didn't know how or who, or from where but, with every instinct he had, he knew it.

Then his phone rang.

Yanking it out, he barked, 'Yes?'

'Jon, it's Charlie.'

The sombre tone of his senior partner indicated that things were about to head south. Shaw fought his way through the crush to the relative quiet of an empty shop doorway.

'I've recently put down the phone to a detective from Devon and Cornwall Police. They want to talk to you.'

So that's what the missed calls were about. Shaw saw his reflection in the glass. Strain tightened his features. 'Did they say what it was in connection with?'

'No, only that it was important.'

'Got a name and number?'

'DS Lee Chester.' Charlie reeled off details. Shaw pulled up the keyboard on his phone and input them under Contacts. 'I told them you were on annual leave,' Charlie continued.

'Thanks.'

'That's not all,' Charlie said. 'Julie took a call from a detective from West Mids, something about a client of yours.'

Deeley, Shaw registered, with unease.

'Jon, what the hell is going on?'

'Sorry, Charlie, you're breaking up. I'll speak to you the second I get a decent signal.' Shaw cut the call and stared at a multiplicity of faces, of every creed and colour; not one familiar or arousing suspicion. For now, the immediate scare of feeling watched appeared to be over, not so the threats from DS Lee Chester, his fellow detective, Nick Stroud, or DI Sam Deeley.

The prudent course would be to get in touch, show willing, co-operate and prove he had nothing to hide. He knew how it rolled. Direct contact would result in a conversation to establish facts, an appointment to meet, a tricky interview to corroborate information, follow-ups, a dig into his private and professional life. No, he had to hold them off for as long as possible. All of them.

To Shaw's mind, the Old Joint Stock Pub and Theatre venue, with its impressive glass-domed roof, chandeliers, drapes and central island bar, seemed an odd choice for a quiet chat. Designed as a library in the nineteenth century, it was bought by the Birmingham Joint Stock Bank. Converted into a pub in the late nineties, it had resisted the march of modernity and retained many Victorian features. A theatre located on the first floor and heralded as 'intimate' (unlike the bar) subsequently opened in 2006. A hub for thespians, theatregoers and corporate clientele, it was popular with lawyers in nearby Chambers. The atmosphere that evening was frenetic.

Shaw downed the rest of a tomato juice spiced with Tabasco and, steering a path through a clutch of young barristers, waited his turn at the bar and ordered another. Quarter to seven and still no sign of Carl, Shaw began to think he was a no-show.

A tap on the shoulder dispelled all that.

'Sorry,' Carl said, 'got caught up and didn't realise the time.'

'What are you drinking?'

'Lime and soda. I'll grab us a table.'

Shaw did the business and found Carl sitting near a door to a fire exit. Shaw set the glasses on the table and joined him. They didn't clink glasses. They didn't say 'Cheers'. Shaw felt like a gunslinger at noon, waiting for the other guy to make the first move. He didn't have long to wait.

'I've considered what you told me,' Carl said. 'Why do you believe Kenny and Mark's deaths are connected?'

'Isn't it obvious?'

'That's my point. Too staged, too theatrical. You're forcing links that don't exist.'

This was not what Shaw expected. It must have shown on his face.

'Different men. Different locations. Different lives,' Carl explained. 'You're not thinking loosely enough.'

'You're saying I have a vivid imagination, is that it?'

'I'm saying that I don't buy your theory.'

Temporarily stumped, Shaw swallowed a mouthful of juice.

'I get why you'd think it,' Carl continued. 'You feel guilty.'

Shaw felt his eyes widen. 'Don't you?'

'Not in my nature.'

'You don't feel a moment's regret about what happened to Mickie Ashton?'

'Pointless waste of energy.' When Carl moved his glass to his lips, his hand was rock-solid, steady. Not one single beat missed.

A flame of anger ignited deep inside Shaw. Carl's absence of remorse was staggering. Did the man feel anything at all? Shaw wished his drink had a big slug of vodka in it. Maybe that would douse the rage burning within. 'You don't feel it's motivation enough for revenge?'

'Revenge is for fools.'

When Danny had first approached him, Shaw thought similarly. Not any more.

'What about the timing? Kenny and Mark were murdered within days of each other. You don't find that eye-catching?'

Carl said nothing, the closest he'd come, so far, to some kind of agreement.

'Can I ask another question?' Shaw said.

'Be my guest.'

'You didn't react when I showed up this afternoon.'

'Is that a question or a statement?'

'I think you expected me.'

Carl's mouth quirked at the edges. Not quite a smile. 'It's true I thought you'd try to make contact. I didn't believe you'd succeed.'

Stupidly pleased that he'd got one over him, Shaw couldn't resist pushing. 'Because you're a difficult man to find?'

'I'm out of the country a lot. In fact, I'm off to Dubai first thing in the morning.'

Convenient, Shaw thought. 'Exports, you said. What type?'

'Incinerators. Industrial-sized.'

'Big market for it?'

'In the Middle East, yes.'

Time for the games and going around the houses to stop. 'What are we doing here, Carl?'

'Having a drink. Having a chat.' Carl spoke with an edge that wasn't there before. 'Old friends, aren't we?'

'Are we?' Shaw leant across the table, looked him in the eye. A vein underneath Carl's left eye flickered. 'What if I'm right?'

'You'd better watch your back.'

'You, too.'

Carl's gaze never wavered. First to break, a burst of raucous laughter drilled through Shaw's left ear. Shaw said, 'If you were a betting man . . .'

'I'm not.'

Shaw forced a smile. 'Indulge me. Who should I watch out for?'

Carl slow-blinked. 'Aaron Waterhouse.'

Chapter Thirty-Four

Carl would not be drawn or explain his reasons for naming Waterhouse. Drinking up, he made excuses to leave. 'Long day ahead,' he said. They exchanged cards for no other reason than that's what civilised people did. Carl's looked authentic but then it would. He had the best people in the business to create a legend for him. Shaw doubted he'd ever hear from Carl again, unless it was to knock him off and make it look like suicide.

Vigilant, attuned to the strange face, the false move, the wrong vehicle, Shaw walked through wet streets. He picked up his car and drove out of the city. The fleeting if genuine sensation of being watched was no longer there. Checking his rear-view revealed no nasty surprises.

Joining the M5 at Quinton, Junction 3, his hands-free set rang. Shaw touched the screen to accept the call.

'Jon Shaw?'

Shaw's ears pricked at the distinctive Devonian accent. 'Yes.'

'DS Lee Chester. Apologies for the lateness of the hour.'

Before he bottled, Shaw arranged his face into a smile. 'It's not a problem.'

'We understand you knew Kenny Sharples.'

'Professionally,' Shaw said.

'Would you be available for a few routine questions?'

No, Shaw thought. 'Yes, of course. When were you thinking?'

'Tomorrow morning.'

Screw it. To make matters worse, some bastard in an Audi was tailgating him in the outside line. Shaw was already doing eighty-five. 'Where do you suggest?'

'We'll come to you. Got an address?'

Shaw gave it and flicked his hazards on. Audi man briefly dropped back. By the time he realised he'd been played, Shaw had crushed the accelerator and was out of sight. If only evading the police was as easy.

On the journey home, he planned his strategy. It wouldn't be simple because he'd lied to Jeffrey Finner about his association with Kenny and handed over five grand without a flicker of doubt. Jeffrey had thought it fishy but Jeffrey had a different agenda. The police, with a murder investigation to follow, would not be so accepting. He was effectively between a proverbial rock and hard place and his only real hope was that the Devon cops were not as smart as someone like Deeley. He still had her to deal with as pleasantly and as convincingly as he could. God forbid Devon and Cornwall Police ever found its way to talking to its counterparts in the West Mids.

Shaw pulled into his drive and let himself into the house. Others would have fled, checked into a low-key hotel, B&B,

or rented a hideaway. Shaw was not minded to move. If he had to die somewhere, it would be here, in full view, where the cops would have a chance of nailing his killer. He didn't openly admit that part of him felt deserving of retribution.

Suspicious of Carl and wired by the thought of a killer making him victim number three, Shaw retrieved the gun from his study, still wrapped carefully in a towel. Taking it upstairs, he placed it, within reach, on his bedside table while he undressed and climbed into bed. If he'd hoped for reassurance, he was mistaken.

Sleep was fitful, disjointed and random. Awake for most of the night, he thought about Waterhouse, about Danny, about possible connections. He relived the chilling sensation of being watched. If Carl was innocent, he could have led a killer to his door. More than a match, Carl could do them all a favour. Except Carl was flying to the Middle East the next morning, Shaw recalled.

He rose early. Gun returned and locked in the drawer in his study, he phoned a car rental company in Alstone Lane first thing and arranged to pick up an unassuming silver Ford Focus at noon. Next, he looked up the address of property developer, Aaron Waterhouse. By ten o'clock, he was as ready as he could be for DS Lee Chester. The presence of the police would surely deter a murderer.

Birmingham is a proper gig. Not as full-blooded as Manchester, yet it displays its criminal underbelly with panache. Its agenda is obvious. I like that about it.

Adopting a professional and authoritative expression, I rap on the door of the apartment. Aware of CCTV, I have ensured my disguise is good enough to put the most keen-eyed observer off his or her game. With luck, it will take them down a rabbit hole for long enough to allow me to do what must be done.

The door swings open. It is early and he is bleary. It's obvious from the shadows beneath his eyes that he has spent the night turning over conversations following unwelcome intrusions from old friends. Nonetheless, he is calm, composed and doesn't appear to mind that he stands before me in a towelling robe. If he's on his guard, which he is, he doesn't display it.

'Yes?' he says.

I flash a warrant card. 'A woman has been very seriously injured in an attack in the apartment above yours. Heard anything?'

He shakes his head. He doesn't say he's sorry to hear the news or apologise for being unable to help. He is not interested in the welfare of my fictional victim, no more than he was interested in a young, desperate woman on a riverbank. Already, he has dismissed me from his mind.

'Could I take your name, sir?'

He doesn't like that, but complies.

'Could we talk inside, do you think?' I glance at his bare legs and give the impression that I only wish to avoid him embarrassment.

'Why? I've told you all you need to know.'

'I'm afraid I have a few more routine questions.'

'Look, I've a plane to catch and I really can't help you.'

I smile and make sure the warmth from the tilt of my lips meets my eyes. 'You'd be surprised how often an unwitting remark from a witness gives us the vital clue and lead we need.'

Scowling, he steps aside and lets me in. 'All right, but I can't talk for long.'

On this we can agree.

'Nice place you got here,' DS Chester said. A stocky man with a shaved head, and whose suit jacket stretched to within breaking point across his broad shoulders, he looked more like one of Shaw's clients than a police officer. Fortunately, his manner was a great deal friendlier. His partner, DC Dan Rees, a much younger man with facial hair that was too long to be considered stubble and not enough for a full beard, seemed of a similar disposition. All smiles and handshakes, they were at obvious pains to put Shaw at his ease. He suspected that the higher ranked Nick Stroud had deliberately sent his B team to persuade Shaw to lower his guard and make a mistake.

'Can I offer you coffee?' Shaw said, equally affable. Chester looked at Rees who looked at Chester. A silent exchange took place.

'Black, two sugars, and Dan's white with one.'

How cosy. All Christian names and mates together. Under the impression that this was part one of the charm offensive, Shaw invited them to take a seat in the sitting room – definitely not the study – and went through to the kitchen. He took his time faffing about with mugs and milk. By the time he returned with a tray, Rees was seated with his notebook out and Chester was studying the garden from the French window.

'Very nice.' Chester spoke more to himself than anyone in the room.

Shaw handed him a drink and left Rees to help himself. While they went through the social motions, Shaw rubbed his hands together as though he couldn't wait to crack on. 'So?'

Chester blew on his coffee and said, 'Mr Sharples, as you now know, was murdered.'

'Mr Finner informed me. Terrible business,' Shaw said.

'What was your connection?'

'To Mr Sharples?'

'Yes.'

'Strictly professional.'

'That's funny,' Chester said. 'Mr Finner was under the impression that you were an old pal.'

'Then he was mistaken unless you call giving someone a business card in a pub the basis for friendship.'

Chester took a swig of coffee. From the look on his face he'd burnt his tongue. Recovering quickly, Chester said, 'You're a criminal lawyer, I understand.'

'Defence,' Shaw replied.

'Was Mr Sharples in trouble?'

'Only in so far as he had gambling debts.'

Rees briefly stopped writing and exchanged glances with Chester, who continued. 'Did you believe that Mr Sharples was under pressure to pay those debts?'

'Put it this way: I'm not sure that the men he owed were that patient.'

'Which men?' Rees chipped in.

'There's a café in Ilfracombe, The Seashell. They hung out there. Mr Finner can probably corroborate.'

'Names?'

Shaw shook his head. 'Kenny was reluctant to say.'

Rees nodded, wrote a note.

'I understand that Mr Sharples was anxious to secure an inheritance from his late father's will,' Chester said.

'Correct. In order to pay them off, I believe.'

'But inheritance is not your area of expertise.' There was guile in Chester's expression.

'As you might imagine, I have a number of contacts who can assist in such matters.'

'Which is why I'm still not clear why you felt the necessity to visit Mr Sharples in person. It's beyond the call of duty, isn't it?'

Shaw arranged his expression into one of grave concern. 'I happened to be in the area and, frankly, I was worried about him. Mr Sharples was a vulnerable individual and understandably concerned by threats made against him.'

'Threats?'

'Yes.'

'What kind of threats?'

'The usual: pay up or else.'

Rees glanced up and flashed a grin. It vanished with one stern look from Chester.

'And what would *or else* mean?'

Shaw shook his head. 'You tell me.'

A pulse in Chester's jaw ticked. 'Was Mr Finner aware of the seriousness of the situation?'

'I assumed he knew. His exact words about the men in the café were that they were a "rum crowd", as I recall.'

'So at no time did you mention the nature of any threats to Mr Finner?'

'Mr Finner was upset enough as it was. At this point I'd no idea that Mr Sharples' death was anything but an accident.' He glanced across at Rees who was scribbling away.

Chester placed his mug on the table in front of him. 'I'm interested to know why you handed Mr Finner five thousand pounds to help with funeral arrangements.'

'Mr Finner was clearly in straitened circumstances and I'm a generous man. I carry out a great deal of pro bono work. You can check me out, if you wish, on the firm's website.'

'I'll do that.' Chester's mouth was smiling. His eyes said he had Shaw down for a well-heeled git.

Rees looked up. 'Do you know why someone might impersonate you, Mr Shaw?'

'I've no idea and I hope you find the person responsible.'

'You don't seem concerned.' Chester was no longer quite as affable.

'Should I be?'

'It's a criminal offence.'

'My line of work is populated by criminal offences.' It was meant to be a throwaway line, yet it resonated. Had he stumbled on something he hadn't properly considered? Violence against criminal defence lawyers by aggrieved clients was not new. What if the killer was solely connected to a professional grudge against him, and his old friends simply collateral damage? Consumed by the possibility, Shaw lost the thread of the conversation. He blinked and asked Chester to repeat what he'd just said.

'I suggest you check your recent client list.'

The signal that they were done with him for now, Rees flipped the cover of the notebook and slipped it into his briefcase.

Chester stood up. Shaw did the same. 'We may need to talk to you again,' he said, extending his hand.

Shaw was sure they would. The firmness of the handshake told him so.

He saw them out and released a breath. Pointing the police in the wrong direction was a calculated strategy. If they were any good at their job, and he reckoned they were, Chester and Rees would report back to Stroud with new information. Stroud would task them to investigate the café connection until it reached its natural conclusion. They'd uncover an illegal gambling ring and/or bunch of loan sharks in the process. It wouldn't solve Kenny's murder but it would buy Shaw the time he needed.

Unlocking the study, he went inside and fired up his laptop. His clients were as varied as the colours of the rainbow. If someone had it in for him, it would be connected to a case he'd lost.

He extended the search period over the past ten years. Many serious offenders were still inside. Of those who had been recently released, some had sworn reprisals that Shaw considered vacuous threats. In his experience, warnings issued, often after a judge has passed sentence, usually cooled by the time of a release date. Yes, there were exceptions:

bad men whose entire reason for living depended on the adrenalin rush of violence and revenge.

It took him a while. Eventually, he narrowed it down to three possible candidates: a man who had murdered a woman he met online, a serial rapist, and an arsonist who'd promised to burn him alive. In all instances the clients suffered from mental health issues and a dismal lack of resources to help them. Without intervention, any one of them could be responsible for turning his life upside down. Shaw expelled a sigh. His training had taught him to view both sides of an argument. In this scenario, it did him few favours.

Deciding to call Charlie, he was put straight through.

'I've spoken to the police,' Shaw assured him.

'May I ask what about?'

'I'm helping them in connection with a murder investigation.'

'Christ Almighty, Jon.'

'I'm not a suspect.'

'Well, thank God for that. Is this connected to you taking time off?'

'No.'

'So?'

'Jo and I split up. I needed some space.'

Never great with personal drama, Charlie cleared his throat and mumbled a platitude. While Shaw didn't enjoy using the truth to cover a lie, he was pleased that it had the desired effect. 'Right, then,' Charlie said. 'Don't go away, Julie wants a word.'

Shaw had no need to guess what about. Julie Strong had been Shaw's paralegal for the past five years. Late middle-aged,

single and with the loyalty of a gun dog, Julie was never seen
at an office gathering whatever the occasion. In the time she'd
worked for him, he'd never heard her call him or anyone
else by his Christian name. The others thought she was a
funny old duck. Shaw liked her and it wasn't only because
she exuded brisk efficiency. When he was in Julie Strong's
presence he felt as if he had to figuratively sit up straight,
pay attention and make himself worthy of her respect.

'Mr Shaw,' she said. He pictured her reaching for a legal
pad.

'I understand that the police spoke to you about a client.'

'That's correct.' Julie gave a factual rundown of the conversation. 'The police officer seemed most insistent that I find
the precise details of Mr Platt's visit and I'm afraid I could
find no trace.'

'Julie, I owe you a huge apology.'

'There's really no need, Mr Shaw.'

'No, I do. Mr Platt collared me on the way out of the office.
I felt rather sorry for him actually and invited him in without
an appointment. I believe you had a day off at the time.'

'I knew there'd be a reasonable explanation.' If Julie was
the type to clap her hands in delight, Shaw was sure she
would.

'I should have mentioned it to you,' Shaw said, contrite.
'There was no actual charge and it must have slipped my
mind.'

'Shall I phone and explain?'

'No need, I have her number. Actually, I wonder if I could
ask you to carry out a little fact-checking.'

'Absolutely, Mr Shaw.'

Impressing upon Julie the need for discretion, he explained exactly what he wanted her to do.

'I'll see to it right away.'

'Could you email the information?'

'Naturally. Will that be all?'

'Thank you, yes.'

'Enjoy your break, Mr Shaw.'

Unlikely, he thought. Looking at his watch, he estimated it would take him around twenty minutes to walk to the car hire firm. If he stepped on it, he could be at Aaron Waterhouse's house by mid to late afternoon.

Chapter Thirty-Five

Shaw had travelled no further than Cannock in the past twenty-five years and, joining the M6 from the M5, felt peculiarly dislocated, as if he were heading to a country on the other side of the world to fight for a lost cause.

The north was pain and dark memories. Long before Mickie Ashton, his mother had carved a scar on his heart that would last a lifetime. For three long, lonely years he'd watched his mam suffer and endure while his father drank himself into a self-pitying stupor and, ultimately, early grave. It was Shaw, a lad, who'd sat with her, held her hand, washed and tried to feed her in the last days. She'd insisted he go to school despite his terror of finding her dead when he got home. He had no idea how he'd carried out her dearest wish, only that if it made her happy, he would do anything. Concentrating on the road ahead, drawn inexorably to a destination he had no desire to revisit, he remembered the confusion and false hope and despair as acutely as if it were yesterday. Watching her hair fall out, her skin shrivel, watching her fade away to husk and pale shadow had ended his capacity to fully love even as it had fired his desire to run. Close to home ground now, Shaw was beset with terrors he could no longer fight.

Skirting the estate where he'd grown up in poverty and only twelve minutes from Wythenshawe, he headed to its glossy cousin, Hale Village, home to one former drug lord and now respectable property developer and buyer of classic cars, if the rumours were true.

From birth, Aaron Waterhouse was a man on the make, a man with ambitions. Shaw didn't know he had pretensions to culture too. 'Hypocrite,' Shaw muttered under his breath. Hadn't he, too, climbed society's greasy pole? Hadn't he, too, tried to better himself? But he'd never given an order to kill. He'd never had a man held down and tortured.

According to Google Maps, a secure gated entrance was the only way in. The property's boundary extended through woodland to a tributary of the River Bollin. It hadn't escaped Shaw that he could be denied access and fall at the first fence. Similarly, Waterhouse and his entourage could be away on holiday. Shaw had considered phoning ahead to check but feared it might elicit a brush-off. To alert Waterhouse would also negate that vital element of surprise.

Shaw dropped the window of his car, reached out and pressed an entry buzzer. A woman with a French accent answered. He explained why he was there.

'Do you have an appointment?'

Waterhouse must be on site, Shaw reasoned. Why else ask the question? 'I don't.'

'Then I'm afraid I can't help. You need to speak to his secretary to schedule a meeting.'

'Tell him Jon Shaw is here.'

Holding his nerve and his ground, he was prepared to camp at the gates for the night if need be.

The line went quiet. Shaw imagined the woman crossing an expanse of hall, tapping on a door, relaying the message in calm and even tones, and receiving a brusque reply. Could take her a minute. Could take her several.

The line crackled and went dead. Cursing Waterhouse, Shaw's hands tightened on the steering wheel.

He switched off the engine and looked straight ahead. About to lever the seat back into a reclining position, he heard the clank of metal and machinery, and the gates swinging smoothly open, granting him safe passage.

Lawn and trees and extensive grounds that would take a fleet of gardeners to manage flanked a drive that was long and sinuous. It reminded Shaw of a recent visit to a National Trust property. Not that Waterhouse would be throwing open his gardens to the public any time soon. The location was clearly designed for privacy and seclusion.

The drive opened out onto a block-paved turning circle with a fountain, and statue of a woman carrying a pitcher in the middle. Beyond, a modern three-storey villa in cream-coloured stone, like an ultra-modern style over substance conceptual piece trying to compete with an old master.

To the left of the property, a garage block for at least four vehicles. Parked near one of the bays, a black Bentley Bentayga with a personalised number plate. By comparison, Shaw's modest hire car felt like a motorised sofa. To the right, a more eye-catching example of wealth: a helicopter, smaller than Shaw had imagined, an oversized black dragonfly. Was

Waterhouse entertaining a wealthy guest or did the machine belong to him?

Shaw pulled up outside. The door was already open. Dressed in a simple grey shift dress, a dark-eyed woman waited. He assumed that this was the same person he'd spoken to moments before.

'Mr Waterhouse will see you in the lounge.' Expressionless, she turned on her flat heels. Shaw followed across an impressive cream marble floor the size of a swimming pool. Wide staircases led off in two directions and converged into galleried landings on three levels. Directly above his head, an ornate rectangular skylight through which light flooded the grand hall.

His guide and temporary host paused by a door and knocked before entering. There was no reply. She gently pushed it open, indicating that Shaw step inside.

The door clicked behind him. The sensation was similar to being trapped in a lift when everyone in the building has gone home for the weekend. Of Waterhouse, there was no sign.

Shaw crossed over to a floor to ceiling window. Manicured gardens and, beyond, a wall of woodland with glimpses of white water through the trees.

Shaw turned back and scoped the room. A combination of state-of-the-art electronics and antique fittings, the lounge matched the entire ground floor space of his home in square footage. From the chandeliers glittering from the ceiling to the antique Persian rugs beneath his shoes, examples of serious wealth were everywhere. Either the occupant had done really well for himself in the past twenty-five years, or he was still in the game.

Above an oversized fireplace, Shaw noticed a conspicuous display of happy-family photographs in a series of large frames. Shaw took a closer look at Waterhouse. The other side of fifty, he carried more cargo, looked well fed and healthy, not overweight. Cut short, his hair was prematurely grey, as were his neatly trimmed sideburns. His face had changed little except that his clean-shaven cheeks were fleshier, making his eyes smaller and less penetrating. The smile, once so dangerous, remained, and yet, Shaw had to admit, in every shot, it looked genuine and warm. In one, Waterhouse gazed adoringly at a good-looking blonde. Another showed him as a doting dad with his arms around three children, two boys and a little girl, the eldest looked to be around nine years old. It was a portrait of perfect harmony.

At the sound of his name, Shaw wheeled round and found Waterhouse striding towards him.

'Jon,' he said, gravel-voiced. 'After all this time.'

Shaw took and shook Waterhouse's extended hand. Unlike Carl's, Waterhouse had a real leader of men-type handshake. A good two inches taller than Shaw, he possessed formidable presence.

'You look well,' Waterhouse said. 'Sit down. Can I get you anything?'

Polite and civilised, Waterhouse's manners had clearly gone up in the world along with his status. 'Water would be good.' Shaw took a seat on a soft grey leather sofa.

'Sparkling? Straight?'

'Tap is fine.'

Waterhouse spoke into a device in the wall and ordered a bottle of still and two glasses.

'So,' Waterhouse said. 'To what do I owe the honour? I appear to be flavour of the month. An old friend of yours called yesterday.'

Danny, Shaw realised, remembering how vociferous Danny had been about Waterhouse being on the straight and narrow.

'Danny Hallam?'

'The one and only.'

'What did he want?'

'He was under the impression that I could find him work.'

Every time Shaw gave Danny the benefit of the doubt that he'd changed, he'd do something that suggested the reverse. In response to what Shaw assumed was his taken aback expression, Waterhouse continued, 'Unfortunately, in my line of business, and as much as I like to do my bit for society, there's not much call for an unskilled man who's done serious jail time.'

So the rumours that Waterhouse was on the straight and narrow were allegedly true. 'And what business are you in?' Shaw asked.

The door swung open and the woman crossed the room and set a tray of drinks on a coffee table. Waterhouse smiled and paused, allowing her to retreat before answering.

'Made my money in commercial property until the financial meltdown and subsequent crash. Fortunately, I saw it coming and had already diversified into residential.'

'I didn't realise it was that rewarding.' Shaw pointedly let his gaze travel around the ridiculously expensive contents of the room.

'Small, high-class developments for the rich and famous,' Waterhouse countered, his smile as slick as his patter.

'And you?' Waterhouse asked, reaching for his glass.

Shaw told him.

'Now someone like you I could *definitely* use.'

'I sincerely hope not,' Shaw said dryly. 'I specialise in criminal defence. My clients are generally on the margins of society.'

From the surprised expression on Waterhouse's face, Shaw could see that it was news. He wondered why Danny had withheld the information. Had he done so to protect him?

'I'm impressed.'

Shaw met his eye. 'Don't be.'

'Ah.' Waterhouse dabbed at an imaginary mark on his tailored trousers. 'Penance for a misspent youth?'

'You tell me.'

Waterhouse studied him calmly. 'As I told Danny, things move on and change a great deal over time. It's called progress.'

'Agreed, but it doesn't negate the past.'

'I think you'll find it does. Look at you. You've clearly done well for yourself.'

Shaw opened his mouth to speak but Waterhouse headed him off.

'Back in the day, we were young desperate men and, sadly, the young and desperate do stupid things to survive.'

'Stupid?' Shaw raised his eyebrows. *Getting kids hooked on drugs? Extorting with menaces? Killing?*

'Come on, Jon, you weren't like the rest of us. Just another lonely starry-eyed kid who hung around the periphery of a gang because there was nowhere else to go. Happens all the time. Please don't tell me you're fretting after all these years?'

Waterhouse was either suffering from selective amnesia or he was the most cunning individual Shaw had ever had the misfortune to meet, and he'd met a few. Time to switch things up.

'People died, Aaron.'

Waterhouse swallowed an immediate objection and narrowed his eyes. 'I hope you're not suggesting what I think you're suggesting, Jon.'

'And what would that be?'

'That I had a connection to that unfortunate woman's death.'

'That unfortunate woman was called Mickie Ashton.'

Waterhouse's green eyes glittered with recollection. 'I remember now. A total tragedy and I can see it's affected you badly. How about I give you the address of an excellent psychiatrist?'

Shaw stared coldly.

'I have his number here.' Waterhouse pulled out his phone and scrolled through numbers. 'He helped a great deal when I was going through a relationship break-up. You remember Esther, don't you? I didn't do right by the girl, to be honest.'

'Thanks for the offer, but I'm good.'

Waterhouse slipped the phone back into the pocket of his shirt. 'Let me know if you change your mind. No shame in admitting past mistakes, Jon, and I'd be the first to admit I've done things that I'm not proud of. But you have to believe me, I'd never sanction the murder of a vulnerable young woman, still less a pregnant one.' Waterhouse raised a finger. 'Never. On my children's life.'

Shaw finally reached for his drink, downing the contents in one go, and placed the glass back on the tray with a clunk. When he glanced up, Waterhouse was studying him with the calm of a magpie eyeing up an ailing lamb before it swoops. It was the first time Shaw detected a crack in Waterhouse's civilised veneer.

'You got any kids, Jon?'

'No.'

'A woman?'

'Not any more.'

'Get one. Settle down. Make a family. It will be the saving of you.'

Too late for salvation, Shaw thought.

Waterhouse lightly slapped his thighs. 'But you didn't come for my advice or to reminisce about old times, did you?'

'I came to find out if you were on the level.'

'And what did you discover, Jon?'

'The jury's out.'

Waterhouse threw back his head and laughed. 'Always a comedian.'

'No, that was Mark Platt.' Shaw stood up. Unabashed, Waterhouse rose to his feet and clamped a hand on Shaw's shoulder.

'It's been really good seeing you. If you ever change your mind about diversifying, the offer of a job still stands.'

Shaw stiffly thanked him.

'Pity Gail isn't around,' Waterhouse said, walking with

Shaw across the hall. 'She'd love to meet you. Another time, perhaps.'

Shaw stopped suddenly, his eye taken by a series of figurative drawings.

'They're good, aren't they?' Waterhouse said admiringly.

Shaw agreed. He especially liked a picture of a naked female, her back to the artist; one leg stretched out, long and lean. Blonde hair coiled at the base of her neck like a Grecian goddess. Slightly turned away, her face was in shadow. The effect was enigmatic, alluring and mesmerising.

'A local artist?' Shaw asked.

Waterhouse snatched a smile. 'I shouldn't think so. I bought them as investment pieces.'

Chapter Thirty-Six

You'd be surprised how many artists cannot draw. They don't know one end of a pencil from another. They can paint, they'll tell you. 'I'm a colourist,' some loudly and pretentiously proclaim. Oh really?

Blood has a multiplicity of hues, lost on painters who reach for the nearest red – scarlet a popular choice, I gather. They don't appreciate that fresh blood has a different shade to dried. Arterial is richer and thicker than blood from a vein, like an expensive Barolo. A spurt from a nose does not have the same shade as a leak from a bowel. You have to see it to believe it. Whatever the injury, we all bleed the same. That's where the similarity ends because the way a wound is delivered will govern blood spatter. It's worth paying attention to the science because if you don't, some clever forensic pathologist will join too many dots, or a cocky Scenes of Crimes officer might reconstruct your moves.

Are you with me so far, or am I blinding you with science?

Born on the wrong side of the tracks, I've known since I was little that cast-off patterns tell their own unique stories: the trajectory of a blow, how often the target is struck, the degree of force used, the actual swing of the person doing the killing. As top-flight cricketers have a particular bowling style, so, too, the murderer. When the 'good guys' bore on about blood pattern analysis increasing the risk of getting caught, they have a point. It's not certain that Danny Hallam knew what he was doing when he set out to kill. I doubt he aimed to be targeted and clean. More efficient than a frenzied attack, a single thrust to the heart can easily result in death minutes later, which comes as much as a surprise to the victim as the killer. One stab (similar to the sensation of being punched) with little external blood loss, and you're talking one second and dead the next. Elegant, isn't it? Hallam chose deep penetration from behind and in the right place. A single wound to both lungs, not always fatal, granted, but, as we all know, can be. The key is precision. Which brings me right back to the value of drawing. The symmetrical pattern of nails driven into Platt's head was not by accident. I didn't just happen to think, 'That would look nice.' It was plotted and planned and mapped and *drawn* long before I loaded up the gun.

Similarly, I sketched the layout of Snare's apartment ('flat' where I come from) before I set foot in it. This is where Google and Rightmove come in handy. One set of quarters is very similar to the one next door. Timing had to be perfect. A few minutes either way could have made the difference between me bluffing my way in and me shown the door. Told you attention to detail is important.

Chapter Thirty-Seven

With uncanny timing, Julie called Shaw as he sat outside Aaron Waterhouse's contemporary villa in a quiet lane, debating what to do next.

'I've got the address you asked for,' she said. Shaw listened and memorised it. After attempting to drown her son, Shaw didn't expect a warm reception from Danny Hallam's mother, Christie.

'Any luck tracking down those clients I asked you to investigate?'

'Tyler Flook accidentally set himself on fire and died of his injuries last year. I'm waiting to hear back from Robert Malsom's probation officer.'

'He's willing to talk?' They weren't generally that accommodating.

'*She*, and yes. I understand Malsom has also issued threats to her.'

Not wise. 'What about our murderer?' The last time Shaw clapped eyes on Nigel King, King had stared at him coldly and drawn a finger under his throat.

'I'm afraid the trail has gone cold on that one. I'll keep trying, of course.'

Shaw thought that only classy pieces of a city looked good in the rain. Poor bits remained mean and miserable and forgotten and the passage of time changed nothing, unlike Manchester, which by all accounts was sparkly and more cosmopolitan and vibrant than he gave it credit for, or could remember. Right now, he wasn't in the well-off patch.

There weren't any flowers in Christie Hallam's garden because, on the twelfth floor of a tower block in Wythenshawe, there was no garden. Potted plants on balconies didn't count.

Shaw took the lift and wished he hadn't. To use it on a regular basis would require breathing apparatus and a strong course of antibiotics.

Stepping out, he was given a fine view of traffic lights on four converging roads. Above his head, crappy strip lighting that crackled and spat. Someone had scattered a load of free newspapers and fled, leaving the remains on a thinly carpeted floor of a worrying colour. The only concession to design: the rainbow-coloured doors, some orange, some green, some purple, and from behind which came the sound of all human activity. Voices and televisions too loud in rooms too small, whose occupants had hopes and passions and cravings that could never be satisfied. Intimately familiar territory for him, this was what he knew and what he remembered. It didn't warm his heart. It didn't make him glad that he'd carved an escape route. It made him sad that so many casualties were left behind.

Shaw pressed the bell for Christie's flat and was surprised

to hear the first few bars of the opening to the theme of *Mission Impossible*, a metaphor, surely, for his current situation. If Christie knew that he'd intended to kill her Danny, she'd claw his eyes out.

The door swung open. Shaw braced himself.

'Well, I never.' Christie peered at him through a prism of smoke from an e-cigarette. Tipping up on her toes, she reached up and gave him a hug. Shaw was immediately enveloped in a cloud of menthol and something less identifiable. Popcorn, he thought. 'Get yourself in,' she said, pushing him inside. 'Fancy a brew?'

'Thanks.'

He followed her into a kitchen that was smart and tidy, apart from a mangy-looking cat parked on a work surface. In one fluid movement, Christie scooped it off, filled a kettle and grabbed a couple of mugs.

'Sit yourself down then,' she said. 'No need to clutter the place.'

'Is Danny here?' Shaw said.

'He was. Milk, sugar?'

'Milk, please.'

Shaw watched as Christie made them drinks. In the intervening years she'd aged and was obviously making no concessions to it, still with the dyed blonde hair that was dark at the roots and going a little thin due to heavy doses of peroxide. Black eyeliner made her eyes compete too robustly with her red painted lips. Her clothes – clingy top, big shoulders and tight skirt – could best be described as retro.

Christie smiled warmly and pushed a mug towards him. 'Hark at you all grown up. Your mam would be that proud if she could see you now.' She sat down opposite and chugged away on the vape. 'I hear you're making quite a name for yourself with the law and that.'

'Danny told you?'

'Right proud of you, he is. And thanks for giving him a place to stay for a few nights. He were that pleased.'

'I'm glad, Christie, but technically he's in breach. He's supposed to be here under the terms of his licence,' he reminded her. 'Danny could be sent back to prison if he isn't careful.' Lifers were monitored closely post-release and their cases managed on a multi-agency basis.

Christie's big black panda eyes peered at him over the rim of her mug. It was like watching a soldier pop his head through a screen of bamboo to better view the enemy. 'What it is, right,' she said, blinking furiously, 'is the probation officer is easy to have over and Danny keeps his head down.

'My boy needs all the help he can get after what happened to him,' she continued, as if in mitigation. Shaw bet she was the only person alive who believed that Danny was innocent of the crime he'd committed. 'I don't suppose you could find him work, could you? He'll apply himself to anything. You can be sure of that. It would mean the world.'

Shaw was reminded of a gallery owner desperate to sell a piece of art before the place finally went bust. 'We don't have any vacancies at the moment.'

Christie's face fell. 'That's a pity.'

'Tell you what – give me your number. If anything comes up, I'll be sure to let you know.' It might enable him to keep tabs on Danny.

'Right you are.' She disappeared then came back and

handed him an old Nokia. 'Never really got the hang of using it but you can probably find what you're looking for.' Christie gave an embarrassed grin.

Shaw smiled back. It didn't take him long. He noticed her contacts listed Clint and Doreen. A quick zip through texts assured him that Christie wasn't a fan of mobile communication. Shaw added his details.

'I've put my number in so we can stay in touch.'

'Sound,' she said. 'You're lovely, you are, not like that scheming louse, Aaron Waterhouse. He doesn't want to have anything to do with the likes of us.' Her face darkened. 'You know Danny went on the cadge to him? I told him not to waste his time, but you know Danny, headstrong as they come.'

'Waterhouse mentioned his visit.'

'Did he now?' She sucked in a quantity of vapour and puffed out. Shaw squinted. It was like driving on a road through thick smoke, care of a bonfire from a neighbouring field. 'What was your business with Waterhouse?' she asked, not too discreetly.

'Looking for Danny.'

Christie nodded, although he didn't think she believed him.

'Do you keep in touch with Esther?' he asked her.

'Waterhouse's ex-missus? You must be kidding. Right old toffee-nose, she is. Made a mint out of the divorce, by all accounts. Not that she'd ever admit it. Always skriking about being hard done by, that one. Sweet on her once, weren't you?'

'Me? No. Is she still in the area?'

'Waterhouse set her up in ever such a nice house, not far from him, but Esther, not as I blame her, hated having her nose rubbed in it by the newer and younger model. They've got kids, and all, something she'd never had with Aaron. Hard for a woman, that is.' Christie stared wistfully into the depths of her mug, as if mourning the loss of her own fertility and youth.

'She moved then?' Shaw asked casually.

'To Chester, a few months ago. Got a sister there. Danny paid her a visit. Fallen on her feet, apparently.'

'Danny? When?'

'Don't ask me – head like a sieve.' Christie hiked her padded shoulders, ran her fingers through her hair. Shaw couldn't tell whether she was stalling or floundering. 'Do you know Chester? It's all black and white houses and posh shops. Esther lives in one of them swanky penthouse apartments in the middle of the city.'

'Sounds grand,' Shaw mumbled, still trying to process why Danny would visit Esther Waterhouse.

'I'll say. There's a gym and a sauna, and what have you. I keep telling my Danny that's what he needs to aim for. Set your sights high, I tell him,' Christie winked. 'I wouldn't mind a bit of the high life meself.' She looked fondly into the distance, as if picturing what that would be like. 'He's a good lad, Jon. You know that. Slipped me a nice bit of cash too. Clint were that pleased.'

'Clint?'

'My partner.'

'Danny had money?' His two hundred quid wouldn't have gone that far.

'Proper minted.'

'Do you know where he got it from?'

Christie shrugged. 'He didn't say. I didn't ask.'

Shaw didn't believe a word of it. 'Did Danny mention when he'd be back?'

'When it was over.' Her eyes connected to his. 'That's what he told me.'

Chapter Thirty-Eight

With a late blast of evening sunshine that created a strobe effect as it sneaked through the trees, Shaw drove straight from Christie's to the chippie on the corner of Gratton Road, in Leckhampton. He couldn't remember the last time he'd eaten anything more than the odd sandwich. Feeling hunted wasn't exactly good for the appetite.

Waiting for his cod and chips with extra salt and vinegar, he considered the possibility that Danny was in league with Waterhouse. Who else would give him a sizeable amount of hard cash? A bigger question: why? And what did Danny intend to do with it?

Whether it was the smell of frying fish, the damp heat inside competing with the wet outside, or the thought of a lot of money, Shaw suddenly recalled him and Danny sitting on a wall stuffing their faces with saveloys. About thirteen or fourteen, they'd fantasised about 'making it big'. Christ, they'd had plans. But dreams without the funds to make them happen were as good as useless. Danny's 'get rich quick' scheme had been to break into the drugs scene. He'd made it sound exciting and glamorous and a laugh. Shaw had grinned and nodded because he didn't want to let his mate down. Danny would have killed him if he'd known what he really thought, that it was a shit idea. Drugs meant dealing with nasty people and he'd had enough of those already to last him, ta very much.

Shaw returned home with his supper. The brief tremor of unease, experienced on walking through the front door, dispelled after a quick walk around convinced him that he'd neither been broken into nor had unwanted company.

Unwrapping his fish and chips in the kitchen and about to tuck in, his mobile rang from a number he didn't recognise.

'Yes?'

'Jon?'

The note of panic made him sit up. 'What's wrong, Lori?'

'It's Terry. He hasn't come home.'

Shaw glanced at his watch. After nine, it wasn't exactly cause for alarm. If anyone could look after himself, Wolf could. *Couldn't he? But what if . . .* Shaw gave himself the equivalent of a mental shake. Doing a runner with a woman was straight out of Wolf's playlist and chimed with the way he'd spoken when they'd last talked. Maybe Wolf had brought his plans forward. Maybe Lori was a panic-arse.

'OK,' he said calmly, pinching a chip. 'When did you last see him?'

'He went out for a run at three. I expected him back by five.'

'Have you called him?'

'His phone keeps going to the messaging service.'

'Maybe he's gone for a pint with a mate. It's a nice evening here. What's the weather like there?'

'That's not the point. Why won't he return my calls?' Her voice crackled with desperation.

'There could be any number of reasons. His battery might have died. He might be out of signal range.' Not uncommon in that part of the world.

'Maybe he's injured,' she said. 'Maybe he's had a heart attack. Maybe I should call the police or the ambulance service, or . . .'

'Slow down, Lori. Terry is a fit and healthy guy.'

'But . . .'

'Have you phoned around his friends?'

'Nobody's seen him, not since lunchtime. Maybe I should check the hospitals.'

'It's a little soon.' Shaw pushed another chip into his mouth, chewed and swallowed. 'The police won't look very hard if the missing adult isn't deemed vulnerable. I genuinely think you're jumping to conclusions.'

'But he's never done anything like this before.'

'Terry's a solitary kind of guy. Maybe he needed time alone. He's probably down your local sinking a few pints.'

'I've already checked.'

'But there's plenty more local watering holes,' Shaw said patiently. 'Does he have any particular haunts?'

'Well, there's the Chinese in High Town. The basement bar is like drinking in catacombs.'

'There you go and I bet the signal is rubbish.'

'You're right.' She gave a giddy laugh, brittle and bright. 'I'm being silly and needy and all those things I promised myself I wouldn't be.'

In the comparatively short time Shaw had known Wolf,

he'd lost count of the instances in Wolf's romantic history he'd heard some poor girl say much the same. Not much had changed. Only now the stakes were higher. An image of Mark dead in the mortuary flashed through Shaw's mind. *What if?*

The line went quiet. Shaw waited. His stomach rumbled angrily. To shut it up, he broke off a piece of fish and popped it into his mouth. It felt greasy and suddenly tasteless.

'Thing is,' Lori began.

'Yes?'

'He's been acting strange lately.'

Shaw rewrapped his dinner. 'In what way?' He kept his tone neutral. Resisted shifting into first gear.

'Going out at odd times. Sometimes he doesn't tell me where. He's become secretive.'

Shaw felt the batter from his fish supper congealing in the pit of his stomach. Still, he refused to believe that Wolf's disappearance meant he'd come to harm. After Shaw's warning, Wolf would be extra careful and super vigilant. There had to be something else at play. 'You think he's in trouble?'

Another pause. 'Yes. Maybe. I don't know.'

'Money problems?'

'No, we're doing all right. Better than, actually.'

'He hasn't fallen out with anyone?'

'He doesn't have an enemy in the world.'

'I don't wish to pry, Lori, and it's a horrible question to ask but—'

'I know what you're going to say,' she said in a small voice. 'You think he's walked out on me.'

No question or surprise in her voice; only realisation followed by a weary acceptance.

'I'm not thinking that,' Shaw lied.

Lori didn't speak. She didn't need to. He could hear her crying softly, something Shaw found difficult to handle.

He waited a beat; gave her time to compose herself. 'Is all his stuff still at home?'

'His stuff?' She repeated it, dumbly, as if her mind was making deductions separate from what was coming out of her mouth.

'Is there the remotest possibility that he's gone away for the night?'

'Not without telling me.'

'So he sometimes goes away?'

'Only for professional purposes.'

'Like?'

'Every year he attends the hospitality and tourism conference at the NEC.'

'Right.' Sounded dull.

'Deep down, I always knew he'd leave one day. Just not right now.'

Shaw winced. 'I'm sorry.'

'Did he discuss it with you?'

'No.' Not in so many words, Shaw thought. 'Anything else strike you as odd, or out of character?

'When he first started running, he'd come back and head straight for the shower. Now he can be gone for over an hour and yet he hardly looks as if he's broken a sweat.'

Shaw had made the same observation. He'd thought the guy was super-fit. Lori seemed to suggest something else.

'Have you found any evidence: messages on his phone, restaurant or hotel receipts?'

She replied that she hadn't.

She'd already looked, poor woman. If Wolf had reverted to type, Shaw didn't think he would simply up and go. That wasn't his style. Which led him straight back to the other more chilling alternative. He told Lori that the absence of proof of an affair was a good sign even as a blade of fear cut into him. No, Shaw thought, don't go there. Not yet.

'What should I do?' she asked.

'Nothing.'

'But I've got a couple of guests for breakfast tomorrow before they check out.'

'He'll be back by then.' *Please.*

'What if he isn't?'

'Tell them the cook is ill and give them cereal.'

'Right,' she said slowly, unconvinced.

'Go to bed. Get some rest. With luck, he'll creep back in, probably drunk, apologise profusely, and give a perfectly reasonable explanation for his walkabout.'

'You think?'

Shaw hated the sudden lift of hope in her voice.

'You must think me so stupid,' she continued.

'I think you care and there's nothing wrong with that.'

'Well, thanks for listening and sorry to disturb you.'

'No problem. Phone me in the morning if he doesn't come home.'

'Night, Jon.'

'Try and get some sleep, Lori.'

Shaw rang Wolf straightaway. He might be trying to avoid Lori but he'd surely answer a call from a friend. Connecting, it went straight to voice message. Shaw asked Wolf to ring and hung up then scooped up the remains of his now-cold supper and dropped it into the kitchen bin.

'God, Wolf, stay safe,' he murmured. 'Whatever the hell you're doing.'

Chapter Thirty-Nine

Shaw almost fell out of bed when his mobile blared shortly after 7 a.m. Lying awake most of the night, one eye half open and trained on the door, his ear attuned for the slightest sound, he'd finally drifted off some time after four-thirty.

He responded to the caller with a muffled grunt.

'He's not back.'

If he thought Lori was panicked first time around, he was way off the mark.

'I'll be with you by nine. Can you hang on?'

'Should I phone the—'

'Don't do anything until I reach you apart from feeding your guests.' And get rid of them, he thought grimly.

Half an hour later, he was on the road. The skies had opened again. It had to rate as the wettest June on record.

Over an hour later, he pulled up outside the guesthouse. Lori was through the door before he'd climbed out of the car. She stood frozen, arms crossed, cupping her elbows with her hands, as if trying to pin herself together. Her hair stuck up in tufts and her eyes were swollen and red. What had happened to the smiling self-possessed woman he'd met a couple of days earlier? It was as if she'd vanished, replaced by an imposter.

He gently led her through to the kitchen and sat her down at a kitchen table covered in receipts, conference details and bank statements.

'Found anything that could help?'

She shook her head.

'No giveaway meals in restaurants?'

'None.'

'What's the situation with your guests?'

'They checked out, said they'd get breakfast in town,' she replied mechanically.

'Anyone else booked in?'

'Not tonight.'

'Had anything to drink?'

She shook her head, looked at him forlornly.

'Where do you keep your coffee?'

She told him. Shaw set about boiling a kettle and preparing a cafetiere.

The doorbell rang. Lori jumped up, sped towards the door. While she was gone, Shaw slipped out his phone and took pictures of everything on the table. When Lori returned, he was reaching into the fridge for milk.

'Postman,' Lori said dully.

Shaw gave her a sympathetic look. 'Where does Wolf usually go for his run?'

'There's no set route.' Good, Shaw thought. Routine was not a great idea in the current circumstances and nobody appreciated that more than Wolf. 'Sometimes he'll run along

the seafront,' she continued, 'and then head up the path leading to the old hill fort. It's called the Poets Walk.'

'Where else?' he said, checking it out on his phone.

'Norton's Wood, locally known as All Saints because of the
church at the entrance.'

Shaw checked this too. Shy of three kilometres, the walk
looked easily accessible.

'Shouldn't we call someone?' she said urgently.

'Let me do a recce first. Someone might have seen him. Will
you be all right?' he asked, setting the coffee in front of her.

'I'll be all right once I know where he is.'

'Keep your phone close. I'll stay in touch. And don't
worry,' he added, heading for the door.

Shaw drove to the seafront where he parked. A couple of
ice-cream vans were setting up for the day along the promenade. Enquiries about a man running that way and fitting
Wolf's description on the previous afternoon were met with
blank responses.

'Thanks,' he said, walking swiftly away. To his right, the
sea churned, more brown than blue, unhappy it seemed with
the recent downpour of rain that morning, although in the
distance, watery sunshine leaked through the cloud.

A solitary swimmer in a wetsuit ploughed up and down a
marine lake. Shaw paused to take a better look. Just a young
guy in his twenties, as slim as Wolf was solid.

The path leading to the hill fort took Shaw past an old
lookout point, a church and graveyard. Each step of the way,
he looked for anything that Wolf might have dropped. His
phone. A wallet. House keys.

Climbing steadily uphill and along the promontory, Shaw

paused by an embankment and scrambled up and onto open grassland. Following in Wolf's footsteps, he imagined what had been going through his old friend's mind. Had Wolf been consumed by that terrible night? Was he reliving every moment of it? In his head, and as he ran, was he chased by demons? Was he worrying that someone was out to get him?

At the top, the earth formed a distinct mound, revealing the remains of the fortification. Beyond, a hamlet of houses that nestled in the valley, like white cubes of sugar on a leaf.

Shaw didn't expect to find a body. The ground was too open, the route too popular. Not a good place for a kill.

Turning back, he retraced his steps, picked up the car and drove to All Saint's where he parked in a street already packed closely with cars. Ahead, rising up into a sky more blue than grey, a hill dense with vegetation and trees. Close by, a primary school and the sound of young children playing at break time. If Wolf had run this way the day before, Shaw realised that it could have been around school pick-up. Shaw approached a couple of women who stood on the perimeter of the playground and asked them. The older of the two viewed him with open distrust. Her friend, a small-boned woman with short, choppy grey hair that framed a wide forehead, answered with a smile that was as warm as a traffic warden's before handing out a ticket.

'Can't help you. Sorry.'

And even if she could, Shaw was only too well aware that eyewitness accounts were fraught with difficulty and could differ wildly for a host of reasons, including mood, gender and background. He'd known one witness to claim the weather was wet while the other swore on his life that it was hot and sunny. Things got even more complicated when witnesses were caught up in hostile, high-pressure situations.

'You might know him. He runs a guesthouse in town with his partner, Lori.' It wasn't inconceivable. The place was small, close-knit.

'Lori Bryant, American woman?'

'That's right.' Breakthrough, Shaw thought, brightening.

'Nice lady,' the blonde said. 'She gave a talk to the kids about Seattle.'

'Do you know her partner?'

Both women looked at each other and glanced away. The older woman crossed her arms.

'I need to find him,' Shaw said. 'It's important. Anything you tell me would help.'

'Terry Whittaker is a player,' the grey-haired woman said, her mouth a short, disapproving line. 'Lori Bryant could do a lot better for herself.'

Shaw wanted to quiz her. The school bell had other ideas. As it clamoured, dozens of little kids tumbled towards the entrance and the two women turned on their heels and strode away.

He'd come this far and was screwed if he was going to give up now, so Shaw headed for the woods. On the approach, he received a text from Lori pleading for news. He texted her straight back with a bland assurance that he was making progress – anything to prevent her from contacting the police.

Passing through a narrow metal gate, he stepped onto a short path and up a steep flight of stone steps. Beneath a canopy of green, the woodland walk before him resembled a scene from a children's fairy story. Ancient trees, enormous in size, stood sentinel. Pale light drifted through blinding green and freckled the earth. And there was no sound. Not a bird. Not a squirrel. No sign of any human activity.

Flat and unassuming, the route ahead would suit a young family out for a stroll, Shaw thought. He walked along a little until he came to where the path narrowed into an alley between two rock faces. He couldn't explain it other than to say that the way ahead didn't feel right, or a direction Wolf would choose. More likely, he'd have taken one of the more challenging paths that led up into the heart of the woods, away from the possibility of people. Isn't that what a secretive man would do?

Glancing down, Shaw's eye caught sight of something shiny and metallic, glinting in an unexpected shaft of sunlight.

He crouched, dug around a pile of old leaves and unearthed a Yale key, suitable for a front door. He pocketed it and continued until he came to a set of wooden steps, which he took, climbing to the top. From there, the trail branched off, zigzagging in different directions. He had no idea which to select and stood, breathing in the silence, unsure. Eventually, he settled on a flatter route that led through a tunnel of green foliage that seemed to open out onto a clearing.

Trees with boughs twenty feet above his head stared down at him, as if in judgement. The air felt thinner.

Shaw picked his way through broken branches, leaf mould and bracken, his footsteps loud in the enveloping silence. There was no reason to press on. Nothing told him that Wolf had passed this way. He had no inkling or intuition. If he were looking for a sign, then he was out of luck. Racked with indecision, he decided give it a few minutes more. After that, he'd retreat and return to Lori. What he would tell her he had no idea.

Tripping over a tree root, Shaw stumbled. Spreading his hands wide to take the fall, he found himself spread-eagled on the ground, his face in the dirt. As he lifted himself up, he noticed that the earth was sprinkled with coins, like they'd been flung from a purse, or left behind by a modern-day Hansel.

Panic spiked inside and Shaw scrambled up and scoped the scenery, narrowing his gaze to see if he was alone. He hardly dared move and when he stooped down to study the cash, the sound he made in the silence was deafening.

A mixture of fifty-pence pieces and two-pound coins littered the soil. Clues or bait or metaphors: *blood money, filthy lucre*? He reached out to pick some of them up and then drew back as if he'd touched fire. No good could come from it.

Straightening up, he tried to snatch at the fear threatening to ensnare him. On he climbed, his breathing ragged and laboured as he ploughed uphill at a steady pace. The terrain was similar to the steep climb up to the barns on Jeffrey Finner's land. There, he'd been hemmed in on either side by hedges. Here, he was flanked by lime and ash. Only the dread of what he might find remained the same.

The deeper into the wood he probed, the more inexorable the sensation of becoming sucked in, the greater the sense of disorientation. Would he ever be able to find his way back?

His boots slid on the uneven ground. Thin branches whipped across and stung and scratched his face. He couldn't turn back now if he wanted to. He was committed. Gone from his mind, Wolf, and the hunt to find him. Kenny and

Mark were absent, too. There was only one way to finish this, Shaw thought. Reach the top. Reach the end. Walk into the trap if that's what the killer wanted.

Danny? Where are you?

A light wind picked up through the woodland. It whispered at first, growing in strength and voice until it whined a lament. Trees swayed in time to its beat. Branches cracked and yawed, everywhere alive until the path converged with dozens of others and flattened out into what should have been a pretty woodland glade.

Shaw gazed up, his eyes shooting wide in horror. He let out a gasp and fell to his knees, overwhelmed with grief.

Chapter Forty

Wolf's body hung lifeless. An unforgiving rope bit into his neck. Twisted to one side, his head. The tip of his tongue protruded beneath sightless eyes. He wore jeans and a polo shirt, not running gear. The soles of his trainers were no more than four inches from the earth. There were higher branches from which he could have hung himself, but he'd chosen one lower.

In a kaleidoscope of mind-searing images, Shaw took them all in. Feverishly glancing at the ground, he saw no giveaway feathers, no symbolic gesture that warned of three men down and three to go. He could see no obvious signs that Wolf had met his end by another's hand. Surely, he would? Forcing himself to stay focused, a dark, offbeat thought slammed into his head. Christ, was it just possible that his old friend had committed suicide?

Shaw let out a breath. He'd never had Wolf down for the suicidal type and yet Lori had mentioned Wolf was acting strangely. Was Wolf a man on the edge? Was this what he'd meant about having plans? Had Shaw's visit tipped his old friend over the divide between wanting to live and wanting to die? Maybe Wolf, buckling under the strain, had decided to beat a killer to it, cheating him of having his shot at vengeance. That scenario seemed horribly plausible and, for this, Shaw bore responsibility. He had not known that Wolf was already in a fragile state of mental health when he'd caught up with him.

Shaw climbed unsteadily to his feet, recalling the haunted expression on Wolf's face when he'd talked about Mickie Ashton's death. To his shame, Shaw remembered his failure to offer the absolution he'd sought.

'We are not bad men. We did nothing wrong. We tried to stop it.'

'We shouldn't have even been there, Wolf.'

And now what? He should call the police. He could do it anonymously, but first he would go back and break the news to Lori. And yet . . .

After he'd left Carl, he'd doubted that he would ever hear from him again, unless Carl wanted to knock him off and *make it look like suicide*. Jaw set, Shaw willed himself to draw nearer. No signs of a scuffle or resistance on the ground. No scratches or bruises on Wolf's arms. It was impossible to detect whether Wolf or another had tied the rope. Shaw frowned. Would he even be able to tell the difference? He realised that to stand any hope, he needed a control sample of a knot made by Wolf. What would Lori think if he asked if he could examine Wolf's shoes on the off chance he'd left a pair already tied because he'd been too lazy to undo them?

Steeling himself and taking one hell of a risk, he removed a handkerchief from his pocket, wrapped it around one hand and, hoping Wolf's mobile phone might offer a clue, slipped it into the pockets of Wolf's jeans. His fingers felt thick and clumsy against the stiff resistance of the corpse. There was nothing to find. No phone. No wallet. No note and nothing that would identify Terence Whittaker to the outside world.

Temple pulsing, he snapped several pictures on his phone and added these macabre attachments to his collection, then clutching at a random patch of forget-me-nots, Shaw placed them clumsily at the base of the hanging tree. With one last glance, he sped away and took a different route back, praying that nobody would spot him. Stumbling back to the car, he wished to hell he'd not spoken to the two women near the school.

The drive to Lori's appeared to take an age. He had no idea how to tell her or how much he should say. He had no right words, only wrong ones. Every phrase sounded trite and devoid of meaning.

The door to the guesthouse was shut and Shaw rang the bell several times. Silence greeted him. He took several steps back from the entrance and, cupping his hands to his mouth, called Lori's name. Expecting to see her appear at an upstairs window, he waited. Still nobody came. Guessing she might be asleep, or in the bathroom, he dropped her a text: *'I'm outside. Could you let me in?'*

Shaw paced up and down. The same two cars that he'd spotted earlier were still in the drive. Assuming she was on foot, she might have nipped to the shops for supplies. She might have taken off to ask around. Willing his phone to ring, it remained stubbornly uncooperative. Slipping it back into his jacket, his fingers bumped up against the key he'd found in the woods. Too ridiculous to think it would fit the lock.

Hands bunched inside his pockets, he strode up and down some more, levelled his eyes towards the road and the pavement and people passing by. Lori was not among them.

Screw it, he thought. Taking the key, he inserted it snugly into the lock. Expecting it to sit tight and refusing to budge, he hoped it wouldn't get stuck.

It didn't.

Smoothly turning the lock, Shaw let himself inside and closed the door behind him. He called out to Lori, waited for a response, one that didn't come. His heart was hammering in his chest.

The kitchen was much as he'd left it: same litter of papers distributed over the table, a half-drunk mug of coffee. Shaw touched it. Lukewarm. A shiver zapped his spine.

Lori's chair was pushed back, he noticed. She must have had a thought or been disturbed and decided to head out, or upstairs.

Shaw went back into the hall. A rack of coats revealed a woman's Mackintosh and light waterproof jacket; below, a neat row of women's shoes, boots and sneakers.

Shaw stood at the foot of the stairs and called Lori's name once more. The only sound was the ticking clock in the hall.

Slowly, he ascended. A reasonable explanation accounted for her absence, he told himself, each step feeling like an invasion. Lori was never in danger, he'd told Wolf. Six feathers. Six men. Then why were Shaw's knees clanking?

Five bedrooms occupied the first storey: Lori and Wolf's, and four guest rooms. Each was locked. Without any idea in which Lori might be, Shaw methodically tapped on each door. He waited patiently for a response that never came.

Doubling back to the staircase, he moved up to the second floor.

There was no landing. The stairs opened out onto a large sprawling room crammed with old furniture, paintings, an exercise bike, racks of clothes and general crap accumulated over a lifetime.

One end of the room narrowed into a corridor. Shaw picked his way through the jumble and found himself in a smaller room with a shower room off it. It looked as if it had been recently refurbished. Lori had mentioned opening up the top storey to create a honeymoon suite so this must be the first step in its transformation.

Shaw ran a hand underneath his jaw. Lori had also referred to what she called the Harry Potter floor. He wished he'd listened carefully and asked more questions.

Retracing his steps back to the main room, he gingerly opened the door to a wardrobe parked along the outer wall. It revealed nothing unexpected and certainly provided no entrance to another part of the house. Similarly, a full-length mirror held little clue to an extra room. It had to be here somewhere, Shaw chafed inside. Then he spotted it. What he'd assumed was a large window with a view of the street and glimpses of sea beyond was actually a trompe l'oeil, a painting creating an image of reality that didn't exist. Reaching for the catch, he sensed movement behind him.

'Jon,' Lori said, wide-eyed.

'Sorry, I didn't know where you were and I was worried.'

'Did you find him?' She talked quickly, her eyes begging for good news. It killed him.

Shaw swallowed. 'Lori, I think you may need to sit down.'

Chapter Forty-One

Lori was inconsolable.

In pale-faced shock, she covered her face with her hands and slid down the wall. At a loss how to respond, Shaw sat beside her on the tatty carpet, drew her close and let her sob. She had no business being caught up in his or Wolf's mess. But how could he explain? Answer: he couldn't.

He didn't know how long they stayed like that. She trembled and her heart raced erratically against his chest. His shirt was soaked through with her tears. Eventually, she calmed a little.

'Why did he do it?' she pleaded. 'We were good together. We had so much to look forward to.' She pulled away, looked up into his eyes. 'Was it me? Did I do him wrong?'

'No,' Shaw said firmly. 'You mustn't think like that. You're not to blame. Terry was a complex guy. Look, Lori, we really should call the police.'

She looked at him blankly, as if grief had suddenly robbed her of hearing.

'They need to be informed,' Shaw pushed gently. There was no getting away from it; it had to be done.

'I suppose . . . Do you think Terry left a note?'

'What?'

'That's what people do when they take their own life.'

'Well, I—'

'He wouldn't just leave me. He wouldn't.' Scrabbling to her feet, she tore down the narrow flight of stairs. Shaw got up wearily and followed. He found her in one of the bedrooms. Beside herself with distress, Lori acted like a burglar rummaging for the choicest pieces of jewellery before the householder comes home. Drawers thrown open, contents unearthed and stuff all over the floor.

'It has to be here,' she said, more and more desperate. He grabbed hold as she sped fast. At first she relaxed but then tensed and pushed him away. 'Why did you come to see him?' Her voice thickened with reproach.

'Lori . . .' Shaw began.

'Why – after all this time?'

Shaw opened his mouth to lie, but Lori wasn't done. 'What did you say? What did you tell him?' She spoke slowly, every word enunciated, like a drunk pulled over by the police trying to sound sober.

He should get the hell out. He should flee and never ever return.

'We talked about old times,' Shaw said as evenly as he could. 'That's all.'

'That's *not* all. He was all right until you showed up.' Her pretty face looked ugly. 'You did something to him.'

'Lori, you're in shock. Understandably, you're not seeing things straight.'

'Don't patronise me. What was it between you two? What were you mixed up in?'

Shaw spread his hands. 'Let me help you. At least let me phone the right people.'

'*I'll* phone the police. That's my job. I don't know you and I sure as hell don't trust you.'

'Lori, please.'

'After you left, he was scared.'

'I know nothing about it.'

'I don't believe you.'

She was right and he was wrong and he could never explain. Advancing on him, eyes like pinpricks, she said, 'What made him crack?'

'Lori, I have no idea what—'

'Get out,' she spat. 'Get out and don't you ever come back.'

'I'm sorry.' It was all he could say, all he could do.

Blindsided, Shaw hurried downstairs and crossed the hall, the front door opening and shutting too loudly behind him.

He picked up his car and drove a way out of town. Strung out, he turned off the main road and pulled over in a tree-lined street. On shaking legs, he climbed out of the car and vomited into the gutter. Lori's accusation had hit home because she told the truth. What hurt more was the loss of his old friend.

Shaw returned to the car and drove away. Using his hands-free, he called Danny's mam. It rang and rang. Judging by his recent foray into her communication history, he supposed it was conceivable that she eschewed mobiles because she hadn't yet got the hang of how to operate them. On the point of disconnecting, a deliberately posh voice he barely recognised said, 'Hello, Christine Hallam speaking.'

'Christie, it's Jon.'

Crackling and beeping preceded a raucous laugh and intermittent phrases that Shaw strained to hear. She sounded as if she were speaking from a tumble dryer.

'Jon?... What... Sod it, Clint, what do you mean I have to stand still? No, I haven't got my thumb over the speaker. Give over, knobhead...'

Shaw ticked with frustration, waiting for the domestic spat to dissipate. No chance. The line swelled with expletives. 'Christie,' he bellowed. 'Can you hear me?'

'I *think* so.'

'Is Danny with you?'

'No, love.'

Was it rotten timing that Wolf wound up dead the second Danny vanished? 'Can you get a message to him? Tell him...' He hesitated, unsure.

'I can't hear you,' Christie said. 'Are you still there? Fuck's sake, Clint,' she hissed.

'Tell him Wolf is gone.'

'Gone where?'

'Christie,' Shaw said sharply. 'Tell Danny to call me. It's urgent.'

Chapter Forty-Two

So what do you think of that, Jon? Was it eye-catching enough for you? And what about my treasure hunt? Like a good little gumshoe, you played along and followed the trail. I wished I could have seen your distraught face when you saw the consequences of your actions close up. Isn't nice, is it, when you lose someone horribly, someone you care about? And before you run away with the idea that I strung him up, let me assure you that Terence was only too keen to tie the knot himself, dirty fucker.

It's all about personality, and mine is *very* persuasive. Tell people what they want to hear and they'll believe any old drivel. It's all about building the right narrative so, naturally, Terry believed me. Well, he would, wouldn't he? Me being a fine upstanding person and all. Engendering trust is a necessary skill in the murderer's manual and I inspire it in spades. I've got that kind of face – lucky for me, not so good for you. Trust counts in my day job too. You *know* what I'm talking about, don't you, Jon? Despite the scepticism against your profession as a breed – who loves a lawyer? – when criminals are up against it, they need a brief like you to believe in.

Are you still getting villains off? I hear you're the man with a plan. Comes as no surprise from the bastard who thought he could get away with murder.

If only those nice people you work with knew the truth. You wouldn't be so popular then. You'd drop straight off the Christmas card list. You'd be shunned. You'd be a pariah. You'd know what it is to feel an outcast. Sure, I know you suffered personal heartache when your mother popped her clogs; just not enough to make a difference.

This all travels through my head as I stand with my right arm at a perpendicular angle and my left stretched out behind me, one foot in front, one behind, a powerful 'fortune favours the brave' stance. Which, can we get one thing clear, it does not? Fortune favours the cunning, the ruthless and the determined.

It's all about understanding the problems and then solving them before they arise.

Take CCTV. How many times have you heard of the film in a camera being grainy or faulty? Technology is no more a silver bullet than DNA and, if DNA were the Holy Grail, no crime would go undetected and unpunished, which, as I've admirably displayed, is not the case. Give me a fully functioning brain any day if you want to be a winner. It pays to get yourself an education, doesn't it, Jon?

And then there's the human element. As you understand only too well, humans are unreliable, weak and contradictory. To correctly analyse volumes of data requires a sharp mind. Most aren't up to it. Some are fucking lazy or plain hungover, or having a midlife crisis or, growing in popularity, have mental health 'issues', (you're a nobody without one). Human frailty, see? But I'm preaching to the converted, aren't I, Jon? How many times have you come across a witness statement that contradicts another witness statement? All those pesky things people forget or never noticed in the first place. It's all about recognising what you're dealing with, about managing risk, exploiting the system and making it work for you. To be honest, I'm surprised you haven't cottoned onto some of this stuff. I can only assume that the shock of your mates' deaths has briefly dulled your senses. You're not the determined and tenacious man you think you are, simply another guy out of his depth and lacking in ambition. (To be fair, most people's aspirations rise no higher than a chair leg.)

'Time's up,' I hear the teacher cry and thank God for that. Stretching out my muscles is sweet pain as I reach for my robe. I have my proper job to go to, another murder to commit. Sharpen up, Jon. You're going to need what's left of that agile mind of yours to maintain pace. Gratifying to know that all your efforts will be wasted.

Chapter Forty-Three

Shaw unlocked the door to his study, took out his phone and examined the shots he'd taken. He started by digitally sifting through the papers that littered Lori's kitchen table. According to a flyer, the tourism conference at the NEC had taken place in March. A petrol receipt from a small petrol station in Tyseley appeared to support it. He checked it out and discovered that it was unmanned, only took card payments, and was open twenty-four hours. CCTV would, therefore, be critical to the smooth running of the business.

Next, he looked for evidence of accommodation bills, something Lori would surely have unearthed. Without a record of an overnight stay, Shaw presumed Wolf had done the trip there and back in a day. Two other petrol receipts, also in the Birmingham area over the next two months, were less easy to explain. Was Wolf in contact with Carl and, if so, why hadn't either of them levelled with him about an association? A less appealing thought: Wolf hadn't actually said he hadn't seen Mark. He'd only mentioned Kenny. Had he lied by omission? However Shaw sliced and diced it, Birmingham appeared to hold a clue. And that meant that Carl *could* be involved in Wolf's death.

Braced, he turned to the image of Wolf in the noose. Any attempt to study the ligature and the direction in which the rope was tied, right over left, or left over right, was impeded by swelling that Shaw hadn't noticed, so deep was his shock. He didn't fully grasp the pathological significance, although suspected it said something about the length of time the body had been there and/or the temperature of the outside environment. About to move to the next shot, Shaw spotted something that took his breath away. With several ideas formulating in his mind, he locked the study, and picking up his car keys, headed over to Hope's. At least he knew she'd be in.

'Wondered when you'd turn up.' She invited him into the kitchen. 'I'm having a sort-out.'

It looked as if she'd had a major delivery from a supermarket. The floor was littered with catering-sized packets of foodstuffs, toilet rolls, tissues, cartons of long-life milk, cordials and seemingly every medicine known to man. Packets of crisps spilled from a cupboard onto the floor, in open warfare with boxes of biscuits that had already taken occupation and set up HQ in the interior. Shaw's gaze drifted up to shelves lined with neatly arranged cans.

'They're colour-coded,' Hope explained.

Not knowing what to say, he cleared his throat and said, 'Can you remotely access CCTV?'

'Depends.'

'On?'

'Most DVR recorders can be accessed using a computer or mobile device.'

'Great.'

'But you need the permission of the host.'

'You don't do permission.' That was why he was there.

Hope gave a crooked smile. 'Tell me what you want and I'll tell you if I can do it.'

Shaw explained.

'Hmm,' she said. 'CCTV is often recorded over.'

'Say it isn't.'

'What are you looking for?'

'Not what, but who. I reckon one of my friends might have had company. If he did, I want to know.'

'Got the name of the petrol station and the date and time?'

'Here.' He pointed at the image of the petrol receipt on his phone. 'The service station is card only and unmanned. The car was filled up shortly before midnight.'

Hope transferred the image to her computer. 'What am I looking for – a man or woman?'

'A man, early forties, tall, well built.'

'A mug shot would help.'

'Ah, that's going to be difficult.'

Hope shrugged her wide shoulders. 'It would speed up results.'

And speed was critical. 'All right,' Shaw said reluctantly. 'But you'll have to make allowances.' He clicked to the shot of Wolf and held it up for her to see.

Hope viewed it as if she were trying to decide which wedding photograph would look best in the album. 'Right,' she said flatly. 'Not perfect but I get the general drift. Did you notice his fly was undone?'

'I did.' As soon as Shaw had spotted it, a light bulb pinged on in his brain. Perhaps Wolf had hung himself during an unorthodox, risky sexual practice. Difficult to prove and often concealed by coroners, autoerotic asphyxia offered an alternative to suicide. It also offered an alternative to murder.

'Ah, so you think Mr Hanging Man had female company?'

'Not necessarily.'

Hope gave him a funny look.

'Come on, Hope,' he said.

'Oh that.' She rolled her eyes. 'Some of the more unscrupulous foreign intelligence services adopt it to pass off their wet work activities.' Her eyes widened. 'You don't think Carl Snare is involved?'

'See what you can dig up,' he said grimly.

Danny's call came through as Shaw walked into the hall.

'Mam told me to phone you.'

'Wolf is dead.'

'Shitting hell, Jon. What the fuck happened?'

Shaw gave him a précis of events. He didn't disclose that Wolf's death might be linked to an autoerotic practice that went badly wrong. He couldn't stomach the resulting torrent of bad taste jokes that would pour from Danny's mouth. He didn't suggest a potential connection to Carl. There was another reason too. He didn't trust Danny. He didn't trust anyone apart from a woman on meds who was somewhere on the autistic spectrum.

'Did you track down Carl?'

'No,' Shaw lied.

'Think he's responsible?'

Carl *ought* to take pole position on the suspect list. He had means and opportunity, yet his motive totally eluded Shaw. He remembered Carl had named Waterhouse when pushed. 'I don't know, Danny.'

'Best keep that gun loaded and by your side.'

'You left it for protection?'

'Why else would I leave it?'

Shaw gave an inner sigh of relief. 'Adding murder to my list of crimes isn't going to help.'

'Better than being dead. I'm buzzing for a scrap. Let him come, whoever he is. End of day, it's down to me and him.'

'You've changed your tune.'

'You're a right dick, you know that?'

Shaw took a breath, then another. 'Danny, what's your game?'

'Same as you. Staying alive.'

'Is that why you visited Aaron Waterhouse?'

'Says who?'

'Waterhouse.'

'Fuck me. You've got some bottle.'

'He said you'd asked him for a job.'

'Did he now?'

'Were you after his protection?'

The laugh pealing down the line had a bitter ring. 'That fucker wouldn't lift a finger to help me.'

'Apart from paying you handsomely.'

'Is that what Mam told you? She's a right gobby cow.'

'It's true then?'

'I got owt from Waterhouse.'

Shaw wasn't sure he believed him despite Danny's vigorous denial.

'Did Aaron Waterhouse give the order to kill Mickie?' As Shaw lobbed the question, he realised that some deep, bleak part of him had always worried that this was the case.

Danny snickered. 'You having a laugh? All that snooping and sleuthing has turned you soft in the head.'

'If anything's turned my mind it's the sight of seeing Wolf hanging from a tree with a rope cutting into his neck.' Speaking it aloud had a depressing and sobering effect. 'What do you want from me, Danny?'

Danny went quiet. Silence and dust and old vows between them. Eventually, he said, 'It was *me* who decided to put the squeeze on Mickie Ashton. *Me* who lost my rag. Nothing you say or ask or do will change that.'

'And was it your decision to visit Esther?'

The hesitation was minimal but it was there. 'What's wrong with seeing an old friend?'

'Never knew you were that close.'

'Fuck you and fuck your shitty questions. I see what you're doing, Jon. You're trying to trip me up. Well, I'm not one of your frigging clients.'

Shaw swallowed his anger and let it go. You couldn't reason with Danny when the red mist descended to enshroud him. Silence, defensive and paranoid, erected a wall between them. It would take skill and goodwill to dismantle it.

'Where are you?' Shaw was softer now, reining in the rhetoric.

'Somewhere safe.'

'Are you . . .'

The line went dead.

Chapter Forty-Four

Shaw grabbed a legal pad from his drawer. Whatever the accused had done, he always trawled through the opposition's side of things. For Shaw, it was war and everything got scrutinised, from statements to exhibits, scene logs, forensics and arrest strategies – amazing how many technical loopholes and evidential weaknesses presented themselves when you knew what to look for. Anything that he could use to discredit an investigation and the prosecution case was fair game. It wasn't a case of corruption, bending rules or hijacking the truth (which often had a tendency to fuck right off), but the strict enforcement of the law. To this end, he made notes about each death, location, method and timing. Each victim had been picked off with speed, guile and planning. This was not a killer who burst in through the front door like a bare-knuckled street fighter, but one that sneaked in like a soft-soled cat burglar, through the back. Shaw didn't care to imagine the fate that awaited him.

Motivation was clear and unequivocal: vengeance, indicating someone close, someone who cared, which was an enigma because Mickie Ashton mattered to nobody, *including Carl Snare.*

Shaw sat back. He'd yet to encounter a murderer whose crime had not taken a toll, either mentally or physically. Taking another life and crossing that divide was only the first hurdle. Maintaining the pretence of innocence was another, and the most difficult. More than once he'd seen relief in the eyes of a killer when finally nailed and justice dispensed. No more lying. No more leading a double life of respectability or pretending you're someone you're not. He understood this better than most. So who was this person? What did he do?

When working a case, Shaw always tried to connect with the accused. If he could, he tried to like them. A two-way street, a defendant with whom he had a professional connection, was more likely to trust his decisions. That was always his starting point. To understand a killer, it was important to look at the crimes and then beyond.

Shaw wrote down *planner, strategist, highly intelligent.* Bearing in mind every one of the old crowd had fled the area and moved on, the killer had remarkable access to information.

Needing a drink, Shaw moved into the sitting room. Two paces in, he froze and stared. Above the fireplace, and stuck to the mirror he'd only recently cleaned after Danny's party night, six black feathers, four of them broken. Danny was clearly alive. That left Carl. But Carl was abroad. Carl would not be easy to kill. Carl . . .

Oh Christ.

Shaw flew outside to the drive and ran to the end of the road, crossing over and into a neighbouring street, where he'd parked the Focus. He examined the undercarriage and wheel wells for trackers. Anything more sophisticated hardwired into the actual dashboard would need a mechanic to tear apart the vehicle. He found nothing out of place, yet wasn't exactly reassured. Shaw thought back to the journeys he'd made recently. He'd been as target-aware as possible. Against a professional, though, he had to admit he was no match. Speeding back home, he carried out the same examination with the stationary Macan. Again, nothing to report.

Back inside, mind ablaze with questions, he examined the locks, windows and entry points on the ground floor. Nothing had been disturbed. Upstairs told a similar story. Shaw went outside to the garden and examined the ground beneath the window ledges, even though he'd already confirmed that the window locks were secure. No shoeprints. No flattening of the grass. No roughed-up flowerbeds. Bewildered, he could draw only one conclusion. Someone had a key and had simply entered through the front door. There was only one obvious candidate: Danny.

Shaw tried to work out the logistics. The break-in must have occurred while he'd been at Hope's, in which case the killer had relied on split-second timing, again, indicating either a professional or someone who didn't give a fuck, which brought him straight back to Danny. But Danny had warned him. Danny had once been his closest friend. Danny had never split on him. Not over Mickie Ashton. Not about Shaw's attempt to kill him. He'd not even told his mam about it.

Shaw checked the study, which was mercifully locked. Retrieving the key, he let himself in. Everything looked the way he'd last left it. He opened his laptop and, hunched over the desk, checked news online for Birmingham. No deaths reported. No links to Carl Snare. Then again, Shaw realised, if Carl were dead the intelligence agencies would swoop. Viewed as a massive cock-up, it would swiftly be followed by a cover-up. The police wouldn't get a look-in.

Best keep that gun loaded and by your side, Danny had said. Now was the time to heed his advice.

Shaw unlocked the drawer, reached inside and grasped empty space. Shocked, he looked again, but he was right first time. Unnerved by the speed with which events were unravelling, he felt as carried helplessly along as Danny Hallam had been when buffeted by a river in full spate. Perhaps Danny had returned to claim what was his after all.

Depressed by the thought, Shaw scraped the feathers from the mirror and reached for the drink he'd promised himself over half an hour before. The moment his rear hit the sofa, the doorbell rang. Instantly on the alert, Shaw took his time answering and hoped that whoever it was would go away. He needed to think, to work the angles. Next, someone banged the door with the flat of a hand.

'Mr Shaw, are you in there?'

Female. Midlands accent. Recognisable. *Shit*, Shaw thought.

He opened the door wide and found a warrant card thrust in his face. D.I. Deeley. Alone.

Shaw glanced towards the police car. Inside, another woman he presumed to be a police officer. She stared directly at him, like a resentful child told to wait in the car. In a distinct moment of déjà vu, he wondered whether West Mids had talked to Avon and Somerset. Were dots being joined and the wrong, if obvious, connections made?

Deeley was stone-faced. 'You're a hard man to track down. Didn't you get my messages?'

'Sorry,' Shaw replied. 'I've been off work and rather busy. Why don't you come in?' He stood aside.

Deeley nodded bluntly. She'd obviously not driven all the way to Cheltenham to have a conversation on a doorstep to then trail all the way back to Birmingham.

Once they were seated, drinks offered and declined, Deeley gave him a long, slow look. Despite being in the hot seat, Shaw had to admire Deeley's gutsy and unorthodox approach. She didn't so much as sit as occupy. It was his home, yet it was her presence that dominated. She was a one-woman invading army.

Smoothly kicking things off in an attempt to prove he had nothing to hide, he said, 'I take it this is in regard to my client, Mr Platt.'

'We wondered whether you'd had a chance to recall any detail that might help us.'

Shaw noted the use of the royal 'we'. 'Sorry, no.'

Deeley nodded as if she accepted Shaw's reply without question. He recognised the dynamic: give the impression that you're on the same side and then lob the verbal equivalent of a flashbang and, while your adversary is reeling with shock, attack.

Shaw sipped his drink and held her gaze. It was so quiet he could hear the refrigerator humming from the kitchen next door. He got it. She hoped he would fill the silence. Well, screw that. He looked. She looked. Finally, she cracked.

'Did you know that Mr Platt originated from Manchester?'

'I might have detected a northern accent.'

'Is this because you're from the same part of the world?'

'Possibly.'

'Did Mr Platt approach you for advice because you already knew each other?'

Shaw felt a trickle of unease. 'I'm not sure I follow.'

'It's a simple enough question.' She spread her hands. 'Perhaps he came to you about a different matter entirely.'

'That's not how I remember our meeting. I think I've been quite clear.'

Her cool smile implied the reverse. 'Where did you grow up exactly?'

Shaw told her.

'Mr Platt was from the same estate.'

'Strange coincidence.'

He thought Deeley's sly smile resembled that of an agent of the court before serving a summons to the unwary.

'The fact we come from the north hardly makes us blood brothers.' A poor choice of words, Shaw immediately regretted it.

'True. Unlike Mr Platt, you've done well for yourself.'

'It wasn't without difficulty.'

'I'd imagine. Must have been tough.'

The surprisingly empathetic response inclined him to think that Deeley had also travelled a rough route before entering her chosen profession.

'Do you know Daniel Hallam?' she asked.

Shaw suppressed any shock by answering her question with his own. 'Should I?'

'His name isn't familiar?'

'Vaguely. A former client, perhaps.' Shaw glanced up and spotted a blob of adhesive stuck to the mirror. Deeley briefly followed his gaze. Shaw tried to divert her.

'What's his significance?'

'He's out of prison after serving time for murder.'

'Then I can assure you that, if he were one of my clients, I'd remember.'

'He isn't.'

'Then I don't see what he has to do with me.'

'That's something I was hoping you could help us with. You see, we believe that Daniel Hallam has been visiting some of his old friends, one of whom was Mr Platt.'

'Like I said, I fail to see the relevance.' Shaw didn't meet her steely-eyed gaze; he took a laser to it. 'Speaking purely from experience,' he continued, 'criminals who serve lengthy sentences are often keen to renew old friendships on release. What they're not keen to do is commit the same crime that put them inside in the first place.'

'And yet you must be aware of the high recidivist rate in this country.'

'I am and, as *you* know, it tends to be for non-violent crime.'

Deeley raised a suggestive eyebrow. Her top lip curled. He had the faintest notion that she was sparring with him and enjoying it. Either that, or flirting, which was insane.

'I don't think I suggested that Mr Hallam murdered Mr Platt,' she said.

'Then I misunderstood you.'

'I think it's me who misunderstood you.' She stood abruptly

and stuck out her hand. Shaw took it, felt the warm pressure of her palm against his. She thanked him for his time. 'I'll be in touch,' Deeley said.

'If I have any thoughts, I'll do likewise.'

Together, they briskly crossed the hall.

'Enjoy the rest of your holiday, Jon.' Her expression was flinty and uncompromising.

She'd be back. Of that, he had no doubt.

Chapter Forty-Five

Esther, Aaron Waterhouse's ex, was easy to find.

Posing as a buyer, Shaw phoned a couple of estate agents with little success. The third proved luckier. The market was thick with centrally located apartments. However, penthouses with balconies and communal facilities, which included a gym and sauna, were in short supply and greater demand.

'Unfortunately, the last on our books was sold a few months ago,' the agent said.

'That's disappointing,' Shaw remarked.

'You'd have loved it. Situated in City Walls Road, it has fantastic views over the racecourse.'

Sounded about right. Before the estate agent tried to flog him something else, Shaw cut the call and went onto the Land Registry site. The apartment in which Esther lived was registered in Waterhouse's name and he'd paid over seven hundred grand for it. Still in control then, Shaw thought, deciding to pay a visit.

He found a car park, stuck a couple of hours on a Pay and Display and set off for City Walls Road.

Christie had been right about Esther falling on her feet. A

handsome building, with Doric columns and sash windows, the exterior resembled an old hospital. Looking towards the upper storey, Shaw could clearly see 'Erected 1761'. He bet there was nothing eighteenth century about the interior.

Unlike Carl Snare, Esther wasn't trying to hide. If she was shocked to hear from him, she didn't show it. Now in her early forties, she had dark hair, cut fashionably short, framing her lightly tanned face. Below carefully plucked eyebrows, the only obvious trace of artifice, her brown eyes gleamed with intelligence and the certain knowledge that she was desirable. She wore a simple cotton dress that displayed a neat waist. Her legs were bare and smooth. On her feet she wore gold sandals and her toenails were painted nude, the same colour as her fingernails. Wealth suited her, Shaw thought, and she wore it well. Esther might have been young and naïve when she married Waterhouse, 'a kid on the make' most had said, and yet she'd grown up in a way that only he could have foreseen. For the life of him Shaw could not fathom why Aaron had let her go. He knew he wouldn't have.

'Danny said you might come.' Her voice was softer and more refined than he remembered. Another person who'd buried her roots deep, he surmised.

'I'm amazed you let him in.'

She clicked her tongue. 'Danny Hallam doesn't scare me.'

'You must have been surprised to see him after all this time.'

She tilted her head to one side and smiled. 'Nothing surprises me, Jon. Shall we go out? I know a nice bar. You can buy me a drink.'

The bar was a fifteen-minute stroll to Love Street. The

weather had picked up and, for once, Shaw felt the heat of
the sun on his back. Some shoppers actually wore sunglasses.

On the way Esther asked all those bland questions people
solicit when they haven't seen each other for decades. Shaw's
answers were in a similar vein. She mentioned that Aaron's
parents had moved out of the city.

'To Barton-upon-Irwell,' she said casually, kicking up a
storm inside Shaw's mind. The river had a history of killing
everything in its slimy depths. It was a miracle that it hadn't
managed to see off Danny.

Part micro-brewery and traditional pub with industrial-
styled lighting, the place was busy with lunchtime drinkers,
most choosing to take advantage of a rare moment of sunshine
and sit outside on a terrace overlooking the street. From a
bewildering selection of beers, Shaw ordered a pint of Golden
Boy, named in honour of Chester-born striker, Michael Owen,
and a fancy gin, from a small distillery, with tonic for Esther.

Taking their drinks, they found a couple of tub chairs near
a table that was private and tucked away.

Esther took a healthy swallow and turned the full force of
her brown-eyed gaze on Shaw. 'It's good to see you, Jon. I'm
glad you escaped.'

'So did you, by the looks of it.'

'It took me long enough,' she said with a wry smile.

'Do you mind me asking what happened between you and
Aaron?'

'You can ask.'

'But won't tell.'

'Probably wise not to.'

'Has Aaron threatened you?'

Esther tipped back her head and laughed. 'He has no need. He holds the purse strings. That's threat enough.'

'But you divorced a while ago.'

'We never married,' she said.

'You took his name.'

'Seemed easier.'

More convenient, pragmatic and advantageous was what Esther meant. Not great for the sisterhood.

'He's done right by me without having to.' She gamely tipped her head to one side. 'Aaron is not the man you knew, Jon.'

Coming from Esther, it was revelatory. Shaw had been away so long, it seemed he'd lost his grip and grasp. 'Is he genuinely out of the game?'

'Has been for years.'

'I find that hard to believe.'

'Lies travel further than truth.' She lifted the glass to her lips, all the while looking deeply into his eyes. 'Don't get me wrong – his wealth didn't all come from property deals.'

'He must have had a lot of capital behind him to go legit.'

'He did.'

'And trusted lawyers and accountants willing to help him make the transition.'

'Jay Kelso has been his go-to lawyer for a number of years. Runs a big law firm.'

'On the level?'

'Straight as a die.'

And there was Shaw believing that Waterhouse wanted to recruit his services so that he could finesse and bend him to his will for an illegal branch of his business. He continued to be wrong about the man and it bothered him.

Esther sipped her drink and continued to view him cat-like, almost with amusement.

'So when did Kelso take over?'

'Got to be ten years ago, give or take.'

'When you were still together?'

'No, Aaron was with Gail by then.'

Shaw sat back and thought about the timing. Important or not?

'I was by his side during the early period when he accrued a fortune,' Esther said.

'That never bothered you?'

'Jon, you know it didn't. We talked about it, remember?'

He cast his mind back. Esther had done most of the talking, as he recalled. Yes, she'd been fond of him, but Aaron had so much more to offer. The pain she'd caused when she'd dumped Shaw had been one more nail in a coffin full of them. He'd thought he was losing his mind. It was one of the reasons he'd gravitated towards the gang and run with the pack on the night of Mickie's murder. Officially, Esther and Aaron Waterhouse had got together shortly afterwards. Shaw knew differently. She'd been seeing Aaron when she'd also been seeing him.

'What happened to make Aaron change?' Shaw asked.

'Unhappiness.'

He hadn't seen that one coming. Waterhouse had led a charmed existence, as far as he could see. 'With what? His life? You?'

The weight of her gaze was crushing. She surveyed him for

a long time before she answered. 'Did you know Aaron came from a conventional background? Not like you and me.' She lightly brushed Shaw's hand to make her point. He felt like he'd been hit with a cattle prod.

'I didn't know that.' Shaw fixed on what she was saying rather than on what he was feeling.

'Aaron's parents didn't have a lot of money but they were decent people,' she continued. 'So Aaron had this notion that couples should have kids. It was important to him. Happy families,' she said with a dry, world-weary laugh. This from the man who had used intimidation and exploitation. Shaw wasn't sure he bought it.

'Aaron needed children and I couldn't give them to him. We were all right in the beginning,' Esther added quickly, as if to assure Shaw that she'd made the right decision for both of them. 'But after we'd been together a while, cracks started to appear.'

'Did he hurt you?' Shaw couldn't bear the thought of it.

'Never physically.'

'But?'

'He could be cold and unpredictable. Something you warned me about, as I remember.' She smiled sadly. 'He spent more time away than he could account for. Usual stuff, seeing his parents who'd moved by then. I wasn't stupid,' she said reaching for her glass. 'When he told me he was busy setting up the business and making sure we were above board from the law and the taxman, I knew he was seeing someone else.'

'I'm sorry it didn't work out.'

'I'm not. He got what he wanted. Nice wife and kids. Properly married this time. And I got my freedom.'

'You make it sound easy.'

She tilted her head to one side. 'Never that. I had to grow up fast.'

'You've moved on?'

'Oh yes.'

He took a deep swallow of beer. She drained her glass. 'Another?' he asked.

'Why not?'

Standing at the bar, Shaw registered that Esther had failed to mention Mickie Ashton. He didn't know whether it was by design or because her death had passed her by. Perhaps Esther had been beguiled and too much in love with Aaron to notice. Shaw had never stuck around long enough to find out.

Setting her drink down, Esther looked up. 'Did you find someone to love?'

Shaw had been deeply fond of Jo. He still cared about her. He desired her. Was that love? 'She didn't stay.'

'I'm sorry. Truly.'

'And now that you're free?'

'There's nobody special. I'm not lonely,' she added swiftly. 'I was only lonely with Aaron. It took me a while to realise that.' Again, that silvery laugh – was it affectation or nerves?

He waited, drank some beer and let her settle. 'Esther?'

'Yes.'

'Why did you see Danny?'

'Why not?'

'A drug runner, a murderer.'

'From what I hear, you let him back in too.'

A fair point except he had a pressing reason to do so: his life was on the line.

'Like I said,' Esther continued, 'people change. Everyone deserves a second chance, don't they?'

He smiled agreement. He could believe it of others and yet he was damned if he could embrace it for himself. 'So what did Danny want?'

She looked him dead in the eye. 'Same as you, Jon – to reminisce about old times.'

Chapter Forty-Six

Lies travel further than truth. What had Esther meant? Shaw felt certain she'd been protecting something. It was true she'd grown up and changed, but not so much that he didn't know when he wasn't getting the whole story.

On the approach to Cheltenham, Shaw went straight to Hope's to see if she'd struck lucky with the CCTV search. Going through the same rigmarole to gain access was akin to Groundhog Day. Hope issued the same instructions. Shaw made the same remarks as he wiggled his way inside.

'What happened to you?' she said. 'You look as if you've been up all night.'

'I'm not sleeping well.'

Hope sniffed. 'You should take better care of yourself. Failing to get seven hours on a regular basis can shorten your life.'

'I'll bear it in mind.'

This time he wasn't offered a bowl of cereal but a pack of Jaffa cakes. When these got rolled out there was usually something worth celebrating. He thanked her and took one to be sociable. This time it was his turn to ask, 'What you got?'

'In here,' she said, as if it was the first time he'd set foot in her digital den.

Pulling up a chair and instructing Shaw to sit in front of one of the screens, Hope clicked the keyboard with a dexterity and speed she failed to display in other areas of her life.

Shaw watched and his eyes widened as a silver Subaru BRZ entered the forecourt of a petrol station. Driver and passenger were visible although Shaw had a tough time identifying either because the sports car was low in relation to the angle of the camera. Not so the registration.

'Plates are false and the car was stolen,' Hope said, squashing Shaw's thoughts of identification flat.

'Where was the vehicle nicked?'

'Saltley, Birmingham. It was found the next day abandoned and burnt out on waste ground.'

Straight out of the Danny Hallam playbook, Shaw thought uneasily.

'There's a better view of the driver here. I've frozen the frame.'

Shaw craned forward, slipped out his phone and took an image.

'There's your man,' she said, pointing.

Against a dark background and beneath a light shining directly overhead, Wolf stood, his hand raised, inserting a credit card into the card reader at the pump.

'You're right.' It felt weird to see Wolf very much alive after seeing him dead. Dropping his gaze, Shaw homed in on the hunched figure in the passenger side. A hood, similar to

the cowls worn by monks, concealed the face, yet the pos-
ture and clothing revealed something he'd failed to consider
properly until now.

'Fuck,' he said aloud.

'What?' Hope said.

'It's a woman.'

'So what?' Hope said.

He looked up at her. 'Got any more Jaffa cakes?'

They say every picture tells a story. I've waited so long to
tell it or, more accurately, paint it because I think of myself
more in terms of artist than storyteller. As such, I regularly
stroll through the gallery in my mind, into which nobody
else sets foot. Only there can I view the images of the dead
in peace. I imagine your portrait joining the collection very
soon.

And a part of me will be lost.

We're not so very different, you and I. You've spent a
quarter of a lifetime covering your tracks, pretending to be
someone you aren't. You know about destroying your roots,
about concealment and reinvention. Both of us hide in plain
sight. Both of us are connected by Mickie Ashton's death.

She cost me everything, but did I love her? You have to be
joking. She was a pathetic, weak-willed, attention-seeking
junkie who cared only about herself.

After her death, I had nowhere to call home. And home
isn't only a place; it's a state of being. It's where you are cared
for, where you feel safe and protected and loved. You and
your friends destroyed all that. For too many years my middle
name became 'Unwanted'. I belonged to no-one. Nobody

listened because I wasn't supposed to exist. But *I* listened. And now *you* are listening. We don't keep secrets, you and me. We *are* the secret.

'Well, say something.' Shaw had expected an offbeat reaction, not a complete absence of one. Hope had demolished the Jaffa cakes and was eyeing up a tub of cashews. A healthier alternative, Shaw guessed.

'I'm thinking,' Hope said.

'The woman changes everything, don't you see?'

'The woman in the car might just be a woman in the car,' Hope pronounced.

Shaw shook his head. He'd never felt more certain in his life. 'The whole cat and mouse element of the killings, the way Kenny and Mark had never foreseen the danger until too late. Easier to trust a woman than another man. Don't you see, Wolf was enticed into a sex game by a killer?'

'You don't know that. Wolf is a player, you said. Even his girlfriend suspected he was cheating on her. It doesn't mean some random woman murdered him.'

There was nothing random about any of this, Shaw thought. 'You think the female passenger is a red herring?' Shaw felt irritation that he might be on the wrong track. 'So I'm back to Waterhouse, or rather someone offing people on his say-so. Maybe he hired a woman for the job.'

'A professional assassin?' Hope scoffed. 'They wouldn't allow themselves to be spotted. They don't leave mess behind. In some cases people are simply disappeared. No remains to find.'

Shaw was alarmed by Hope's casual admission of what

sounded like state-sponsored murder. Shaw pushed the thought firmly aside. This killer definitely wanted everyone to sit up and admire the handiwork, the subliminal message: *This is what you did to me and now you're going to pay.*

'I still reckon there's a personal element and Waterhouse is involved somewhere.' He simply needed to find out where he fitted. Anyone would think that Waterhouse had got religion if Shaw were to believe the picture Esther painted.

'Doesn't stack with what you told me about the nice little life Waterhouse carved out for himself,' Hope said. 'Why rock the boat? What would be his motivation?'

Shaw had said the same, he recalled. Every time he tried to forge a link, he was forced to bow to the evidence.

'Did Mickie Ashton have any siblings?' Hope asked.

Not according to Danny, Shaw remembered. 'No siblings, no parents.'

'Kids?'

Shaw swallowed and shook his head.

Hope fell silent.

'There's something else you should know,' Shaw said. 'Out of six of the old gang, four of us are dead: Mark, Kenny, Wolf and now someone else.'

'Obvs not you,' Hope pointed out with a gummy smile.

'It's unlikely to be Danny Hallam because I spoke to him moments before I found out. That leaves Carl.'

'Carl Snare?' Hope scoffed. 'That's impossible. The guy is a trained killer.'

'Even trained killers get caught out.'

Chapter Forty-Seven

The call had come through on Deeley's watch. The shout lines were suspicious death, male victim and a flat in Marshall Street. Short-staffed, Dillane had told her to get herself down to the crime scene.

'The coroner's been informed. I've already liaised with Dr Speight. If you look sharp, you and the SOCOs should arrive at roughly the same time.'

Deeley smiled while bridling inside. Dillane had made it obvious that he was disappointed with her apparent lack of progress in the nail-gun case and he'd done so under the malicious gaze of Angela Finch. With her cheeks aflame, Deeley had explained that the homeless had a natural antipathy to talking to those in authority, that they closed ranks.

'Excuses,' Dillane had said.

But Dillane had no idea about her evening visit to the lawyer and she was going to keep it that way. As far as DC Bailey was concerned, she could be relied on to stay quiet. Wouldn't look good for it to be known that she was interviewing a man solo, not after what happened before. Her only regret was the picture she'd clocked of Jon Shaw with a woman. They'd looked like a couple. Deeley felt a familiar tug of what most would describe as jealousy. She called it animal attraction.

A uniformed police officer stood outside the apartment, which had already been cordoned off. He logged Deeley's presence on a scene log.

'What's the story?' Deeley slipped on a white paper scene suit, hairnet, mask, gloves and overshoes.

The officer, a newbie by the look of him, consulted his notes. 'A cleaner, Marsha Willis, married, fifty-four years of age, found the victim. She identified him as Carl Snare, a forty-four-year-old male. According to Mrs Willis, he lived a quiet life and kept himself to himself.'

Deeley wished she could have a quid for every time she'd heard that one. It was the quiet ones you needed to watch. Deeley did her best to ignore the sudden tightness in her chest.

'Where is Mrs Willis?' Deeley asked.

'The Q.E. Being treated for shock,' he explained.

'OK, we'll need a statement. No sign of forced entry?'

'No.'

'Well done, PC . . .'

'Barnes,' he said. 'Lenny,' he added.

'Good work, Lenny.' Inside, she cringed. She had so few friends and colleagues who rated her, she found herself going over the top when trying to solicit respect. However she played it, she couldn't seem to gauge it right.

On entering the crime scene, Deeley thought the contrast between the setting of her last murder and this could not be more stark. Industrial minimalist chic here versus squalid clutter there.

Taking care to avoid the most obvious route between the doorway and victim, Deeley located Speight bending over the deceased. Standing next to her, Harvey, the crime-scene manager, poised and waiting to discuss forensic strategy. Deeley acknowledged her with a smile and nodded to a couple of SOCOs, including Nicole Draven, and an officer already designated to handle exhibits.

Dressed in a towelling robe that was rucked up to expose his genitals, the victim looked as if he were either preparing to shower or had recently bathed. He had short closely cut hair, no distinguishing features, other than the bullet wound that created a third eye in the middle of his forehead. Seemed he'd been killed at point-blank range.

'Unfortunately, one of the paramedics chucked a blanket over the body out of a misplaced duty to preserve his dignity. I've had a word,' Harvey said ominously.

Knowing Harvey there would be several words, Deeley thought. Anyone who screwed with her crime scene could expect a tongue-lashing. Perversely, she could be quite sympathetic if one of her SOCOs cocked up.

'Looks like we have the correct location.' Speight's nasal voice was a dull monotone. 'No evidence to suggest that the body was moved.'

'It's been alleged that the apartment belongs to the deceased. We'll check and confirm. Can you give me a ball-park time of when he was shot?' Deeley expected a vacuous, non-specific answer.

'Taking into account room temperature, dry interior

conditions, absence of clothing and build, I'd estimate he's been dead for two or three days,' Speight answered, to Deeley's immense surprise.

'Chimes with the airline tickets on his desk,' Harvey said. 'He should have flown to Dubai on Tuesday.'

'OK, we need to check his last movements. Do we know what he did for a living?'

Harvey shook her head.

'See if you can find anything that helps drill down the detail. The uniform says there was no sign of forced entry.'

'Correct,' Harvey said. 'It would appear the killer came to the door and the victim let him in.'

'Which suggests a prior relationship,' Draven chipped in.

'More importantly, the victim trusted his killer. You don't normally invite someone into your home when you're half dressed.' Deeley looked to Harvey. 'We need a ballistics team down here. I don't suppose the murder weapon's been found?'

'Unlikely, but we'll look.'

She didn't need to say that she wanted the place meticulously examined. She knew that they'd do a good job.

'You crack on. I need to have a word with DCI Dillane.'

Deeley stepped outside. Before she'd scrolled to her contact list, she heard a shout behind her. Hurrying back inside, she found Harvey crouched down on the floor next to a sofa.

'Oh my God, we need a firearms unit here,' she cried. 'There's a gun underneath.'

Chapter Forty-Eight

'If anything's happened to Snare, it will be sanitised,' Hope argued. 'The intelligence agencies don't like to admit to losing one of their own. Bad for street cred.'

'But there would be something in the press, surely?'

'Not unless the victim winds up in a sports bag. Anyway, you still don't know if it's happened, when it happened, and where.'

'That's a lot of variables.'

'I'm in the variables business. One thing you can be absolutely certain of, the intelligence agencies will be looking at targeted assassination and every possibility from foreign states to personal contacts.'

Which was good, Shaw thought. It would buy him time.

'And that means you,' Hope said darkly.

'And you.'

'Me?' Hope blew out through her cheeks. 'My tracks are well and truly covered. I'm a batty has-been, remember?'

Taken aback by Hope's flash of self-awareness, he wished he shared her confidence. 'I should never have dragged you into it. I'm sorry.'

'I'm not. What will you do?'

If Carl was dead, what could he do other than go to the police? He couldn't outrun the past forever and he'd come to the point at which facing the consequences was a better alternative to death. After his last conversation with Danny, Shaw no longer felt he could rely on him. This was the straightforward, sanitised version of what he believed, the alternative darker and more complex. His best and only bet was to spill his guts to Deeley. She wouldn't be sympathetic but she might be fair. He shared his thoughts with Hope.

'They'll arrest you.'

'I know.' The police could uncover enough circumstantial evidence to fill a vault. He made a mental note to get rid of the shovel from the farm.

'They'll charge you for everything.'

'I know a good lawyer.' He sounded flippant. He didn't feel it.

'I know what I'd do in the circumstances,' Hope said.

'What's that?'

'Go dark.' In response to Shaw's vacant expression, she added, 'Disappear.'

'I've hidden all my adult life. Look where that got me.'

'Well, you'd better hope that the Deeley woman is having a good day.'

Deeley darted back inside the crime scene and knelt down next to Harper. Swivelling her head, she could see the weapon staring straight back at her, grim and ugly.

'Fantastic.' Deeley knew the drill. The weapon needed to be made safe so any DNA or prints could be protected. 'I'll get firearms down here right away.' Chucking a gun under a sofa in flight was a reckless, amateur act. It spoke of a killer who'd made a bog-standard mistake. Probably a drugged-up youngster hell-bent on rich pickings. Thrilled at the prospect of an easy collar, she allowed herself a few seconds to enjoy it. This was her time to shine. This would set her back on the right path. All that crap back in Worcestershire could be glossed over and forgotten. Her colleagues would look her in the eye once more. Angel Finch would be forced to eat a huge portion of humble pie. Deeley would even hand her the bloody spoon.

Deeley was still on the phone when she heard PC Barnes raise his voice. 'You can't go in there, sir.'

At the threshold of the crime scene and beyond the police cordon, a tall, lean man stood erect. He had sharp grey eyes and even sharper cheeks that made his face look as if it were sculpted from stone. His gaze cut straight to Deeley who was now on her feet and barrelling towards him.

'Who the hell are you and which bit of *you can't go in there* did you not understand?'

The man's face flickered. Not quite a smile. The rest of his body didn't move a muscle. He was dressed in a lightweight jacket that probably cost more than the contents of Deeley's kitchen. He wore an open-neck shirt over designer jeans, and tan leather Chukka boots. His look was expensive, which went with the superior expression. She hated him on sight.

'You must be DI Deeley.' He looked her up and down in a way that was unnerving and vaguely humiliating. Never had Deeley wanted to rip off her forensic suit with such speed.

The hairnet and overshoes made her feel a right tit. 'I've already spoken to your boss, DCI Dillane.'

Done deal then, Deeley thought, livid. 'And you are?'

'Shall we talk somewhere more private?'

Deeley felt the collective heat of several pairs of eyes boring into her back. She glanced over her shoulder. Speight remarked that she had plenty of dead people waiting to be seen. Harvey stood mute, the rest like statues.

'Tell your team to stop what they're doing and vacate the crime scene,' the man hissed under his breath.

Her stiff. *Her* team. *Her* investigation. Who the hell was this guy?

'Pause everything,' Deeley stuttered.

'Shall we?' The man indicated that she follow him.

'This had better be good,' she said, ripping off her forensic suit.

The man walked a little way down the corridor to a window with a view over the city and out of earshot of PC Barnes. Deeley dug her hands into her pockets and joined him.

'Jeremy Langley-Jones, Counter-Terrorism.'

Fuck me. 'I see,' she said, although she didn't see very much at all. She longed to run back and yell at Harvey to spirit away the gun or, better still, slip it to the exhibits officer.

'We'll take the investigation from here,' Langley-Jones said smoothly.

'We've already begun collating evidence.'

'Which is very good of you, but we have our own people.' Deeley's rethink was fast and furious. Counter-Terrorism had no remit to investigate domestic criminal offences, but counter-terrorism officers often worked closely with the security services so it amounted to the same thing. Screw that. She decided to maintain resistance.

'And you have no formal involvement in my murder investigation.'

Langley-Jones's smile was thin. 'In matters of national security, you have no jurisdiction.'

Deeley wasn't at all sure about that. She stubbornly believed it was her role to keep MI5 in the loop, not the other way around, unless there was something unofficial going on. 'I've already ordered a firearms unit to attend,' she said bullishly.

'I'm sure it's simple enough to make a phone call to stand them down.'

Mutinous, Deeley didn't move. This was several kilometres outside her comfort zone and she had no idea how to respond. The sensible, rational approach would be to comply, without complaint or question. She didn't feel sensible or rational. This bloody stooge from the powers that be was tanking her chance to redeem herself.

'I'm not happy.'

'I can see.'

'It's a waste of my time.'

'Tedious and tiresome for you and for which I can only apologise. We should have arrived sooner.'

'We?'

Langley-Jones tipped his head in the direction of a door next to Snare's apartment. 'My team is already setting up.'

Deeley's eyes narrowed. 'Is Carl Snare a spook?' *If that's who he really was.*

The grey eyes hardened. His mouth stayed shut. Perhaps he found the term 'spook' pejorative.

'A lot of bother for someone on the margins,' Deeley relentlessly pressed.

'I couldn't possibly comment. I'm sure you understand.' He spoke soft and low, the implication that if she didn't, she was a moron and morons got punished. In essence, she could be demoted to directing traffic. *Wouldn't Angela Finch be thrilled?*

Deeley stood up to her full height. Her eyes locked onto his. 'Will I be kept informed?'

'I'm sure DCI Dillane will share any relevant information with your good self. No doubt you'll be mentioned in dispatches,' he said crisply.

Before Deeley could retort, he tipped his chin towards the occupants of the room. 'Now if you don't mind, I'd like you to ensure that everyone gets out. Pronto.'

Chapter Forty-Nine

Shaw had believed he'd be dead by now. He'd run through the permutations, from brakes failing, a hit and run in the street, to an open attack and blade in his gut. He hadn't considered poison, a favoured method of dispatch by mothers of their children. Which brought him straight back to the possibility that the person who had six reasons to kill was, against the odds, a woman.

As far as he knew, Mickie was straight – her pregnancy appeared to support it. But she could have been bisexual. Did the vengeful lover scenario fit?

It had been a week since Danny had smashed back into his life. It could only be a matter of time before Shaw's luck ran out. At any second, he expected a call from the cops connecting him to murder.

In crisis about whether or not to talk to Deeley, he took a few precautionary steps. Wearing gloves, he wrapped the shovel he'd used to unearth Fred, Kenny's dog, in a commonly used refuse bag. Slinging it into the boot of the rental car, he drove to Kingsditch and the recycling tip on Swindon Road.

Throwing the damning piece of evidence into the designated area, he felt like a killer disposing of body parts.

Back home, he called Jay Kelso, the lawyer now handling Aaron Waterhouse's affairs. According to the company website, Kelso Jenner and Forbes was a law firm offering a range of legal services, including a bespoke service for individuals with property portfolios. Kelso, its fifty-five-year-old senior partner, enjoyed cycling and running. Shaw studied the picture of a bald-headed man with a slim build who looked for all the world as though he'd won the lottery. His teeth were so white they looked false.

Shaw introduced himself as a lawyer. True, and yet in the past week, he'd effectively shed one of his skins, his real identity lurking several layers beneath. Not unlike the killer.

'Aaron Waterhouse is one of your clients,' he said.

'He is.' No hesitation, consternation or trepidation.

'I understand you've provided services for him for several years.'

'Correct. I'm not quite clear why you're asking.'

'A potential criminal matter connected to your predecessor.'

'Ah, I'm with you. You mean Dale Hook.'

Shaw wrote down the name. 'Have you any idea how I can find him?'

'Probably in prison. He was struck off for carrying out transactions involving thousands of pounds, for which he could not account. Insolvency deals were his speciality.'

'Cash in from mystery client, that type of thing.'

'Which often strangely stayed in his personal account.'

Shaw scratched his ear. If Hook had cheated Waterhouse, he'd be lying under several layers of concrete on the M6.

Kelso said, 'There is absolutely no suggestion that Mr Waterhouse acted in any way inappropriately or above the law, I might add.'

'Understood.'

'Someone said that Hook had become a *debt collector*.' Kelso's disapproving tone suggested something dark and sleazy. He might as well have said *rent boy*. 'I heard he had some rather unsavoury dealings with some unscrupulous members of the police.'

'Are you implying corruption?'

'Put it this way: he kept strange company.'

Lawyer to lawyer, Shaw thanked him and signed off. He wondered why Esther, among other omissions, had failed to mention Hook. He intended to find out why.

Esther wasn't in. He pushed a note under her door. Around lunchtime, he headed to the bar in which they'd shared a drink the day before. She wasn't there either. He decided to eat and return to her apartment afterwards.

Halfway through a plate of sausage and mash, Esther appeared. He saw her before she saw him. Tipping up on her toes, she scoped the room, her expression tight. He half stood and stuck his hand up. Her eyes found his. With a peremptory nod, she walked smartly to his table. Today, she wore a pair of black trousers and red heels. She looked different, less carefree.

'I hadn't expected to see you again so soon.' She sat down, a little distracted, he thought.

'Can I get you anything? G&T?'

'Coffee,' she said firmly. 'You stay there. Finish your meal. I'll get it.'

She sprung up and cut to the bar. Obviously a regular, she was served quickly. Shaw had lost interest in what he was eating, took a couple of mouthfuls and pushed the rest away.

Esther returned. In the space of minutes, she'd recovered her cool. 'So?' she said.

'Dale Hook was Aaron's lawyer. I need to find him.'

'Why?'

'To talk about Mickie Ashton.'

Her eyes never left his. Her face was a mask. 'What makes you think I can help?'

'You've always kept your ear close to the ground.'

At this she smiled. 'That was then, a lifetime ago.'

'Where was Hook's office?'

'I'm not sure he had one.'

'C'mon, think, Esther.'

She puffed out her cheeks. 'He worked from home mostly.'

'Where?'

'Hale.'

'But he's not there now?'

'I doubt it. Probably wound up in Shitsville.' Shaw recalled a number of places that could fit that bill, his old housing estate included. 'He got struck off for dodgy dealing.'

Corroborating Kelso's information. 'Did he ever cross up Aaron?'

Esther raised an eyebrow. *Are you serious?*

'Last I heard he'd gone into debt collection,' Shaw told her.

'Sounds about right.'

'So you've no idea where Hook lives these days?'

'Why don't you Google him, or something?'

'Not sure Hook is big on social media. When you've done time, you tend to keep a low profile.' Deeley flickered in and out of his mind. What was her reason for maintaining the social media equivalent of radio silence?

Another smile. Esther's eyes danced left and right.

'Are you expecting someone?'

'No.'

'You seem nervous.'

'Tired, that's all.' She muted a yawn. About to push it, the arrival of Esther's cappuccino derailed the opportunity. She picked up a spoon, dug into the frothy surface and lifted it to her mouth. A fleck of grated chocolate clung to her top lip. He leant forward slowly and brushed it away with his index finger. She didn't recoil.

Low, he said, 'Talk to me.'

She exhaled. Shaw could feel her breath warm against his face.

'This is about you, isn't it? It has nothing to do with Aaron.'

'What do you remember about those days, Essie?'

She didn't react to the endearment. 'A gang attacked Mickie Ashton and Danny Hallam stabbed her. That's what I remember.' Her look was stiletto-sharp. She knew of Shaw's involvement somehow. Was it conceivable that Danny had told her?

'What else?'

'Ugly rumours about Aaron.'

'Lies?'

'Yes.'

'Like?'

'Aaron sleeping with Mickie Ashton before she died.'

Shaw felt his head drum. A child at that point in Waterhouse's life was an encumbrance. Her murder would have suited his plans. 'Did you know she was pregnant?'

Esther's eyes creased at the edges. She burst out laughing.

'What's funny?'

'If Mickie Ashton was pregnant with his child, Aaron would have married her on the spot.'

He wanted kids, Shaw recalled. The scenario that seemed so right seconds ago disintegrated. Shaw had to admit that he'd personally witnessed Waterhouse as a contented family man, both physically and caught on camera if those photographs were anything to go by. Aaron's second chance had worked out a whole lot better than his own.

'Was there ever a suggestion that Mickie was bisexual?'

Esther gave a start. 'Whatever makes you think that?'

'Doesn't matter,' he said. 'Only trying to figure stuff out.'

'Figure what out? She's dead. Gone. Danny paid the price. Mickie would shag anything but I never heard she was into girls.'

Shaw nodded, acquiescent. He wasn't ruling it out until he knew otherwise. 'You said rumours. Plural.'

'The classic: Aaron gave the order to have her removed.'

'Did he?'

Colour fled across the tops of her cheeks. Her mouth creased in irritation. 'Why would Aaron bother with a two-bit junkie when he was raking in thousands?'

'To make an example of her and ensure that nobody else screwed him over?'

282

'Why take the risk? Invites all kinds of trouble.' And if he had, Aaron Waterhouse would be right up there on the shit list. Maybe he was, but that would mean seven feathers, not six. No, he had to accept that Waterhouse was in the clear.

'I've asked myself the same question,' he said mildly.

'Which means you're asking the wrong question to the wrong person.'

'Then what question should I ask and to whom?'

'Jon, you're the problem here. Why can't you let it go?'

'You sound like Aaron.'

'This is me talking, not my ex.' She took another sip of coffee, taking care to wipe her mouth afterwards with a tissue.

'Is that what you meant when you said that lies travel further than truth?'

'Did I say that?' She rolled her eyes theatrically.

'You did.'

'Then probably.'

'You didn't mean anything else by it?'

'Like what?'

Shaw shrugged. He could fence with her all day and all night but it wouldn't save his life and put a stop to the violence. It wouldn't nail a killer with an obsession. *Only him and Danny left ...*

'Aaron was a lot of things, but he would never hurt a woman. Not his style. Not in his nature.'

'I thought you said he hurt you.'

She held his gaze, vice-like. He saw steel and ruthlessness that only a woman intent on survival can engender. It's one of the things he'd admired about her. Now he feared it.

'Not like that. Never physically, never intentionally.'

'Why are you so loyal?'

'Because that's who I am.'

And yet Esther's loyalty had not extended to him, Shaw recalled. 'Did Danny mention Mickie when he visited?'

'Danny's moved on. I suggest you do the same.'

'Sounds like a warning.'

'Friendly advice.'

Shaw laughed lightly. 'For a moment there I thought you cared.'

She laughed with him. She didn't agree or disagree.

'Did Danny mention money?'

She frowned, not understanding.

'Did he ask for any?'

She shook her head. 'I got the impression he was flush.'

'Recently released from prison, it's unlikely.'

She gave a shrug. 'He said he had some deals in the pipeline.'

The drumming in Shaw's head increased. Danny was back to his old tricks. How else could he score a lucrative amount of cash? Having warned him of a killer on the loose, Danny had picked up right where he left off, which wasn't logical but it didn't take a massive leap in thinking to understand why he had shored himself up with easy money. The problem lay with the hard men who would necessarily be involved. An untethered Danny complicated things massively.

'Jon,' she murmured.

'Yeah?'

'Are you in trouble?'

'You could say.'

She didn't ask why or what. She shook her head and said, 'When people are in trouble, they often make the wrong decisions. Be careful, Jon.'

Chapter Fifty

Dale Hook worked for 'Pay-Back Services' in Greater Manchester. There was no difficulty in tracing him because 'Pay-Back' registered high on the list of debt collection agencies for the area and Hook's name cropped up on a list of case handlers. According to the blurb on the website, the legal system was a joke and 'Pay-Back' succeeded where others had failed. To be part of their team, it appeared brawn mattered more than brain. 'A vigorous approach is taken to debt collection,' it said next to the image of a man looking moody. Shaw pictured Hook as a twenty-stone heavy with fists like piledrivers. No doubt Hook's training as a lawyer stood him in good stead for getting around pesky legal niceties.

Shaw emailed Hook directly, stating his name and phone number. Under 'Best Time to Call' on the online form, he typed, *'Now, urgent.'* Regarding the 'Amount Owed' section, Shaw paused. What would be tempting? As an individual, Shaw thought a lower figure sounded credible. Another idea in mind, he settled on £17K.

Shaw waited in his car. From Chester to Manchester, he

could do the trip that afternoon. He only hoped that Hook was available.

Shaw's phone rang. After Hook introduced himself, Shaw asked straightaway for a meeting.

'First, why don't you tell me what the problem is, Mr Shaw?' Hook's vocal cords sounded as if they had been filed down with coarse-grade sandpaper.

'It's a delicate matter I'd prefer to discuss face to face.'

Shaw listened to a quantity of air snatched into lungs and puffed right back out. Hook could have been smoking, weighing him up, or thinking, *yeah, yeah, heard that one before.*

'Thing is,' Shaw said. 'I've cocked up and my firm don't know it yet. I really need to get the money back before they find out.'

'Got you,' Hook said. 'What line of business are you in, Mr Shaw?'

'The legal profession.'

'Aha.' Shaw surmised his answer had resonated. 'Got far to travel?'

'I can be with you in an hour.'

'No can do. Five o' clock best I can manage.'

'Great. Where?'

Hook gave him the address of a working men's club near Gorton. Shaw thanked him.

He'd got an audience. Whether or not Hook would play ball was an entirely different matter.

'Langley-Jones took the investigation from right under our noses. How can that happen?'

'Above my pay grade to find out,' Dillane said.

287

Deeley pinched her thumb and index finger together. 'We were that close.' She couldn't help sparking with frustration and anger.

Dillane regarded her with an expression that told her she was petulant, naive and unsophisticated. 'To what exactly?'

'The gun left at the scene was our best chance of nailing a killer.'

'Depends if it was used to perpetrate the crime.'

'The victim is shot and you reckon the weapon was irrelevant?'

'It could have belonged to Snare for all we know.'

Deeley bit her lip. In her rush for answers she hadn't been loose enough in her thinking. How could she have been so thick? 'But you have to . . .'

'Admit that there are other possibilities rather than one? You need to calm right down, Samantha. In matters such as these, ours is not to reason why.'

'But the gun—'

'Will be analysed and any relevant results forwarded. I have Mr Langley-Jones's word on that.'

Didn't Dillane realise that Langley-Jones was stringing him along with false promises and platitudes? Standard practice to give the impression that the police were in the loop when, in reality, they were being closed down. Not uncommon for counter-terrorism, in cahoots with the intelligence services, to be less than straight with those they regarded as lesser mortals. And Dillane made out that *she* was unsophisticated?

'What do I tell the team?'

'To forget all about it. We must ring the incident with a wall of silence until told otherwise.'

'That will be difficult.' Gossip was a popular pastime. She should know.

'See to it,' Dillane said crisply. 'Going forwards, any progress on the homeless man investigation?'

'I have a lead.' Forcing a smile, she explained the connection between Platt and a recently released lifer who happened to be an old mate. The 'mate' was Danny Hallam and Hallam had grown up with Platt. She wasn't bluffing when she'd spoken to Shaw in Cheltenham. 'Hallam was seen in the area days before Platt was murdered.'

'Then what are you waiting for?' Dillane blazed. 'Bring him in for questioning.'

Humiliated, Deeley bowed her head. Open-plan workspaces were good for communication, bad if you were receiving a dressing down. During the walk of shame back to her desk, everyone's eyes were averted, apart from Angel Finch's. Fixing Deeley with a look, Finch cupped a hand over her mouth and muttered something to a new DC sitting next to her. Intending to rile Deeley, Deeley was riled. She'd become accustomed to being shunned but she could not tolerate Dillane's open contempt. To hell with all of them. She stared right back at Finch, who had the temerity to smile.

Grabbing a packet of mints from her drawer, Deeley fled to the changing room and her locker. Using a combination code, she opened the door and reached inside for the emergency miniature vodka that kept her from losing the plot entirely. The smell of neat spirit promised the hope of instant gratification and confidence.

Shards of pain fled from the tips of her fingers up her arms. Warm liquid ran down her wrist. Cursing, she withdrew her hand and found the skin in shreds. Her eyes filled with tears as she pulled out a piece of glass embedded in her palm. Bastards, she thought. Someone had been inside and smashed her fix. Then she noticed a piece of paper, already stained. Sliding out the note, it said: *Blood on your hands.*

Chapter Fifty-One

A flat-roofed, slab-sided building, it was like an island surrounded by a sea of double yellow lines. With nowhere close to park, Shaw was forced into a street some distance away and arrived ten minutes late.

Brown and orange decor gave the interior a seventies look. Pink and white balloons hung from the ceiling. An old guy shuffled around a stage, setting up for what Shaw presumed was an evening of karaoke. Early drinkers comprised as many women as men. Most drank beer and lager. Lighting was brutal and, since the smoking ban, nobody smoked and yet Shaw fancied he could still smell nicotine in the fabric of the club.

Acutely out of place and knowing it, Shaw identified Hook because he sat solo. He was nursing a pint with yellow-stained fingers and had the face of a man who'd done five rounds with Tyson Fury. His eyes were slits, his nose and lips thick, and his skin the colour of a corn-fed chicken. Too big for his narrow shoulders and chest, his shirt strained over his gut. In short, he resembled a man not long for this world.

At Shaw's approach, Hook squinted and gestured with his chin.

'I've signed you in.' Hook spoke with a slight wheeze.

'Drink?' Shaw said.

'Pint. They know my poison.'

Shaw went to the bar and ordered two pints. 'Whatever he's having,' he said, glancing in Hook's direction.

'If you're a mate of Hookie's,' the bartender said, 'you're a mate of ours.' Shaw smiled stiffly. Dale Hook seemed the most unlikely local hero.

Shaw paid for the drinks, which were the cheapest he'd purchased since 2006, and sat down opposite Hook.

'Thanks for seeing me at short notice.'

Hook lifted the remains of his first pint to his lips, drained it, moved the glass aside and pulled his fresh beer into pole position. Smoothly choreographed, it had obviously been done hundreds of times before. He sat back, folded his arms and studied Shaw's face, gauging him.

'I'm going to be straight with you,' Shaw began, 'because I don't believe you're a man who likes having his time wasted.'

Hook's dead-eyed gaze intensified. He said nothing.

'Forget chasing the debt – I'm going to offer you easy money.'

Hook grimaced. 'Take it from me, there's no such thing.'

'I assure you there is.' The clarity of his words seemed to penetrate Hook's hard exterior.

'And what would you want in return?'

'Information.'

'Are you wearing a wire?'

'No.'

Hook half smiled, like a man who has heard it all before. It quickly vanished. 'This is a set-up.'

'I'm on the level.'

'Nothing straight about you, pal.'

Shaw had always thought that to rise above corruption, a lawyer needed to be incorruptible. Did the offer of hard cash rate as a crooked act, or was paying for information strictly transactional? He favoured the latter. Half his professional life was spent doing deals, negotiating trade-offs. Like it or not, and he mostly didn't, a finding of guilt was a flexible commodity.

'Look, I'm sorry I lied. It was the only way to meet you.'

'Then you've had a wasted journey.' Hook took a deep swallow of beer.

'I can put money straight into your account here and now.' The same figure he'd asked Hook to recover. This way, Hook would receive a great deal more than the usual percentage of the spoils of war.

'I regret to inform you that money means very little to me.' Hook made to get up.

'Then how about saving a life? Does that mean anything?'

A shadow passed behind Hook's eyes. Shaw wondered how long the man had got. Hook sat back down. 'Whose life are we talking about?'

'Mine.'

'I don't know you.'

'I think you do.'

Hook didn't confirm or deny. He sniffed the air as if scenting fresh blood.

'You used to work for Aaron Waterhouse,' Shaw said. Indirectly, he'd done the same.

'Long time ago.'

'Then you'll remember his association with Mickie Ashton.'

Hook stared and said, 'Ashton's been dead for twenty-five years. Got set upon by kids down by the river. The bloke who did her got caught and banged up. What's there to talk about?'

'Someone bears a grudge.'

Hook's eyes gleamed with insight. 'So that's why you're here.'

'I never laid a finger on her.'

'I only have your word for that.'

'It's the truth.'

Hook studied his face in the way a blind man reads Braille. The pouches under his eyes swelled. 'You saying someone's out to get you?'

'Three of us are already dead.' He recalled the four broken feathers in his sitting room. Until he'd received confirmation, he was in denial about Carl's death.

'My, my. Cops must be well and truly delighted.'

'They haven't yet made the connections.' Shaw gave Hook highly edited highlights. Hook sat, belly out, like an all-seeing, all-knowing Buddha. Shaw hoped he had the same level of enlightenment.

'Have you been questioned?' Hook said.

'By officers from Avon and Somerset and a DI from West Mids, which was my idea.' Shaw explained why he'd taken the risk. He wondered how long before investigating police from one constabulary or another would bear down on him.

'And now the sharks are circling the bleeding body?'

'In a manner of speaking,' Shaw replied.

'You know they'll throw the book at you. Nothing the police enjoy more than to unearth a dodgy lawyer.'

'I'm not like you.'

Hook raised an eyebrow, as if admiring Shaw's spirit, and tapped his nail-bitten fingers on the glass. 'Do these officers have names?'

Shaw shook his head. 'I don't want them leant on.'

Hook slow-blinked. 'Nothing could be further from my mind.'

Shaw didn't like the direction of travel. Best to get Hook back on track. Quick.

'Did you know Mickie?'

'I knew *of* her.'

'What did you know exactly?'

'Same as everyone else: a junkie who was not averse to putting it about a bit.'

'Tastefully put.'

'I tell it how it is.'

'What about her family?'

'I need to see the colour of your money first.'

'I thought you weren't interested.'

'I changed my mind.'

'A grand for starters.' Shaw whipped out his phone.

'Make it five.'

'Three,' Shaw insisted, 'And I need something tangible, not hearsay.'

Hook wiped his mouth with the back of his hand and, reaching into his wallet, produced a card with his bank details. 'Ever ready,' he said, with a throaty laugh, smacking it down on the table.

Shaw did the business, showed Hook the on-screen transaction, and swallowed some beer, which wasn't the worst he'd drunk. 'You were saying.'

'Ashton didn't have any family to speak of. Her mam, Dawn, lived over in Gorton.'

'Near here.'

'That's right.'

'What was she like?'

'A bit of a looker, by all accounts. Blue eyes, pale skin, dark hair. Irish blood somewhere along the line. She married a lorry driver. Evans, I think his name was.

'Anyway, the marriage didn't last after Mickie got offed. Dawn took bad. Drink.' Hook raised his glass for emphasis. Simultaneously, the stage burst into life as the old boy who'd set up launched into a Neil Diamond number.

'What happened to Evans?' Shaw was forced to raise his voice over the din.

'Went back to Brum.'

That Birmingham connection again, Shaw jinked inside. Evans's life had taken a significant turn for the worst with Mickie Ashton's murder. Yeah, he could imagine Evans as a bitter man, but was it enough for him to bear a grudge for a quarter of a century? And how old would he be now? Did he have the energy, the stamina, the sheer versatility to kill so many without detection? It seemed a long shot.

'How old was Evans?'

'Oooh, younger than Dawn. Looked it at any rate.'

Maybe not such a long shot after all.

'Mickie getting offed, well, it did for her mam,' Hook continued. 'They were that close, see? She had her when she were eighteen. Nowt but a kid herself. Loses her daughter and her old man fucks off – well, you can see how that would destroy a woman. Not long after, Dawn kicked the bucket.' Hook stared morosely into his pint, as if contemplating his own mortality.

'Did Waterhouse sleep with Ashton?'

Hook's head flicked up. 'How the fuck should I know?'

'You two were pretty tight, weren't you, from what I hear?'

'What you hear and what is are not one and the same.'

'So speaks the lawyer.'

This raised a genuine smile. 'Those were the days,' Hook said fondly.

'You miss it?'

Hook nodded with a sigh. 'I help people when I can.' He glanced around the bar. 'The boys and girls at Pay-Back are glad to have a tame legal beagle on board.'

'Tame?'

'Semi-tame,' Hook flashed a cheeky grin. 'Still got my contacts,' he said proudly.

'Coppers?'

Hook's answer was to raise his eyebrows and down the rest of his pint.

'Same again?' Shaw said.

Hook met his eye and smiled. If there was more money on offer, why not, his expression said.

The club was filling up and it took longer to get the drinks. Mercifully, 'Cracklin' Rosie' had finished.

When Shaw returned, a man was talking to Hook on the quiet. He sprang up at Shaw's approach.

'I'm sure we can come to some arrangement,' Hook said confidentially. The man patted Hook on the shoulder and nodded to Shaw before moving away.

'Undertaker,' Hook explained matter-of-factly. 'And I'm not talking in euphemisms.'

'I'm sorry.'

'I'm not. It's my liver and it's buggered.'

'Then what do you have to lose by telling me what you really know?'

He looked at Shaw, looked away and then back again.

'Are you being threatened?' Shaw asked.

'Me?' Hook snorted. 'You credit me with too much import-ance. I don't know where the bodies are buried, if that's what you're suggesting. That *is* a euphemism,' he added.

'I'm really struggling here. All I hear is that Mickie Ashton was a sinner who nobody loved and Waterhouse is a saint that's seen the light. There's a disconnect.'

Hook gave him a sharp look. 'You really want to know?'

'I do.'

'Christ, do you want me to spell it out?'

Blistering with frustration, Shaw assured Hook he did.

'Aaron Waterhouse was never the same after Mickie Ashton's death.'

'It scared the hell out of him?'

'I'll say. He was afraid of where it might lead.'

'Back to him, you mean. His drugs therefore his kill?'

'From a business perspective, it didn't look good. But it was more than that. It changed him. In here,' Hook said, pressing a fist to his chest. 'And I should know because I was there. He were that upset he visited her mother to pay his respects. Even offered financial assistance.' As an inducement to keep her mouth shut, Shaw wondered. 'Afterwards he did everything he could to get out of the business and go legit,' Hook continued. 'And before you go running away with the idea that Waterhouse is on some crusade of vengeance, you can forget it. Utter shite. Family became his everything.' Hook spoke with the forthrightness and sincerity of a dying man with nothing left to prove or lose.

So it was true, Shaw realised. Ashton's death had genuinely brought about a change for the better. How strange it should benefit a man who Shaw considered to be a double-dealing snake, while Shaw's friends were hunted down.

'I stayed with Aaron for another eight years until my own troubles caught up with me,' Hook said plainly. 'Aaron saw me right then too.'

Shaw thought about that. Esther had said her troubles with Waterhouse began around ten or so years ago, which would be around fifteen or sixteen years after Mickie's death. No point looking to Hook for information that might throw light on it. He was already under arrest and out of the picture by then.

'You said you had police contacts.'

'I don't think I actually *said* anything.'

Shaw had to admire Hook's ability to evade commitment. He'd have made a decent politician. 'At the time, what was the word on the wire?'

'Oh, plenty of coppers gunning for Waterhouse. They'd have liked nothing better than for his paws to be on the blade that killed her. I don't mind admitting that I had to pull a few strings to make sure he wasn't fitted up. Truth was, the evidence simply wasn't there. That mate of yours has a lot to answer for, I can tell you. He caused a world of trouble.'

Which explained why Waterhouse had failed to lift a finger for Danny.

Chapter Fifty-Two

Deeley had spent the afternoon at A&E. An outsider would believe that she was staring at a poster about how to spot the signs of a stroke, something she felt in imminent danger of. Her brain obsessed on one thing: that bitch Angel Finch. She was the only person who could have played such an evil prank. How she'd managed to gain access to her locker was a mystery.

Many officers used their four-digit collar codes for the combinations. As security-conscious as when accessing an ATM, she'd always avoided it. That also ruled out the possibility of her being observed. Whenever Finch was around, she immediately triggered Deeley's radar and Deeley would have noticed her loitering. Unless Finch had put someone else up to do it, like the new DC. Even then, Deeley would have spotted him. As to how it was done, the simplest conclusions were usually the most plausible. She must have forgotten to lock it.

Deeley thought about that. Desperate to impress with her professionalism, she'd failed spectacularly. She could count none of her colleagues as friends. She wasn't even sure anyone would have her back in a crisis – a truly terrible situation for a copper, potentially dangerous too. She'd been in a state for months, years if she included events leading to her transfer. In short, she was a woman under a great deal of pressure and stressed-out people made dumb mistakes.

And then there was the Shaw factor.

Her attraction to him had been instant, like a spark igniting. Seeing him again had only fanned those flames. Now she thought about him all the time and not necessarily in connection to the case. She imagined them together, intense and out of control. She reckoned that the only thing Shaw wore in bed was a woman and she wanted it to be her. Consumed, no wonder she'd been stupid enough to leave her locker open.

Eventually it was her turn to be seen and her wounds were painfully dressed and her palm stitched. She now had a bandage the size of a boxing glove on her right hand, enough to piss anyone off.

While waiting to pick up painkillers from the pharmacy, she set the wheels in motion for Danny Hallam to be picked up from the address approved by his supervising probation officer, which happened to be at his mother's house, only to discover that Hallam wasn't there. Worse was to come when she reported in to Dillane.

'Where the hell are you?'

She gave an explanation that sounded naff to her ears and quickly covered it by impressing upon Dillane that, despite the injury to her hand, which, she was careful to stress, had not been caused on police premises, she had not been a slacker in the investigation.

'Absconding in these circumstances is run of the mill,' she told Dillane on the phone.

'You're several steps behind the news,' Dillane informed her thinly. 'Hallam has been picked up by the men in suits.'

Had Dillane told her that she was to be promoted immediately, she could not have been more shocked. In effect, the intelligence agencies had lifted her only suspect for the brutal slaying of Mark Platt and, possibly, Carl Snare. She told Dillane this.

'Nothing we can do, DI Deeley, it's outside our remit.'

'But that's totally unorthodox. MI5 should have no formal involvement in the Snare investigation, only be kept informed as a courtesy.'

'I wasn't aware that you were an expert on the internal workings of the security services,' Dillane chucked back. And he hadn't asked about her hand. She felt murderous. And her fingers throbbed.

Back home, she downed two Nurofen, washing them down with a glass of red, and settled down for a night in with the TV. Forty years of age, washed up, chewed up and spat out; this was what she'd been reduced to. The obsession that had led to her downfall threatened to take hold once more. She could feel it burrowing its way into her bones. Jon Shaw had a girlfriend, she told herself. He also had a life that was as flaky as hers.

For Chrissakes, get a grip, she told herself sternly. This did *not* mean they were made for each other. But it might mean that she'd need his help.

Chapter Fifty-Three

Shaw had hoped to go to Deeley with a theory. All he had was a random piece of family history and a tenuous connection to the Midlands. Not enough to prevent the spotlight of suspicion from casting him out of the shadows. Before he called Deeley, he ran back through his conversation with Hook, particularly the part about Mickie Ashton's mother and the effect it had.

Loses her daughter and her old man fucks off – well, you can see how that would destroy a woman.

Shaw called Dale Hook who answered after two rings.

'You're back smartish,' he said. 'What can I do you for?'

Shaw asked a straight question. Hook gave a straight reply. Why Hook hadn't clarified this when he'd first spoken, Shaw had no idea. There was no note of deception in Hook's voice. Like the lawyer he'd been, he probably didn't feel it relevant when, to Shaw, it was a key piece of information.

Wired, Shaw phoned Deeley from the car. The number rang out several times and she appeared to fumble the phone as she answered. He heard *'Fuck it'* before he heard 'DI Deeley'.

'Jon Shaw here.'

'Jon,' she said gamely.

After the personal visit and grilling days ago, it wasn't the reception he'd expected. 'I'd like to talk face to face.'

'In relation to the Platt investigation?'

'Among other things.' Feeling suddenly claustrophobic, he reached up to undo a button on his shirt.

'Are you bringing a lawyer with you?'

'No.'

'Just you and me?'

It wasn't a date, for God's sake. 'I'd prefer it. Shall I come to Lloyd House?' Police HQ.

'No, I'm on a rest day. Do you know Northfield?'

A suburb of Birmingham, he registered. He told her he did.

She gave him the address of a café. 'Nine o' clock tomorrow morning.'

'What happened to your hand?'

'A tangle with a broken bottle.'

They were sitting in a café near the Northfield Shopping Centre. From the window he could see three lanes of traffic whizzing by.

Deeley sat opposite, nursing a mug of tea, her gaze intense. It felt oddly intimate, he thought. He glanced at her left hand. No wedding ring.

'So?' she said, once they were settled and he had a drink in front of him.

'You asked about my connection to Danny Hallam. I lied when I said I didn't know him.'

Her top lip tilted with interest. 'A lawyer that lies, well, well. And why would you do that?'

'Because I did something I regret a very long time ago.'

Deeley's skin tone lightened a shade. A fleeting shadow passed behind her eyes even though she attempted to cover it with a steady look. 'Are you going to tell me a story?'

Shaw's eyes found Deeley's. 'I'm going to tell you the truth.'

It was like a confession. He told her about the night of the attack on Mickie Ashton, assuring her that he was never personally involved. The horror did not diminish in the telling. Deeley looked like she'd been rabbit-punched.

'I didn't lay a hand on the victim,' he stressed, 'but I realise I should be convicted under the new joint enterprise law.'

Her cold and disappointed expression didn't disabuse him.

'If it's any consolation, I'm deeply ashamed.' He explained how his friends had gone their separate ways. He told her about Kenny and how he'd found Wolf. With each revelation, Deeley's jaw grew slacker, her eyes wider. She was like a kid watching a Disney movie for the very first time.

'Don't you see, we're being hunted?' he finished.

'Honestly, Jon, I don't know what to say. Kenny could have been killed for getting into a gambling debt. Your mate, Wolf, from your description, died during an autoerotic experiment that went wrong. Not that unusual, to be honest.'

'C'mon, you know how this looks.'

'It's *exactly* how it looks. As for Carl Snare—'

'What did you say?' So what he'd feared was true. It didn't soften the blow.

'He's dead – with a bullet to his head.'

Hope's words instantly came back to haunt him: *If any-thing's happened to Snare, it will be sanitised . . . The intelligence agencies don't like to admit to losing one of their own. Bad for street cred.*

The MO was very different, Shaw thought, and odds on, the authorities would presume his death was connected to Carl's line of work.

'Has anyone been arrested?'

Deeley nodded warily. 'Counter-Terrorism picked up a suspect.'

'Who?'

'Danny Hallam.'

Shaw gave a start. It raised a whole new terrifying prospect that had implications for the gun missing from the drawer in his study. What if Danny had shot Carl?

'Did the intelligence agencies find gunshot residue on Danny's clothing?'

'Well . . .'

'Did they find any evidence when they swabbed his hands, face and neck?'

'I can't tell you.'

'Can't or you don't know?'

She slumped a little in her seat. He got the picture. She'd been sidelined.

'There's only me and Danny left,' Shaw said quietly.

'Which means,' she said, rallying and holding his gaze, 'one of you is a killer.'

'No,' Shaw said feverishly. 'You're wrong.'

'Hallam was seen talking to Mark Platt. He was in the area at the time of the killing.'

'That's purely circumstantial.'

'And if I talk to officers in Devon and Cornwall, and Avon and Somerset, what will they tell me?'

She had him. He thought about Danny's impersonation. He thought about a borrowed and burnt-out car. He thought about Danny involved in slippery deals, no sign of change or a desire for a fresh start. None of it made him a killer, Shaw reminded himself, silently cursing that Danny brought out such conflicting emotions in him. One minute he was prepared to believe he was a murderer, the next that he was a victim. Exhaustion crept over him like a shroud.

Deep in thought, Deeley tapped the fingers of her good hand against the surface of the Formica table.

'Who's Danny's lawyer?' he asked.

'I told you. I'm not in the loop.'

And if she was, she wouldn't be sharing information with him because it would put her own position in jeopardy. 'Anything that could help would be greatly appreciated.' He understood he was asking the impossible. Where he went from here if she refused, he didn't know.

'You mean we help each other?' Deeley coughed, sat up straight, not quite meeting his eye.

Obviously, she wasn't comfortable with it, yet also resented being left out in the cold professionally. He needed to persuade her that making him an ally would improve her situation. 'We trade,' he said. 'I've been straight and honest with you and, should I uncover anything, you'll be the first to hear. Now it's your turn.' He waited, watching her eyes. She still didn't look keen.

'What I *can* tell you,' she said cautiously, 'is we found a firearm at the scene.'

'Did you identify it?' Most Midlands police officers were familiar with makes and models.

'Sig-Sauer.'

Shaw put his head in his hands. It would have Danny's prints on it. He told her about the weapon Danny had gifted him.

'You were given an illegal firearm from an ex-offender and you kept it at your house?' Deeley's voice rose in pitch.

'Wouldn't you if your friends were being murdered and you were next?'

'Where the hell did you keep it?'

'In a desk in my study; both drawer and room were locked.'

'Do you have a cleaner?'

'No.'

'A lover?' She arched an eyebrow.

'Not any more.'

The eyebrow stayed arched.

'You're asking who knew, right?' Shaw had asked the same question.

Deeley nodded.

'Danny.'

'Then you have your answer.'

'If Danny had used the gun to kill Carl, he would not have left it behind. Prints on a murder weapon were what did for him first time around. He wouldn't make that same mistake again.'

Deeley scrubbed at her forehead. Shaw read it as an

unconscious sign that she was trying to get her head around the mess of it all. She was not alone.

'Do you seriously think that if Danny Hallam were guilty, he'd abandon the one thing that connects him to the alleged crime?'

'What about you?'

'Me?'

'What about your prints?'

Shaw gave her a long level look. Was she implying what he thought she was implying? 'I didn't kill Carl.'

'That's not what I asked.'

Shaw shook his head. 'I was careful.'

She stared at him as if she was seeing him in a new and calculating light. To his surprise, she didn't appear fazed.

'Look, Danny had no reason to kill his mates. If he'd wanted to drop us in it, he could have done so twenty-five years ago. Danny's a hothead,' Shaw said in response to Deeley's obvious cynicism. 'He acts on instinct. This killer is a planner.'

'Why the hell are you so loyal?' Deeley stared at him as if she were looking down the barrel of a sniper rifle.

'Hard to explain.'

'You like him?'

'Not particularly.'

'Then what is it between you two?'

Shaw's heart swelled in his chest. Danny had been like a brother. Their childhoods spent wandering streets. They'd played football on dog shit-strewn playing fields. They'd gate-crashed any and every party, uninvited and often illegal. They'd nicked cars. Danny always drove, Shaw riding shotgun. Crushing the accelerator, Danny had held the power of life and death in his hands. He'd scared the crap out of Shaw, and yet he had felt so alive at a time when most of him was dead. Trust, a rare commodity, and yet Shaw had trusted Danny. Implicitly. One question remained: did he *still* trust him?

'He matters.'

Deeley pursed her lips. 'Isn't that contradictory?'

'Complicated. You may not like members of your family, but you don't give up on them.'

'And Danny is like family?'

'Yes,' he replied firmly. 'Even the crazies, the wild cards, the black sheep need to be taken care of. It's why I became a lawyer.'

Deeley fell silent. Shaw gave her the space to reflect. No point rushing her. When she finally spoke, it was a long time coming.

'In your opinion, Danny is being framed by the same person out for revenge.'

At last they were on the same page. 'Exactly.'

'Anyone in mind?'

Shaw nodded and explained.

Chapter Fifty-Four

'*If* I set aside your less than glorious role, there are obvious difficulties associated with any case that is twenty-five years old,' Deeley said. 'We're not looking for the murderer because he's already been caught and served his sentence. According to you, we *might* be looking for someone affected by what happened and yet you're telling me that possibilities are thin on the ground, apart from Dawn Ashton's ex-husband, who must be knocking on.'

'He isn't. Think about it, he's a lorry driver. He can go anywhere, any place, any time.'

'A lorry driver with impeccable skills.'

'You don't buy it?'

'I wouldn't give you fifty pence for it. It's not a strong enough personal connection.'

'Then there's only one other possibility – Mickie Ashton was pregnant. Airlifted to hospital, her child was delivered prematurely. Word on the wire was it didn't make it.'

'And?'

'A source tells me that the child survived and, without anyone to take care of it, was taken into care.'

'So said kid waits twenty-five years—'

'Coinciding with Danny's release,' Shaw butted in.

'To pick you off one by one.'

'Why not?'

'Because that kind of thing only occurs in films, plays and books.'

'Right,' he said.

'Don't look so crestfallen. Do we know the sex of the kid?'

'Check this out.' Shaw produced his phone and showed Deeley the grainy image of the hooded woman sitting next to Wolf at the petrol station.

Deeley stared at it and then looked him in the eye. 'How the hell did you get hold of this?'

'Does it matter?'

'If it isn't legal, yes it does.'

The air pulsed with tension. Little he said or did now would reduce it.

Deeley let out a long *setting aside and moving on* breath. 'Had Ashton given birth to a son, it would offer a more viable line of investigation.'

'Isn't that sexist?'

Deeley opened her mouth to retort, thought better of it.

'At least consider the possibility.'

'You really believe some woman is running around the country with a different MO for every day of the week?' Her eyes drilled into his. 'It's laughable.'

'I'm not sure I find it funny.'

They had reached stalemate and he, quite possibly, was about to enter an interview room.

Shaw put away the phone and asked, 'Are you going to arrest me?'

'For what?'

'I can think of a number of charges. Possession of an illegal firearm for one.'

'Only if you admit to it.'

'Are you asking me not to tell the truth?'

'I'm doing no such thing but, from where I'm sitting, Jon, the truth is a little thin.'

This had been a mistake and massive balls-ache, Shaw realised. His thoughts zoned in on Danny. He asked Deeley when he'd been picked up.

'Yesterday.'

Shaw worked it out. No way could the police detain for any length of time without the accused having access to a solicitor. Similar applied to the security services unless an urgent interview was required in extreme circumstances. He knew of one case where the accused had been detained for over nine hours. In his dealings with GCHQ, they'd pushed their luck with Hope too because she'd been an employee.

Shaw pictured Danny sitting for hours, alone, in a dank, brutally lit basement facility in a bid to 'soften him up' and where brave men cracked. Danny's 'Keep The Fuck Out' façade wouldn't work with people like them. He could well crumble in the face of an onslaught from the intelligence services. Without someone to empower and guide him, Danny was at risk of digging his own grave. He would fail to keep his mouth shut. He'd ramble and protest in the crudest terms. Answering one question would elicit others. Danny wouldn't realise that he was under no obligation to speak until he had

314

a lawyer by his side. And that person could not be him, Shaw realised. He thought about approaching Charles. Not an easy conversation. Maybe Julie Strong could be briefed. That way he could keep a tight rein on proceedings. The best outcome would be if the intelligence services failed to nail Danny and threw him back to the police. Either way, there was every chance that Danny was going back to prison. At least there he'd be protected. The alternative was far worse. The security services' main interest would be whether Danny was a terrorist or affiliated to a foreign power. If that were the case, all bets were off. He wouldn't be shipped out to a black site; he'd be shipped off the planet. And when a connection was made, and it would be, Shaw stood a high chance of being next in line. There were plenty who resented him getting Hope Castleman off the hook.

He drained his mug, about to leave. Simultaneously, their phones started to ring. Shaw reached for his first. At the sound of Danny's voice, he stood up and slipped outside, taking the call in the wind and the rain and on the pavement.

'Danny, where are you?'

'Cop shop in Birmingham.'

'Have you been arrested?'

'Arrested? I've been swabbed. I've had my clothing confiscated. My new trainers nicked. I've been peered at in every fucking orifice.'

'Is anyone listening?'

'Fuck no. I told them you were my brief. Pile of crap, but police think I'm good for Mark's murder. And that's not the worst of it,' Danny burst out. 'Did you know our Carl were a spy? I've spent the last sixteen hours being grilled by faceless pricks with the insane idea that I'm the northern equivalent of Osama bin Laden.'

'But the intelligence services passed you on?'

'Too fucking right, the fuckers.'

'Danny, I need you to calm down.'

'And I need you to get me out of here.'

'It can't be me.'

'What?' Danny gave a nervous laugh. 'It has to be you, Jon.'

'I'm not the right person. I'm too involved.'

'No, no, no.'

'I can find someone else. Somebody highly experienced, a specialist in these types of circumstances.'

'I want you, Jon, I'm begging you.' Danny didn't do pity or fear or despair, yet Shaw, registering all three, was briefly jettisoned back to another time and a similar plea. Then Danny had been cold, hungry, lost and scared.

Danny lowered his voice. 'Please, Jon.'

'OK, OK, I'll be right with you. In the meantime, behave and do not speak a word to anyone.'

Shaw disconnected, went back inside and found Deeley slipping on her jacket. 'I have to go,' she said, her expression inscrutable.

'Same here.'

Deeley trailed behind him to the door, which he held open for her. 'Rest day over?' he said as she breezed past. 'See you at Lloyd House,' he called over his shoulder.

Chapter Fifty-Five

Deeley's mind ran in double time as she picked up her car and drove towards the city centre. Dillane had called, delivered the good news about Hallam and, after discussion, given the go-ahead for the analysis of Snare's crime scene. After she'd revealed the fact that Platt and Snare were childhood friends, Dillane had also authorised for further tests to be carried out by forensic scientists in the Platt case. Dillane already knew about the friendship between Hallam and Platt, so asking and granting had not been a stretch.

If she believed Shaw, she was on a road to nowhere with Hallam. Shaw was right when he said that Hallam's association with Platt and Snare was purely circumstantial. She had no smoking gun, not even a gun with prints on it if Shaw was right. But she knew that Hallam had handled the Sig Sauer and so had Shaw. In theory, she should be able to put both men inside. In practice, she was the only person who could see the big picture and she knew that, if squeezed into a corner, Shaw would deny ever having the conversation. In this respect, the scales were evenly balanced. She'd taken a huge risk consorting with and leaking information to

Shaw. Found out, she'd be heading straight for a misconduct charge, which, on top of her previous history, could sink her. It's why she'd chosen a location where she was unknown. Looked like her reckless gamble had paid off.

So what did she, Detective Inspector Samantha Deeley, want out of it? She wanted a collar. She wanted a prize and she wanted a big win. More than this, she wanted respect. And Shaw with his monumental fuck-up had handed her the opportunity to achieve every one of her goals because now she had a chance to nail a multiple killer. Try as she might, she didn't think Danny Hallam was it.

Bubbling inside, she needed to keep Dillane sweet while working her own agenda. She'd go ahead with interviewing Hallam so she had something to show. Dillane knew nothing about the personal relationship between Hallam and Snare but, bearing in mind that Snare's murder was back in their court, she could study anything turned up by the SOCOs with a view to finding any evidence-based connection. She would also follow up the murders in the West Country. She reckoned she could pull it off without raising too much suspicion because it was almost a mantra that police were reluctant to connect cases. The fact that the MOs were diverse, which had seemed an obstacle, would be her greatest asset. Nobody would be thinking along multiple or serial killer lines and screwing with her investigation. Things were looking up.

Entering the building held no horrors and Deeley walked with a lightness she hadn't experienced in a very long time. She headed straight for SOCO HQ, as she liked to think of it. Unusually, everyone was milling around. Harvey looked up from monitoring the jobs coming in on-screen. 'Hiya,' she said. 'Slow morning.'

'Well, that's about to change,' Deeley announced.

'Thank God,' Nicole Draven chipped in. 'I've arrived to find it quieter than a crime scene. Another day like yesterday, I'll keel over with boredom.'

'What we need,' Harvey said, 'is a break in the weather.'

Kevin Sutton, one of the older SOCOs said, 'As soon as it turns hot and sunny, emotional temperatures rise and an upsurge in crime guaranteed.'

'Can't wait,' Harvey said, with a wink.

'Am I missing something?' Deeley said.

'She's on leave tomorrow,' Draven replied.

Deeley informed the team that forensics resulting from the Platt case were to be reviewed. Harvey's face fell. When she spoke she looked as tetchy as she sounded.

'Are you suggesting that evidence has been contaminated, or not collected according to correct procedure?'

'Not at all,' Deeley said soothingly. 'I'm sure you've done a brilliant job as usual.'

'Then why the re-run?'

'There's a new development in the investigation. I'm simply letting you know as a courtesy.'

'Has the Head of Scientific Services been informed?'

'Dillane's sorting it. Meanwhile we're back on with the murder case in the apartment.'

Harvey turned around, glanced at the screen. 'Rightio.' She stood up, stretched. She'd lost weight and looked like hell, Deeley noticed. A break would do her good.

Travelling to the main ops room, Deeley bowled straight

into Finch, who stared at Deeley's bandaged hand. She wasn't smiling but she wasn't hatchet-faced either. She looked smug, Deeley thought. Well, she was shortly going to out-smug her.

'Dillane wants to see you,' Finch said, already clip-clopping away. 'Rest area. Urgent.'

Deeley glanced at her watch. Shaw would be with his client for a while yet. Yes, she had time. She stood up straight, feeling a swell of confidence she hadn't experienced in years. A cliché, but she was like a different woman, a similar sensation to having a new man in her life, which in a weird kind of way she did.

The room was empty apart from one officer making a mug of tea, and Dillane, who sat hived off in an alcove in front of a feature wall painted a soothing grey. There was nothing soothing about his demeanour. He pecked furiously at a laptop and glanced up coldly as she approached.

Dillane glanced across to the tea-maker. 'You going to be long?'

'No, sir. Just off now, sir.'

'Take a seat,' Dillane told Deeley. 'We have a problem.'

Deeley didn't like the sound of that and dutifully sat down. Oh God, she thought, she'd been sussed. Someone must have seen her talking to Shaw.

'This has come to my attention in the past five minutes.' Dillane turned his laptop around and pointed at the screen to a newspaper article with a national. Deeley hunched over and felt the contents of her stomach tunnel up to the back of her throat. Stupefied, unable to absorb it, she saw the words in snatches, like watching a foreign film with subtitles.

Underneath *'Code of Silence'*, *officer transferred* . . . *failure to act* . . . *death of woman* . . . *affair* . . . *coroner's verdict* . . . *suicide*.

What had been a private low-level investigation, fuelled by innuendo and rumour and, inescapably, shared between forces during background checks, had just gone public. The only reason she hadn't faced a disciplinary hearing at the time was due to a cock-up and an inability to prove a solid case against her. But truth had a habit of exploding when least expected. She felt as if a grenade had been lobbed, the pin already pulled, blowing her to a million pieces.

Deeley closed her eyes to prevent the tears pooling at the corners of her eyes from surging down her cheeks. When she opened them, she found Dillane staring at her, not with anger but with pity. She understood then that she was sunk.

'Unfortunate timing,' he said.

'Why now?'

'A relative of the victim.'

'It's not an anniversary.' She counted those.

'It would have been Beth Elton's birthday today.'

Deeley felt her heart contract. Her lips drew apart to speak but, temporarily confounded, snapped shut.

'I see your hand's still heavily bandaged,' Dillane said.

She nodded blindly.

'Then we will use that as an excuse for you to go on leave.'

'But—'

'It would be for the best until things calm down, wouldn't you agree?'

No, sir, it wouldn't and I don't agree, she wanted to say. One terrible mistake and she was paying over and over again, like her life was on a loop. When would it stop? Would she ever be able to find a way back? Was she forever condemned? She thought of Shaw. Hours ago she would have believed that their shared misfortune welded them together. Now she thought them both sad losers, destined never to succeed.

'I have an interview to conduct,' she said stiffly.

'Ah yes – Hallam? I was rather thinking DI Finch could take over.'

'But, sir, I—'

'Has new evidence come to light?'

'Nothing admissible.'

'Then make it quick and then get Finch up to speed.'

Shaw had lost count of the many times he'd advised clients in tight situations. The basics were always the same: Don't change your statement. Don't lie. Unlike what most are led to believe, 'No comment' is a lousy idea. Straight silence is worse. You might as well say 'Come and get me.'

Danny enveloped Shaw in a man hug. He smelt of sweat and fear and vulnerability. An image of an earlier time skittered through Shaw's mind. Him comforting thirteen-year-old Danny after his mam's latest bloke had beaten him senseless.

In a matter of days Danny had bulked up. His face was fuller, his neck thicker. He viewed Shaw with bloodshot eyes. Shaw asked him about the bruise above his left eyebrow and his split lip.

'Bastard spooks beat the shit out of me when I resisted arrest.'

'How many?'

'Two of them.'

'Did you get any names?'

'Did I heck.'

'Didn't you realise that you were under no obligation to speak to them, especially without a solicitor?'

Danny shook his head and ground his jaw. His body was as rigid as a clenched fist.

'Where were you picked up?'

'Me mam's.'

'Good.' And lucky; at least Danny couldn't be done for failing to be at his designated address.

'So what happened next?'

'I got bundled into the back of a van with blacked-out windows and driven to Christ knows where,' Danny scowled. 'Proper cloak and dagger.'

'Were you restrained?'

'I'll say. Kept me on my own for hours and then some bloke wanders in, offers me a cigarette and a cup of coffee and asks me a load of questions about Carl. Anyone with half a brain could work out I knew fuck all. But on and on he droned.'

Shaw visualised the scene. Once Danny engaged, and he would, the questions would escalate. The security services' entire reason for being was to gather information. He imagined them poring over every word coming from Danny's loose mouth.

'Why pick on you specifically? They must have had their reasons.'

'A bar bill for a hotel in Birmingham was found at Carl's place. When they checked CCTV, they spotted me.'

'You were meeting Carl?'

'Nope.'

'C'mon, Danny. The two of you in the same hotel is more than coincidence.'

'He approached me, honest to God. I were that gob-smacked.'

'When was this?'

Danny told him. The same day he'd turned up at Carl's apartment. He remembered Carl's urgent meeting. He hadn't realised that Carl was seeing Danny. Carl must have tracked Danny to the hotel. He certainly had the resources and ability to do so.

'What did he want with you?'

'Same as everyone wants with me. Be good, Danny,' he said, adopting a faux falsetto. 'Go on the straight and narrow, Danny. Keep your nose clean, Danny.' He stared at Shaw reproachfully.

Shaw saw how it rolled from the perspective of law enforcement. Danny had form. Danny knew the deceased. And it could be argued that Danny had broken the conditions of his release. Wonderful.

'And what were you doing in a Birmingham hotel?'

Danny dropped his gaze and took an avid interest in a coffee ring on the table. 'A side hustle.' At Shaw's sharp intake of breath, he looked up. 'It was only a small quantity of weed. A man's gotta eat.'

'I'm sure that will play brilliantly with the police when you're questioned,' Shaw said with heavy sarcasm. 'Did your interrogators mention a firearm?'

'Mention? They never shut up about it.' Which explained why Danny had been hung onto for so long, Shaw realised. Technically, analysis could be done in a day if fast-tracked.

The weapon would be subject to chemical treatment, any marks photographed and swabbed for DNA. If a connection was found to other crimes, the firearm would be sent for further examination and test-fired so comparison of striation marks could be compared to bullets from other scenes. Shaw asked Danny about his handling of the weapon.

'What do you take me for? I wiped it clean.' Danny's face split into a wide grin. 'Maybe they'll be knocking on your door.'

The thought had crossed Shaw's mind. He wondered about Deeley. He bet she was pacing up and down outside, champing to get inside. He needed to get to her first.

Danny tipped up on his chair. 'You never answered my question on the phone about Carl.'

'I knew he was an intelligence officer.'

'You spoke to him?'

'I did.'

'You never said.'

'Neither did you and it wasn't relevant.'

'Says who?'

'It wouldn't have materially changed anything,' Shaw said.

Light-thinking and nimble, Danny said, 'You've found something, haven't you?'

'Maybe.'

'And?'

'First, tell me why you visited Esther.'

Danny glanced at the wall. Shaw waited. 'It was rumoured that once upon a time, Waterhouse carried a torch for Dawn Ashton.'

'Dawn?' Shaw said in surprise.

'Mickie's mam. Anyway, she gave Waterhouse the push.'

'That was bold. When?'

'Pre-Esther and pre-Gail.'

Shaw thought about that. According to Dale Hook, Waterhouse had offered Dawn Ashton financial assistance after Mickie's death.

'It would explain why he threw me out of his house. Fuck, was he angry.'

Not how Aaron had described the meeting. 'What did Esther say?'

'She denied it.'

'Think she's telling the truth?'

'Deffo.'

'Why's that?'

'Dawn Ashton was too old for the likes of Aaron Waterhouse.'

Shaw felt his eyebrows shoot up to his hairline.

'Duh, I'm saying Aaron liked his women young, not frigging kids. You only have to look at Esther and Gail. Ask Esther about his little fling – that's what did for them.'

Yet Esther hadn't mentioned a word.

'So what did *you* find out?' Danny said.

Shaw told Danny about Mickie Ashton's child.

'Well I never,' Danny said, the fact he didn't swear a measure of his genuine shock. 'Reckon she's good for it?'

Not according to sharp-thinking Deeley. 'It's the only lead I have. First, we need to get you out of here.'

'Thank fuck for that. Thought you'd forgotten.'

Shaw gave him a dry look. 'The fact the security services released you goes in your favour with regard to Carl. As for

Mark, the police have circumstantial evidence. Enough for arrest but not enough to charge.'

'They'll cook something up.'

'No, they won't.'

Danny planted both his elbows on the table. 'What aren't you telling me?'

'The police officer about to question you – she knows about the gang.'

Danny growled. 'Not going funny on us, are you, Jon?'

'She's on our side.' A stretch, but it was important that Danny believed it. 'She's aware of what's happening.'

'Are you out of your tiny mind?' Danny's fists balled, knuckles white.

'So we keep it cool,' Shaw said through pursed lips. 'We don't get rattled. We answer every question honestly and calmly. I *will* get you out of here.'

Chapter Fifty-Six

'For the hundredth time, I saw Mark because he's a mate.'

'Same reason you saw Carl Snare?'

'Are you deaf, or what? I already told you Carl bumped into me.'

'Do you own a nail gun?'

DC Bailey had asked the question, the woman who'd sat in the car while Deeley spoke to him at his house. They'd been going for the past hour, Deeley strangely disengaged, Shaw thought, as if she wasn't really with it.

'Oh sure, I carry one with me at all times. Dead 'andy.'

Shaw rested his hand lightly on Danny's arm, a gesture of restraint. Sensing a minor victory, Bailey looked pleased. Deeley didn't display any emotion. It was a strange sight. Shaw had expected a robust interview if only for Deeley to show him who was boss. She worked and reworked the facts, not to unbalance Danny but as if she couldn't understand them and needed to remind herself. She seemed listless, off her game, deflated somehow, unsure and lacking in confidence. He only wished that Danny could respond with better grace. Interviews like these were very much an orchestral piece. Tempo varied according to which party took the lead. Shaw tried not to wince at Bailey's shrill line of questioning, the discordant harmony made deafening by too much volume from the wind instrument sitting next to him.

Shaw intervened, not for Danny's sake but for Deeley's. 'The past twenty-four hours have been an ordeal for my client who is understandably frustrated. As we've already covered all the bases and your only evidence rests on Mr Hallam who was, once, a friend of the deceased, I see no further reason to continue this discussion.'

'To be a friend of one dead man is unfortunate,' DC Bailey jumped in. 'To be a friend of another who died a week later is frankly worrying.'

Danny started forward. Everyone jumped, including Shaw. Bailey ducked and Deeley went the colour of cottage cheese. 'Where's your proof?' Danny demanded.

In the absence of a reply, Shaw stood up. 'I think we're done. Get in touch if you have any further questions and my client will be only too happy to oblige.'

Shaw looked at Danny, who stood. They all clattered out. Clear of the interview room, he told Danny to go and wait for him at the entrance. 'Could I have a word?' he asked Deeley.

Expressionless, she nodded.

'Are you all right?'

'You need to muzzle your client.'

'Noted. He was, however, speaking the truth.'

'I wish I could have a tenner for every time I hear that one.'

'Do you believe *me*?'

'It doesn't matter whether I do or don't.' She turned on her heel and left Shaw, mystified, to head for the exit.

He found Danny underneath a growling leaden sky, smoking a cigarette. 'Thought you said she was on our side.'

'She is. She cut you an enormous amount of slack.'

'I could have decked that other copper,' he muttered.

'Thank God you didn't.'

'I enjoyed the way you stood up to her at the end.'

Shaw ground his jaw. 'My car's that way.' Deeley bothered him and he wondered if he'd blown it with her. 'I'll give you a lift to New Street.'

'I don't want to go to the station.'

'Yes, you do. You're staying at your mam's until this gets sorted. You will not leave, break the conditions of your licence, or get yourself involved in anything dodgy.'

'But . . .'

Shaw stopped and faced Danny. 'For Chrissakes.'

Danny clasped the back of his neck with both hands. 'OK, OK.'

'Any breaking news, I'll let you know, and for fuck's sake, look after yourself.'

Anxiety tugged at the corner of Danny's mouth. They were both thinking the same thing. Nowhere was safe. The killer had taken their pals out of the game. Maybe, just maybe, Shaw had got through Danny's thick skull, although he wouldn't take a bet on it. 'I'll buy your ticket,' Shaw said more calmly.

'Ta,' Danny said. There was a pause. 'Jon, are we good?'

Shaw looked into Danny's tired eyes. The man he wanted

to throttle was also the man he wanted to throw his arms around and hug. 'Yes, Danny, we're good.'

'What are you going to do?'

Before he could answer, his mobile rang.

'Shaw,' he said. The line crackled, or so he thought, before realising that it was the person on the other end. Dale Hook sounded a lot sicker than when he'd met him in person.

'I can't talk for long,' Dale Hook wheezed. 'Got an address for you. Joel Evans, Dawn's ex. He might be able to give you some info on Mickie Ashton's kid.'

Shaw listened and memorised. 'Why are you helping me, Dale?'

Hook gave a wheezy chuckle. 'I'm sentimental.'

'Really?'

'Lawyers don't like me generally. They treat me like I'm scum. Let the side down and all that rubbish. Not you. You treated me with respect. I suppose I wanted to prove I'm a man of honour and . . .' He broke off, convulsed by a coughing fit. Shaw ignored Danny's curious expression and waited for Hook to recover. 'I want to see how the story ends.' His voice was thick with phlegm and the distillation of hundreds of cigarettes smoked over a lifetime. 'If you don't wind up in a shallow grave, you'll let me know?'

'I will.'

After Shaw finished the call, Danny said, 'Who was that?'

'Someone with a lead.'

'Be careful.'

'Always.'

Danny grabbed his arm, looked deep into his eyes. 'You promise.'

'I swear.'

Still Danny clung on, the air fizzing with tension and regret and disappointment.

'Jon?'

'Yes, Danny.'

'In my story you're my friend and the fucker who tried to kill me. Who am I in yours?'

This was it, Shaw thought, the moment he knew one day would come. Time to tell the truth.

'Home isn't a place, Danny. It's a person. And that person, for good or ill, is you.'

Chapter Fifty-Seven

New Street Station: full tilt, full volume, same concessions and brands and eateries as in a hundred other stations. Same crush of people.

Shaw bought Danny a single ticket to Manchester Piccadilly and walked with him to the barriers.

'You take care of yourself.' He clamped an arm awkwardly around Danny's shoulder.

'You too, mate.'

'You'll be all right?' He thought Danny looked absolutely beat.

'Sound.'

'You'd better go then.'

Danny nodded, stayed put.

'Go on then.'

'Jon?'

'Yeah?'

'Watch your back.'

Shaw gave him a playful shove. 'Go.'

Shaw watched as Danny loped through and towards the

escalator. Abruptly, he stopped, turned back, his face split into a grin, and waved.

Shaw waved back. He hoped it wasn't for the last time.

Deeley drove home and went to bed. Pulling the duvet over her head, she wanted nothing more than to sleep the day away, to forget the past and obliterate the present.

She was not the first police officer to sleep with someone she shouldn't. Officers engaging in sexual relationships with other officers, married or not, was almost a cliché. Fodder for gossip around the water cooler. Nobody got disciplined or fired. Divorce was rife to the point of banality; so much so that in every crime novel she'd ever read, the lead detective was either a lush or a divorcee, sometimes both. She ticked each box. Working in tandem in a pressurised environment, it wasn't exactly surprising. But she hadn't done the usual. She'd done something worse.

She turned over, caught her hand and let out a yell. In retaliation, she gave her pillow a bashing.

It all began with a missing teenager and finished with a suicide.

Holly Carlotta was the girl's name, her parents of Italian descent. After Holly was dragged from the River Severn, a post-mortem revealed that she had not drowned but had been strangled.

During the course of the investigation, there was a call from a witness who believed he'd seen the seventeen-year-old crying in a park hours before she vanished. Piecing together a timeline and tracing the last people to see Holly alive, Deeley had visited the man, an IT consultant, in his home.

She remembered Gareth Elton as if it were yesterday. Gareth wasn't her usual type, meaning he was a nice man rather than a bad and exciting man. A shade taller than her, he was built like a rugby player, solid, dependable – oh, the irony – and had a smile that could light up the dark. He was also married. And she knew it. And so was she.

Too hot, Deeley threw off the covers. Things hadn't been right with her husband, Ross, for a while. She wasn't making excuses. She'd long ago stopped blaming him or circumstance. According to her divorce papers, she was the guilty party and, 'fair cop', accepted it. She had acted on instant mutual attraction. She had behaved badly. If only it had stopped there.

When Gareth's wife, Beth, found out, she called Deeley, told her to back off. Deeley denied the affair. The next call, there was a lot of swearing and cursing. As the phone calls stepped up, Deeley calmly suggested that the Eltons needed to sort themselves out as a couple. She didn't mean a word of it. Predictably, Beth contacted Ross. The weekend he moved out, Gareth moved in. They were in love. They were meant for each other. But lust lasts only so long.

Several months later, Beth turned up at Deeley's door drunk and took a swing at her, blacking her eye. Gareth took his wife home. Deeley feared that he would not return. Men so rarely left their wives for mistresses and, like she said, he was a decent man. She waited that night, going to work the next day, coming home. Repeat. Her phone calls went to voicemail until the line was disconnected. Needy as hell, in desperation, she showed up at his place of work. She went to his house. She pleaded. She cajoled. She begged him in the same way Beth had done. Only she grovelled too. He was cold. He didn't want to know. He was staying with his wife. He threatened to end Deeley's career. He reported her for harassment and, at first, was disbelieved. After that, he was told to change his number, avoid social media, advised to move. Publicly, others had covered for her grave errors of judgement. Privately, she had been ostracised, and rightly so. Deeley could not account for her blinding obsession other than she knew she had a screw loose when it came to the opposite sex, and the entire works fell apart when it came to Gareth. But she had tried to make up for it since. She had really tried.

Deeley scrunched her eyes up tight in a doomed attempt to squeeze the memory of what happened next out of her mind.

When, out of the clear blue, Beth killed herself by downing weed killer, Deeley's world, as she knew it, ended.

A roofer was convicted for the murder of Holly Carlotta. Deeley was blamed for smashing up two marriages, hers and the Elton's. She was also held responsible for an innocent woman's suicide.

It was like being back home.

Towering post-war blocks of flats, interspersed with patches of council-owned green, competed with pylons. One of the poorest parts of the city, the view from the top would be a sprawl of metal shutters and brick, graffiti and alleys. Below, and overshadowed, rows of terraced seventies-style houses, entrances jutting out at right angles, satellite dishes and aerials clinging precariously. Every car and van was old, mostly diesel, all that was affordable. And there was the hallmark underpass. That piss-filled, graffiti-plastered corridor in which you walked at night at your peril.

Joel Evans lived on the ninth floor of a block next to a row of shops and units that looked as if they'd been empty for some time. Nearby, a gaggle of lads hung out, swearing, drinking and smoking. One had a kid's bike, nicked maybe from a younger brother. He had sharp eyes, a pinched face and swagger, and reminded Shaw of a young Danny – he of the big mouth and attitude. Shaw should have felt threatened, but he didn't. He'd considered himself to be a man who had journeyed a long way from his past. He'd been proud of his achievement. Now he perceived it for what it was: an illusion.

Nobody stopped him as he walked by because they saw right through him. They recognised one of their own, that below the expensive clothes and clean-cut lawyerly, upstanding image, underneath the skin he was feral.

The lift was broken. From above, Shaw heard a mother hurling profanities at a crying child. Up two flights of steps, he met them. Both had frightened, vulnerable eyes. He doubted either was living the dream. That was the preserve of the privileged and the rich, the highly educated and the lucky.

The door to the address that Dale Hook gave him was freshly painted lime green. Shaw knocked and stood back. A man in his fifties answered. He was slim and wiry, looked strong, Shaw thought, with hair cut super short. He wore glasses and chewed gum. He said, 'All right?' with an upward Midlands inflexion.

'Are you Joel Evans?'

'Yeah.' More chewing.

Hoping to God that Evans would not connect him to the same Jon Shaw who'd hung out with Danny Hallam, Shaw introduced himself.

'A lawyer?' Evans's clean features crumpled. He momentarily stopped chewing. 'This is about Danny Hallam, isn't it? I hear he's out. Don't tell me you've found new compelling evidence that makes him innocent?'

'No.'

'He's killed again?'

Shaw shook his head.

'Then what?'

Shaw looked beyond Evans. 'Could I come in?'

Evans took a moment, sniffed and opened the door wide. 'Take off your shoes,' he said.

Shaw did as asked and followed Evans, who moved with lightning gait.

Cream painted walls, laminate floor and minimalist decor made the living room seem big. Shelves built into a recess next to a window housed books. Shaw glanced at the titles. Among interior design and gardening were action adventure and true crime. On the window ledge, houseplants, none that Shaw could name, and cacti in a variety of pots and colour. It was the very picture of ordered and sanitised living.

Evans followed Shaw's gaze. 'My little beauties,' he said proudly. 'Are you much of a gardener?'

'Can't say I am.'

'I love my plants. Used to be a lorry driver but I gave that up to work in a garden centre. Clean air and healthy living, that's me. Can't beat it.'

Shaw salted the information away as something to check later.

'I'd like to talk to you about your stepdaughter, Mickie Ashton.'

'What's there to say? She's dead.' Evans spoke without sentiment. A man who had moved on, he'd not only started a new episode but a new series.

'I know and I'm sorry to drag up the past.' Shaw felt on decidedly shaky terrain. He was hoping for a strong reaction and there was none. He'd made a mistake with Joel Evans. To take the man back to that appalling time was cruel. Perhaps he should walk away now.

'I'm over it,' Evans said, bullish. 'Got to, haven't you? No point sitting around moping. Life goes on. Me and the missus had split up anyway before she did herself in.'

'She killed herself?' This was not what Dale Hook had said.

'With the drink.' Evans continued to chew. Light glinted off the lenses of his spectacles. 'Might as well have taken a load of pills and be done with it instead of dragging it out and leaving the rest of us to pick up the pieces.'

Shaw shifted uncomfortably. The tone was ugly and resentful and accusing. Shaw realised that Evans would have been in his mid to late twenties at the time, younger than Dawn and out of his depth.

'So what's this really all about?' Evans said.

'As you're aware, Mr Hallam has served his time.'

'Not long enough.'

'Unfortunately, I don't make up the sentencing guidelines. I'll come straight to the point: Mr Hallam's life is in danger.'

'No surprises there, the sort of company that man keeps.'

Including his, Shaw thought grimly. 'We think it's connected to someone who bears a grudge.'

'Never,' Evans said with a loose grin. 'Wait a minute. You think I'm some kind of threat to Hallam? Jesus.' Evans took off his glasses and tipped back his head. He laughed so long and loud the thin walls shook. Unnerved, Shaw mentally estimated the distance between Evans and the front door.

The laughter stopped as if someone had switched it off. Evans wiped his eyes with a tissue and put his glasses back on. 'Sorry about that,' he said. 'Caught my funny bone.'

Shaw pushed a smile. *No problem.*

'Look,' Evans said. 'Wasn't my fault.'

'What wasn't?'

'The kid. Mickie's child. Sickly little thing. In hospital for months, it was. Touch and go for ages. Dawn wanted to take it in but I put my foot down. Dawn wasn't fit to look after a gerbil. Well into the bottle by then. I told her the social would look after it, no worries.'

Professionally, Shaw had come across those who'd been in the care system. For every one who made it, there were others whose lives were forever blighted.

'God, the rows we had,' Evans said with feeling. 'Mickie was a pain in the butt when she was alive; her kid was a pain after her death.' Evans blew out between his lips. 'That kid did for us in the end. Sounds harsh but it would have done us all a favour if it had died.'

Shaw felt the heat of a familiar emotion: fury. He tethered it, arranged his face into a picture of neutrality. 'The child, was it a girl or a boy?'

'Girl. Jane, her name was.'

'Did she keep her mother's surname?'

Evans puffed his cheeks out and ran his fingers through his thinning hair. 'Dunno.'

'Do you know who the father is?'

'Could have been anyone's the times that girl spread her legs.'

Shaw tamped down a desire to push his fist into Joel Evans's face. When Dale Hook had said much the same, it was without rancour. Anything that came out of Joel Evans's mouth had a nasty, unpleasant tang.

'And Jane. Where is she now?'

'How should I know? I told her what I'm about to tell you—'

'Hold up. You've seen her?'

'Not recently. Must have been nine or ten years ago. I gave it to her straight,' Evans droned on. 'I said I was a young man with a life ahead of me. What would I want with someone else's kid?'

Dizzy with the unfairness, cruelty and sadness of it all, Shaw thanked Evans for his time and left.

Chapter Fifty-Eight

'Are you asleep?'

'No.'

'Have you been crying?'

'Yes.'

The last woman who had cried in front of him had been poor Lori and it hadn't ended well. The thought of Deeley weeping was not an elevating thought.

'I've had a breakthrough.'

'Good for you.'

'Is that all you have to say?' He thought he heard the sound of water running. Shit. Relationship bust-up. Had to be. Why did women always take a bath when they were unhappy or got dumped?

'I'm off the case. In fact, I'm off *any* case. My career is in tatters. Does that explain things adequately for you?'

So that's why she'd behaved so strangely during the interview. 'This isn't connected to what I told you, is it?'

'Don't flatter yourself.'

'Or because you were seen talking to me?'

'No.'

'What happened?'

'Long story.'

'Then tell me.'

'You'll like me even less than you do now.'

'I'm prepared to take that risk if you are.'

The water stopped running.

'All right,' she said slowly. 'I'll give you my address on one condition.'

'What's that?'

'Bring booze.'

'So there you have it. I'm a home-wrecker and, if you believe everything you read in the newspapers, a murderer.'

'I stopped looking at the news a long time ago,' Shaw assured her. 'And who am I to judge?'

'Fair point.'

'Did you love him?'

'I thought so at the time.'

They sat in Deeley's kitchen. She drank white wine. He drank coffee. Scrubbed, no make-up, her cheeks were shrimp pink and her hazel-coloured eyes paler in the reduced light. Her feet, which were bare, were small and her toenails painted blue. She seemed softer and more approachable in her home environment. Nothing like a public fall from grace to plane sharp edges and reveal the softer individual beneath.

'But you didn't come here to listen to me. You have news.'

Shaw took a swig of his drink and told her about Jane Evans.

Deeley exhaled. Shaw expected a re-run of the argument

she'd so elegantly delivered only the morning before. Instead, he detected a shift in her previously strongly held conviction.

'So running with your theory, after a crap life with no free handouts, Jane Evans grows up into a troubled and resentful individual. Somehow she tracks down the members of the gang. How?'

'I haven't yet worked that one out. I suspect she located Danny – easy enough to find – and then used him to trace the rest of us.'

'She'd have to get around in her tea break. What the heck does she do for a living? In the removals business, do you reckon?' Deeley smiled playfully.

'You're still not buying it, are you?'

'I'm finding it difficult.'

'Plenty of jobs involving travel.'

'How do you explain the versatility of the MOs?'

'It's a stumbling block, admittedly.'

'More of a mountain. A woman, for Chrissakes?'

'You're not really helping.'

Deeley reached for the bottle, topped up her glass. 'Helps me think,' she said. 'Easy stuff: she has access to transport. We know she's smart. We reckon she gains people's confidence. How else would she kill Carl Snare?'

'She inspires trust. She's probably superficially likeable.'

'Sounds like a sociopath.'

'Or psychopath.' Shaw didn't need booze to riff.

'Maybe she's in the army, or ex-army.'

'What are you saying? That all British soldiers are psychopaths?'

'No,' Deeley said as if speaking to a very small child. 'You have to admit it would account for her killing skills.'

'Fair enough, could be a possibility.'

'Did you know that a large population thinks lawyers are psychopaths in suits?'

'Snakes,' Shaw said, 'not psychos.' He spared a thought for Wolf, who'd suggested that Carl fitted into the category.

'Same difference.'

'You think she's a lawyer? Might as well say she's a police officer.' Shaw sat up. 'Fuck,' he said.

Deeley's eyes widened. 'Holy fuck.'

'It would explain how she accessed records, addresses, locations,' Shaw said, counting them off on his fingers, 'knowledge about forensics and breaking and entering.'

'With a warrant card, you immediately assume authority.' Deeley put down her glass. Her lips very slightly parted.

'What?'

'There's an officer at work. Right age. Gym-fit. Cold and calculating as winter.'

'Every workplace has a resident bitch.'

'Granted but this?' She raised her hand.

'She did that to you?'

'I'm pretty certain.'

'Pretty isn't good enough. What's her name?'

'Angel Finch. She's a DI and wannabe DCI and she's taken over my investigation. Allegedly, her daddy's a big police cheese.' She faltered. From the expression on Shaw's face, she could see the hitch in her theory.

'Not sure she fits our profile,' Shaw said bluntly. 'And

she's the kind of woman who's already got it made. Sorry to disappoint.'

'Pity. I'd have liked nothing better.'

'I can tell, but it could be another police officer.'

'Whoever it is has probably changed her name by deed poll.'

Which was up his legal street. A deed poll was a contract. A solicitor would be involved and would, therefore, be aware of the previous name. Anyone can start using another name provided it's not for illegal reasons. Surely something like that would raise suspicion if she wanted to join the police? It would look dodgy even if it was on the level. He told Deeley, who agreed. Then it hit him.

'She might have a connection to the police in a clerical or civilian capacity.'

'She'd still be vetted.'

'Maybe she ghosted by creating an ID from someone already dead.'

'That works,' Deeley said. She put the cork back in the bottle, filled the kettle and flicked it on. Her movements were energetic. She looked less downtrodden. Talking and coming up with a theory had helped her get her mojo back, Shaw thought.

'Jane went into local authority care, you said?'

'That's what Evans told me. She'll be twenty-five, twenty-six now.'

'Which gives us a problem,' Deeley acknowledged. 'If we're right, we have no idea where she's based. We don't know how she got to where she is now. We have no idea about the trajectory of her life or career.'

'So we start with the local authorities.'

'It won't be easy. Jane would have been kicked out a decade before. Records will probably only reveal the date she left and maybe the address of her first home.'

'Can you find out?'

Deeley nodded eagerly. 'I'll make a start first thing.'

'Be careful. If the killer gets wind and senses we're closing in, she could cut up rough.'

'I've been watching my own back for the past two years,' Deeley said. 'No change there.'

Chapter Fifty-Nine

Shaw called Danny on his way home. 'Did you board the train ... Good. Now listen.' After he revealed the game plan, he promised to stay in touch.

After nine, daylight lingered as he parked in a spot opposite the Queens Hotel. From there he walked the short distance back home. The shutters closed, a token attempt at security, the house looked unperturbed, as if it wondered what all the fuss was about. Shaw saw nothing amiss. He heard nothing. He sensed plenty. Alert, he unlocked the front door and was greeted by a swell of water that immediately engulfed his shoes. A torrent cascaded down the stairs, soaking the carpet and carrying books and ornaments with it. In an instant Shaw was transported back to the night of Mickie's murder, the dim grey light, the river's rush, the sound of yelling and slapping and screaming and silence.

He plunged inside, calf-deep, his jeans immediately drenched. In his head he told himself a pipe had burst or a toilet had clogged. He knew better. Someone had been in his house some time between seven-thirty that morning and nine-fifteen that evening. Maybe the killer was still there.

He sloshed his way to the kitchen and saw that the taps were on full. He turned both off and, crouching down, soaked his arse. He found the stopcock in the cupboard underneath the sink and closed it. Wading to the cloakroom, he turned the taps, clearly on, off. Furious, he splurged back to the kitchen and grabbed a heavy-bottomed saucepan strong enough to fracture a skull. Armed, he strode through the lake that was the ground floor. Shoes squelching against sodden carpet, he went upstairs, crept into each room, primed for attack. He welcomed it. Bring it on. But whoever had entered his home was long gone.

Close inspection revealed that every tap in every sink, bath and shower had been switched to full. Water had loosened tiles, lifted floorboards, damaged plaster and destroyed furniture. Tables upturned, photographs had splashed into the shallow depths, ruined. A favourite vase that Jo had bought sailed past and smashed against a chair. His home must have been flooding for hours. And it hadn't happened by accident. Any forensic evidence would be entirely washed away.

Shaw surged into the bedroom, reached for a bag on top of the wardrobe, grabbed a change of dry clothes from a shelf inside that had escaped a soaking and sloshed his way back downstairs. Outside, he called the twenty-four-hour emergency response number for a specialist company that restored water-damaged properties. Explaining the situation, he was told he'd receive a call back. Next, he called a high-class B&B in Hales Road and booked in. Throwing his bag onto the back seat of his car, he climbed inside and drove away. He needed a hot drink and a shower and then, as late as it was, he'd call Esther.

*

'Wet on wet' is an exciting technique used by water colourists. It describes dampening the paper with water and laying one colour into another, allowing them to diffuse together. The lack of control often creates 'happy accidents'. I try not to smile at the thought of Jon Shaw finding his very own, specially designed watercolour. 'Happy accident' it was not.

I'm on my back, one knee bent, my arms raised above my head. Recumbent, the arty types call it. My head is tilted towards those who sketch my naked body, my eye fixed on a point in the distance, mind tuning out. It's a pleasant release after a day at the coalface of crime.

My victims are piglets. They run and squeal in all directions, snuffling and grunting for the truth. I hate pork. Talking of pigs, a shame the detective had to involve herself with Shaw. Having cosy conversations was a very bad move, surely a hanging offence in the circumstances, Detective Inspector Deeley. A professional pariah with something to prove sucking up to a murderer turned lawyer – you couldn't make it up.

The instep in my sole threatens to cramp. I'm desperate to flex my toes, to lift my leg, to relieve the pressure. Focus on something rewarding, I think. Like the afternoon I saw the three little piglets together. Who knew that Shaw would lead me to Carl who would lead me to Hallam? Come to think of it, who knew Snare was a spy? It could have rocked me to my core if I were capable of shock. Killing him was quite the coup. He didn't see it coming, in the same way he didn't notice me drinking quietly alone, or saw me lift the cash receipt from the hotel bar and insert it into his apartment.

Shame about the gun. I was so sure it would be covered in their sticky prints, certain it would condemn Hallam to spend the rest of his days in prison, or get Shaw a lengthy jail sentence.

To get the job done, I'll have to take some leave.

'Why do you want to know?'

'Is it a state secret?' Talking to Esther on the phone, Shaw, wrapped in a large fluffy towel, sat on the edge of a double bed. Dry and warm, he glowed.

'It's personal and none of your business,' Esther retorted.

'And yet you told Danny.'

'That was different.'

'How so?'

Esther clicked her tongue. 'I was at a low point. I'd had too many gins. I didn't think. I should have kept my mouth shut.'

'I' carried a weight of responsibility, Shaw thought, and there were a lot of them.

'Because Aaron told you to?'

'Because it's not nice when your partner chooses a kid he's just met over a relationship that was solid for years.'

'A kid?'

'Sixteen or seventeen, no more.'

'Tell me about her.'

'I don't understand what this has to do with anything other than satisfying your curiosity.'

'Trust me, it's important.'

Esther went quiet.

'*Please*, Essie.'

'There's nothing to tell.' Humiliated, she was clipped, buttoned-up and spiky.

'How did you find out?'

Esther let out a gale of a sigh. 'I went shopping and, halfway into town, realised I'd left my purse in my other handbag. I went back home and there she was.'

'Where? Bedroom—'

'The lounge, all right?'

'Clothes on?'

'God, yes.'

'So how is there a problem?' he countered. 'It all sounds innocent.'

'Anything but. He had his arms around her. They practically sprang apart as I bowled in.'

'Did Aaron introduce her?'

'He said she was a daughter of an old friend of his.'

'You didn't believe him?'

'Did I hell.'

'And her name?'

'Jane,' she said.

Gotcha, Shaw thought.

'And plain she was not,' Esther continued. 'She had incredible blue eyes, like distilled violets. Piercing.'

A thought, which he couldn't quite nab, dinked at the back of Shaw's brain. 'Did she come to the house often?'

'How should I know? Aaron wasn't about to confide in me. At that stage I was going out more because things had got so bad between us. Aaron also started spending more time away. He *said* he was visiting his parents.'

'In Barton-upon-Irwell?'

'Good memory,' Esther said.

'How does Gail fit into the picture?'

'Search me. If you're asking when Aaron finished with Jane and when he picked up with Gail, I have no idea. Knowing him, he was probably seeing them at the same time.'

Like you did with me, Shaw thought but didn't say. 'Are Aaron's parents still in the village?'

'Aaron's dad died last year. His mam's in a care home. Alzheimer's,' Esther said.

'A village seems a strange place for them to uproot to.'

'Why does anyone move anywhere?'

To escape, to hide, not from others, but from yourself, Shaw thought. And it didn't work.

'When was this exactly?'

'I don't know, pre-split; definitely not post-split.'

'So they moved on a whim, for no good reason, that right?'

'A family connection. Long story, short: Aaron gave his parents a ton of money to finance a venture with his dad's eldest brother, Uncle Russell.'

'What kind of venture?'

'A pub restaurant.'

'Risky.' Restaurants came and went in Cheltenham faster than you could order a takeaway. Big chains able to afford rent hikes had replaced many independents. Perhaps it was different outside Manchester.

'They were doing alright,' Esther said, 'but everything fell apart when a lorry driver piled into Russell and his wife on the M6. Aaron's auntie was killed outright alongside her children. By some miracle, Aaron's uncle survived.'

'And Aaron's parents stayed in Barton after the accident?'

'Jon, why the questions?'

'Please, Essie. It's important.'

He heard her sigh. He also thought he heard the chink of ice against a glass. 'They stayed, although they sold the business. Aaron's dad is buried at the church there next to his sister-in-law and the kids.'

Shaw considered what he'd heard. If he was on the right track, he needed Esther's co-operation. 'Are you in touch with Aaron?'

She hesitated. 'On and off.'

'Tell him I've been in touch, that I've been poking around and asking questions about his family.'

'Are you cracked? Why would I do that?'

'Because Jane is still very much in the picture,' Shaw said. 'Surely you'd like to get your own back on the woman who you believe screwed you over?'

Chapter Sixty

Deeley cocked open one eye. Someone had taken a drill to her head. Her tongue tasted as if coated in tar liberally sprinkled with birdseed. Somewhere in the recesses of consciousness, she registered that her mobile was ringing.

Scooping it up, she grunted a greeting.

'Angel Finch, what colour are her eyes?'

'Good morning, Jon.' She propped herself up. 'Thought we'd eliminated her from our enquiries.'

'We have, but I don't want doubts or loose ends.'

'Dung brown.'

'You're sure?'

'Certain.'

'Hmm.'

'Are you telling me it definitely rules her out?'

'Unless she wears coloured lenses, yes.'

'Disappointing.'

'Are you up?'

'Washed, dressed and ready to go.'

'That's keen. It's six o'clock in the morning.'

Deeley cleared her throat and felt her neck flush with embarrassment. 'Thought I'd make an early start.'

Shaw put himself in the younger Jane's shoes. It wasn't difficult. He'd burnt with anger at anyone or anything when he lost his mum. Denied the chance of time spent with someone who truly cared, Jane Evans's childhood had been violently cut short from the moment of her birth. And he took responsibility for his role in that destruction. Abandoned in a system that was as damaging as any prison, Jane had grown up with despair in her heart. She had every reason to want revenge. Eventually finding out about her wealthy biological father, the life she could have had, must have been crucifying. But Esther, he was certain, had got it all wrong about the nature of the relationship. Jane Evans was not Aaron Waterhouse's lover; she was his daughter. Shaw would probably never know why Mickie had failed to reveal that she was pregnant to Waterhouse, a man who'd longed for a dynasty like some fictional Italian mafia don. Perhaps Mickie had genuinely not known who had fathered her child. She maybe feared Waterhouse as much as she'd loved him. Waterhouse appeared to inspire that kind of devotion in his women, Jane Evans no exception.

Had Waterhouse discovered that the baby was his all those years ago, his instinct would have been to take her in. Of that, Shaw was in no doubt. But to do so then would have associated him too closely with a dead woman and draw attention from the cops. Waterhouse could not afford to take that risk. So instead he'd salved his conscience by offering to pay Dawn Ashton. For all Aaron's sins, he believed in the sanctity of family, which explained why he had not turned his back on his child years later.

But many questions remained. Shaw hadn't yet worked out how Jane had reconnected with Waterhouse or how she squared away the fact that it was her father's drugs that had got her mother into trouble in the first place. He wasn't sure whether Waterhouse was aware of his daughter's murderous intentions, still less whether he was an accomplice.

But he understood how Jane had reinvented herself. The truth lay in a graveyard.

Deeley, upright and on her third cup of coffee, was rocking it from the comfort of her own small living room. She'd contacted Social Services and spoken to one social worker, two health visitors and a child protection officer, none around when Jane Evans had been put into care. She had, however, discovered that a 'package', including housing, health and education, would have been put in place for Jane on her entrance to the big bad world.

A long time ago, Deeley had once visited a local authority care home. It had her reaching for a drink the second she got home. Poor little bastards, she'd thought.

'Up to a year beforehand, each child is prepared for the world of work or further education and given a designated social worker,' a head honcho at the local authority assured her. He had the cool and impartial manner of those paid a lot of money to orchestrate and influence lives, despite not being at the sharp end, or feeling the heat from any ensuing carnage or fallout when things went pear-shaped.

'Is it possible for children to fall through the net?'

'As with many things in life, it doesn't always pan out the way it's supposed to.'

Tell me about it, Deeley thought sourly, ending the call. She thought of herself at sixteen years of age. It was a hell of a thing to expect a young person to go out and fend for his or herself, especially someone as damaged as a child from a care background often was.

She glanced down her list. One more call to make, to Jane's designated social worker.

'Is that Jess McNally?'

'It is.'

Deeley went through her usual spiel.

'I've been retired ten years.' The relief in McNally's voice suggested that she had no regrets about leaving. 'I'm not sure how you think I can help,' she said with more caution, as if she feared an action she'd taken during a professional crisis was somehow coming back to bite her on the rear. How well Deeley understood that emotion.

'I gather you were Jane Evans's designated social worker.'

'Ye-es.'

'What can you tell me about her?'

'The girl with blue eyes, we used to call her. Bit of a tearaway.'

'Oh yeah?'

'Her file wasn't pretty. She'd been placed with three foster parents. Sadly, none worked out for her.'

'Any particular reason?'

'She was highly disruptive and not very nice to either pets or other children.'

Deeley scribbled a note: 'psychopath', and underlined it three times. 'What happened after she left the care system?'

'She refused any assistance at all.'

'She was allowed to up and leave?'

'Of course. There's always a choice. Most youngsters are not automatically kicked out at sixteen. Having had enough of institutionalised living, there are always some who reject the help on offer. It was a pity because she was a bright girl. I'd hoped she'd go on to further education. It was discussed.'

'Do you know what became of her?'

'She said she had friends up north. Poor child had it in her head that she was related to a wealthy family. It's not uncommon for children to believe in a shining knight in armour. Sometimes it's all that gets them through the day.'

'I understand.' Deeley shared that much in common with Jane Evans.

'Is she in trouble?' McNally said.

'Too early to say. At this point we need to find her and, hopefully, eliminate her from our enquiries.'

'I do hope so. Given the right environment she was the type of young woman who could excel and make a genuine success of her life.'

A watery light drifted through the clouds upon the sleeping dead. Older gravestones squinted myopically at their more youthful, upright neighbours.

Shaw followed a meandering path, scoping the long grass for signs of monuments and new graves. He fancied he heard the sound of children's voices on the breeze from a nearby school. Perhaps it was pure conjecture. Hard to remember if he had ever been shrill and light and happy as a kid, Shaw thought. Times with Danny, when he thought his heart would burst with laughter, emanated from the thrill of doing something they shouldn't and not getting caught. There was no joy in being good or well behaved.

Breaking from the path and under the watchful eye of an angel, Shaw skirted late spring flowers and found himself in a densely wooded section, in which headstones choked on ivy and where the air was cool and still. Only old bones here.

Tracing his way back out onto the main path and, after a painstaking search, he found Aaron Waterhouse's dad, a man called James, 'Jimmy' to his friends, beloved husband and father and devoted grandpa, laid to rest beside a rowan tree. Next to him, a grave that charted a family tragedy and facilitated a crime. Paying scant attention to the male line, Shaw focused on Aaron Waterhouse's aunt whose maiden name was Draven. The daughter who died with her in the accident had been sixteen years old at the time. Not a Jane, but a Nicole.

Shaw looked up to the heavens, as if giving thanks, the sky so impossibly blue and . . .

The SOCO who'd followed Deeley out of the maisonette and crime scene, where Mark had been murdered. Her eyes had been a blizzard of blue, like 'distilled violets', Esther had said.

He pulled out his phone. Before he made the call, he had an incoming.

'Yes?' he said.

'Jon, it's Aaron.'

Shaw waited several beats. Above his head, the whir and

chuff of a helicopter. How apposite, Shaw thought. 'What can I do for you?'

'I want to straighten things out between us.'

'I wasn't aware they were snarled up.'

'I think we both know what we're talking about.'

'Your daughter, or the fact you've aided and abetted a murderer?'

Waterhouse's voice was characteristically bombastic. 'Jon, for a lawyer you have a vivid imagination.'

'Nothing imaginary about seeing your friends dead.'

'Very sad, but I'm afraid you've got it all wrong.' Waterhouse sounded like a man sure of himself.

Unnerved, Shaw narrowed his eyes against a shaft of sunlight breaking through the cloud. Was he mistaken? Had his obsession with Waterhouse made him shoehorn the evidence to fit the crime?

Shaw's most challenging clients were often youngsters whose parents were seriously wealthy. Immunised from the strain of paying bills, finding rent or earning a living, those kids also believed that they were exempt from justice. Doting parents sometimes fuelled this delusion. They'd even been tagged with a label: 'snowplough parents', those who removed any obstacles, however serious, from their children's lives in order to create maximum opportunities and protect them. Was Waterhouse simply another father blind to a daughter's faults, or was he complicit?

The helicopter circled back on itself.

'Come to the house today,' Waterhouse said, puncturing his thoughts.

Trap, Shaw thought. He also knew he had to end it. For too

long he'd stood idly by and let events unfold. Most regrets came from the things you failed to do rather than the things you had done. This time, he had to 'do', whatever the cost. 'What time?'

'Noon.'

Two hours, Shaw registered. Plenty of time for a man in flight who wants to cover his tracks and tie loose ends. 'I'll be there.'

'Nicole Draven?' Deeley burst out. 'Are you tapped? She's nice, for God's sake, and utterly professional.'

'That's rather the point,' Shaw said. 'If anyone can get away with murder, it's a Scenes of Crime officer. Plus she's perfectly placed to gain access to the police database.'

'Illicitly, but you're right.'

'Giving her access to a criminal's history, associates, aliases, addresses.'

'The whole bloody works. SOCOs also provide fingerprints and DNA for elimination at crime scenes.'

'Which would nicely cover her involvement in Mark and Carl's murders.'

'God, are you sure about this?'

'I am. She's Waterhouse's daughter.'

'You think he's an accomplice?'

Shaw had thought long and hard about it since the conversation in the graveyard. Perhaps Waterhouse was a man driven by guilt for what had befallen his firstborn child. Kingpins didn't always know what was going on at the lower levels of their businesses. While he must have known about Mickie's drug habit, it was entirely plausible that he was ignorant of the debt she'd racked up with Danny. As likely, he was afraid for his current family and sought to protect them, not simply from his past, but from Jane's murderous ambitions. Easier to assist than resist.

'It would explain how Draven could be in so many places and yet hold down a full-time job. Waterhouse has a helicopter pilot's licence. You can legally land one anywhere providing there's the space the size of a tennis court to do so.'

'If he's involved, it makes him an accessory to murder. I'll call it in right away. It shouldn't be too hard to pick her up.'

'Best of luck – she'll be long gone.'

'We'll circulate her as wanted and send out an All Ports warning.'

'There's something else you should know.' Shaw told her about his intended meeting.

'You're not serious?'

'I have to.'

'No, you don't, and for all you know he could be harbouring Nicole.'

Shaw's stony silence told her she was wasting her time.

'Have you got a death wish or something?' Deeley turned her head, briefly listened. She heard a tap at the window as if a bird had misjudged its flight path.

'I want it finished,' Shaw said. 'And I'm the only person who can.'

'You're a stubborn bastard but, if that's what you want, I'll talk to Dillane and arrange back-up.'

Deeley cut the call, reached for her car keys and, halfway through punching in Dillane's number, the doorbell rang. Breaking off to answer it, she felt an arm snake around her neck, the combination of forward momentum and backwards motion as powerful as G-force. The phone flew out of her hand and hit the wall. With intense pressure on her throat, she could neither gasp nor scream. It was like carrying a piano on her back. Her assailant's breath felt hot against her face and smelt of curry.

'Down,' a man's voice bellowed, nasal and northern.

Yanked backwards, her knees buckled, body falling with a painful thump, elbows bruised, ribs screaming. Danny Hallam, beneath, had broken her fall but his legs were wrapped tight over her own. It was like being rolled by an alligator about to drown its prey.

Chapter Sixty-One

'Have you got that all down, Julie?'

Shaw was in Julie Strong's office and she was tapping away as if communicating the last desperate message from a doomed submarine before the air ran out.

'Yes, but Mr Shaw, I really think . . .'

'Give it to me.'

'But I haven't finished.'

'Could you step on it, please?'

Julie didn't do anger or irritation. Passive aggression was more her thing. Her lips pinched. Her body stiffened. But she did, indeed, step on it. She finished with a flourish and printed out the document for Shaw to sign, after which she counter-signed it.

It didn't provide insurance but, if he failed to escape with his life, he had the satisfaction of knowing that the police would look at Nicole Draven very seriously for multiple murders, and that Danny would go clear.

'If you don't hear from me tomorrow, make sure that everything is sent to DCI Dillane at West Midlands Police,' Shaw said.

*

Upended and pinned down, Deeley heard the doorbell ring again. One long note this time, urgent, and similar to an alarm before an imminent air raid in an old war movie.

Hallam had one repellently sweaty hand clamped over her mouth. He squeezed her cheeks with his thumb and fingers as if her face was a piece of dough to be kneaded. She hadn't yet processed the scenario other than either Shaw was wrong about Hallam, or Shaw had duped her.

Attempting to twist her head, she received a smack so hard her teeth rattled. Tears springing to the corners of her eyes, she willed the person on the other side of the door not to go. She prayed they'd look through the letterbox and, reading the situation, call for help. No, *yell* for it. The dread of her potential saviour leaving without being able to raise the alarm rendered her slick with fear. If only she could work her mouth free, she could scream the bloody street down.

'Fuck's sake,' Danny snarled as she wriggled. 'Stay fucking still.'

He increased his grip. Her heart raced in her chest. Her head ballooned through lack of oxygen due to a restricted airway. Spots danced before her eyes. Her body was like a tuning fork, every muscle and sinew taut and fit to bust. He was going to crush the life out of her. *Obey*, she thought. Maybe if she did, he'd loosen his grip. She willed herself to let her body go limp.

'Better,' Danny hissed in her ear.

The doorbell stopped ringing. It went suddenly quiet. Deeley caught her breath, strained to listen, praying she wouldn't hear receding footsteps. She'd sometimes considered her own death in the line of duty. Show her a police officer who hadn't. It would be on the street, she'd reckoned, from a wound that penetrated a stab vest, a shot to the chest, or a vehicle employed against her like a battering ram. Or, giving chase, she'd fall through a skylight and her head would smash open, gore and brain tissue decorating the concrete, and every bone in her body broken. It would happen in the dead of night or before the grey light preceding dawn. It would *not* occur in her own home in broad daylight with a man she'd interviewed only the day before.

Terrified she'd missed her chance, she dug her elbows in. The vice-like grip loosened and, filling her lungs with air, she raised her head. Any scream was curtailed by a popping noise and the crash of splintering wood. Deeley was fairly sure her hair parted as a bullet sped from behind the front door and embedded itself somewhere in the building.

'Stay down,' Danny Hallam yelled, another shot zinging past.

'Jesus Christ,' Deeley let out, swiftly recalibrating the situation and, as importantly, Danny Hallam's role in it.

'Move,' he shouted, hauling her backwards.

Shoulders and backside scraping painfully against the coir matting, which had seemed so chic when she bought it, she fixed on the hole in the door that grew bigger with each shot. Seconds thudded past like hours. If this were her destiny, then it was crap. She would not go down easily. Someone would hear the commotion, wouldn't they? She simply needed to hang on long enough for the cavalry to arrive in the form of armed response. With the terrorist threat, there could be as many as a dozen members of the public calling the police at this very moment.

Somehow, Danny Hallam had lugged her to the foot of the stairs. He scrambled upright, dragged her to her feet and gave her a shove. 'Up,' he commanded. Perspiration streamed from his forehead and into his eyes. His lips were pale with fear.

'I need my phone.' She crouched, pointed to it by the door.

'OK. I'll get—'

Danny grimaced and glanced down. Blood bloomed on his T-shirt and spread. Deeley caught him as first his face and then his knees crumpled.

And then the shooting stopped.

Chapter Sixty-Two

The gates swung open and closed behind the Macan. Shaw did not have a death wish, but was tired of running and now it was going to stop. Walking away, without facing the consequences of that night, was not an option.

He didn't believe there would be time to explain, let alone connect with a determined killer. Reasoned argument was not going to work with a woman whose entire life revolved around paying back those who had taken so much away. He'd briefly considered strapping a blade to his wrist before sanity had prevailed. Little point in taking a knife to a gunfight and, anyway, what was he going to do with it? Stick it in her like Danny had done to Mickie Ashton? It would count as the ultimate hypocrisy. His only weapon was that he knew his enemy because she was broken the same way. They'd both been fashioned in a cauldron of violence, abuse and neglect from which you never quite recover. They shared the same sense of isolation and abandonment. They had both clawed their way out of what life had thrown at them, and remade themselves in images neither of them recognised. They roamed freely among their interior worlds, with similar trains of dark thoughts. He'd been wrong when he believed Draven was motivated by revenge. Draven was driven by grief. Sociable on the outside, she was angry and she was lonely. And the lonely like to talk when they have someone to listen and even when they don't. Every killer Shaw had ever known wanted to grandstand, to explain his or her warped point of view in a bid to justify seemingly incomprehensible actions. They loved the sound of their own voices. That was where the similarities ended. Unlike Draven, he had not received a wealthy helping hand. He was no murderer. And, crucially, he possessed the ability to forgive, if not yet able to forgive himself.

Shaw climbed out of the car. The helicopter, he noticed, was already gone. He allowed himself a smile. Waterhouse had made the call when he was already in Birmingham. But Shaw had already second-guessed Waterhouse's moves and arranged for Danny to protect Deeley. A coward, Waterhouse would flee.

Shaw glanced at the sky. Deeley should have made the call by now. In minutes, the cops would arrive.

'Stay with me, goddammit.' Deeley pressed her hands into the wound in Danny's chest to staunch the flow.

Danny moaned. His eyelids fluttered, his lips trembled and his teeth chattered. His skin was pale as stone.

'I'm going to get help.'

Danny muttered a few indecipherable words. Deeley leant in close to hear. 'Behind you,' he rasped.

She felt before she saw. The space around her was contained, airless and in shadow. Glancing over her shoulder she saw why. A man stood in her hallway, sweating. He wore sunglasses. Why would he do that, she thought giddily, on a dark, wet day? She knew it was a stupid thought because the bigger problem was the gun held in his gloved hand. When he raised it she read how it would end. She imagined she'd go down screaming and cursing, making some kind of deluded heroic statement, but she cowered while Danny Hallam leaked blood and was dying in her arms. With that certain knowledge, she realised that she was too late to save Jon Shaw.

'Please,' she said. 'Don't do this.' She could not plead for her life on the grounds that she had children or a significant other, or a dependent relative, or, God help her, a duty to fulfil, a societal debt to repay, and even if she did, it would make no difference.

The man, who held sway over her hallway, said not one word. He was cool and bold and cold. Karma was not a bitch, she realised, it was a bastard man stamping his size tens, and he had a gun in his hand and retribution in his heart.

She heard two shots and saw, or imagined, two thin streams of smoke. It didn't hurt as much as she thought it would. At first. Then the pain kicked in, strong and hard, and her breath snagged, the blood ran and, as she slumped, she heard the sound of fast retreating footsteps and distant sirens.

The door to the big house was ajar. Shaw cracked it open and walked into the vast hall with the nude paintings.

There was no housekeeper to greet him. Aaron's kids would be at school, his wife away; only Nicole Draven left to form a welcoming party. He was her prize. He was what she wanted most. For Draven had no idea that he hadn't touched her mother or that he'd tried to protect her. Even if she did, she wouldn't buy it because it wouldn't fit with her warped narrative. He'd been there so, in her head, he was one of those who'd got away with murder.

Shaw had moved beyond fear to a state of being in which he didn't care and the world no longer mattered.

His eyes fixed on every corner from where an unpredictable woman might strike. Aside from his footsteps, all was quiet as if the house, built on blood and death, was cocooned and slept.

He crossed the floor towards the room where he'd sat and talked to Waterhouse. Shaw walked calmly inside as if he were about to reunite with an old friend, for he and Nicole Draven knew each other well.

Her back to him, a woman as tall as Deeley stood in front of open bi-fold doors that gave an expansive view of the garden and woodland beyond. She lifted her head and breathed deeply. Getting into the zone, Shaw suspected. Draven had calculated and choreographed the endgame to the last detail. She already knew he was there.

When she turned, it was as if a flashbulb had gone off in his face. Immediately he was back on the street, outside the place where Mark had been murdered, and saw Draven, the SOCO, talking to Deeley.

Draven's build was athletic, toned and, he suspected, powerful. Her feet looked big or she wore oversized boots. She had skin the colour of cool sand, hollow cheeks and a slightly long jaw. From an objective view, she had an interesting face. Her light brown hair was scraped tightly back into a ponytail, traces of thin white scalp visible like ley lines. In her earlobes, gold studs, not showy. Draven had Waterhouse's small mouth and thin lips. There was a surprising quietness about her demeanour betrayed only by the blizzard of blue that were her eyes. They burnt with light and resentment. The big giveaway was the gun in her hand.

She circled him, inserting her body between him and the door. Shaw backed up. He could charge her right here and now, or turn and make a run for it through the grounds. He doubted he'd get much further than a few paces either way, the only satisfaction to be had: his blood spewing all over Waterhouse's thick pile cream carpet.

'You achieve nothing by killing me,' Shaw said.

'I disagree. With you dead, it's the end.' She had a low voice, with a hint of northern roots.

'There is no ending, Nicole. There never was. There never is. For you there's only a lifetime of smashed dreams and the inside of a prison cell.'

'Where you should be.'

'For trying to prevent a murder?'

'Prevent?' She let out a husky laugh. 'You were there. You were part of the baying mob.'

'Guilty as charged but there was no intent to kill. About that you're very wrong.'

'I'm never wrong.'

'So says the killer who got sloppy.'

The thin lips parted with indignation.

'I've gathered enough evidence of your crimes to condemn you. It's already en route to the police.'

'Oh yes, Deeley, the discredited police officer. Did you know she stalked a man until his wife committed suicide?'

The blue eyes hardened. 'I'm a scenes of crime officer. You seriously think the police will believe the word of a cheap lawyer who's led a double life to cover up his murderous past?' Her voice cut through the air like an arrow shot from a crossbow.

'The only person with a knife in his hand was Danny Hallam and he's paid his debt to society.'

'But not to me. My world fell apart when you had your fun. I died inside because of *you*.'

Shaw shook his head. Sorry wouldn't cut it. Sorry wouldn't end her despair, or his. 'I know what you endured,' Shaw said softly.

'You have no idea.' Her hand tightened on the stock. Shaw chilled at the thought of the damage it would do.

'I spoke to Joel Evans,' he said.

'The man's a cunt.'

'And so is your father.'

Draven broke into a proud smile. 'He made me.'

'Then he created a monster. The one thing I don't get: why side with the man responsible for your mother's addiction and debt?'

She stared straight through him. 'I should drop you here and now.'

'But you won't because you're not ready. You don't have an audience.'

She smiled, appreciating his logic.

Except Shaw was convinced Waterhouse wouldn't come. Danny wouldn't let him. 'The hit list – was it Aaron's idea?'

'We're done with talking. Move.' She gestured with the gun towards the garden. 'Outside.'

Chapter Sixty-Three

He stepped onto the terrace, Draven behind him, the muzzle of the gun pressed tight against his spine. Nicole's gaze was like an axe cleaving the centre of his back and spread-eagling his ribs.

Under a darkening sky, Shaw crossed to a set of stone steps that led down to the gardens. In the distance, he heard the unmistakable sound of an approaching helicopter. It could only mean one thing: Waterhouse's return. Nervously, he wondered what had become of Danny and Deeley? Where was back-up? Shaw felt a sudden hollowness in the pit of his stomach.

Against the growing clamour as the machine made its descent, Draven shouted, 'That way.'

Shaw crossed a precision-mown lawn with cultivated borders and ornamental trees. He passed a gardener's hut and outbuildings, none of which were occupied. Through a gate next and onto a gravelled path that led down from the main gardens into an expanse of woodland. Raindrops spat and crackled against beech and sycamore, the sound like the prelude to a wildfire.

He entered a coppice. A light breeze had picked up. Leaves shivered as if with dread at impending disaster. Each time he slowed, Draven dug the muzzle of the gun into his back.

Eventually, the track branched in three directions and he heard a distant roaring in his ears.

'Fork right,' she said.

They pushed on in tandem through sharp rain that drilled the ground like machine-gun fire. He was like a mine detector sweeping the ground for unexploded ordinance, Draven stepping into the exact prints the soles of his shoes left behind. Consumed, his thoughts were of Deeley and Danny, Danny and Deeley. He had to survive if only for them and that left him with a problem. Despite gender equality, in Shaw's book a man didn't hit a woman. Don't call him old-fashioned. Don't call him politically correct. Call him a man traumatised by a violent past. Played out, imprisoned, he could not bring himself to attack Draven. Too much like history repeating itself. And if he didn't act, he stood no chance at all.

The route zigzagged and he finally reached a glade flanked by whispering willows. Here the terrain was marshy and pitiless. Rain in his eyes, cold in his soul, the air smelt of wet vegetation and reeds. The noise in his ears accelerated and he knew what it was: a turbulent river in full spate.

Shaw no longer saw his surroundings. He didn't register time. In his mind he was back to a cold night where the polluted waters ran and the fish died, a woman screamed and bled and finally expired. He was on the riverbank. Trainers sliding. Bruises blossoming. Sweat pouring. Him fighting. He remembered it all like yesterday. He remembered the pain and the hate and the fear.

Draven pushed him sharply in the back.

On he trudged until the earth opened out and they stood at the side of an inky-looking river that had burst its banks and splayed out onto the land. Trees, overwhelmed, struggled to stand erect, their branches waving in the breeze like the hands of a drowning man. He understood, like he'd never understood before, the terror inspired in Mickie Ashton.

Nearby, the river's pulse was slow and sluggish. Where the wind licked the surface of the water, waterfowl bobbed up and down on the waves. But only a little further out, the river moved with stealth and speed, gathering pace and churning with white water. Where it swirled, the current doubled back on itself, ready to suck the unwary under. Shaw's heart fought hard against his ribcage in a losing battle. Did he have the balls to jump?

'WAIT.'

Shaw followed Draven's gaze to a familiar figure, smug and satisfied, striding towards them. 'Job done,' Waterhouse announced. 'The bitch is as good as dead and that piece of shit, Hallam, is playing a harp.'

Shaw opened his mouth to yell but no words came out. How could Danny, his mate, the boy with the dirty laugh, the kid who had patched him up, who'd led him into all the wrong places and helped him live when he wanted to die, be gone?

'Good riddance,' Draven said.

'What? Got nothing to say, Shaw?' Waterhouse gloated. 'No fond farewells?'

The grief Shaw had contained exploded like mustard gas, releasing a toxic cloud of anger. Fuck forgiveness and restraint and despair. Screw the past. The street fighter in him finally won out. He wanted to kill Waterhouse and he wanted to kill Draven.

Waterhouse turned to his daughter. 'I'm surprised you haven't done him.'

'I was waiting for you.'

'That's my girl.'

'I'm not your girl.' Draven twisted with speed and raised the gun with an outstretched hand. The shot that clapped the air went straight through Aaron Waterhouse's throat.

Eyes wide with horror, Waterhouse clutched at his neck. Blood streamed through his fingers, spurted and spewed down his shirt onto the wet earth. Choking, his jaw opened and closing, chest pumping as his lungs tried and failed to take in oxygen. Through some monumental effort, he took several paces, staggering like a drunk in a pub car park, and clawed at the air with bloodied hands. Knees giving way, he went down with a soft thump as if the earth was already primed to receive him.

'Who said I sided with him?' Draven casually stuck out her foot and pushed him into the river.

It was the break Shaw needed.

Shaw lunged as Draven trained the muzzle dead centre. Braced to have holes drilled into his chest, Shaw kept moving. Nothing happened other than a dull click. Draven gawped at the gun as if someone had handed her a plastic replica.

Already in motion, and before she could pull back the slide for an action replay, Shaw powered into her with a thump that winded him and sent the weapon flying from Draven's hand and splashing into the water.

Draven recovered with vicious speed and let out a scream. To Shaw's ears it was a war cry. A big woman, and holding steady, she wasn't backing off.

Shaw felt his bottom lip split from a cross hook delivered to his chin with astounding force. Blood trickled into his mouth, coating his teeth and tongue. Next a punch to the side of his head that made his ears ring. She was strong — fucking strong.

Another clout to his ribs so hard he was sure one had cracked.

Everything around Shaw closed down. The river didn't exist. There was no sound. The only flavour on his tongue was the metallic taste of his own blood. He felt void because he registered nothing other than him and her; his hands balled into fists as were hers and she was using them. So far he hadn't landed a single blow.

Shaw stepped back in time to avoid a flat-handed finger jab to his eyes. She feinted left and then right. A front kick dangerously close to his groin failed to fully connect but made him gag. To disable her, he had to change the dynamic, to switch the tempo. He had one advantage. With each landed blow, she got cocky. In her head, she'd already won. Danny had made the same mistake all those years ago.

Shaw jabbed with his fists, danced from one foot to the other like a tennis player waiting for a serve; in truth, positioning himself on less boggy ground. Oblivious, Draven closed in, slid, and Shaw struck. In a risky move, he aimed at her throat, temporarily stalling and forcing her to reassess her options. Grabbing her shoulders, Shaw thrust his knee up and pulled her body towards him. Breath knocked out

379

of her, Draven pitched forward, gasping. Shaw advanced to finally cut her down.

Suddenly, an unrelenting force drove a piledriver into his gut, sending him backwards. Shoes slipping, head down, arms manacled around his, Draven was pushing with all her body weight. Against the slimy ground, Shaw was powerless. Water seeped over his shoes, up the bottom of his jeans. With one push, he would be in the river.

But if he went in, she was bloody well coming with him.

Chapter Sixty-Four

Lightly dressed, he might as well have been wearing a concrete overcoat.

Shaw fought to stay afloat, to breathe without gulping in water. Scum coated the surface, run-off from surrounding fields and who knew what.

He'd already ripped a hole in his leg from a half-submerged tree. His eyes stung. Cold dug its talons into every part of him. It would kill him before the river had a chance to get its filthy claws around his throat. He didn't think he'd ever be warm again. Cut off from the impulses in his brain, his limbs were thick and heavy. Nothing worked the way it was supposed to and he had zero sense of coordination. It was like being clubbed over the head with a claw hammer.

Draven was nowhere to be seen.

In the wrong direction, he was moving away fast from the riverbank. He kicked with his leg, flailed with his arms in a feeble attempt to reach safety. The river had other ideas. Stretching out, it caught hold and sucked him into deeper water. It tore at his clothes, intent on stripping him naked.

Shaw tried not to panic. Carried away against his will, his head dipped and he struggled not to inhale.

He was in the river proper now. Faster flowing, reeds and high bank on either side. Go with it, he thought. What choice did he have? Maybe this was his time to die. Maybe this was how it was supposed to end.

Disorientated, Shaw had a choir of competing voices in his head: Danny's raucous rattle; Deeley arguing the toss; Charlie booming for him to get in another round; Jo moaning in abandon. He didn't know what was up or down, what was land or river, what was real or fiction.

Exhausted, Shaw's head sank lower. First, it was his chin and then his mouth. If it rose over and into his nostrils and entered his lungs, he would lose the will to fight and he was fucked. He'd once heard that drowning was a decent way to go. He strongly disagreed. Water invading every part of him, like a despot bombing his own country, it was cruel and humiliating.

A random memory of Danny larking around at a swimming baths flashed through his mind. Shaw, a crap swimmer, had spent most of his time on his back, sculling the water. He listened out for Danny's laugh. He heard nothing.

Shaw rolled over, gaze fixed on a sky that jeered at him. Heavy and leaden, it threatened more rain to come. The distance between cloud and river seemed infinitesimally small. Soon he would be gone, washed out to sea, never to be found.

Must not sleep, Shaw thought, so he shouted instead, a pointless waste of energy. Caught in a torrent, Shaw was buffeted along, painfully aware of the fragility of his body, how easily its walls can be besieged, made vulnerable, penetrated and attacked. There was a chattering in his ears that erupted into a roar.

He glanced madly behind him. The route had significantly narrowed, following a course around a steep-sided bend. If he could grab onto an overhanging tree branch, he might be in with a shot.

Shaw rolled onto his front. He saw two things: a bridge, far in the distance and out of reach, and white water churning.

He was heading over a waterfall.

Careering defencelessly towards it, Shaw's body cartwheeled over the edge. It was like powering down a flume upside down in a glass coffin. Panic marauded as he fought his body's instinct to breathe when doing so meant drowning and death.

A mesh of fear smothered his face. His stomach collided with his heart at the sudden drop in gravity. His limbs, extended, felt wrenched out of their sockets.

He landed feet down, crumpling painfully against a collection of tree roots. Every bone in his body jarred. His ankle twisted. Yet, by a miracle, he was in the shallows. He'd missed a boulder by a feather's width. Draven had not been so lucky.

A fallen tree, its branches spread out like a helping hand, had saved her from being carried downstream, but she was face down and still and had a deep gash to her head.

Shaw waded over. He had no idea how long she'd been like that. He scooped a hand beneath her face, lifting her clear, and put his ear to her mouth and nose. She was barely breathing. He felt her pulse with frozen, shivering hands. A slow erratic tic, maybe, although he couldn't swear to it.

Grabbing her underneath her arms, he half hauled and dragged her across slippery rocks and stone and onto dry land. White as bone, she looked dead. He had no formal first-aid skills, only what he'd casually gleaned from movies and medical TV dramas. He placed the heel of one hand over her chest, his other on top and pressed firmly, pumping up and down. He counted aloud up to one hundred in a voice that didn't sound like his. When he covered her cold lips with his own, he did not think of Draven the killer, the woman who'd murdered her father in cold blood and had wanted to shoot him. He thought of a child, bereft and lost and inconsolable.

'Come on,' Shaw yelled, 'do not die.' One life saved in all the chaos was all he asked.

Increasing speed and pressure, he believed with each compression he was inching her back to life and yet she remained stubbornly resistant. In a blizzard of desperation, he barely noticed a black retriever join him at the water's edge.

Glancing up, he noticed a middle-aged woman speeding down the track towards him. 'I'm a nurse,' she cried, pulling out a phone.

And with that, Nicole Draven spluttered into life.

Chapter Sixty-Five

The bitch wasn't dead.

Contrary to Waterhouse's assertion, Deeley sat up in a hospital bed, tubes coming out of her body and attached to an array of complicated-looking machinery that bleeped and winked and made Shaw feel giddy. He'd been in to see her every day since she'd technically died and he'd almost drowned.

'How are you feeling?' he said.

'Like someone who's been shot twice.'

He caught the glimmer of a smile. A good sign, he thought. Deeley would be OK. That was something. Nicole Draven, on the other hand, would remain in custody until her trial for multiple counts of murder. He had no doubt that she would be handed a whole life order, meaning life imprisonment without any possibility of parole or conditional release.

'I'm truly sorry about Danny, but there was nothing I could do, Jon. Fact is he took a bullet for me and saved my life.'

This was not the first time she'd said so and it wasn't the first time Shaw had muttered platitudes in reply. *He understood. He was grateful for her efforts. He knew deep down that Danny was capable of good things* ... In truth, he was stuck in the stunned *I don't believe this happened stage*, which was dumb because what had this all been about if not people dying, one by one? Extended conversations with the police, and Danny's mum, Christie, over the past few days, had fogged his brain. He didn't know if he'd ever emerge from the smog of grief.

'Hot news off the press,' Deeley announced. At times her manner was too feverishly bright. Shaw put it down to the cocktail of drugs coursing through her system. 'Flakes of paint from Kenny Sharples' quad bike were found at Nicole Draven's home.'

'Careless of her.'

'*Stupid* of her. How did you get on with Dillane? You remember what we discussed?'

About countering Nicole's allegation against him and clarifying to the police how he'd been so closely involved with many of her victims, yes, he remembered.

'What you're really asking is whether I confessed to being present at Mickie Ashton's murder?'

'I bloody hope not. What would be the point of that?'

Shaw had asked himself the same question. In the end he'd weighed up how much good he could do if he were free against how much he would be unable to do if he were banged up and struck off. Did one life saved cancel out another lost? With Danny and his mates gone, he felt as if he'd been handed a life sentence. Maybe that was as it should be.

Deeley was still waiting for a reply. Despite her insistence on saying nothing, it didn't feel great to use a lie to cover the truth.

'I explained that they were my mates back in the day . . .'

'True.'

'That I did not run with the gang.'

She stuck out a hand, wobbled it, *'sort of'*.

'And as such, I could not have possibly taken part in Mickie Ashton's murder.'

'Also true.'

'Not sure he bought it.'

'Suspicion runs through Dillane's veins more thickly than blood and, in case you hadn't noticed, there's precious little of that. The fact is he can't prove Nicole's allegation.'

'Guess I'll have to live with it then.'

'Guess you will.' She let out a terse sigh. 'Jon, you made a choice and you saved a life. Had it been me, I'd have left her floating face down.'

He believed her. He also believed that Nicole would have preferred to drown. Eager to change the subject, he asked, 'What's next?'

'Once I'm back on my feet, I'll go back to work. They might even thank me, you never know.' She pushed a little smile. Tiring easily, she suddenly looked frail and drained.

Shaw patted her hand and stood up. 'I'll drop in tomorrow.'

'I'll be here. You can count on it.'

Shaw walked out of her room and followed a maze of corridors to the main entrance. People of all ages coming and going, every emotion conveyed. Shaw tuned into each and every one of them. Grief and pain tempered by joy and relief. He wondered what Danny would have made of his life had he lived. Pathologically unable to conform, fiercely resistant to routine, unwilling to submit to any form of authority, he would have struggled. No place in the world for misfits and miscreants and those with dreams far exceeding their ability to attain them. As for Shaw, he would have to learn to tick to a gentler beat, the way people do when someone they love dies. If he could do this, it might provide a fresh start.

Shaw had one last phone call to make, to Dale Hook, if the man was still in the land of the living.

Acknowledgements

If you're reading this, chances are you've shelled out your hard-earned cash at a time when financial constraints are tight so this is, first and foremost, huge thanks to you, the reader. Writers don't survive without your support.

As ever, my deepest gratitude goes to Broo Doherty, agent and dependable friend, who has steered me through the turbulent waters of publishing. Thanks also to all at DHH Literary Agency.

This book could not have been written without incisive advice and technical information from Graham Bartlett, former Sussex Chief Superintendent, and Kate Bendelow, Scenes of Crime Officer for Greater Manchester Police. No question was too much trouble and your good humour knows no bounds. If I've made a mistake, the fault lies with me alone. It should be stated here and now that Kate bears absolutely no resemblance to Nicole Draven in the story!

Thanks to Oliver Goom for his legwork to ensure an authentic description of the woods in Clevedon. Some of your 'finds' were amazing.

Every writer needs a supportive writing mate and I could

not ask for a better 'co-partner in crime' than 'Supersuze' Davis. You keep me grounded, Susie, and can always be relied on to make me laugh.

Finally, it's not easy living with, or even being around, a writer. Half the time we're not really 'there' but tuned into another fictional world, which can be frustrating for those closest to us. So a big hug goes to my five fantastic 'Big Kids': Bex, Milly, Kate, Ollie and Tim.

Finally, and importantly, my husband, Ian Seymour, has walked every step of my writing journey with me. I couldn't wing it with anyone but you.

Credits

Orion Fiction would like to thank everyone at Orion who worked on the publication of *Six* in the UK.

Editorial
Francesca Pathak
Lucy Frederick

Copy editor
Clare Wallis

Audio
Paul Stark
Amber Bates

Finance
Jasdip Nandra
Afeera Ahmed
Elizabeth Beaumont
Sue Baker

Contracts
Anne Goddard
Paul Bulos
Jake Alderson

Design
Debbie Holmes
Joanna Ridley
Nick May

Editorial Management
Charlie Panayiotou
Jane Hughes
Alice Davis

Production
Hannah Cox

Publicity

Will O'Mullane

Sales

Jennifer Wilson

Esther Waters

Victoria Laws

Rachael Hum

Ellie Kyrke-Smith

Frances Doyle

Georgina Cutler

Rights

Susan Howe

Krystyna Kujawinska

Jessica Purdue

Richard King

Louise Henderson

Operations

Jo Jacobs

Sharon Willis

Lisa Pryde

Lucy Brem

Don't miss G.S. Locke's first gripping, nail-biting thriller . . .

A detective desperate for revenge. A hitwoman with one last job. A killer with both on his list.

Detective Matt Jackson's beloved wife, Polly, is the latest victim of a serial killer – Neon – who displays his victims amongst snaking neon lights.

Suicidal but unable to kill himself, he hires someone to finish the job. But on the night of his planned murder he makes a breakthrough in the Neon case and offers his assassin, Iris, an irresistible opportunity: help Jackson find and kill Neon in return for his entire estate.

What follows is a thrilling game of cat-and-mouse between detective, assassin and serial killer. But when Jackson discovers it's not a coincidence that their paths have crossed, he begins to question who the real target has been all along . . .

'Vivid and stylish, it rushes along like a rollercoaster before plunging to an intense conclusion – to be read in a single sitting'
DAILY MAIL